What people are saying about

A Westerly Wind Brings Witches

Honourable Mention runner up in A Woman's Write 2021 novel writing competition:

I'm enchanted by Walker's fresh — yet dry! — sense of humour and I know readers will be also. It's rare to find a writer so adept at making fun and pun of even the simplest or most ponderous material, while balancing it with intelligent observations and diligent historical delving. Within a framework of irony and exaggeration and vibrant settings, Walker places a credible, likable central character — Moira, who becomes a witch. A strong story with an enthralling premise that will attract female readers especially!
Barbara Bamberger Scott, author of *A Woman's Write*

This novel balances rather knowing humour about modern Pagans, with well informed dives into history. It's a remarkable blend of comedy and compassion that manages to both make jests about some of our standard witchcraft fantasies while offering a compelling view of reincarnation and personhood. Full of unexpected things, entirely charming and well worth your time.
Nimue Brown, novelist and author of numerous books on Druidry and Paganism, including *Druidry and the Ancestors* and *Pagan Planet*.

A Westerly Wind Brings Witches is a cunningly woven tale, reaching back from the present unto the ghosts of our past. Within its pages Sally draws together the threads of community (its power and its pitfalls), patriarchal abuses of women and endurance, inner strength and transformation amidst the heady presences of the Land and the Otherworld. Thoroughly enjoyed.

Gemma Gary, author of *Traditional Witchcraft, A Cornish Book of Ways* www.gemmagary.co.uk

A Westerly Wind Brings Witches

A Cornish Odyssey

With many thanks to mum and dad,
for your love and support
in life and since.

A Westerly Wind Brings Witches

A Cornish Odyssey

Sally Walker

MOON BOOKS

Winchester, UK
Washington, USA

JOHN HUNT PUBLISHING

First published by Moon Books, 2024
Moon Books is an imprint of John Hunt Publishing Ltd., No. 3 East Street, Alresford
Hampshire SO24 9EE, UK
office@jhpbooks.net
www.johnhuntpublishing.com
www.moon-books.net

For distributor details and how to order please visit the 'Ordering' section on our website.

ISBN: 978 1 80341 458 4
978 1 80341 459 1 (ebook)
Library of Congress Control Number: 2022922018

A CIP catalogue record for this book is available from the British Library.

Design: Lapiz Digital Services

UK: Printed and bound by CPI Group (UK) Ltd, Croydon, CR0 4YY
Printed in North America by CPI GPS partners

We operate a distinctive and ethical publishing philosophy in
all areas of our business, from our global network of authors to
production and worldwide distribution.

All characters are fictitious. And despite what the witches say about coincidences, any resemblances to the real members of my own Moon Group are purely accidental!

Part I

Woman Goes West

Chapter One

Moira was "the plain one".

And not just the plain one of the family – though she was that. And this family was plain to start with. Throughout Moira's interminable childhood, they squeezed themselves into a basement flat in Feltham (an unassuming suburb tacked onto London's outskirts like a tatty frill) where they were looked down on by the neighbourhood as the unpresentable, unpreventable Box family. Comprising of loud-mouthed, wide-berthed Mr. Box, sad sagging sorry Mrs Box and three or four little spotty Boxes, of whom Moira was the most pimpled and pitiable of all. (She was the latest, worst-rated edition to the Box set, born merely – they grumbled – to debunk the family catchphrase: "Things can only get better!")

Not just the plain little kid in dowdy hand-me-downs, trailing behind the rest of the small fry on the council estate (scruffy end) either. Though she was that too. It wasn't that Moira was picked *last* for the little girls' games, she wasn't picked *at all*. It had been gravely debated, while the stodgy six-year-old Box child stood stolidly at the garden gate (chewing her fingernails), and decreed that she wasn't fit to fit in. She jeopardized the serious business of play. She fell over and bled on the skipping rope (someone else's skipping rope). She didn't invite anyone to her birthday parties (she didn't have birthday parties.) Her only Princess Dress was sadly shabby, on the skimpy side and too tight to fasten properly (everyone agreed it would never get her into a Royal Ball.) And to top it all she ate liver sausage! (A secondary food choice, Daddy Box got to the cake first.) The Lower Feltham Girls' Gang, all potential management material, closed ranks and voted her expendable. Moira (redundant) took to watching other children's friends through gaps in the hedge. Naturally, it was a prickly hedge.

Neither was she just the continually overlooked plain-Jane of a bulging class of forty-five pupils in a 1960s primary school, though she ticked this box as well. Mrs Hartfield meant well and indeed often made a point of giving Moira a jovial "Good Morning!" But it doesn't do for a shockingly overworked teacher to offer deprived children a kind word for they are apt to want another and another and *another*. They tend to attach themselves like ticks, especially at tea break. In addition, the Boxes stinted dreadfully on baths and clean laundry. So Moira was seated at the back of the class near an open window. (From where she spent the day dreaming of being in the central hub.) (Or any sub-hub. Even the teensiest bubble!)

Furthermore, Moira wasn't merely that poor gnome of a child, plainly standing all by herself at the end of the queue into school every morning. Though had there been a certificate for this she would have got one at the end of term assembly. In the playground, the Big Girls baited her unmercifully on account of her gabardine mac. This dour garment reached down to her shins (it had belonged to a long lean cousin). And this in an era when the mini skirt was the only fashion – it being imperative for self-respect to flaunt your knickers. Only Moira, amongst the bevy of Class 4D girls, blushed with mortification every time they practiced handstands against the Elliot Hut wall; it went without saying that Moira's translucent bri-nylon knickers were the wrong sort of knickers...

As children, like adults, judge by appearances, Moira was teased or ignored and got dumpy and grumpy. She played alone, ate sweets, collected stamps and grievances.

"I'm not just the sitting duckling that even the certified gawks and dorks take pot-shots at, sitting out the scout-hut Valentine Disco by dilly-dallying in the cloakroom all night," Moira wailed despairingly to herself. She'd reluctantly given in to adolescence and made herself yet more hideous with thick powder-blue eye shadow and Barbie-pink blusher, while electrocuting her lank hair by frizzling it with electronic tongs. Adding to her own efforts, the hormones of puberty contributed acne, undesirable hair in unacceptable places and menstruation, bloating her tummy and swelling her into an emotional flood plain. She draped her body in 1970s scanty synthetics of large fluorescent or polka dot design. These emphasized her hip rolls – that is on body not dance floor. She danced like a drainpipe, inflexible from the ankles up. She was called "The Biscuit Barrel" (amongst other things).

"I am in fact The Plain One of the *whole world* and *all sublife in the universe,* including those green pus globules found inside daleks!" So she concluded with all the agonizing of Sour Sixteen, her flat face further flattened up against the mirror.

But in this she lied, or at least exaggerated. Teenagers are apt to have illusions of grandeur and this was hers. Yes, Moira Box was plain, and in the plainest sense, but she didn't have it in her to reach the Truly Appalling Pinnacles of Ugliness. Now *that* would have been something! Heads would have turned in the street! It would have been cause for public acclaim, just as great beauty is but with the advantage of being comic and so more popular. But alas the sad truth was Moira didn't warrant a second glance. The first was uninteresting enough.

At secondary school, the careers advisor looked bleakly at the Box girl and found herself unable to suggest the run-of-the-mill shop work or "starting a family" she normally offered the low achievers. She resorted to "opportunities for working from home, um.... sticking envelopes and things." Moira, slowly simmering in her overstretched bottle-green uniform, continued to sit sullen, substantial and as responsive as a beetroot – despite a lightning bolt of pure inspiration suddenly striking Miss Jarvis.

"Do you like the seaside, pet? There's an exciting opportunity near Bognor for a lighthouse assistant!"

By the time Moira had lurched into her twenties (living, not in a lighthouse, but in a pokey bedsit in Slough) she was too nondescript to be even an unpaid extra in someone else's drama. And she certainly didn't have any of her own.

"If *'All the world's a catwalk'* for all the men and women to strut their stuff – and I'm beginning to think that's exactly what it is! – then I'm the lame duck left backstage in the reject box," she confided to her stripy brown roommate (having decided that boyfriends are, after all, just cat substitutes).

People sometimes went out of their way to be unkind, but generally they simply failed to notice her. On the rare occasion another young woman might try a little out of pity (as "there for the grace of God and my denim genes go I") but on the whole they left her alone. They were secretly afraid that her visual boringness – short, blobby and ploddy – might reflect badly upon themselves. Besides, guys hunt in pairs and come August Moira sweated so.

Moira slogged hard to adapt to the laws of survival. She dressed in camouflage, lowered her low expectations, and avoided hairdressers and cosmetic counters as places of public humiliation. (Though, in secret, she also possessed a surreptitious and totally superfluous wardrobe of pretty clothes; ordered by mail catalogue, hidden in a locked box under the bed and only worn within the confines of her room, while her throbbing boombox serenaded her with Prince's *The Beautiful Ones*.)

By her thirties she was accustomed to her rotund figure, the shape of an unopened kitchen roll, and gave up diets. She'd accepted her workplace in the grungy back office so as not to threaten profits, and had made a few like bodied friends. They were totally united in supporting the wall at the dreaded staff Christmas Party. Apart from these she didn't get out much; she kept a now extensive stamp collection and had become an escape artist into mushy gushy romantic fiction, fantasy films as far from reality as faintly feasible, and *Star Trek*. She identified with the Ferengi.

It was not enough. When approaching the fearsome forty, Moira awoke one morning (raining again) and decided she wanted to live. Her life was (always had been and worse still looked like it was going to carry on being) a big flat, morose and moping, indeterminate Nothing-Very-Much.

"And clearly Fairy Godmother isn't going to bother showing up, gifting glass footwear, at this late juncture," she reluctantly acknowledged, looking down regretfully at her Extra Wide Fit feet.

So she resolutely gave away *The Dress* from under the bed to someone who looked less daft in it and her last lingering delusions, along with some untouched lace lingerie, were ditched with the box. As skedaddling had always been her one successful strategy, she posted her key to the landlord, packed cases and cat into her Ford Fiesta and drove out of Sloughdom, Heading West.

Bombing down the M3 – as if there were Mynocks sucking at her back bumper – Moira couldn't shake off the uneasy sensation that she, cat and car were attached to a long length of elastic, like a giant bungee jump cord. She'd always thought of herself as an inadequately encased tortoise, doomed to spend eighty plus years laboriously clambering across a Sahara-sized desert of sharp jagged rocks but now, *phenomenally*, she was in the clear, in the sunshine and running!

"Too easy surely? At any minute someone'll start reeling me back into my crate," she pessimistically predicted, putting her foot down heavily on the accelerator until the little Fiesta shuddered in protest.

She hadn't given much thought as to what she was running to, only euphorically grateful for what she was leaving behind. Yes, yes, somewhere over the rainbow might be good, and at the back of her mind she had a hazy vision of wandering over windswept moor looking interestingly demented in a trench coat. But she wasn't particularly bothered as long as it was *Far, Far Away.*

"Quite frankly I don't give a damn!" she shrieked out the window, feeling rather tiddly on a brew of reckless and ill-advised decision making; not at all in keeping with her habitual "keep your head down, stay in the slow lane and try-to-please-anyone-who-doesn't-actually-spit-at-you" behaviour. She wasn't even sure what had finally tipped her into this utterly unprecedented probable lunacy – that last mouldy straw of hopelessness perhaps, or awakening to the faecal fact that she had *nothing to lose that she wasn't secretly wanting to lose anyway!* Moira was just relieved to be fleeing from her life and vaguely surprised that she hadn't had to wait to die to do so.

"The tortoise has arrived at the Funfair and boarded the roller coaster!" she announced exuberantly, as she screeched into the A303 main roadway crossing middle England. "Here goes – WHEE!!!"

Moira and Tigger took the A30 to Penzance. From there they cut across moorland to St. Just with its squat church tower and bunched up houses, and then followed the coastal road overlooking Bronze Age strip fields and a sparkling Atlantic Ocean. They stopped at Zennor for scones for Moira and Cornish cream for Tigger. A side road slips down steeply into the village, which appears a mere blink-and-you'll-miss-it clump to the eyes of a London Sprawl girl, though it has a shop, tearoom, little wayside museum and church with a mermaid.

A small ad sellotaped to the shop window read: *Cottage to rent, apply Mrs Applebee, Wica,* and giving a phone number. Wica turned out to be even more minute and remote – which suited Moira just fine. (In a past era women like Moira would have disappeared into convents, the far edge of Cornwall is simply the modern equivalent.)

So she transplanted herself, like a refugee from Mordor, into the wee cottage with its old warped wooden door and new PVC windows inserted against the wild winds and soaking sea fog that hugs the coast there. The cottage had charm, spiders, uneven floors and small windows with deep ledges set into hard granite walls. So hard that Moira was unable to hammer in nails for pictures, so she hung these on string pinned to the ceiling beams. She filled the larder with crucial provisions and some jam jars with pussy willow. There was a diminutive wood burner in the lounge which she lit, dabbing Tigger's paws in butter so he could lick them in front of the blaze. Although this left greasy prints on Mrs Applebee's rug.

As the light faded on her first evening of not needing to eat away the day's discomforts, and as the amber glow warmed her knitted slipper socks, Moira heaved a huge sigh of relief for discovering that, despite being put on "Pause" since birth, she *could* change her monotonously loathsome lifestyle. (She'd give anything that cropped up from now on an "improvement" rating.) She was feeling cosily snug and smug at having opted for the Opt Out option and had real hopes that Grim Reality might not catch up with her in this well westerly hidey-hole. Additionally, she felt *spectacularly* excited that tomorrow wouldn't have an *office* in it!

But before starting life afresh, there were a few weedy roots to pull up from her previous hardly-amounting-to-an-existence-even. Moira grudgingly unpacked pen and pad to write letters of explanation and justification. She dolefully considered the inevitable responses. Her family would write her off as an idiot, nothing new there then. Amongst her few friends, Jeanette and Pamela would endeavour to make her face the woeful truth *for her own good*. (Their solicitude invariably felt more like TCP than

TLC, and listening to their advice was much like gargling with TCP – better to spit out than swallow.) She could just imagine what they'd have to say this time:

"Good gracious, Moira, didn't you know that the Cornish, who are cranky in character, aren't renowned for welcoming eastern invaders, calling them *emmets* (roving ants) and 'the bloody English'?"

And, well, they didn't like to mention it but, even if Moira hadn't the social skills of a bladder worm (tee hee), didn't she think she might find it hard fitting in?

And at *her time of life too!* For Pete's sake, she's coming on *forty!*

They wouldn't *sleep* for worrying how she'd manage on her own!

Wouldn't she miss her friends and family *terribly?*

Cornwall is such a long way away – the ends of the civilized earth (the only Primark there is in Devon). *And what about her secure job in Staines!*

Then they would indulgently laugh at her funny freakish behaviour, label her "the Gullible Goose" and a dear imbecile who would be lost without them. Meanwhile they would ruthlessly organise her return. And there she would be – back where she'd started. Well not quite. Without a doubt, there would be 'The Big Joke' of Moira's nutty breakout / breakdown of '98 which for years after would be festively pulled into conversation like a Merry Christmas cracker, never failing to put everyone else in stitches! Moira firmly crossed out "Pamela (Egham)" and "Jeanette (Hounslow)" from her slim address book.

She nibbled her pen top. Now *Tina* could be relied on to enthuse over Moira's escapade. So much so that she would plonk herself on the doorstep with make-up bags and emotional baggage within a week. From then on, she would commute between fridge and sofa with sole possession of the TV remote.

She'd just about galvanise herself at mealtimes and, in between, issue orders such as "make us a marshmallow butty, hun". But inevitably Tina's Will to Live would be too depleted to help with the washing up. She might manage the beach when it got warmer, and she might hang around until it did! In case of future amnesia, Moira tore out the page with Tina's entry.

In the end, she just sent a postcard and friendly invitation to her dentist, who wasn't married and rather good-looking. Well, you never know.

Chapter Two

During the following months, an enthusiastic Moira bought an Ordinance Survey map and eagerly explored. She developed a passion for folk museums and for a local species of ice cream topped with clotted cream and honey roasted hazelnuts called a hedgehog. Hedgehogs can be purchased at Chapel Porth, a narrow rocky inlet on the battered North Coast. She'd eat it standing on the pebbles, in woolly hat and stripy mittens, while watching the waves crash in.

The folk museums totally licked stamp collecting as her new nerdy hobby. They crop up in most market towns and even villages may boast their own converted barn full of rusty hoes, sickles and pitchforks. They offer – in what Moira felt was a sympathetic spirit – a pile of faded guidebooks on the counter, a draughty side room serving tea and saffron cake, and a welcome refuge for the disgruntled holidaymaker when it rains. During a wet summer they'll be packed and steaming with sopping waterproofs and cross children. But now they were deserted and silent, echoing only with memories of a dingy distant past and Moira's stomping footsteps. Amongst the old washtubs and mangles, leaky buckets, wooden dolly pegs and early sepia photographs of Cornish miners in tin hats topped with tallow candles, Moira was happily absorbed for hours.

"The most comfortable sort of past to remember," she realised, "is one I'm not in."

So she glimpsed (well gaped really) into a Cornwall of long ago. Browsing from room to room, she peered into the drab brown prints of the Victorian family grouped stiffly around the laburnum tree in the manse garden; the upright father, the promising sons, the seated daughters with restricted opportunities and restrictive corsets. Back further and there was the panting smelly beast, the steam powered beam engine, setting all the land chugging and spewing out smoke and tin ore. Around the stamps and dressing floors of the mines laboured the balmaidens with their thick muscles and ribald jokes, wearing gooks and hobnailed boots on workdays and bonnets, worsted stockings and second-hand finery on Sundays. (Moira briefly fantasised about being a balmaiden – who would mess with a woman who wielded a sledgehammer for a living!)

In her fascinated mind's eye, she followed the ghosts of the ragged children and tough tinners down into the hot hewn out tunnels threaded through the rock, where life was cheap and working men seldom lived past forty. She swore she could virtually hear the clanging doors of the old workhouses (now hospitals) and the hymn singing Wesleyites, whose chapels (now deluxe homes) outsized the parish churches, hanging their hopes on Eternal Glory. And she miserably mourned the double coffin rest under the lychgate at St. Euny, built to bear the multiple deaths of the barefoot Redruth poor.

At the end of each visit, Moira found it a wrench to step back out onto the modern high street with its anonymous superstores, speeding cars and passers-by who passed her by.

As the season progressed she ferreted farther afield, until one sunny April morning took her to the quaint and curious little witchcraft museum at Boscastle. After her tour, while she mooched her way through the gift shops where the unfortunate shop girls were dressed in green tights and pixie outfits, and later on as she sat on the wall of the crooked harbour to chomp her pasty, Moira pondered upon the museum's odd items. It had displayed a peculiar mixture, alongside the orthodox portrayal of the rancorous old harridan with broomstick were images of a village Wisewoman, adept in herbal lore and midwifery. And, as she'd moseyed around its sundry sinister exhibits, chants venerating the Goddess piped out over the museum's loudspeaker system.

Moira toyed with the idea of a medieval job description:

Vacancy for position of witch. Desirable attributes: female, repulsive appearance, prepared to work nightshifts on full moon basis, scraggy hair and warts essential, knowledge of ragwort and hemlock an advantage. High public profile and notoriety guaranteed in terms and conditions.

Moira reflected that, ill qualified for most jobs though she was, she would have several of the right credentials for this one. She rather fancied frightening Christians out of their beds and complacency on Halloween. With very little practice she felt she could be a dab hand at cackling and cursing. And she'd always liked wearing black, such a slimming colour! Wondering whether it was a possible career choice today, Moira retraced her steps back to the museum to enquire. The proprietor, who took her questions seriously (creepy that) gave her some contact numbers. She walked out with a list of itemised witches, plus a pagan shaman in the Treliske Hospital religious services catalogue.

Moira was a trifle gobsmacked but she liked to follow things up. She phoned the next day.

The following week was foggy and wet, ideal weather for researching her new project. Moira loaded herself down with books and retired to the café at Geevor Mine, which feeds you well and claims sensational sea views in better visibility. Information was surprisingly plentiful. Historical stuff and stacks of paperbacks on contemporary witchcraft, ritual and magic, channelled wisdom of Ancient Egyptians and Indigenous American Indians plus helpful tips from bardic Druids, just lined the shelves of Smiths and Olivers. Such a prominence of Wicca studies caused Moira some anxiety that the subject was in danger of becoming respectable.

Hence it was a relief, once she'd actually met some local witches at the Penzance Moot, to find that they were reassuringly unlikely to feature in the more cosmopolitan of the women's magazines. Not one resembled the lofty personas they aspired to (High priestess, Isis and the like), in fact several had really quite interesting personal problems. On the whole they had some pith and backbone; some were frankly terrifying!

Shakti Crows Wing (christened Debbie) advertised her witchy services and spell charge rates in the *Yellow Pages* phone directory. This sassy sage had jet black hair (improbably natural), a ginormous cast iron cauldron blocking her hallway and lived in Towednack, a village renowned for its history of witchcraft. It's built around a crossroads, perhaps witches used to hang about there. Or hang there.

Cait, the editor of a Cornish Mystery Lines journal, looked most unwitchlike with bright blue eyes, a cherubic face and bubbly body, curls and personality. She also possessed a Virgoan obsession with collecting mounds of archaeological evidence of Ye Olde Goddess matriarchy nestling amongst the Penwith hills. Not a stone was left unturned in case fecundity, fertility and vulvas lay beneath it!

The scariest of all was Mage from Mousehole, who refused all men entry to her property, including the postman and the poor chap who tried to read the meter. Instead of a black cat she kept a quarrelsome Rottweiler and an Argentinian Mastiff, with a nasty glint in its eye, as her Familiars. She took her chosen archetype of Sarama, the Bitch Goddess who led the Vedic dogs of death, very seriously!

Gwenda, a pagan potter, was flint eyed, dagger tongued and hadn't stopped rebelling since sauntering down the aisle to get married in red leather hotpants and fishnets (her parents had insisted on a church for her first wedding, they'd just rolled over for the following three). Her sensible nine-year-old daughter, Violet, confided that when her mum had given a talk on assertiveness skills to her Brownie group nearly all the mothers kept their daughters at home with colds. Gwen showed Moira around her studio, it was overflowing with colourfully confrontational canvasses and hair-raising sculptures of naked lascivious figures, several with snakes erupting from their genitalia.

"Um, very nice." Moira, blushing and studying the carpet, had managed.

It was Gwenda who introduced her to the Great West-East Divide. Whenever Moira mentioned her address the Penwith witches of West Cornwall would ooze jubilation, divulging in voices saturated with awe and homage: "You'll discover that very *special* people are drawn to this part of Cornwall, it's a very *enchanted* place!"

As a Kerrier woman, Gwen had snorted on hearing this, "What they mean is that anyone east of the Hayle estuary is just not pagan enough! Of course, to have real credibility you're expected to have Celtic blood in your veins and boast direct lineage to Gaelic speaking ancestors who wove cloth and sang a lot."

Moira, whose descent from the London suburbs clearly didn't count for much, was again deflated.

"Shucks," she mourned, "yet another status hierarchy with me at the bottom – down with the scum Anglo Saxons this time."

On a higher note, the Wicca dress code mainly consisted of ethnic cottons, big baggy sweaters (preferably with pentacle motif) and generous natured stretchy leggings. The hand of the hairdresser was thankfully not evident, long and tangled being the established mode. Men were thin on the ground (though thick in beard) amongst the pagan groups and excluded altogether from the witch covens. The majority of Wiccans were post-divorce and wickedly irreverent. Had they been around in feudal times they'd have all got a dunking on the ducking stool for sure.

Moira was accepted into a full moon group. ("Perfect," she rejoiced, "my cheek size. All four in fact!") Her new coven colleagues were very pleased to share their advice and opinions with her. They let her in on their secrets (well mostly other people's) and initiated her into the benefits of belonging to a whole caboodle of stroppy women of a certain age when it comes to dealing with hoodies, hooligans and Jehovah's Witnesses.

Sadly though, they refused to take her seriously when she requested a spell to make herself gorgeous before the end of the bikini season. Only Veronica, an incongruous slinky blond witch in floaty pastel chiffons, kindly recommended positive affirmations and mirror work. Moira declined the mirror work. She'd done enough of that in her life already – usually involving painful manoeuvrings with tweezers. Gwen's contribution to the Love Yourself Formula was to "dance naked on your lawn at dawn". Moira hoped the neighbours were either exceptionally broadminded or exceptionally short sighted.

The regular topics of conversation at the tarot card and rune stone meetings did not cover boob jobs, boring besotted boyfriend blabberings, nor panic-at-putting-on-a-pound freak outs. Sometimes they would chat for ages without a calorie count cropping up once! Moira, who hadn't previously mixed much with older women, kept waiting for the usual sarky slights and derogatory digs, taking much comfort when they didn't come. She started saying "Roll on cronehood!"

Chapter Three

It was the day of the Summer Solstice. The Moon Group were having a picnic by the Neolithic Men-an-Tol. With a full stomach of banana bread and blueberry muffins, Moira was lying flat on her back contentedly contemplating the sunlight bouncing off specks of quartz in the granite monoliths. She had embraced her new witchy life like Fat Cat Meets Cream. She was at heart – slowly defrosting from cold storage where it had been (partially) protected from past pummellings – a nice, well meaning, simple soul. She didn't attempt to analyse the Jungian complexities of her metamorphose, she just felt a lot more cheerful without needing to find reasons to be. She'd flushed her Prozac down the toilet.

The lazy drone of a bumblebee hovering by her ear drowned out the bickering coven. (They'd eventually reached a consensus that the universe is malleable, in keeping with the old English word Wicca meaning 'to bend or shape', but were ferociously squabbling over the extent to which it is permissible to create one another's reality. Is weather magic and rain dancing ethically sound for instance?) There was a skylark singing overhead and the smell of yellow gorse in the air from the heath.

"It's on such a day as this" Moira mused "that old white-haired rabbits wonder which way Time went. Or maybe, when twilight tints the shadows purple, a doorway opens in the ageless hills leading to the Faery Halls!" She'd been indulging in tales of Morgan le Fay and Tintagel, Tristan and Iseult, the giant Cormoran and legends of Madgy Figgy of Tol-Pedn-Penwith. Today her soul was being pisky led into the lavender and lilac realms.

The mayhem of the group packing the picnic remains into their rucksacks broke Moira's reverie and recalled her to coven controversy. Discussion had moved on from the morality of manifestation magic to whether the central holed stone of the Men-an-Tol symbolised Mother Earth's vagina. Moira declined both an opinion on the terrestrial anatomy debate and the traditional squeezing through the granite orifice. Local custom guaranteed pregnancy; although she was getting no more sex than an amoeba, Moira wasn't taking any chances.

"You think you're safe and then angel Gabriel turns up," she warned.

On reaching the remote Nine Maidens stone circle across the moors, with Ding Dong engine house standing sentry in the distance, they encountered a group of Americans armed with what Moira supposed to be mangled coat hangers.

"Dowsing rods," Shirl amended, "made from mangled coat hangers".

They seemed to be reverentially placing their foreheads against each standing stone, though all moving at different speeds and directions around the circle. Consequently, there was a pile up forming in the top left-hand corner.

"Widdershins!" a woman in green with a red face was shouting, waving her arms to indicate an anticlockwise route.

"St Just woman," Maddie whispered. "She runs the Gaia Goddess Tours Ltd during the summer season. It caters for tourists with legs. Your average coach trip only stops off at the Merry Maidens because it's on the road to Land's End and has a car park."

Gwen rushed forward to greet the overheated green woman, interrupting her spiel on the St. Michael and Mary serpent ley lines.

"Hello Pat!" she waved. Pat shook her head severely.

Maddie nudged Moira again, "She's Ceres the Great Mother in work hours and Pat out of them," she explained.

"Business is thriving," Ceres-returning-to-Pat told them, having abandoned the Americans to their own devices with instructions to "close your eyes and tune into the Land's currents". (Though the resulting spate of bodily collisions amongst the megaliths didn't abate until she specified "*a stationary tuning!*")

"But I'm having trouble with the hate mail," Pat complained. "The local evangelicals have started a crusade to rescue their Holy Isle from the witches. Can't somebody tell them we had it first? They're accusing me of having a pact with Lucifer. Nonsense of course, I never truck with male immortals, neither God the Father, God the Son, nor God the Holy Ghost if it has a ghostly penis."

No one noticed that the ground shook.

Pat and Moira struck up an unlikely friendship. Moira enjoyed Pat's pungent put-downs of all things respectable / mainstream, while Pat found Moira's candid naivety endearing. (Moira was now feeling safe enough to start opening her mouth and letting things spill out, jettisoning her timeworn south-eastern survival strategy of appearing mute when possible and mumbling short insincere fabrications when not.) Pat, who was in her sixties, was kind and honest though as unbendable as her miner's cob terraced house which, like Pat herself, was unrenovated, undecorated and a bit jumbled. But also homely and warm. Her kids had outgrown it and flown east to become city sophisticates, leaving their less pretentious belongings behind to clutter up the place in their absence.

There was a shiny brass plaque on the front door, such as you'd find at a doctor's, which read in elegant italics, *Pat Trenoweth. Witch of the West.* On first seeing this, an embarrassed Moira had squirmed from foot to foot on her friend's behalf. Pat came bounding up the path behind her, beaming and booming:

"Like it? I'm thinking of adding a logo. What do you reckon – pointed hat or broomstick?"

After some preliminary cosmic ordering exercises, Moira secured herself a part time job in a bric-a-brac – referred to as 'Cornish curios' and extortionately priced for the tourists – shop in St. Ives. (Home town to the Seagull Mafia, with a sneaky beaky mobster on every post, all strategizing your bag of chips…) Moira spent her half days off in Pat's laidback lounge, which was filled with big bulgy cushions and a surplus of little tables – the sort that ought to fold into each other but didn't. Pat dished out mugs of strong tea and yummy homemade flapjacks. She talked a lot, at length and loud enough to be heard from her lofty soap box on the moral high ground. Moira nodded at regular intervals, borrowed her books and, when she wasn't looking, cleaned her kitchen.

They often walked the cliffs together as the sun was setting its burnish over the sea, sometimes they walked on until the moon rose up to sheen it silver. They followed the Tinner's Way or past Pendeen to the lighthouse. On damp days they'd trek through the eerie mist with the foghorn bellowing like a marine monster in labour. Moira found that when she talked Pat listened. This was an unusual experience, "It never happens in Staines" as she remembered.

Moira tried to expound to Pat, and to herself, on how she was feeling.

"I wake up in the early hours and for no apparent reason I start sobbing. And I can't stop. I don't know why. I'm happier now than I've ever been. My life's been fuller in the last four months than it has in the previous four decades! And I'm hardly a tragic figure, I've not suffered any heartbreaks, shark attacks or disfiguring fungal infections. Yet I feel like I'm in mourning. When I'm on the beach I keep turning to scan the horizon, as if there's something I've just missed. Something important. And it's too late to find it now. It's a sore, itchy sort of sad sensation."

Moira shuffled about a bit to help relieve the discomfort of opening up to emotions, hitherto kept securely buried somewhere in the earth's central iron core. Pat nodded sympathetically.

"Perhaps it's too late to reclaim your past but it's not too late to claim your future."

Moira thought it over, "Maybe if I get up extra early, I might squeeze more in to make up for lost time."

"Start with more marmalade on toast," Pat advised.

Chapter Four

After a spot of physical coercion, Moira attended the *Five Rhythms* dance class at Sancreed. When dancing in public had first been suggested she had replied with a definite "I'd prefer to pick stinging nettles naked, chew cacti, suck slugs, bathe in a tub of swarming wasps and fill my knickers with red ants, thank you all the same."

Pat had soothed her impending panic attack with a "That's fine, we'll leave it," and then collected her on the day and drove her there, holding her hand in a friendly gesture as she dragged her out of the car. Moira's heels left tracks along the entire length of the drive. Despite her acute trepidation it had been O.K. Nobody wore high-cut designer leotards and the women came in assorted shapes and sizes. In Wave Dance there are no steps or sequences to struggle over, and it felt deeper and more meaningful than aerobics.

One particular dancing session, about a month later, had been especially exhilarating and embarrassing. Moira had acted totally out of her normal passive nature. She'd got cross, *very cross* – well, ballistic blinding red-eyed rage really! And she'd shown it. It had spewed out of nowhere during the relentless drumbeat of the "Chaos" crest of the wave.

Moira had found herself roaring and snarling, barring her teeth and pounding the wooden floor in fury. And had she howled? Yes, she distinctly remembered throwing back her head and howling like a wolf! She growled and yowled and scowled magnificently, without a thought as to what a fright she was looking! She'd boiled in furious frenzied sulphur and thrashed about like a rampaging squid! Three people were scared off the dance floor. And, although afterwards they said it had been very expressive, Moira noticed they didn't come too close while they were saying it.

Whilst in the midst of – what Sarah, the empathic dance facilitator, delicately described as "getting in touch with your Lilith and Eris energy" and Pat curtly dubbed "a whopping big strop" – she'd run amok around the hall smashing faces. Not physically but in her head. The faces of all those callous work colleagues, condescending bosses, condemning relations, cruel lads, false friends, sneering hairdressers, judgmental train commuters, dismissive teachers, sniggering schoolgirls and oblivious acquaintances who blanked her, dumped on her, patronised her, ridiculed her and left her feeling ugly and unacceptable. She cursed them all, and one by one shoved them off Hell's Mouth cliff. Then she drove a heavyweight rotary mower over their corpses. And fed the seagulls. She felt a bit better after that.

Moira resolved no more playing the Doleful Doughnut role assigned to her. She stormed and fumed and railed to the spectres of her past (and to the room at large) that she "hadn't been given a *flea's* chance to like herself! And *they* could have afforded to be charitable, they were the Loved Lovelies after all!" Majestically and with relish, she swiped the blame back from herself and heaped it, sizzling with hot coals, on everyone else. She didn't care if this was unreasonable. She was *fed up* with being reasonable; she wanted to be as temperamental and selfishly wilful as only pretty girls and seductive women get away with. *So, she would so!*

At the end of the dance, she limped out with blood blisters on both big toes.

Pat made her talk. "After a major clear out in the shit house you need to discuss new interior design," she insisted as they sat in her car, engine firmly switched off.

A distressed Moira, still churning like a butter barrel, kept looking longingly at the ignition key, trying to silently indicate that her duvet was waiting for her to crawl and hide under.

"I guess you're right about the shit," she whimpered. "It was. My life stank. And I never even sussed how crap it was; it's not as if I could wake up and smell the roses above the stench!"

She attempted to communicate the great big Full Stop at the end of this confession and again stared hard at the ignition. Pat waited. Clearly going nowhere. After an overdue-date-pregnant pause Moira was induced to confide, rather reticently as she was afraid of what else might spurt out of her atrociously behaved subconscious.

"Well, following my frenzy, I just slumped in a corner panting a lot. And the strangest thing happened. More memories but older ones, ones I'd forgotten, started seeping up into my mind. I remembered, I must have been about seven or eight at the time, lying face-down in the muddy grass with a boy's boot in my back. I was desperately pretending to be lifeless in the hope of escaping more agro. I was always bullied on my way home from school. I used to call it *The Walk of the Tin Can Maiden* because I ended up with dents.

"That was at primary school. At secondary school it was more wit than thuggery, which hits harder and leaves deeper scars. (One smart Alec once commented that my backside reminded him of a planetary gas giant, so – unhappily ever after – whenever I lifted my bottom off a chair to stand up, the class would chorus 'Jupiter ascending!'. That joke was milked until the geriatric cows came home.)

"Yep, the teen years were the worst. I used to die of humiliation daily – hourly! And yet that kick in my back at seven did something to me which never went away. It was like a vaccine injection of distrust and fear which stays in your bloodstream forever. If life had a dial, that kicking set mine on a background static of Unremitting Misery. I survived, survival of the unfittest, but I didn't become who I might have been."

She took a gasping breath at this point, like a shipwrecked sailor struggling up from the mucky depths with a mouth full of seaweed.

"Then this really trite image popped into my head, of a young me – not as a child but as a fledgling. A fledgling which never got airborne because someone was always putting the boot in. And I had this vision of lots of dowdy little brown sparrows, dragging broken wings, under every bush in Britain. Because some of us never got off the ground. We never learnt to fly. We didn't get the chance. Does that sound pathetic?"

Pat shook her head and produced a tissue. Moira gulped, mopped up a bit, and plodded on.

"The other day a psychic fair Reiki Master told me that my solar plexus chakra (the seat of self-confidence) is badly debilitated. I'm only amazed it hasn't shrunk down to threadworms and wriggled away completely!"

Moira paused but Pat didn't laugh – not fooling no one.

"Oh, O.K. then... The truth is I've been screwed up, thrown away, kicked in the gutter, squashed down and walked over as if I'm an unwanted soggy paper bag. And I still feel damp." Moira sniffed loudly and sighed.

Pat gave Moira a long soft look, "Come on home, Mogs. I'll fix you a stiff drink."

"How stiff?" Moira snuffled, but with a return to the reason for living, "Can I have a Hot Chocolate thick enough to stand a spoon up in?"

It was pitch black when they got to St. Just. Pat made Moira a Horlicks (oh woe! no chocolate in the house, liquid or solid). She kindled a fire in the lounge grate and lit candles instead of switching on switches, possibly out of respect for Moira's swollen eyelids and blotchy face.

"First fire for months. It's only the end of August but the nights are drawing in and there's already a nip to the air," Pat commented, as she coaxed the twigs to catch. "It seems only a moment ago we were celebrating Lammas. Now that's a deceptive festival, there you are in the height of summer, surrounded by ripe wheat and flaxen corn, with the juicy fruits of harvest hanging in abundance and the freshly baked plait loaf smelling heavenly. But underlying all this bounty lies the sharp edge of the scythe, the approaching sacrifice to appease the ruthless winter ghouls waiting in the wings! The Corn God mercilessly cut down by the Grim Reaper. The red evening sun burns without heat and everything is at its fullest before it begins to fade from the world."

In honour of the approaching doom and gloom, and to make up for the lack of chocolate, Pat mixed a saucepan of warming punch. The spicy aroma wafted deliciously about the room and Moira, who enjoyed being pampered and fussed over, started to cheer up – though still a little limp from her unaccustomed energetic and emotional expenditure. (She was also beginning to cringe, now that the steam had subsided and lava congealed, in hot sticky plum-faced mortification over her public eruption and was thoroughly considering the possibility of Life in a Cupboard. Preferably a kitchen cupboard.)

"And tonight, my poor lacerated lamb, because it's a blue moon and because digging out the debris from old scars is a sore and sopping process, you get to peep inside my Treasure Chest!" Pat pledged in thrilling accents, dramatically whipping the tie-dyed cover off a leather and brass trunk standing in the corner.

"Ooh goody!" Moira squealed, and fell to.

Pat's treasure trove was a kooky cache of ritual objects, several of which Moira had seen in both the psychologically intense lunar meetings and in the wayward celebratory solar festivals. There was a ceremonial wand, with a pointed clear crystal inserted at one tip and a smoky quartz at the other. Lying in a lead scrying bowl, very heavy with Norse cyphers around the rim, was a silver paper knife,

"An Athame," Pat corrected, "used for cutting a gateway in the sacred circle – on account of my dodgy bladder."

There were ceramic bowls of small shells collected at low tide, gemstones and polished pebbles. A deep blue glass chalice cast an indigo shadow when held to the candle flame. *Mother Peace* tarot cards lay scattered about and there was a smudging stick of buzzard feathers bound in red and green wool at the shafts. A velvet alter cloth, slightly muddied from outdoor use, had been embroidered with phases of the moon in silver thread. And from the bottom of the trunk Moira drew out an old circular mirror, badly tarnished, set in a dark oak surround.

"Ah," Pat whispered mysteriously, "my witch's mirror. Incredibly ancient and doubtless used by some aged hag up to mischief many centuries ago. Look into the glass to see enchantment unfolding before your very eyes!"

"Hocus-pocus," Moira derided stoutly. Pat acquired a quizzical look. Moira half believed her and shivered.

Mustering up a sturdy show of bravado, she took a deep breath, "O.K. then, here goes. I wish to see my Life's Meaning!"

She held the mirror resolutely before her face, with its oaken back to the fire. With her thick eyebrows drawn together in concentration, she stared fixedly – like a kid with her first conjuring set – fiercely willing the magic to work.

Neither of them moved nor spoke; slowly the shadows shifted and the silence started to shout. As her eyes ached and blurred, a misty form took shape in the glass. The swirling grey haze steadily settled into a softly oval face, not her own, with heart rending almond eyes reflecting back at her. Moira caught her breath in a gasp and Pat moved closer to peer over her shoulder. As she did so another face appeared, the deeply lined visage of an old woman, stern enough in aspect to make Moira scream and drop the mirror. It smashed.

"Look out!" Pat warned, "Here comes the seven-year Bad Luck!" Then she whacked Moira smartly across the knuckles with the punch ladle.

Chapter Five

Moira was pacing the floorboards. After leaving Pat's (as soon as she could without appearing too much of a cowardy custard), she'd driven back home through the darkness; slowly to avoid the rabbits which nibble on the grassy verges and also because that stretch of coastal road twists sharply and unexpectedly, especially at night. Moira could have sworn the road was wriggling into fresh curves, like the long slither of an adder, whenever she nervously glanced in the rear-view mirror.

She'd slept fitfully and awoke at daybreak in a fidgety state resembling an overcharged electric toothbrush. She'd been doing housework ever since; which, after yesterday, felt a blessedly humdrum activity. While she wiped and hoovered, she puzzled over the evening's events. There must be a key to explaining it somewhere. But where do you find missing keys to open hidden doors to uncover lost answers? Hell's teeth and Hecate's gums! She wasn't even sure of the question.

By eight o'clock Moira had mopped the kitchen floor, degrimed the sink, polished the cat's bowls, removed the dead mouse from under the cooker and was hanging up the washing on the clothesline. Her next-door neighbour, Bev, was likewise hanging out her laundry, in an identically compact garden (though neater, with more patio tiles and plaster garden ornaments). Beverly was a spotless person, inside and out, a house-proud housewife (anxious to assist her more grubby neighbours) who smiled continually like a Tupperware party hostess and described everything as "*lovely!*"

"Cooey! *Lovely* drying weather!" Bev had called to gain Moira's attention. "You're busy early!" she flagged up with a note of approval.

"Couldn't sleep. Would you like tea and toast with me?" Moira offered, knowing that Beverly was the very woman to admire so much manic cleaning.

Bev and Des were a very normal couple in their thirties who couldn't have been married very long as they were always scrupulously polite to each other. There was a chrome framed wedding photograph on their sideboard revealing the happy couple in all their white frilled glory. On the lawn in the background of the photo, Moira spotted two toddlers in tangerine taffeta thumping each other and the unmistakable outline of a black Labrador having a poop.

"Oh my Goodness! Your kitchen's looking *lovely!*" Bev effused as Moira burnt the toast whilst making the tea.

"Here, let me do that," Bev insisted, decisively removing the breadboard from Moira's grasp.

"Sorry," Moira apologized, trying to conceal a tablecloth stain from her neighbour's rigorous scrutiny. "I can't seem to get my head straight this morning," she excused herself. "It's buzzing like a cicada bug on crack cocaine!"

She was feeling jittery and increasingly on edge, and Bev's chipper chitter-chatter about which foods were on special offer at the Co-Op really wasn't helping. In fact, she realised, if she didn't confide in someone soon, she might just have to grab the food waste caddy from the draining board and empty it over her hygienic neighbour's head! So, risking being thought crackers (but – hey – news of last night's Irate Stomp would doubtless be spreading across the district like one of its heath fires at this very moment), Moira sat down to tell her about the queer goings on at Pat's house. Above her hot buttered toast Bev's eyes grew rounder and rounder, her eyebrows heading Heavenwards as she listened. When Moira had finished, and was waiting for comment and critique, Bev remained dumb and gawking at her. Moira tried to open the debate:

"You probably think I'm gaga?" she volunteered.

"Oh no!" Bev breathed gravely. "I'm sure it happened just as you described! But you *must* be more *careful* about what you're *getting yourself into!*" And with that she gathered up her handbag and scuttled back next door to Des and her dishcloth.

Moira felt snubbed and deflated, so she talked to the cat instead. Tigger proved a better audience (cats considering it undignified to register anything as vulgar as common shock. Though they do a good line in disdain when it suits them) and he got a tin of tuna in recompense. Moira made herself a sandwich for elevenses and set off to Cot Valley cove to clear her head with the smell from the sewage outlet.

By the end of the day, Moira only needed a sensible man with a perfectly rational explanation to convince herself it had all been a trick of the mind. She was to have one. At six o'clock on the dot the doorbell rang. Standing on the front step, looking self-important, was her next-door neighbour and a man in a suit. He was middle aged, paunchy in the stomach, balding with a pasty complexion and he looked like a Man on a Mission. Which indeed he was.

Bev introduced her accomplice, "Ah Moira, this is Mr Hoskings, our lay preacher at St Edwyn's Chapel. He'd like to have a word."

"David," the man of a word spoke. "Pleased to meet you, Miss Box. I hear you're new to the neighbourhood. I do trust you're settling in well?"

"Yes, thank you," Moira replied, wondering why this ecclesiastical welcoming committee hadn't occurred back in March when she'd moved in.

There was a pause in which her visitors smiled in determination at Moira until she invited them in.

"Tea, coffee or something stronger?" she offered.

"Tea, black, no sugar, if you please," Mr Hoskings instructed.

"He's teetotal," Beverly whispered loudly enough for them all to hear.

They sat at the dining table which felt rather business like. David cleared his throat,

"We'd be delighted to see you at St. Edwyn's any Sunday, Miss Box. Des and Bev are regular attenders and would be happy to bring you, I'm sure." (From the other side of the table Beverly elevated into an angel.) "You'll meet some smashing people who will do their utmost to make you feel at home – *decent, trustworthy* folk I mean!"

At this he looked significantly at Moira. Bev joined in. Then he leant forward to be virtually eyeball to eyeball. This was the most intimate Moira had been with a man for years. She wondered if he had any amorous intentions. He was no oil painting but then neither was she for Elysium's sake! He also pervaded an off-putting well-scrubbed soapy smell. Moira began to deliberate upon which aftershave she could give him for Christmas, *Brut* didn't seem appropriate somehow. Moira tried to adjust her expression to look adorably puppylike and waited hopefully.

"I'm very concerned for you, my dear," he prosed on in a solicitous tone (so far so good). "I hear you're being drawn into some unsavoury company. I feel it's my duty as a Christian to *warn you of the danger*. I've lived in this part of the county for a long time and believe me when I tell you there's more to West Penwith than cream teas and holiday homes. There's a nasty sinister secret hidden in this peninsula, you only need scratch the surface and you'll discover the canker beneath the pretty picture postcards! *Witchcraft and Satanism!* The Devil isn't dead but walks in disguise in twentieth-century Cornwall! He preys upon the naive and innocent who are new here. I fear you're being manipulated and mislead. We've come to sound the alert and help you avoid the *gaping pit before your feet*! It's all too easy to fall in!"

As he spoke Moira began to see him standing on a plinth in a pulpit. She was rivetted by the way he stretched his eyelids back so the irises gleamed in two large white pools. There were little pink blood vessels creeping across from the corners and Moira wondered if he suffered from high blood pressure.

As he continued, he upped the tempo by a further octave, "People muck around with the paranormal as if it's a party game! They don't realise the strength of its *Destructive Power!* Mental institutions are full of poor gullible souls who foolishly dabbled with the occult! *Be warned!* It can scorch your mind until it burns to the socket!" (The whites of his eyes were positively raspberry-rippling milky lagoons by the time he had swelled and amplified into his grand finale.)

"You look like a common-sensible young lady," he appended his denunciation, coming down in decibels and wiping his brow with a blue checked handkerchief. "Check it out. Be vigilant and wary. Call upon us, day or night, if they pester you. Remember, we're here to save you from *Moral Peril!*"

After an impressive silence, David got up to go and Moira's charitable neighbour, eager to walk in his footsteps, hastily followed. (So hastily she trod on his heels – rather ruining the solemnity of his exit amidst profuse apologies.) At the front door, Mr Hoskings warned again "Beware of the Dark Side!" just like in Star Wars. Only he wasn't joking or a Jedi.

"We'll be praying for you!" was Beverly's parting contribution. She crossed herself as she left the premises.

Moira took the good Mr. Hosking's advice and checked it out. On her next visit to Redruth, she called in at the psychiatric hospital (built next to the viaduct to save on overdoses).

"I'm very worried about my Susie, you see nurse. Would you say many of your clients have a personal history of involvement in occult practices?" she enquired at the end of an impassioned monologue, clutching a mumsy handbag and adopting a native Cornish alias for credibility.

The staff nurse looked overworked and underpaid, but answered patiently and without undue interest.

"I really wouldn't stress out so much about your daughter, Mrs Cow Meadow," he reassured her. "Certain personality types suffering with mental health issues may well grasp on to anything mystical which feeds their delusions, but we've just as many fanatical Christians here who wear open-toed sandals and believe they're the Saint Augustine of Hippo, bless them! You see, Mrs Cow Field, there's really no more likelihood of your daughter developing psychoses from buying crystals and playing with her astrology starter kit than if she joined your neighbourhood church. It's probably best that you speak to your doctor next time you're worried, Mrs Cow Herd."

Moira then asked if there was an abnormally high percentage of psychiatric cases in her locality. She was told that "If the shape of Cornwall is like the Sock of England then Penwith is in the toe. Well, we all know where the nuts fall to."

Pat chuckled copiously when she got to hear about the Holy Delegation.

"David and I go back a long way unfortunately. The rest of the clergy have given up on me but Hoskings is like a pesky Jack Russell – always getting underfoot, scampering around with raised hackles and once he's got his teeth into your trouser hem there's no shaking him off at all! Don't get me wrong, I enjoy a good row – er, I mean discussion – but he will keep quoting scripture at you, as if it were some sort of final clincher on the ultimate truth. Most irritating."

"I just want to find out about my mirror maiden," Moira persisted with a touch of truculence. For days now, it felt like she'd accidently wandered into some impenetrable maze and got stuck in there, repeatedly bumping her head on dead ends. With the bull-headed stubbornness of a minotaur, Moira was tenaciously determined to get to the bottom of it all but the strain was making her tetchy.

"Then start looking in the right places," Pat admonished, "you won't find her in a psychiatric unit!"

"I know that – I'm not stupid!" Moira thundered back, surprising herself. (In her previous life of Heavy-Duty Dreary she'd been too depressed to achieve anger, merely operating in the standby mode of Low-Level Grumpiness, not ever saying anything confrontational but huffing a lot.)

"I do wish everyone would stop telling me what to do all the time!" she grouched on, finding that channelling one's Lower Self is really quite fun. "If it's not you, it's some lay preacher or the woman next door! I came down here to get *away* from being bossed about!"

"Ooh!" Pat grinned, "MOO, MOO, BLOODY MOO!"

Chapter Six

One mellow gold and faded blue twilight, the ending of a fine September day, Moira went on a vision quest, searching for the almond-eyed girl who was haunting her.

There's an open well at the top of a steeply stepped path, which mounts the cliffs from a secluded seashore on the rugged coast between Porthcurno and Sennen. At one time infants were baptised here and it still has the faint aura of a holy well, especially on such a silken evening with its soft light and white gulls soundlessly winging across the ocean.

This freshwater spring fills a small pool, enclosed by well-worn paving slabs and thick with viridescent waterweed growing beneath the rim. Moira had no offering so she emptied out her canvas pumps and dropped in a handful of grounded shell grains from the beach. Fervently gazing into the jade water, she called upon Nagini, the Vedic Serpent Goddess with her snaky tail, who lives in underwater temples and guards the sacred wisdom of springs and wells.

"Nagini, listen to me! I am one of yours. In pain I shed my outgrown, red raw, scaly skin as I rattle and hiss and spit venom! I've come to you seeking the understanding under the truth. Share your Serpent Mystery with me! Don't send me back with hollow heart and shallow self. Unable to catch the kite strings of my soul, unable to leave the empty Wastes! I am prepared to pay the price of the depths in salt tears. If you summon me, I will descend to the Lost Lands beneath the sea." Thus Moira made her invocation.

The rolling waves slowly smoothed the sands below, and the tranquil air veiled a numinous presence around her. She had the sensation of being invisible and apart. The Evening Star shone low in the western sky and, upon the still waters of the well, a girl's bronze-green eyes spoke of an unspoken tale. Moira left not knowing what would come. But knowing something would.

Moira dreamt that night. In her dream it was winter. She was seated upon a three-legged stool, placed to one side of an inglenook fireplace in which a wood fire burnt. There were bunches of drying herbs hanging from rafters and a cream pottery jug on the dresser.

Aside from the crackling twigs, Moira noticed a rhythmic murmur which had been disturbing, or maybe adding to, the restful lull of the room. She moved her head to see that it came from the turning of a spinning wheel, worked by the bony hand of an old woman. The spinner, wearing dark woollen garments with a shawl about her shoulders, didn't look up for she was intent upon her task. Moira recognised the hag from Pat's mirror, no longer frightening, merely weathered and worn and gnarled as age-old oak bark. Moira turned back to the open hearth to watch the logs blazing, whilst grey smoke rose in wispy coils. Somehow, she belonged here. The dream stayed with her on waking.

The next day was the Autumn Equinox. Moira celebrated it with her witchy group on Porthtowan beach. All the women managed a chilly afternoon dip, albeit a quick flash-and-splash one with much squealing; some only venturing up to their knees, others braving the elements and taking the full plunge. Most skinny-dipped. Moira wore a sensible swimming costume under an apricot flannelette bath robe, flip-flops and a spotty shower cap.

Afterwards, sitting on blankets and clasping hot flasks to chest, they thawed out their frozen extremities by a lot of friction rubbing with towels. They talked about the meaning of dreams.

"Some forms of knowledge cannot be accessed directly," Jan began. "Messages from the psyche, for instance, may only be seen obliquely, through omens, coincidences and dreams."

She gave them an example. "In my dream it's prehistoric Britain. There are two sisters: Abira and Dajen. One day Abira leaves the safety of the encampment to climb the Hallowed Mountain. Lighting a burning torch, she enters a cave mouth there.

"Meanwhile, Dajen stays with the tribe and marries a handsome warrior. But it turns out that good looks are all he has, besides syphilis. So she crosses the war-torn barren scrub, the territory of the dangerous Musgothians who punish their prisoners by binding a rotting corpse on to your back, to join Flavanna, Ancient Warden of the bluebell wood, learning her wisdom and in time becomes Warden herself."

"Yes, go on then, what do you reckon it means?" Rianne queried as Jan switched her attention to getting the sand out from between her toes.

"It's really quite obvious – in the language of dreams," Jan clarified, taking pains to talk down to her audience. (Rianne, behind her back, stuck her tongue out.) "Both sisters are aspects of myself. Part of me wished to pursue an Otherworldly Journey but another part, Dajen, prefered to stay in the paddock grazing with the flock, getting married and making do in a materialistic society where people live like dead things having lost all sense of meaning and the Sacred, hence the Musgothians."

"Well, what about Abira? Did she have an easier time of it?" Olive asked.

Jan raised her eyes in blatant astonishment, "Good Grief no! Whoever said the spiritual path was easy? Sadistic savages and cosying up with rotting carcasses are *nothing* to it!"

Afterwards, Pat and Moira went for a stroll along the coast. The tide had rolled right back allowing the two friends, tall and gaunt and short and tubby, to walk the golden stretch from Porthtowan to Chapel Porth with no more than wet feet.

"This wise old woman theme which cropped up in Jan's dream and in mine, you don't see it much in films do you? Moira brooded, as she squelched over the soggy sand. "And even when you do see an actress over fifty on glamour commercials, she normally has to look ridiculously young and attractive for her age." She thought for a moment, before remarking more hopefully, "But then again there *is* Maggie Smith."

As Pat on her long legs strode ahead and Moira on her little ones pattered behind, they continued to stew over the indignant fate of elderly women.

"She's generally put down by society and put upon by her grown up children as free childcare. Apart from that she mainly goes unseen – practically the Western equivalent of purdah!" Moira bemoaned.

"No sex appeal you see, Mogs. She's not going to sell any cars or brands of beer," Pat pointed out with asperity. "Though she is beautiful, the Crone, in the way of Tibetan Art. (The Tibetans say that 90% of the beauty in their art is invisible.)

"The churchmen had in for her too. Hecate, the Greek Grandmother Goddess, was renamed as the Queen of Witches by the early Christians – and it wasn't meant as a compliment! There was only one thing that terrified men more and that was *death*. Oh, not other people's, they were quite happy to slaughter thousands in war or in the Inquisition's bloody trail. But their own, quite another matter! No wonder the Crone Goddess was so hated, She represents death and endings. – Also rebirth and reincarnation but the Church isn't big on recycling either."

Pat and Moira broke into a slow jog at this point with a wary eye on the incoming tide. Conversation was suspended and all breath reserved for getting to the next cove before the Fish Mother caught them. On reaching Chapel Porth they collapsed panting on the pebbles, having first checked out that the café was, tragically, closed. Moira, whose thinking was still gnawing on the same spot, apart from the fleeting hope of ice creams, carried on where she'd left off.

"But anyway," she announced on a chirpier note, "I was forgetting, in my new career as Hex and Hindrance I don't have to bother about any of that. I can positively relish getting old!"

"And so you should, duckie!" Pat approved. "The long awaited Come-back of the Crone is coming! The third aspect of the Triple Goddess will rise up from the back burner!

"Hopefully, once Elder-status has become a thing, I'll get some well-deserved recognition at last," she pursued, exposing her number one private grouse, "and if only everyone would stop banging on about youth and beauty, then you and the Loathly Lady Ragnell can advertise Lamborghinis."

"As well as old age for women, I intend to reclaim the word *hag*." Moira proclaimed, determinedly ignoring Pat's (kindly meant but horrendously tactless) unfortunate last comment. "I heard that it derives from the Greek *hagia* meaning 'holy one'. 'Hag' used to be a cool word! And she was worshipped, both as the *Hag of the Dribble* in Wales and as the *Feast of the Hag Goddess* on New Year's Eve (*Hagmenai*) – and what about the much-loved Scottish haggis?" Moira quizzed

"Oh, she had many forms and followers once upon a time," Pat hastily followed up – anxious to move speedily on from her faux par. "She was Minerva, Shakti, Kali Ma, the Morrigan and the Caillech. In ancient China their Fireside Goddess was described as a 'beautiful old woman in red garments'."

"Well now's a good time to reinstate her, with an aging population and longer life expectancy for women, there are going to be too many of us to be restrained! Let's make the first of November an annual *Fab Hag Day!*" Moira proposed. "All the crones can come out of their closets and care homes to upstage the delectable young hotties on *Baywatch* and *Hollyoaks!*"

"What a nice idea, sex over seventy will be back in!" Pat applauded, "And when society at last appreciates its golden oldies for their wealth of knowledge and discernment, coach companies could arrange excursions to the most outstanding geriatric venerables. Then I can pass on everything I know. Sort of *Day Trips to the Elderly*".

Shortly after this Moira came across a poem about the Crone in a pagan periodical. And, so as to constantly remind herself of the figure she's aspiring to, she cut it out and stuck it on her fridge door (just as women's slimming clubs recommend).

Crone Woman,
Spirit Seer,
Stern Guardian,
Beloved Elder.

You walk on the edge of Mystery,
Looking beyond our world,
And back across the storms
You have weathered.

Perceiving past the illusions of living,
The disillusions of experience.
Knowing the source,
Reaching the heart of the labyrinth.

You are winter winds howling,
Blowing away dead leaves,
Stripping down stark boughs
Knit against a stony sky.

You are sunset's soft afterglow,
Moonlight on luminous snow;
Wearing a cloak of the Initiate,
You are Night.

The Gateway,
The deepest trance,
The last stance
On staunch cliffs before the sea.

Youth appears more than it is,
A glossy magazine of adverts.
Age, barely visible in the shadow,
Expands further than eyes can go.

Wisewoman, you wear your wild spirit
Warm with the heat of the hearth.
I hope, growing old, that I may too
Soar soul-strong and hold heart true.

Chapter Seven

After the Equinox the weather took a turn for the worse and by the end of October was plummeting into a drab winter. Both the mornings and evenings were enshrouded in darkness, and the hours in between with wet cold fog. Except for those days when the whole peninsula was battered by the infamous Atlantic winds which blast the breath out of your lungs. Zilch chance of keeping the cat flap closed.

Moira, who was a product of the Yorkshire Ripper era, always avoided walking alone after nightfall. Consequently, she felt trapped and depressed at this time of year and no amount of chocolate fudge could perk her up before March. As her spirits plunged downwards she began dwelling on the bleakest scenarios, fretting over what she had done and what she hadn't done, worrying about what she might be unable to do and what she might inadvertently end up doing! She became morbidly obsessed with finding a clue to the Mirror Maiden Mystery and would wake up too early and gnaw her fingernails, unwilling to get up and be constructive at such a dismal uncharitable hour.

Pat found her in this sorry state on the last day of the month, scooped her up and took her to the Samhain celebrations on Gwenda's land. The barns were decorated with autumn leaves and red berries, and the pagan merrymakers with long cloaks (Moira's was a converted rayon curtain), ivy garlands, black eyeshadow and lashings of silver glitter. As well as the motley haggle of witches and pagans, there were also a lot of over excited dogs and hyper children, plus a couple of brave Christians from Plymouth come to suss out the opposition – which has to be taken seriously now it can't be burned.

One of the more mythically minded men wore antlers, which looked impressive until they got caught up in the grid on the barn wall above where the luckless would-be Herne the Hunter was sitting. Another hopeful chap was adorned in full wizard regalia complete with tapering wobbly hat. Moira wondered, as she listened to his irritating "let's all go skyclad" (pagan for naked) chat up line (not to her), why the poor old witch has traditionally got such bad press whereas the Merlin / Gandalf look has always been the Beloved Darling of the Nation?

Lanterns were lit for the ritual with a bumper bonfire and fireworks to follow. Gwen talked to her captive audience (the adults) in the old cowshed and banished the uncapturable ones (kids and canines) to play in the field. As it was, they only just packed in, everyone having to sit with someone's knees in their back and to shallow breathe.

"Samhain is the end of the pagan year when the wheel winds slowly before taking another spin, when nature is at a low ebb and the life force withdraws down into the roots and out of sight," Their relentless priestess hostess elaborated at length. "It marks the start of the descent, reaching its darkest hour at the time of the December Solstice, after which the hard climb back to the light begins."

But being a true Scorpio, Gwen wouldn't let the Dark be put down as the bad guy. (In fact, she seemed to be in such raptures over everyone's abysmal fate that Moira questioned how her numerous husbands had ever dared turn their backs!)

"Without the Descent, scary and painful though it is, we stay stuck in toytown eating the candyfloss Big Brother spoons us. Cycles of birth, growth, decline, death and rebirth are necessary cycles of Gaia. What is gone is not lost, what dies is reborn, what decays nourishes new life."

Next, Nellie led a creative visualisation, pushing everybody down spiral steps into the vaults of the Abyss and tipping them into a bottomless underground lake. Once there, floundering in sub-zero water, Nellie relented a little and allowed them to transmogrify into whichever water creature they felt akin to. Moira tried hard to imagine herself as a graceful mermaid with long raven tresses but, overriding all her efforts, she kept shapeshifting into a manatee – a roly-poly, substantially blubbery marine beastie, like an egg with flippers and stumpy snout, commonly known as the sea cow. She got rather annoyed with her subconscious for being so literal minded and churlish.

Down in the inky depths they encountered the Cave of the Ancestors. A gift, personal to the receiver, was awaiting them there. Moira found a box with "Pandora" written on the lid. At the bottom, after the bugs had buzzed out and stung her, was not "hope" but "wholeness". Nellie brought them back; Moira was looking disgruntled.

Everyone then got to throw a pebble into the cauldron along with a negative quality. People threw away "indolence", "guilt", "celibacy", etc. Moira threw away "pimples". There were murmurs of "dear of her!" After this, apple and pomegranate slices and sparklers were dished out and so there was no keeping the kids away any longer. The partying began.

Queuing up for quiche and jacket potatoes, Moira fell into conversation with a Roger from the Christian division of the S.W. Ecumenical Association. He seemed genuinely interested in Moira's beliefs, and not overly anxious to save her soul for Jesus, so she was encouraged to elucidate on how a religion which has a male godhead and male representatives, had left her (as a little girl deposited at Sunday School each weekend so her parents could copulate undisturbed) feeling second rate. The majority of figureheads in her era were male – albeit, in the case of the religious ones at least, often wearing long frocks. (Most little girls had aspired to a mass-produced plastic doll permanently standing on its toes, with an impossible hourglass figure and a painted pink smile which never fades, as their female role model.)

The devout Roger seemed to be listening attentively and bobbing his head a lot. However, when Moira made an aside about how difficult it is to grapple with the concept of the Divine Creator, an inconceivable all-powerful deity, his instant response was "That's easy, just think of Him as *Dad!*" Moira, discouraged, gave up and went off to eat a tofu burger.

Later on, after the food had gone, people began drifting off home or gathering around the fire to bang drums. Moira and Pat pulled up a hay bale and sat warming themselves, their hands stretched out before the smouldering logs. At its birth the monster bonfire had been a red-hot fire dragon, disgorging a swarm of darting sparks up into the black sky and billowing its smoke into the stinging eyes of any who dared to approach, but now in its mellow old age, it lay domesticated and quiet as a warm mound of glowing embers and white ash flakes. Pat started ruminating while Moira's wellingtons were toasting nicely:

"All Hallow's Eve – Samhain – is the time of restless earth-bound shades, when Inanna has been butchered and hung on the meat hook in Hades. It's when the veil between the worlds is at its thinnest, when the Gates of the Dead stand gaping open, when the Unreal becomes real enough to drift amongst us. On this night we mortals are bidden to summon up our long-gone forebearers. Perhaps it's time for us to get a splodge of Otherworldly info, eh Mogs?"

"Come on then, let's get on with it!" Moira commanded, imitating Pat (who didn't spot the joke).

They borrowed a large scrying bowl from their hostess and carried it up to the top pasture, filling it with rainwater from the horse trough. Pat cast them a circle of protection, invoked the four quarters and drew down the moon, which was waxing. They sat on bin bags upon the cold ground and gazed into the glistening metallic bowl, occasionally dimming as wispy Cirrus cloud skidded across the night's sky. Moira began to go boss-eyed.

"Don't look away," Pat directed, "it's when your rational mind's befuddled that the Second Sight takes over. Just do as I do."

After twenty minutes of bone chilling Pat slunk back to the bonfire. Moira, whose parents had called "the world's most obstinate child", stayed to freeze.

Once alone, the empty pasture seemed a strangely eerie place. Without Pat's puffing, the silence felt lead heavy, the air crisp and as sharp as knives. Moira could almost see the frost settling upon each blade of grass and the moonlight shafting off them. The reflections in the brimming bowl began to glint and pull. Dragging her down into the icy water. Drawing her out of her mind into the black.

An hour later, after a sudden torrential downpour from cloud coverage which sprang up from nowhere, Pat in mackintosh came up to retrieve a chubby drenched rat. Moira's hair was sticking to the sides of her face in wet streaks from which rain still dripped. Pat had to shake her to achieve a dazed look and vacuous murmur.

"Are you staying out all night?" Pat barked, shaking her again with even more vigour, "You feel like stone, have you turned troll?"

"Um… How long have you been gone? Has it been raining?" an almost absent Moira mumbled.

"If you're going to start going into trances on me I'll take you to a professional tomorrow!" Pat threatened. "Now come on, for Goddess sake! Don't you know how late it is? Tigger will be having kittens!"

The professional's name was Alec James, a specialist in reincarnation and past life regression, who Pat booked an appointment with when it became clear that Moira just wasn't going to drop it until she got a proper explanation for her time lapse. The P.L.R. man was full of zest and bounce, and wore hectic colour combinations of patchwork pattern as if he'd stepped straight from a pantomime. He reminded Moira of the Pied Piper and she fell at once under his entrancing spell.

She and Pat went for weekly regression sessions throughout the winter. The results were recorded and labelled according to the date in a sixteenth-century incarnation that each was catapulted back to. Some entries appeared as if the events were unfolding before their very eyes, others as if the day was reviewed at the end of it. Each was spoken in a voice unrecognized by its owner, of remembrances from before memory.

Alec told them that the life we're living is just a tiny pinch of us – like the proverbial protruding tip of the gigantic iceberg submerged in an Ocean of the Unremembered.

"Past lives are our deepest roots, they are hidden and furthest down out of reach. But they bleed into the us nevertheless. Should one emerge just beneath the surface it has a message to tell you and the message is for the present, not the past. Listen to it, for the gone and forgotten may yet be twisting and distorting this life's growth."

The regression process resembled bubbles leaking up from some closed off subliminal chamber; slowly and separately at first but then gathering speed and frequency so that they merged together in a stream of continual consciousness. The accompanying sensations also came thicker and more pungently, until Moira became immersed in them, sometimes losing track of who she now was so that Alec would have to do some vigilant grounding exercises involving much foot stamping.

The first images that filtered through were static pictures. Moira would receive a vivid view of a lane, enclosed above by buckthorn trees and edged with dogwood. There was a stile set in the hedgerow and fields rolling beyond it in gold and russet tones. It felt like memory rather than imagination for there was an attached tug of feeling, and she experienced a strong pull to cross the lane to the stile as if she did this daily, heading down to the village with a basket over her arm.

As had happened so many times since arriving in Cornwall, Moira – grasping her metaphorical witch's broom – was having to brush out her old beliefs from under the rug. It was as if her life had a false bottom, which was now giving way to show a second life buried beneath it. Like an excavated Pompeii with a personal agenda.

Moira had opened a can of caterpillars. Who knows what they might grow into? Each Wednesday Alec spooned them out and Moira chewed on them till spring.

Part II

Martha's Mirror

Earth, Air, Fire and Water,
remember the lost magical daughter;
fruit of temptation, coil of lust,
the witch is burning with passion and love.

Copper leaves turn and fall from the tree,
twisted truths around us creep;
flesh into fungi, lore made mute,
corruption covers our hidden roots.

For the Craft of the Wise, staking their lives,
hang by the neck at the crossroads of time;
history smothered, the dug-up dirt,
long-time buried beneath the skirt.

The witches return.

8th *July 1589, entry by Hannah*

I am the daughter of Jacob and Tamsin Greene. My parents' names are written in the church register at St. Oswald's of Durlow, Herefordshire, along with the names of my brothers, Joshua and Samuel, listed under *Births of the Parish.* My name is also there, Hannah Greene born 23rd October 1576. I am now twelve years of age.

I have not seen my family, nor heard word, for a perturbing length of time and know not whether they are alive or dead. Sometimes, when I am sorely missing them and most fearful of their fate, I will go down to St. Oswald's to look upon the recordings and to run my finger over the mark my parent's inscribed there on their wedding day. As a little girl it brought me some comfort, for I held some fanciful belief that, should God see me tiptoe timidly into His church upon my errand, He might spare an angel to watch over my family wherever they should be. I still pray it is so.

Before their departure we lived on a small farmhold but in the year of our Lord 1583 the tenancy charter expired and our landlord, Yeoman Crouch, who owns several furlongs of fertile land in the valley below us, raised the rent too steeply to meet the half of. My parents, now dependent on poorly paid seasonal work, determined – being able bodied and sanguine in nature – to make a new life for themselves in the city. Being the youngest by several years, I was left behind to live with my grandmother, Martha Herrington, whom they trusted and with good reason, for she has been as a mother to me ever since.

After their departure Nan met with some difficulties for my father left many debts behind, and his name is still unpopular in the village.

One of my earliest memories, I must have been four or five summers perhaps, was a distressing one – though trivial enough to adult eyes. But the very young view the world from a lesser height, things closest to hand are vast enough to fill a child's whole vision whilst remote and abstract matters, which the grown-ups fret and fume over, are as high above young heads as the geese flying north in the spring.

One Sunday, as on any other, the village was at worship in church. I was hardly aware of the Reverend Hickes delivering his sermon, though the sound of his voice bounced and echoed off the bare stone walls, for I was intent upon a poor butterfly trapped inside the window, battering its soft felted wings again and again against the pane. Occupied thus, I was shaken to my toes to suddenly perceive the vicar, with his ecclesiastical robes billowing, swooping down upon me like a great black-backed gull!

To my infant terror he seized my knitted mitten, pulling me from the pew and along the length of the nave, to stand petrified before the congregation. I took one dazed look at the rows of parishioners, all their solemn faces directed at me with one accord, and I shook in fright and would not again lift my eyes from the flagstones on the floor. A heavy hand pressing down upon my head forced me to my knees, where I remained trembling so violently that my little legs were blue with bruises after.

"Let us watch over these innocent babes, so ignorant and weak, lest they fall by the wayside and cannot be redeemed!" His words boomed out loudly to reach any deaf ears of body or soul. In my exposed position beneath the blazing minister they blasted like trumpets to wake the dead!

"Four laws I would counsel to your children," and with this he thrust his fearsome face into mine for a long dreadful moment, "to tread the road of Righteousness."

"First and foremost, to serve the Almighty Father with your utmost endeavour your life through. Next in sanctity, to honour and obey your earthly father and mother in all things. And parents beware! Your Christian duty is to chastise your children's reprobate acts and to beat out wilfulness 'til they repenteth. For the soul that sinneth, eternal torment shall be its damnation! The third commands constant attendance, and with reverence, at each and every Sabbath service to learn Godly instruction here. Lastly, I bid of you most vehemently to prepare for your life's task as diligent husband or dutiful wife, without question nor weakening."

I was sent back to my seat after this, too scared to utter a whimper, my face crimson and crumpled which I sought to hide beneath my bonnet in shame. The rest of the service passed in a blur of burning cheeks; in my childishness I believed 'twas the heat of Hell that roasted me thus!

As we left St. Oswalds and made our way back up the lane, I kept my head bent down, occasionally stumbling as I walked, for my eyes were filled with the tears I struggled to withhold. My father chucked me under the chin and, with a guffaw, called me "his little lambkin to the slaughter". He did not consider the incident to be of note, nor so my mother who rushed ahead after my brothers in trepidation of harm to their Sunday-best clothes.

But grandmother Herrington, my dear Nan, stepped up and took my hand in hers, straightaway setting my little world to rights and as the relief came the tears gushed out. Without a word Nan lead me away from the chattering villagers, into the meadow we went, now golden green with merry buttercups. She sat on a fallen tree trunk there, settled me upon her knee and wiped my wet face dry with her kerchief.

When I'd finally managed a wonky smile, she spoke to me in earnest, cradling me close – though the day was fine – as if against a cold wind blowing.

"Hannah, my little one, I also would like to give you some good advice. Not to constrain or frighten you, but to aid you to live happy and content. To the vicar's four I would offer three decrees, a sacred number of long ago.

"To take joy in life is the bedrock to all blessings, to follow where your heart yearns to go, though in ways that harm none. The second leads on from the first. Just as I would caution you to harm no other, so would I entreat you to forebear from harming yourself. Do not rebuke yourself unnecessarily, nor listen to others when they unjustly put you down as they are all too wont to do. Be not downcast when you make mistakes for thus we learn, nor despairing that you have failings for so have we all. Be your own best friend, Hannah.

"Thirdly, my darling, do not swallow wholemeal the 'truths' and dictates others thrust upon you. For several will give you indigestion of mind and disease of heart. Think for yourself, weigh up and sieve what your eyes see and your ears hear. It will arm you better, my angel, than the swords grand gentlemen wear about their hips."

23rd *October 1589, entry by Hannah*

It is my birthday today and I have reached thirteen at last! It seems I have been *forever* waiting for this day! Everyone makes such a fuss about the number thirteen. The girls shriek and flee if they pick it in games, and the old folk cross themselves and say 'tis an ill omen. All manner of people creep about on the day of Friday the thirteenth as if it is a boggart set out to jinx us! We look for odd things, bad things, things that send the shivers skidding up your arm, sliding over your shoulder and slithering down your backbone! And what uncanny, ghoulish happenings might befall *me* over the next twelvemonth, during the span of its thirteen moons, now that I carry my own thirteen years like a banner to tempt the Fates? 'Tis so exciting I tap my toes in anticipation!

'Tis well past sundown and I am sitting within the inglenook with Whisper, my black tom kitten, a-purring on my lap. Mellowed by the whirl of Nan's wheel spinning, I watch my hopes sweetly unfurl in the glowing heart of the fire. The smell of burning tallow from the candles and of the hemp between Nan's fingers blows about the room, driven by the draughts creeping under the door and squeezing between the tightly closed shutters.

We have not spoken for a while and the warmth seeps up and down between feet and forehead. As drowsiness slips around me in wisps, I begin to hear voices in the sizzling, spitting flames. Nonsense words like the gobbledygook of goblins:

Spittle spattle, hiss and hackle,
Hear your fate in the fire's crackle!
Throw the dice and stake your life
Or live to be a dead man's wife!

And indeed, as my eyelids begin to droop, I see miniature figures with sharp-chinned faces descending from the chimney, gliding down upon the curling smoke. How they heckle and mock, and – look there! – here comes a fiendish oversized head looming up from the hearth, leering and beckoning with its knobbly finger! Its black eyes glint wickedly in the firelight, while the jeering hobgoblins jiggle in the wavering air. I blink to shake myself free and they are gone.

A knock at the door jerks me fully to my senses. It's Hugh's knock, so I leap up and fly across the room before Nan has time to say, "It's too late to play with your friends now." As I lift the latch though, it is Hugh's ma who steps across the threshold – almost before I have time to get out of the way! But all is well for I spy Hugh hiding in the shadows. He winks at me as she rushes into speech:

"I've hurried up to see you, Widow Herrington, on account of my Thomas's chest. He's got this dry ticklish sort of cough which is mortal bad in the night hours, he protests he cannot sleep at all, try as he will, and I thought I'll just pop up the hill and ask my good neighbour Martha for a potion, as I'm sure she'll have something handy, what with all her balms and syrups for every affliction a poor soul may be stricken with goodness knows and more to boot I wouldn't be surprised! So lucky we are, as I was telling our Hugh here, to have such a skilled medicine woman right on our doorstep as we do and always so helpful and friendly like, 'tis good fortune indeed as I've said many a time! Why 'twas only last week you gave me that charm to keep the ants out of my larder and worked a treat it did, never an ant nor beetle I've seen since, crawling with its dirty six feet all over my meats and syllabubs!"

Nan reaches for her knitting, clicking the needles in time with our guest's quickly pace. On Edith's last visit, when she wanted my grandmother to use her second sight to find a lost pewter spoon, Nan finished an entire stocking.

I slip out and join Hugh, who's sitting on the low wall mimicking owl hoots to entice the shy nocturnal birds out of the woods. Hugh is my dearest, darlingest friend, I hope we'll be best friends always! I fill my lungs with the cool evening air and scan the dark skies for the moon.

"If you're looking for the Crescent Princess, I can tell you she has retired to her boudoir of fleecy clouds, where she adorns herself in silver and dreams of the glimmering wedding gown she'll wear when she's fully grown." Hugh says in his soft singsong voice.

"As do all we maidens!" I reply, giving him a pointed look to which he grins.

"I would give you the moon in your lap if I could catch it," he smiles with a mock bow, and I am content with that.

"Kitty the Cat's been hassling all evening," Hugh tells me. "She wanted Ma out of the way so she can slink down to the village to hang outside the tavern with Bessie and Leah Pond. They've had their ears to the ground like a pack of hounds all week, trying to sniff out when Ralph Crouch and his gang are drinking there. Looks like it's tonight."

Kitty is Hugh's sister and our senior by two years, though you'd think 'twas twenty to hear her talk! She banters him as only an older sister could get away with and Hugh as easy-going as he is. She calls me "her gullible babe" and sometimes gives me trinkets from discarded admirers. Hugh calls her "The Cat" or "The Devil's Vixen" and he bears a few scratch and bite scars to prove it!

"Does Ralph admire her?" I ask, for the handsome Yeoman's son has always been disdainful of us younger girls.

"Nay, not he! When he deigns to drop his glove, I warrant it will be for the very best on the market! Kitty's pretty enough for the other louts but not near fine enough for the Great Ralph! As I told her," he adds, showing me a fresh fingernail mark down his cheek, "and then I assured Ma that she needn't worry that some rogue might steal Kitty's virtue for she'd sell it cheaply enough given the chance!"

I jokingly make pretence of searching for more scratches but he shakes his head and says:

"No, not there. Look instead for the premature bald patch on my maligned scalp. The Vixen tried to sow my hair to the wind to feed next year's crop as fertilizer!"

I laugh and cannot resist tugging gently at his tawny locks myself. They slip deliciously through my fingers like silk.

28th *September 1591, entry by Hannah*

I walked along Baddons Lane today, on my way to Yeoman Crouch's farm where I've been hired to help gather in the apple crop. The hedgerows were all aflame with the reds and oranges of ripe berries – the bright shiny rosehips, the hard wine-red hawthorn fruit, the fleshy Lords and Ladies, the pithy Bryony berry and the Bittersweet. They're threaded through the twigs like beads of an autumn necklace and their piquant display gladdened my heart, adding a skip to my step.

I sang as I worked, filling three wicker baskets, with the sun low in a cornflower blue sky. I love the heady smell of the fallen fruit fermenting in the grass, where the wasps buzz and hover drunkenly. I was humming with the drowsy insects when I noticed a sudden silence from the birds which had been chorusing cheerily a moment before. I stopped, straightening my back, aware of the change in the atmosphere but unable to account for it, until I spotted Ralph Crouch leaning against the orchard wall with his eyes fixed upon me.

Brushing aside the discomfort at being spied upon, I greeted him and asked after his sister, Parnella, who sometimes joined us in play when we were children. Though she had been more aloof of recent years because, or so Kitty claims: "Her mother fears we may outshine the mutton charms of the dull Parnella and filch away the suitors she takes such efforts to procure! Mistress Crouch has convinced her precious lanky daughter that she is a cut above us." Ralph always knew he was.

"How long have you been there?" I asked.

"Long enough but I could watch you longer," he replied, and I misliked the way he leisurely cast his arrogant glance over me, "You've been growing up little Hannah, not now so little and grown into a real beauty besides!"

I felt the annoying fingers of a blush steal up my cheeks as he came several steps closer.

"How old are you?" he insisted on knowing.

"Fourteen," I answered, keeping a wary eye on him for I distrusted the leer upon his face.

"Fourteen is ripe enough to pluck a kiss then!" and he lunged to grab me with his long arms but I was too quick and eluded him, darting between the trees and out through the gate to run home.

22nd October 1591, entry by Hannah

Night has fallen and heavy rain is sheeting down outside. Nan has gone to the village to help Rachel Barnes with the birth of her fourth child for it has been a difficult pregnancy. But Hugh is keeping me company and we're sitting together in front of the hearth. He's feeds sticks to the ever-greedy fire, while I gaze into the flames trying to track my scattered thoughts leaping there. 'Tis the eve afore my fifteenth birthday but somehow this birthday feels disturbing, unlike the merriment of those that have gone before. I attempt to put this nagging unease into words:

"It's as if the comfortable gaiety of childhood has slipped a little. As if the firm fabric of life has become fragile, shrunk down to a facade hiding some horror I hadn't known was lurking there."

Hugh pauses and looks at me sideways. It crosses my mind how unlike he is to other lads, who cannot forebear to tease and taunt and turn all to rowdy jest. He gives me his attention and waits for me to say more.

"You know how it was when we were little and the grown-ups fed us pretty tales like toffee apples? I believed then, that once the land freezes all the birds and tiny creatures of the fields curl up in their nests and burrows, to be snug and cosy until the thaw. And with that assurance I was thrilled with the winter world and welcomed it in all innocence. But the truth is the White Weather is cruel, its seeming softness bringing cold and hunger beneath each thicket. And all those small cries of suffering are unheard and those little lonely deaths unnoticed, as we laugh and throw snowballs or sleep sound in our beds."

I hesitate, my vision inward and brooding, "When I was young and saw an old woman bent double from relentless toil, somehow the ache of that crooked back passed me by, whereas now I feel her bones grating with every throbbing step! And once the punishing reality cracks through the fairy-tale you can never again return to the child's safe haven, for you have found the world is of a darker hue and will remain so for evermore."

"This wood is from an elder tree," Hugh observes, indicating a burning log. "It makes me think of our own Elders. They bear the weight of responsibility upon their shoulders for they must carry the grimness of reality for us all. The callous truth they try to hide, wanting to wrap us in the fey fleece a little longer. *They* know there are few happy endings on the other side of it. I have seen this in your grandmother's eye when she speaks to you sometimes. But what I also witness – always, day and night, year after year – is the love she bears you! A whole life story in this dismal world has failed to extinguish that love, rather it has grown stronger in the shadow."

I look at his fine sensitive face in the glow of the firelight and I think again how unique he is, how special. Always so swift to follow my hazy meanderings, always several steps before me and diving deeper into the depths. As if this were his natural element, as if he has matured a hundred years in some mythical realm to return to us aged fifteen in body alone!

"But it isn't the ferocity of Nature I rail against, for though She is implacable She's abundant withal in Her bounty. No, it's the petty savagery of man that makes my blood boil!" Hugh rails with burgeoning anger. "Look at Rachel Barnes, fighting for her life at this very moment with only your grandmother at her side. For where is her husband? In prison on bread and water for a month. And why? Because he dared to plead for pay sufficient to put food into the mouths of his bairns! And so it is always stacked against the poor!

"Hannah, we live in a time of crisis! It is harder than ever before to eat by honest sweat alone. These last decades of the sixteenth century have seen prices soar, and the rich gobble up the livelihood of peasants like cattle munch upon grass, pulling it up by the root!" And I could wring out the frustration in his voice. "But laws to keep down wages are no longer needed, the population has mushroomed, the shortage of paid work ensures that we will slave for a pittance. I tell you, Hannah, in this remorseless world the well-fed man sucks the scant nourishment from the bare bones of the starving!"

"Wait!" I command, jumping up and running to my truckle bed to drag the straw pellet across the floor, flinging it down between us. "Here lie all the fat land owners and bigwig law makers who would stint on a miserable labourer's pay and charge a fortune for food. We're granted two minutes of their valuable time!"

We set too with gusto, punching and thumping the straw, at first in earnest and then with a return to the juvenile glee which a moment ago we'd claimed to have put behind us forever! It ends with us rolling around in helpless laughter and sitting up dishevelled and tousled, but with a return to hearty cheer. Hugh hugs me, declaring I am his tonic for melancholy and bile.

Wrapped within his warm arms, I know in my heart that life is really very, very good.

I continue to sit after he leaves, quietly pondering his words. Recalling his respect for the elders I think of my own dear grandmother. The village folk have always come to her in times of strife, especially in sickness for physicians are out of reach of our thin purses but Nan works as a natural healer for only a jug of milk or slab of butter from the dairy, and for thanks alone as needs be.

I believe that when I'm really old – not just playing at it – and looking back on my life, I will consider it well spent if I have helped just a mite as much as she has done. And so it is, with the last spark of the smouldering wood, I make my birthday vow. I will endeavour to follow in my grandmother's footsteps, I will commit my life path to serving my community. For how could I live with myself if I did less – when, for so many, life is such struggle?

13th *March 1593, entry by Martha*

The new vicar of St. Oswald's, Gregory Gifford, delivered a sermon this morning sour enough to curdle milk. Reverend Hickes' ranting used to churn the food in your stomach but it was lullaby in comparison! Gifford, if I do not mistake the gleam in his eye, is brimming over with holy fire and brimstone. He has dedicated his life to saving us – Heaven help us!

Our ways, it seems, are depraved. He abhors as indecent licentiousness the Sunday afternoon sports, while as for the table card games popular in taverns and alehouses across the country, these he condemns as Satan's vice, a bane upon the godly! He would forbid us to sing any but solemn hymns while we labour in the fields, and he would chain our feet for fear they might dance a jig!

The congregation sat meekly throughout, with bowed heads and humble countenances. Nevertheless, after the service the same were out again, men and women alike, with their bowls and stoolballs upon the village green. The only dour faces were those of the little ones kept in the cold church to learn the Creed by rote.

I linger awhile, perched on the stile, to watch their revels. My granddaughter, leaving the knot of young people who have been her friends since her first wobbly steps, comes over to join me. Now sixteen and a young woman, she is more fair of face and form than any I have seen in my long years. Beauty that is just skin deep and dulls fast in the eyes of the discerning but Hannah's shines forever bright. For 'tis the sweetness of her nature as well as of her smile, and the warmth in her hazel eyes as well as in her words, that reminds even such a crotchety old crone as myself that there is still some blessed purity amidst the dross.

"Well, grandmother mine, how do you esteem our devout new minister?" she teases for she can see I'm itching to spill my spleen.

I sniff in disdain, before letting the stopper out in defence of those who normally only serve to irk me!

"He would do well I think – granddaughter mine! – to gain some understanding of the hard lives of his parishioners. Gifford would steal what scarce moments of harmless jollity exist in their short drab lives," I reply tartly. "But until he doth bend down a little from his outraged righteousness, and attempts to somewhat curb his pious zeal, few will go to him for advice or solace. The only impact he will bring to bear upon Durlow will be a blast of indigestion before the Sabbath luncheon!"

With a more thoughtful look, Hannah remarks, "I hope the new Reverend is not of an envious disposition and is as lenient towards you as was his predecessor."

"Maybe Hickes didn't find it necessary to persecute the Wisewomen or to bar the laity from following the ageless traditions and folkways of the countryside," I grant grudgingly. "But Gregory Gifford is of the new breed, a Puritan who serves a Jealous God!

"I foresee that our sanctified new Ministry will brook rivals no more. For fear of mice nibbling the holy cushion on its throne of power! In dread of worms burrowing into the stronghold of its coffers! In terror of wild gatherings plaguing the soft slumber of its clergy! The Church must defend its Divine Right to have the sole ear of the Soul of England."

I spoke part in josh but, alack, 'tis all too true. The Church must rule us from the cradle to the grave. Non-attendance is met with formidable punishment in court, excommunication means social ostracism from the community life upon which we all depend. One day I fear that they will invent a device to fit into the privacy of our own homes to continue dictating our thoughts all week long!

Hannah takes my hand to pull me up, saying lunch is calling her to make haste, and that she does not believe I'll ever be so old that I cannot still talk whilst we walk! I chuckle, but sigh too, for she is too young to remember what we have lost.

The Church, since the Reformation earlier this century, has been so changed and upended it has become as a stranger to my generation. The austere stone buildings have been stripped of their sacred objects so lovingly crafted. Where once glorious stained glass filtered the light in golds, emeralds and royal blues, now the rain and grime show up starkly against the plain windowpanes.

In like manner the beloved rituals of our celebrated saint days, which once breathed warm blood into religion, have been banished from the lives of the common people. Mary the Mother, who held a faint reflection of the Great Goddess long ago revered in this land, has been struck down by her officials and denigrated to but a minor role in the holy hierarchy.

For whatever rational reasons these familiar cornerstones of our faith were revoked, their disappearance has taken some hallowed feeling along with them. And England is still in mourning.

5th *January 1594, entry by Hannah*

The festival of Yule glitters like a brilliant bauble set amid dull grey winter. Albeit I've turned seventeen and no doubt should know better, I can hardly resist the urge to leap and caper about, holding my kirtle up to my knees in happy abandon! For tomorrow is Epiphany, the Twelfth Day of Christmas, and this night, on its Eve, we are assembled in the Crouches' farmhouse to party!

We have rosy countenances from twirling around in dance; even the crippled feet of the old dames, with sore bunions and painful calluses, are tapping away to the jolly tunes the musicians play us. We've feasted upon pies, cakes, nuts and brawn, and passed around the wassail – the brown bowl of hot spicy mead – many times in honest fellowship. Gifts have been exchanged: gingerbread and nutmegs, plump pincushions dotted with pins and fat apples studded with pungent smelling cloves. There are to be riotous games later, as much for the adults as the children – and indeed it is hard to tell them apart by conduct alone! For we're as merry as the woodland faery folk, who we seek to entice in from the wintry clime with the evergreens bedecking our homes.

The central hall of the house looks enchanting, with a huge Yule log burning in the grate, and so many candles lit that their reflections twinkle like fey lights upon the shiny green leaves of the holly, bay and ivy. There are festoons of mistletoe tucked up on the beams and the air is scented with rosemary and sage.

Many of my friends are here amongst the bustling guests, also in high spirits and eager for fun. Parnella, the Crouches' daughter (herself hung like festive decorations, so many gaudy adornments does she wear about her person!) is in her element playing the gracious hostess. She flits back and forth, often pausing to twitter in my ear about the compliments she has been paid by her "courtiers" as she calls them. Kitty Kemp turns her head to listen and gives me a suggestive nudge.

"Our Noble Lady Parnella speaks a different language to us lowly bumpkins! She hears extravagant praise in a simple salute of 'good morrow to thee,' and sees courtship in a young man's civil nod. Woe betide the lad who comments upon the weather for she will take it as a declaration and low, he will find himself wed! At twenty she should have married half a dozen dashing bucks by now, so hotly is she pursued – or as she would tell us!"

Kitty speaks in a loud aside, loud enough to make the girls giggle and to infuriate Parnella. The minx would continue her sport but Mistress Crouch's sharp eye is on her. (Alice Crouch oft accuses Kitty of being a fast unruly young woman, though Nan says she was such another in her day.)

After eating our full, mummers arrayed in outlandish costumes and bizarre masks perform their Yule pageant, which is a delight to me and I applaud 'til my palms sting! The traditional Misrule fruitcake is then shared amongst us expectant young people. But it is I who finds the dried pea in my slice and Hugh – oh bliss! – calls out that he has the bean in his. This makes us the King and Queen of Misrule for the festivities, I am elated clear through the roof!

We are seated side by side on the fake thrones, while the company encircle us to witness our performance. I persuade Hugh to go first, who sings a crude comic song to much laughter for he never lacks nerve! Next, I attempt a lullaby which I choose for its lilting melody. The mood of the room changes with this, there is a hushed pause and then kind applause before our audience return to their chit-chat and merrymaking.

As I make my way across the room Ralph, the eldest son of the house, steps deliberately into my path and demands my attention.

"The voice and face of an angel," he avows. "Oh lovely serene Queen, I entreat you for a dance!"

Not heeding my pleas, he grabs my hands and would have pulled me onto the floor had not Hugh – bless him for his constant care of me! – promptly stepped between us, jutting his chin out and reaching his hand to the hilt of an imaginary sword.

"The lady has no wish to be manhandled, Sirrah, and is betroth to me as my Queen of the evening. I will fight you to the death for the sake of this dance with her!" Hugh challenges, his eyes sparkling with mischief.

Although this is done with a laugh in the grand manner, there is a nasty look upon Ralph's face, who doesn't much relish such impertinence from a lad five years his junior. For an awkward moment an ugly scene hangs in the balance, until I seize my gallant Galahad's arm to pull him away and Ralph moves off with a sneer. Though I fear the jibe beneath Hugh's defiance will long fester between them.

Hugh grins impishly but I cannot scold, and I for one have soon forgotten the incident in the pleasure of dancing some reels with my darling boy. Fuelled by his boisterous humour, we cavort around in circles, upsetting furniture and bumping into other guests. Once the room stops spinning, I collapse on a chair to watch the raucous game of Hot Cockles in which one player must hide his head in another's lap and guess who it is who spanks his bottom!

Whilst this is afoot, I could not but notice Kitty striving to charm and coquette with the still offended and scowling Ralph, who turns his shoulder upon her with an indifferent shrug. I am not the only one who observes this, Parnella watches exultantly and with a smirk tries to catch her eye. Kitty foils her by bounding over to perch beside me with an arm about my waist, gossiping in her own giddy animated way.

Once Parnella has given up, however, Kitty's flow of vivacious patter tapers off and she becomes unusually pensive and subdued. Pushing the dusky curls off her forehead, she turns to fix me with a long hard stare. When at last she speaks her voice is more serious and low-pitched then is her wont:

"You know, my gullible babe, that this God we worship is an unjust one? He makes a mockery of us in His divine dispensation of gifts! Look at all the fire and scheming I spend trying to captivate the man I desire to be rewarded with scant return. Whilst you, young Hannah, have but to walk into a room, sit quietly in a corner uttering no more than commonplaces in that soft voice of yours and the men clamber over each other to reach you, like ants around the jam spoon!

"You know nothing of the arts of cajoling and flattering a man, of slanted glances, of flirting with your eyelashes, of tantalizing with your lips. You have no skills in repartee or quick wit and, worst of all, you have no more notion of how to take advantage of your looks then doth a kitten! What use will you make of them? None! For you'll throw away your Heaven-sent prospects, handed to you on a gilded plate, to marry my kid brother.

"The face and body to attract men and the gumption to catch a wealthy husband who can offer you a better existence than squalor – this is the only power women have! If I had your beauty, I would not squander it as you do. Oh, by God's Dines! Wouldn't I get value for investment! Yet I am bestowed with an average quotient and God throws all away on you!"

I am disturbed by Kitty's hostile words and the bitterness of her tone.

"My hopes are as high as yours, Kitty. I wish for happiness with the man I love and who I could not be content without." I contend in sincerity.

"Oh, grow up, child!" Kitty snaps scornfully, "Do you really think you can live solely on love? It doesn't last, it'll be bled out of you in the daily struggle to fill your children's bellies! You two will live in grinding poverty which will wear away romance, sour your dreams and wither your youth. Leaving you exhausted and infirm with a belching, ungrateful, peasant husband. What twaddle you talk! I swear you're as dopey and dunderheaded as Parnella Crouch. I've no patience with you." Upon which she jumps up with a swirl of her skirts, sauntering over to join the lads.

I am left perplexed with a sordid taste in my mouth, but Nan approaches to take me home, "before the cock doth crow", and the world gradually rights itself from the depressing one Kitty is apt to drag you to. As we wend our way up the hill under a frosty starlit sky, we natter and laugh over the evening's events until we reach and fall sleepily into our beds.

9ᵗʰ *January 1594, entry by Hannah*

Today is Plough Monday and we have met in the fields to bless the plough with prayers for the year's growth ahead. It takes an act of faith to imagine the ripe corn for now the ground lies frozen as hard as stone, the clods of dark brown earth barely visible beneath a thin coating of crisp snow, becoming brittle and crunching underfoot as the afternoon wanes. Low leaden clouds are gathering in the north and more snow will fall ere the feeble day departs.

After the age-honoured invocation, the villagers disperse back to their homes or to mend walls and repair tools for we use the time as best we may before the thaw. Hugh and I tramp off in the opposite direction to collect kindling, walking arm in arm against the cold blustery weather. Up here, high on the common, we can just make out the church tower in a gap between the rolling hills and hear its bell chime, though the peal sounds muffled and uncanny in the icy air.

As the afternoon fails to an ominous half-light, the dim winter sun is blacked out by dense cumulus. Immense fluffy snowflakes flutter down, lifted and spun by gusts of wind so they swirl in wreaths about us. Before the distant church bell rings again, we are pushing through mounds of mounting snowdrifts.

"What do you see in the snow fall?" I ask Hugh, who follows the wild flurry with his eyes though he says nothing. He has worn a faraway look since we left the others, which I feel the need to break through. There are times these days when I do not know where Hugh is or how to reach him.

"I see the weak sun and wan moon eclipsed. I see the familiar blown away, whilst the unknown and spectral seep in through the shifting mists. I do not believe that our stout homesteads any longer stand where they have always stood. The life we lived has been ground to powder, which will dissolve away in milky floods when the world melts. The people have flown, along with all I was sure of, gone with the migrating flocks. Only the wraiths remain and they are without substance. I am disembodied and cannot remember even my name. I have vanished into the white wilderness, banished to wander through the howling gales which carry my words to where they'll be forgotten."

Hugh speaks in a dull monotone which stirs in me an inexplicable sense of dread. I can find no reply to answer him, for I do not understand this well of sorrow and anguish into which he is apt to drop. I must wait until he returns to me, as I wait 'til the storm breaks, draining itself before the sunlight can shine again. I place my arm around him as we battle the last windblown stretch before the shelter of the trees.

Once under cover the wind gives up, for although the branches are bare of leaf the trees are sturdy and grow close together forming a tight cobweb of interweaving twigs over our heads. Underneath the air is musty and almost still. Released from the buffeting, we can move more easily here, and walk with loosely linked hands. We come upon the old twisted beech we used to play around as children, the massive girth of its trunk spiralling round as if a giant's hand has wound it like a spring. We both stop beneath the tree, sensing that we are being watched. Looking up, I spot an owl upon a lower bough. But it is an owl such as I have never seen before!

"Look at the size of it!" I exclaim in awe. "Twice as large as a buzzard. And those unearthly orange eyes that stare at us so piercingly!"

"It's magnificent!" Hugh agrees in a hushed voice. "I do believe it is an eagle owl! I'd thought them all extinct after King Henry's onslaught upon the species, retribution for their prey on young deer bred for gentlemen's sport. During His Majesty's reign a guinea was paid for each dead eagle owl presented to his huntsmen; a whole year's wages for many and so they were hunted down in every woodland and wooded grove in England."

He steps closer and speaks directly up to the owl:

"Hail, my lone survivor! Are you the last of your lost kind? How does it feel to be so persecuted?"

As if in reply, the bird spreads out its great wingspan and lifts soundlessly up into the twilit sky.

"Pray we'll never know," I murmur with a shudder.

As we collect dry deadwood, we move further into the dense forest. Carefully we cross a woodland stream, ordinarily bubbling and cantering over pebbles like frisky foals but now caught and held captive in strange frozen shapes by the hard spell of winter. Within the tangled undergrowth I begin to see hostile spiky faces, half-hidden amongst the entwined ivy leaves, up high in the foliage and crouching down amongst the bracken. I try to shake the phantoms away but am brought up short when I realize Hugh sees them too. I pull at him to turn back, to get out of this haunted place, but in so doing we slip on a sliver of black ice underfoot. Together we slide downwards on an incline into a rounded dell within a clearing, trying to cling to each other for support only to crash down upon the ground with a thud.

At once, though for but a moment, we are encircled by a troop of fierce Elven men, ash pale and lithe, holding thin reed spears with needle tips all targeting us! The next minute they are gone. Only the grey outline of the saplings remains, and I am left trembling with racing heartbeat.

"Spriggins!" Hugh whispers. "Faery warriors, driven down from the hills and high places to shelter until the snow has passed. They do not welcome our intrusion!"

"Let's go," I beg. We pick up our bundles and leave more swiftly and quietly than we had entered.

I've never been so relieved to reach the homely safety of Nan's cottage as this evening. I crouch before the fire and scoop up my sleek black tomcat, hugging him tightly until he mews in protest. Nan sets me upon my stool with a hot bowl of broth to cradle and warm me through.

After listening to my tale, she speaks about the myriad of different life forms with whom we share this world, who have moved apart from humans since the early days when the Fey were known to us. Although old housewives still put out dishes of milk beneath the stars to tempt the faeries into good will. Nan recounts an almost forgotten story of the Little People, while I stroke Whisper upon my lap, until silence falls between us and the dwindling embers settle into a fading glow.

9th *January 1594, entry by Martha*

I witnessed again this evening that my Hannah has the Sight. It has long been our family inheritance, though sometimes skipping a generation as between my granddaughter and myself. Whilst out in the woods today with a neighbour's boy, she was blessed by a rare encounter with the fair folk. It is of significance I feel sure, though of what I cannot say.

Nor for whom. Hugh Kemp is a restive soul beneath his dreamy exterior. That one would run blindly where whim or passion took him! I sometimes wonder whether he'll be content to settle at home with my gentle Hannah as we all predict for them. Would that I could keep them safe from the warps of life which jab and rip at us! But then, that's what we are born for, it's upon the sharp stones we learn.

As soon as Hannah was tucked up in bed, for she was weary and heavy eyed, I raked over the ashes, donned my cloak and cloth bonnet, and set off for the tavern. Plough Monday is also named Distaff Monday and is dedicated to the work of women, many of whom were enjoying a tankard or two of Mad Dog within. I arrived late, despite striding full pelt down the hill upon my long shanks (another family inheritance), to find them well ensconced on the high-backed settles with several empty jugs littering the long table.

My neighbour, Edith Kemp, had joined me on the way. Directly I'd passed their cottage, I heard her scurrying footsteps pit-a-patter from behind and her shrill voice cooing. Poor silly Edith, she's hit hard times of late. Her brute of a husband has taken to his bed with a wasting disease, while Edith herself suffered a fit last year which left one side of her face slightly eschew. Sometimes when excited her mouth on that side will go slack and she'll dribble from it.

The villagers are quick to treat her with ridicule and smile derisively at each other when she's talking. I try to shield her as best I may but she bleats round Alice Crouch, Janet Butterworth,

Margery Fisher and their cronies like a tiresome sheep, insisting that such sharp-toothed minxes are her "very good friends". She always speaks as if her words are escaping her and she must constantly run to keep up.

"Oh Widow Herrington, I was hoping to catch you! I did so fancy a tiny tipple – naughty little me! – and a comfy chinwag with all our neighbourly wives, always so pleasant and friendly like. But I'm not one to go out after dark on my ownsome, my husband doesn't care for me to do so there being so many vagabonds and cut-throats about now. I don't know what things are coming to, it's scandalous, my Thomas says he doesn't know why we pay our taxes! I shake like a leaf in my bed at night, really I do! Now what was it I wanted to tell you? Oh yes, um, well I never did, 'tis gone again!" And so her incessant flow continued until we reached the village green.

The tavern is full with the usual crowd, the womenfolk sitting to one side, clearly in rollicking mood by the time we arrive. I am greeted with affable calls to "Come share a glass of Father Whoreson and the latest title tattle," while Edith is rudely overlooked. Due to my craft I amount to a public figure of sorts, though there's a certain amount of unease amongst the younger women – not helped by my grim appearance, for mine is a stern face with harsh jaw line and grey hair scraped severely back into a knot beneath my widow's cap. Hannah did not get her comely looks from my side of the family for sure!

I look around with what no doubt is ill-concealed displeasure. There are few of my peers left alive now, the price we pay for living too long, and I still miss their genial trusty friendship. I've surely grown extra crabby of late for I can find little to commend in those assembled here; they seem merely shallow, self-obsessed and as bitchy as pooches snapping together in their kennels!

Alice Crouch – a gossip pint pot if ever there was one – hails me, she always presumes friendship when in company.

"Neighbour Herrington, see we are drinking a toast to honour women's work on this Distaff Day. Who knows, perhaps we're toast the work men do best as well, if they give us a taste of it, that is!" She hollers out, raising a smutty laugh from her clique and a tittering from Edith beside me.

I wonder which particular man Mistress Crouch intends to favour this night, not her ponderous dull husband I'll be bound! Alice Crouch was frequently to be found behind hedgerows and up haylofts in her younger days, and she bitterly resents the fleshy fingers of middle age sagging her best assets, along with the decline in illicit opportunities it carries in its wake. She applied to me for a beauty potion once and I told her she flatters me beyond my powers! I hope that still rankles.

Twenty minutes later the answer to my question walks in, I'd hazard a guess, in the rotund and worthy form of Leonard Bambrick, for she sits up and adjusts her cleavage. The women are all too apt to fall over themselves toad eating this galling man who is my counterpart, so to speak, as the Cunning Man of Durlow. Why they fail to see him as the pompous jack bragger and blatant charlatan he is beggars belief!

Alice, as quick as ever to catch my derision, tries to turn it against me:

"What an admirable figure of a man! But then you've never succumbed to his charm have you, Widow Herrington? So surprising as you are colleagues or is that the root of your aversion?" Implying petty jealously on my part.

"Nay, I'm not one to intervene in another's domain, whether trade or husband!" I purred, knowing she'd catch my drift – Alice being nobody's fool.

"Yes, you were never one for competition, Martha, but then better to know one's capability I always say," she simpers back.

"Oh indeed, Mistress Crouch, I have the greatest respect for the man's magic, you have shown me how successful are his love spells!" I counter, which turns the mirth against her and scores me the point.

But I soon tire of it all, and sit back in my corner nook to watch the men and women at their antics. It's perhaps as good an entertainment as any travelling players could perform but it's one I've seen all too many times before.

15th *January 1594, entry by Hannah*

I sat shivering in church today; it was not from the midwinter chill, nor from the damp clinging to the mildewed stones of the old building, but from the ferocity of the Reverend Gifford's sermon, surely designed and delivered to smite my grandmother down! His formidable frown was repeatedly directed towards her, as he roared at us from the pulpit:

"The Devil himself doth walk amongst you, *godless dissolute reprobates that you are!* Even here, in this quiet backwater of Durlow, he doth stalk and sidle up, pouring his pestilence into your ear. And you – *you feeble mislead dullards* – do listen to his iniquitous duplicity and sell your souls into his diabolic keeping! Take heed! *I know all your transgressions!* How many of you have succumbed to black bewitchment? Yea, to shamelessly seek demoniacal counsel from *Satan's hand woman!* And could there be such a malignant miscreant, blasphemous and steeped in wickedness, even in this sanctified church of God! I quail for you wretched sinners for the Accursed One *sits down alongside you at this very moment!*"

And his glower fixed upon my grandmother had the blast of a furnace. But while the congregation quaked at his accusations, Nan sat calmly, her blue orbs raised to his with the expression of a saint upon her face. She gently twiddled her thumbs and smiled benignly. The minister is right in a sense – the devil is in her today!

On the way home she made light of it, "So our Holy Herald has found me out at last and is full of wrathful indignation. No doubt he will summon forth the whole Heavenly Host and egg them on to vanquish me!"

But when I spoke my concern, she lessened her bantering to reply,

"Don't fret, Hannah. He'll be defeating some other heinous sin before the week is out, I know not how God would manage without him! Besides, this wet weather is sorely aggravating the poor man's rheumatism, it upsets his timorous, mild disposition. Let us pray for a dry spell!"

15th January 1594, entry by Martha

So, Gifford hath declared war against me. 'Twas only to be expected I suppose, for here am I – a poor cottager and an old woman – with more villagers coming to me in a week than our good vicar receives in a year. And I refuse to quiver at his ridiculous rumpus as his cowed parishioners do, in fact I shall much enjoy being the thorn in his flesh to chaff and needle him!

Yet it riles me that now, in these hard times, the Church would suppress the Wisefolk and ban what help we strive to give. Undoubtedly, it is tied in with another holy war and stacking the odds against us. For most of the Wise are women, who have ever been the guardians of the secret – now forbidden – knowledge, and against whom Christians have borne a malevolence since Eve first gave Adam the apple. There is a published sermon called *The Homily of the State of Matrimony* which according to Ecclesiastical Law must be preached annually from every pulpit throughout the country. I have heard it so many times in my long life that I can quote it by rote:

> *Woman is a weak creature, not endowed with strength and constancy of mind; therefore they be the sooner disquieted, and they may be more prone to all weak affections and dispositions of mind, more than men be.*

We are instructed to obey our husbands in all things (even should they be heavy fisted bullies like Tom Kemp who beats his featherheaded little wife halfway to death). And we are bidden to confine ourselves to the house and dairy.

Nature hath made women to keep home and to nourish their family and children, and not to meddle with matters abroad, nor to bear office in a city no more than children or infants, the holy homily dictates. We are hardly rated God's creatures at all. If it could but be admitted that God makes mistakes no doubt *woman* would be decreed his biggest cock up!

But when I look ahead, I am afeard for the future and for the young folk. If the Ancient Wisdom is forced to retreat still further behind cottage doors after sundown, to disappear into nooks and crannies out of sight, then what is there in this severe religious doctrine which will uplift the people when their hearts are heavy?

How shall the girls, like my beloved granddaughter, find a place and respect for themselves as they grew into womanhood when the prevalent creed of Church and State only bludgeons them into submission? Starvation of the soul is more corrupting than starvation of the body. The meagre cold crumbs the ministers throw us will never keep the internal flame burning in our breasts, one cold snap and 'tis snuffed out forever.

It is for this, that England has desperate need of its sacred inheritance, that I honoured today. Hannah did again beseech to be entrusted with the mystic lore of our forebearers. As my mother had taught me, and my grandmother and great grandmother before her. So, for the sake of the people, this time I said yes.

1ˢᵗ *February 1594. entry by Hannah*

It's been a raw February day, with such a nip in the air the frost remains untouched and my breath's visible as rivulets of white vapour as I set out across the fields. Since Plough Monday I've avoided the forest beyond the common, but go instead to the little copse of alder, hazel and ash which lies a stone's throw from our hill. The trees are coppiced every seven years for the sake of their straight and pliant rods to be interwoven into our wattle and daub houses. The younger shoots are used for baskets and for our brooms with which we sweep away the old rushes from the floor before laying down fresh.

Already catkins are dangling from the branches, where they sway in the breeze like lambs' tails, and soon the leaf buds will swell as a welcome sign of approaching spring. In autumn too this little spinney delights, with a profusion of toadstools sprouting up on the woodland floor. Hugh and I gather the edible giant puffballs, parasol mushrooms and honey fungus for the stew pot, filling our bags with the common field mushrooms which leave faery rings in all the nearby pastures. The bold beauty of the poisonous red capped fly agaric, and the vivid violets of the wood blewit and amethyst deceiver, we feast upon with our eyes alone.

As I return home at dusk with chilled fingers and a hefty appetite, the evening star shines like an auspicious gem above the horizon; people call it the Wishing Star. My own wishes are crystal clear to me now. It is Hugh's dearly loved face that floats through my dreams at night and calls to me in the gloaming hour.

Nan says it is exciting to be at the beginning of things but I yearn to rush further in. Sometimes when he sits beside me, his long legs pressed close, hot waves of excitement flame through me in a thrilling flush! Forcing me to catch my breath and to steady myself. For my hopes are held captured in a treasure chest which I would prize open before I give fate a chance to turn the key.

Our cottage is aglow with candlelight when I reach it, and Nan sets a crock of hot pottage upon the table, seating me with a kiss. Today, is the Feast of the Purification of Mary once celebrated with a ceremony of light. That was before my time and now this Holy Day is banned, but we make do without the Church's sanction, lighting extra candles in Her honour here at home. Tonight we will spread the ashes across the hearth in the hope of seeing Saint Brighid's footprint there in the morning, and Nan has hung wool from a hawthorn bush outside to absorb her healing powers. Another name for Brighid is Bride and, with a white willow wand, I wish for my own bridal one day – and not too long in coming!

14th February 1594, entry by Hannah

Valentine's Day. Will he? Won't he? He will, won't he? Surely he will? He does, come noon Hugh is standing on my doorstep looking adorably sheepish with a posy of snowdrops in his hand. I take his arm and try to set him at ease, for Nan says that men will bellow and bluster quite naturally but need encouragement to be civil! Pinning a blue ribbon onto his jerkin, we exchange tokens and kiss briefly before he bolts back to the ploughing for the spring crops of beans, peas and oats. I float through the day.

By late afternoon my work is done and I skip down to the well where I'm meeting Kitty, Leah, Bessie and Sue to pick Valentine lots. We've been doing this since we were little girls, gossiping and wondering about the romances of older sisters. With great deliberation I dip my hand into the basket to choose my mate, but it plays a knave's trick, causing me to groan aloud, for I've selected the mark of little Joe Tenbale whose round face is pork marked and who slobbers like a puppy! We all pull out poor luck in our mock solemn game except for Kitty, who will not give us the name but looks pleased and tells us to listen out for the banns at church.

On the way home we're joined by Ralph Crouch who walks close beside me, too close for my comfort, whilst telling Kitty to "run along like a good little girl" – a calculated jibe guaranteed to provoke the sophisticated Kitty whose eyes spark dangerously. In a whisper I beg her not to leave me but she turns a haughty shoulder and flounces away. I also try to escape but the discourteous Ralph catches me around the waist and insists upon fastening his gift to my bodice before he will let me go. Later I offer the offensive brooch to Kitty, who at first refuses in pique and then changes her mind, saying "It's pretty enough."

25th February 1594, entry by Hannah

On the morning of Valentine's Day, Parnella Crouch was betrothed to Godwin Colebatch. We heard about the event at some length from Parnella the day after. And again, the day after that, and then again, and again, with ever more embellishment! Kitty took to wearing blobs of wool in her ears for a week following. The villagers chuckled over this but Parnella became so enraged that she tried to clobber Kitty with a broom! To which Kitty threw back her head and laughed and laughed, and continued laughing until Parnella was out of earshot.

28th February 1594, entry by Hannah

During the summer months when the demand for farm labour is greatest, we work as long as daylight permits. It is during wintertide, when the dark comes early and departs late, that my grandmother has more occasion to teach me her Craft. While we spin hemp or knit stockings to bring in much needed pennies, Nan instructs me in the magical lore, herbal medicine and sacred ritual.

It's the healing arts that draw me most. I see such suffering through sickness and I would give much to help ease it. Mother Earth freely lends Her aid, for as the Old Ones say, "there is a doctor in every hedge". So we scour the land for curative plants during the growing season, as well as cultivating a stock of herbs in our own garden strip which we dry out in bunches hanging from the rafters.

I have learnt which poultice to apply for reddened irate skin, that elderflower and angelica leaves steeped in boiling water will relieve the worst of colds, and ground ivy bound about a wound draws out the poison. Clubmoss gathered on the third day of a new moon is beneficial for dimness of vision, while chamomile leaves cropped beneath a high sun can loosen stiff painful joints. These are but a handful of a whole wealth of recipes passed down from generation to generation and added to by each.

Good health and good fortune may be lost overnight like the petals of a flower blown bare by the wind. And those like ourselves who live hand to mouth throughout the year are ill prepared to cope with the swinging scythe of Fate. We have no savings to spare on expensive apothecaries or book learned physicians; though, as Nan caustically remarks, money to burn on such is oft a curse in itself.

"Declining health is the price the rich pay for the services of physicians, who have but one fixed formula through thick and thin, from sickbed to coffin. Bleeding, leeching and purging from one end or t'other is both their prescription and death sentence for their unlucky patients! You need to be stout indeed to survive their practice, it leaves the strong weak and finishes off the ill and ailing before the week is out."

Nan maintains that "Healing is an art of many levels; the bookmen reduce it to a single physical dimension alone. This is altogether inadequate. Though ointments and nostrums may soothe the body's symptoms, the mind and emotions must also be engaged to hinder reoccurrence of disease. Worrying doubts and anxieties will nag around nature's good work, overthrowing it in time for thoughts act as drops of water falling perpetually upon stone, in the end they'll dissolve away your very bones!

"Revengeful obsessions boil the blood until the joints swell, while self-pity and melancholy slow your body organs until they fail altogether. But faith, gratitude and good humour will amend the ailment over time as surely as the medicinal properties of herbs assist in the immediate crisis.

"You must offer both, Hannah, we need to dish out hope with each poultice, clarity and generosity with every tonic. Seek for noxious emotions, growing over time as slowly as hardwoods but as deep rooted and unyielding to pull up. Long repetitive incantations and daily work with charms are necessary to replant more wholesome habits of thought. Folk do believe the magic is in the spells, when in truth the magic is in their minds."

5th March 1594, entry by Martha

Washing the laundry in the Wandle River can be a chilly business but this morning is a mild one with warm sunshine to tempt us out. Several women are here, busy upon the paving slabs laid down long ago so we might avoid the mud. The girls, Hannah, Jane and little Annie Lissett, slip away to pick primroses and early violets which they lay in bunches upon the grass, one for each of us.

Beating the wool and fustian garments with paddles is tough work and somewhat tricky too, beat too weakly and the clothes do not come clean, too vigorously and we are all drenched. – Sometimes on purpose and, as we are all in lively spirits today, our morning task ends in a raucous water fight until we are wetter than the washing!

Relaxing on the bank after, with the Wandle babbling past more quietly than ourselves, we make our plans for today is Ash Wednesday. We have constructed an effigy of sticks and moss to represent Jack-a-Lent, which we nail to a trunk and pelt unmercifully with stones, shouting "Go shoe the goose Jack!" as we do so.

It's a light-hearted but timeworn custom for the first day of Lent and if nothing else it serves to release the ache from the winter's hardships, which like most has taken its toll upon the elderly and weaned out the weakest infants. Poor Jack, symbolizing all our grievances, does not long survive the onslaught! When at last he is no more than a scattering of twigs, we sit down again to share out fritters and pancakes left over from Shrove Tuesday.

It's an inopportune moment, as the talk is bawdy and boisterous, for the Reverend Gifford to come by but so he does, frowning at the signs of our late activity. The man is a fool to be perpetually putting people's backs up with his moralizing and condemning. Fie! If his purpose is to make saints and prudes of the villagers then he is doomed to failure!

Gifford picks out my Hannah, as the men invariably do, and begins to cross examine her about abstinence from flesh and fish, to which she answers politely and with her usual tranquillity. He inclines his head in a sanctimonious manner and moves on to Mistress Kemp whom he bullies shamelessly in spite of her meek subservience. I step up behind her and pleasantly observe the bristles rising on his neck. He begins to bluster and grows heated for he dislikes me mightily. Whilst still in mid flow (but then when isn't he?) I civilly invite our choleric vicar to join us and partake of a bite.

Amidst an awful silence, he attempts to outstare me. After a while, it becomes just too ridiculous – is he awaiting a thunderbolt? By our Larkin', I cannot resist giving him a quick wink! Gifford, now resembling the turkey cock amongst my poultry, puffs out his chest and pulls himself up to his full height (alas a full three inches less than mine) demanding to know what I'm surrendering for Lent.

"Well Reverend, I'm pledged to forsake all love liaisons, just for a few weeks like." I reply innocently, which raises a laugh from the women on account of my age and wrinkles. Gifford goes quite pink in the face, the man will surely have an apoplexy one of these days! Our good Servant of the Cloth is too zealous to have a sense of humour.

"Unless you yourself have desire to deny me my resolve?" I brazenly add, caught up in the day's reckless mood, and then – in for the briers now! – grossly flutter my eyelashes in his direction. Forsooth this is going too far, without doubt I will lose my tongue 'ere I die!

There is some suppressed spluttering and gasps at my irreverent nerve. No doubt this piece of audacity will be much talked about later over Durlow suppers.

"Wash your filthy mouth out, woman! How dare you mock one in the Holy Orders! Learn your lowly place and tremble lest the Almighty shalt smite thee leaden!" I am rebuked.

Well, that was the start of it anyway, a long torrent of godly wroth follows. After my personal berating, he then rounds upon us all for our heathen behaviour and pagan rites. We can expect additional purgatory at next Sunday's sermon for sure!

30th April 1594, entry by Hannah

When I was a small child and apt to gurgle over in delight, my father used to say that I must have tiny wings tucked inside my petticoat for my feet did not touch the ground as I pranced about! So I still do to this very day, the Eve of May Day – Apostles Day as it's now called or Beltane as was the old name.

It is altogether a celebration of expectancy, a confident anticipation of the harvest's bounty ahead, an eagerness for all the treats summer has in store, undaunted by the flaws of real life but as ripe in perfection as only promises can be. 'Tis the wildest of the festivals and the favourite of the young – though some of our respectable matrons look askance at us for even the most modest maid may become wayward, giving in to sweet seduction on this heady eve.

I'm secretly hoping for the chance to misbehave! Should Hugh, with his arm about me, lead me into the forest for the ancient Greenwood Marriage I would not risk even a token resistance. For May is the lovers' month; to be candid, many a hasty summertime wedding has followed upon the back of lusty Beltane! And who amongst us, young, as yet unwed and with the blood running quick in our veins, can deny that loving union is our upper-most thought and our most flaming desire? Our future lives like the season to come lie as an unopened book, viewed only by the allure of its cover and read but in our dreams.

It is a glorious day, as bright and beautiful as April and May will sometimes be, all golden sunbeams and dulcet breezes. As if bestowing Nature's blessing upon youth, both of season and creature. The sky is a heavenly blue, the trees abloom with the pale pinks, delicate lilacs and downy peaches of spring's flowering. Nan has woven me a crown of cherry blossom and I wear the traditional flowing white gown of the May Maiden; it is of the softest, smoothest cotton I have ever touched!

The colourful ribbons of the Maypole on the village green flutter gaily on currents in the air, and the music of wooden flute entices us to come together to intertwine in the ritual dance. To me it echoes the lilting melody of the elven pipes you think you almost hear drifting across the hilltops on a midsummer's evening.

1st May 1594, entry by Hannah

I tossed and turned in bed last night for I was excited with thoughts of the day. It must have kept Nan awake for she scolded me on rising.

"Must you look so fresh and glowing this morn while I look every one of my sixty odd years? I'm too old for sleepless nights, my cherub!"

"Never mind, granny dearest, who knows, perchance you'll have the bedroom all to yourself tonight!" I made sport, skipping out before she could reproach me.

Kitty holds to the dreary view that all the tales of knights rescuing fair damsels are as improbable as the existence of dragons. But me – well I believe in dragons! For yesterday evening, while treading the merry dance around the Maypole, weaving in between the rainbow ribbons, Ralph Crouch whispered audacious words into my ear as we passed. But dear Hugh was watching, he came hard on the heels of the objectionable Ralph and would bump into him from behind, or step upon his feet, before dodging out of range of Ralph's hand raised to cuff him. Maybe Hugh is more a mischievous imp than noble knight, and I did try to warn him not to push Ralph too far but he merely laughed, saying,

"The splendid swanking Yeoman's son, awaiting his fat inheritance, will bully me no more, Hannah! Or else he will discover that I am no longer the little docile boy he was wont to push into the muck of the pigsty and who he thrashed for recreation."

Today, May Day itself, is again all benign sunshine and periwinkle skies. Durlow is decked out in full glory for the festival and likewise its residents wear sunny smiles upon their faces. Time enough for laboursome toil when the hay harvest comes and the growing season demands every ounce of our time and strength. But that's for tomorrow, for now the whole village plays. And plays with gusto for we do nothing by halves on this longed-for day!

The lads were already engaged in a noisy game of Cockshies when we arrive, which seems but an excuse for a romp and ruckus. A new game is proposed next, to raise money for the parish funds – or so 'tis claimed!

"We men, armed with ropes, will chase you girls through the village and, when caught, will tether you to us until put in receipt of ransom for your release," we're told.

"Indeed! And what are we to be armed with pray?" Leah enquires haughtily.

"Why, with your maidenly virtue to be sure! Pray 'tis safeguard enough to keep my ardour at bay once you're in my power, my sweet rose!" Ben, the impudent scamp, gives answer, causing Leah to blush up to her hairline.

"Oh yes?" Kitty retaliates, swift as an arrow, "and if we are to trust such gentlemanly restraint as yours, we'll need to start henceforth upon the swaddling clothes!" And she shows us the red marks left upon her neck from last night's mauling. "'Tis well we have our wits as more than match for your thick heads and boorish muscle!"

"'Twould take more than a rope to tame our tempestuous Kitty Kemp!" a cheeky chap ribs back, "We need an armour apiece to protect us from her scratching!"

And so, the banter continues with our cocky boys until the game begins, the rules still unspecified. I'm off as fast as I may for I see a look of determination upon Ralph's countenance, and I dodge him around the houses before I'm cornered and roped. Gasping for breath, I gladly offer up my ha'penny tribute but the unchivalrous Ralph will have none of it, insisting instead,

"A kiss alone will be your ransom, my long-legged pretty maid, or else I will take you home with me this night and keep you 'til the cock crows!"

But before he can bend to take his kiss, out of nowhere springs Hugh, seizing the rope and snatching me away in a trice! Together we speed off, giggling like babes with Ralph left bemused and furious, his mouth standing open like a gapeseed.

After that, I suppose it was inevitable that Hugh and Ralph should be opponents in this afternoon's wrestling match. By the look on their faces, it'll be no frivolous contest. Spectators gather and the girls are no further back in cheering their heroes on with catcalls and raunchy comments than are the men.

"He's a fine figure of a fellow, you must admit," Kitty whispers into my ear, admiring the muscular Ralph who is stripped to the waist.

"Your brother will beat him for all that," I refute.

"A coddled mummy's boy fed upon milksops!" Kitty scoffs until I move away, vexed at her for her disloyalty.

Although I dislike wrestling, with Hugh a participant I watch without lowering my eyes until the last struggle ends. Both lads fought fiercely (as if to the death) but for the first year of late Ralph is not the victor. My pride in Hugh is not for his triumph however but for the honourable manner with which he offers his routed opponent his hand, saying "Thank you, Cos, for a splendid fight, though I reckon Lady Luck was in my favour or the outcome would have differed!" Which is generous indeed. As to be expected Ralph takes his defeat badly, churlishly swearing and refusing Hugh's gesture of goodwill. There are boos from the onlookers and the scowl upon Ralph's face is as black as murder.

I carry off my brave champion for cake and ale, and we enjoy the Morris Dancing before making entertainment of our own with games of Penny Prick, Barley Break and Blindman's Buff. Before the sun sinks down behind the hills, many young couples tiptoe off, hand in hand to the meadows to gather flowers for the market cross. And not all return. I notice by the light of the bonfire that Kitty and Ralph are absent both, though the night has long fallen. Ralph was not amongst the flower pickers but stormed off after the fight, with Kitty running behind attempting to placate him. For once she received no rebuff.

Hugh and I are sitting together, a little apart from the merrymakers, beneath the old oak and I thank my darling boy for his chivalry this day. While I praise him, he looks down in embarrassment, tracing the protruding knobbly roots of the tree beneath his fingers. Finally, he looks up and grins.

"'Twas a pleasure," he says, and kisses me.

19th May 1594, entry by Martha

Out on the moors, in a dip where a small grove of silver birch trees grow, a spring bubbles up that is hallowed to us. Curative powers have been attributed to this sacred well for as long as people can remember, and the earth's goodness bestowed here since time began. The night of the year most blessed by its enchantment is that of the full moon in May.

For there are three elements to healing. In addition to working with the body and mind, there needs to be an exchange, a gift, of energies. The source of this Divine Bequest may come from the Spirit realms or, most potent of all, from the Goddess Herself in the cool waters syphoning up from the land's bowel.

So tonight, I have come to enact the ancient rites and to harness the restorative potential of the living land. A motley gathering of folk have crept out under the cover of darkness, making their way in the illusory moonlight across gullies and over hummocks, scrambling through fern and bracken, to assemble in shadowy silence around the crescent pool. They have come with their pain and ailments that time and effort have failed to cure. They have come as on a pilgrimage and they have come in faith. The Lady will ask no more.

Hannah, her cloak and hair streaming out behind her, raises her arms to implore the moon to descend and wed with the earth currents so their strength may magnify. As she draws down the moon, she herself, her face as white as marble but as softly fluent as dew on blossom, becomes the embodiment of the Moon Maiden for us all to behold.

But be warned, Our Silver Mistress has withal a dark face also, a hidden side. Yes, She may awaken the Sight and bestow Otherworldly endowments, but Her gifts are perilous for the key to the Gateway is not lightly given. Better for most to hide under the bedclothes and to fasten the shutters tight! For the full lunar glare shatters the flimsy locks of civilization. Disturbed emotions and shady delusions crawl to the surface to hoodwink and beguile us, 'til we too wail like the wolf beneath her baleful pull!

The elementals of moonshine steal away our wits until our minds are emptied. They hound us with howls of desolation, they hurl our hopes into the abyss. They tug at all the tears we have interred, to flood into a churning sea into which we are cast to drown. They distort our dreams to nightmares that gallop up behind us across the fells, and they gorge upon our security like maggots on a corpse!

The Maze of Mystery is walked by the foolhardy alongside the mystic, is trod both by Initiates in quest of the magical labyrinth and by the lost who wander the winding alleyways of madness. In my great grandparents' time, the medieval minstrels would sing of the souls of the insane flying off to the moon, leaving strips of pale mist like the sails of ghost ships across the sky.

But if you can pass through the mirror unbroken to the Midsummer Lands beyond the brink, you will secure the immortal prize most worth the winning. For there you will encounter the mysteries of the Old Wisdom and the secrets of Fey.

I scope up the blessed water, luminous in the ivory light, to trickle through my fingers as each supplicant kneels upon the pool's rocky floor, and I can feel a surge of vitality streaming over their bodies to purify and empower. As I bend to the last pilgrim a dark shadow crosses us, breaking the reverie. I start up to see the outline of a black figure standing above me, pointing an accusing finger. So intent have we been upon our ceremony we failed to notice the Reverend Gifford's stealthy approach. He comes seeking the evidence to condemn me as a witch.

22ⁿᵈ *May 1594, entry by Hannah*

On the way to market today, Mistress Crouch singled me out and bade me walk with her.

"Hannah, my dear girl! I've been wanting to drop a soothing word in your ear. I've heard about the great defamation cast upon poor Martha, and have seen how pallid and strained you've been looking. I do declare I see now an anxious crease across your brow! Wait! Let me smooth it away. There, tis gone! You're too young and bonny for such blemishes!" she protests caressingly, with her face perched close to mine.

In truth I am surprised by the apprehension she seems to behold in me, for my mind has been set at ease by Nan's assurances. I hasten to relieve the good yeoman's wife of her misgivings:

"Nay, mam, my grandmother says there is nothing to fear from the ecclesiastic courts, that they are merely a pigeon coop allowing the clergy to strut and fluff out their feathers but with no more clout than a peck from the dainty beak of an indolent pullet! The worst sentence for witchcraft they may authorize is but an apology at church on Sunday, nothing more."

"Ah child, but what disgrace to stand a penitent before the entire congregation! And she will be dressed in a white sheet too and made to carry a wand like a toy – 'tis a grievous affront to her dignity! I know that fierce pride of hers, Hannah, if the villagers chasten and deride our ill-fated Martha the abasement will surely be the death of her! My pretty girl, you must not be frivolous now, chasing fun and giddiness, for believe me your grandmother has need of you in this time of tribulation!" she implores, with such solemnity as to shake me, though to puzzle and distress me too in her mistaken belief that I would ever put pleasure before my love for Nan.

"No, no, I assure you, Mistress Crouch, Nan would herself make a farce of the performance, laughing all the while up her sleeve and making a jackass of Gifford into the bargain! And as for the villagers, they attribute her great respect for Durlow has always needed it's Wisewoman. My grandmother has helped so many in her time, they'll not turn against her now." I assert with confidence.

"You'd be surprised how rapidly the tide can turn, Hannah," Alice Couch drily cautions. "Widow Herrington is a brave upright woman but she is also headstrong and reckless. She's too blunt in her speech and has shown little care for the whims and sensitivities of others. Most of the folk hereabouts are shallow in their petty concerns, they will follow wherever the flock go – nay, even over a precipice if fashion dictates it! And what is even more pertinent, my lovely, the world is changing. Tolerance for the old traditions is lessening. I know it to be the case for my husband keeps abreast of public events and foresees the rolling crest of the country's climate of opinion."

Our neighbourly matron again speaks so convincingly that I can no longer doubt her, and the furrowed brow she'd imagined before must now have sprung up for real upon my forehead.

"Your grandmother is perilously behind the times!" she counsels. "Aye, and it does not do to goad a Reverend for the clergy are powerful men and have the ear of the wealthy. It is but a short step from the docile church courts to the death trap of the State's legislation. It has happened before, you put one foot on the slippery slope with the mighty set against you, and your destiny leads through prison to the noose awaiting at the bottom!"

While recounting her fears, she fixes wide horrified eyes upon mine. I am scared now, cold to my marrow.

"My young Hannah, I tell you these things because I think of you as a daughter," she adds, giving me a sidelong glance. "And I would not have my dear old neighbour go to Heaven in a string, as the saying goes! I cannot lie to you for you are her only kin, but I dread to one day see her remains hanging in the gibbet for the crows to pick at!"

I can only thank her for her solicitude, but I continue on my way to Hereford with fear like a rock in my breast and the screams of the gallows clamouring in my ears.

23rd May 1594, entry by Hannah

When I returned home that evening Nan endeavoured to allay my alarm but I could not still my disquiet of mind, and that night I was plagued by dark disturbed phantasms. One dream struck me as bizarre and haunting a night vision as any that have overshadowed me before.

I was dancing at a festival. It was May Eve for there was the Maypole – but all was a parody of our jovial celebration, it merely mocked the Beltane spirit of freedom and zest for life! For instead of taking place upon the village green, this strange sombre masquerade was set within the brick walls of a gaol courtyard.

In place of a vivid array of the many-coloured ribbons of custom, its Maypole was hung only with black strips which blew about the pole like a swarm of night bugs, and the lyrical melody of the flute was replaced by the slow hollow beat of a drum. Instead of the boughs of blossom with which we garland the day, here were coffins tipped up upon their ends, set around the yard as if in macabre decoration. Along the top of the high walls sat chains of inky rooks, spying upon our every movement.

The revellers were set in pairs, swirling about the cobbled yard, following the steps of some stately dance. Although I was dressed in my simple white gown, everyone else was adorned in deep purple garments of a transparent flowing material. They had donned preposterous elaborate hairstyles and their faces were partially obscured by masks.

I knew my partner to be my own Hugh, and as we slowly threaded between the couples some would reveal the familiar faces of the villagers. Bessie and Leah giggled and nudged me as they passed. Kitty winked broadly, with a jackdaw sat upon her shoulder winking in unison. Edith Kemp cheeped and cooed to her husband, who looked ashen and stiff as if he'd risen from his deathbed. Yeoman Crouch and his wife inclined their heads condescendingly. The face of Alice Crouch was grotesquely painted like that of an aging trollop, the peaks of her upper lip picked out so sharply in scarlet as to resemble the twin blade points of scissors.

Across the cobblestones, I spied my parents linked in dance. I waved frantically but only my father saw me. Opening his mouth to grin, he exposed a row of rotting stumps and gaps where his teeth should be. As I strove to keep them in sight I was knocked off balance by two lads running past, engaged in a mad chase with hoops. Recognizing my brothers, now young again in my dream, I shouted their names but with a wild yahoo they sped out of the gates and beyond, while my mother rushed after them calling out not to soil their Sunday-best.

My partner witnessed my distress at their departure, for he bent to wipe my tears with a lace handkerchief. I looked up in surprise that Hugh should possess such a dainty item, and laughed up at him on account of it. He opened out the delicate cotton so it lay across his palm and I saw a wedding ring gleaming within. I smiled, held out my third finger and, standing on tiptoe to kiss his lips, I raised his mask to expose – not Hugh's loved countenance – but the cynical face of Ralph Crouch ogling me!

In horror I tried to break away but he gripped my wrists tight, and we struggled in slow motion while the dancers continued to whirl around us. Desperately biting into his skin drew forth drops of blood and he released me. I flew to the wooden gates only to find them locked and bolted. As I beat upon them with my fists in mounting panic, the rooks began to hurl themselves, one by one, against the heavy panels to fall dead at my feet. At last, in defeat, I turned round to see the people all vanished and the courtyard empty, except for the corpses of the black birds which littered it.

24th May 1594, entry by Martha

My granddaughter has never lost the trusting openness of childhood but she looked tense and troubled on her return from market this Saturday gone. Someone had been dropping doubts and demons into her ear, and I know this to be the cultivated skill of our neighbour yeoman's spiteful wife!

Since they were girls, Alice Crouch was an intimate friend of my daughter – but never a good friend! You cannot speak the name "Alice" without a hiss in the tail, as if a snake resides there. Like the word "malice" which, upon my troth, would better suit her! Always wearing a false face to my Tamsin, she was perpetually pandering and insinuating affection where there was none, while all the time her sharp beady eyes would be darting about seeking the main chance for herself.

And a clever miss she was too, flaunting her corpulent bosom whenever it served her interest best. By twenty she'd netted herself a wealthy husband with a hundred plump acres of farming land. No matter that he was forty with a former wife not twelve months in the grave! But still this did not satisfy that greedy roving eye of hers, soon she was turning her attention and bust full upon my daughter's worthless but handsome husband.

Jake Greene was all too pleased to exercise his shallow charms and oily strokes on his wife's best buddy; his paws were inside her bodice and his todger inside her cunny-burrow the moment she flashed the all go! Which was quick enough. They carried on their sleazy affair right under Tamsin's woebegone gaze, doubly betrayed and broken hearted, poor romantic dupe, but harnessed to her lousy husband by law and babies.

I might have forgiven Alice (for Jake, the filthy oinker, would copulate anything with a hole in it) were it not for her hypocrisy. It's the gall of the woman that rankles and sets my fingers itching to slap her! Long after Tamsin's departure she continued to talk of "her boon companion" who she "weeps for", lamenting her poverty and downfall – and this from her own husband's avarice, a fact that is never mentioned. With Alice Crouch the nasty truth always hovers unspoken in the air between you, and if you hint at it, she flings up her hands as if at barefaced lies!

Pah! I've only contempt for the doxy! I have much relished the loss of her buxom good looks and fleshy endowments, eaten away by passing time that rights all wrongs in the end. She's still the same vulgar lightskirt clothed in the fake fabrics of gentility, but her days of romping in the hay with lusty husbandmen are dwindling to a close. Her power now lies solely in her deceit and treachery, and in the razor tongue that never rusts from lack of use.

But her snide suckling to my granddaughter I have watched with suspicion for well I know the jealousy behind it. Hannah has always stood to her Parnella as a peony to hogweed, and ambitious Mistress Crouch dislikes her son's pursuit of a penniless girl. She slips slivers of poison into Hannah's ears and speaks honeyed compliments that stick and bind and suffocate like the fronds of a creeping ivy!

I can stem her venom with a look, for in truth she fears me and my witch's curse a little. She would never stick her neck out and put herself at risk, her sly way is to wait until sentiment begins to turn and then to whip it to fury against her chosen prey. If t'were not for knowing that spells of ill will rebound upon the sender threefold, I would have roughened her path long ago for all the mischief she has caused! But I will not perjure my soul for the likes of slithering, fork-tongued Alice Crouch.

6ᵗʰ *June 1594, entry by Martha*

It was a simple enough task to gather half a dozen "honest neighbours" to swear my innocence. The Archdeaconry Court restored my good name and dismissed the case, leaving me free to put myself directly in Gifford's sight as often as I can contrive. It's torment for him to see me now but we are instructed that suffering is balm for the Christian soul! Sweetmeat though this is, I enjoy still greater pleasure in seeing the sunshine return to Hannah's smile.

I strive harder than ever to pass on the Old Lore to my granddaughter, for there are few who still possess the true wisdom of the Ancestors and it must not be lost. Certainly, it is not to be found in the tawdry forgery of Leonard Bambrick and his like! Alas that the villagers are such dolts and halfwits as to believe the showy trappings of this crafty fox. Sometimes I hear of his shoddy malpractice from one of his credulous dupes and I would crack my ribs laughing were it not for the tragedy of his victims' lives.

At last night's spinning bee, I was seated beside Mother Nokes who confided her woes to me and, though I pitied her distress, I could not but be entertained by her discourse.

"Widow Herrington," she lamented, "my life has been clouded with strife since ere I saw you last! I do not know what will become of Nathaniel and me!"

As I unravelled her tale, while ravelling my yarn, it became apparent (though not to her) that she has suffered a little bad luck from fate and a lot of bad advice from Durlow's so-called Cunning Man.

The Nokes work a small farm, mainly arable with a few livestock, which allows the couple to barely scrape by most years. So when their best milk-yielding cow, Betsy, dried up, the Nokes gathered up their few pennies and called upon Leonard Bambrick as their salvation. Bambrick sold them some tincture to be swallowed and salve to apply. As the man has little knowledge of the healing properties of herbs and roots, this worked not at all and poor Betsy violently vomited. He cunningly proclaimed it a necessary purging and honoured them with a visit.

"Betsy," he pronounced, "is bewitched in her udders." Blaming witchcraft is frequently used by the unscrupulous to save reputation when a patient stubbornly refuses to respond to phoney treatment.

The next task then, was to find the foul hag who had it in for the Nokes' cow.

"Breathe three times upon the Mirror of Merlin and gaze into the mist," Bambrick instructed, fixing his awe-inspiring eye on Nathaniel and uttering a monologue of gabbled hexes, while the old chap miserably huffed and puffed upon the glass.

"Have you or your kin ever been stricken with peculiar swellings? Have you woken in the night to feel the weight of bricks upon your chest? Has your mule fallen lame? What crone with squint eye, hare lip and noisome breath has cast you malevolent looks? Somebody once offended, a beggar turned away, a fulsome spinster ignored who cursed you for it!" he continued to probe whilst the quaking Nokes, peering into the steamed-up mirror, began remembering insignificant incidents that now took on sinister shape in their scared rabbit minds.

When Mary Nokes confessed to an unexplained rash three weeks past, the evidence was declared absolute: it was the evil work of Widow Smithe, who had requested a favour that day and who keeps a black dog. To remedy Betsy's harassment, they must contest the widow in court and burn some object belonging to her. I foresee a fiery end to their long friendship and no need to use my second sight for that prediction!

For all I blame Bambrick for swindling such simple-minded folk and creating discord between neighbours, the canker really lies in the beliefs of the people. There are and always will be a hundred Bambricks, men and women alike, to be found in every county of England who will prey upon ignorance and gullibility. What grants this corrupt fetid pack their success are the fears that distort our thinking and throw us into their greedy grasp.

Life is harsh and hazardous for most, with real dangers lurking behind every corner and within each passing hour. Illness, hunger, accident and violence may strike a man down to leave his family destitute before the sun again sets. We have no safeguard against such hellish uncertainty, and we are told it is the Wrath of God. The Gospels would have us look for sin within but it is more comfortable to look for sin without.

Easier to find dark deeds in a wrinkled face and gobber tooth, in the crooked back that stoops in old age, than to search amongst our own actions or accept that we live in a precarious world without rhyme or reason. For centuries, throughout this Christian Europe, our forebodings have been housed in women; the State makes punishing laws against them and the religious men preach of their corrupting nature and devil worship. And so we swop our fears for changelings! We twist our natural anxieties into the monstrous terror of Europe, into the Fear of Witches.

It is *they* we say, who create the havoc fate plays with our lives. This lends us an illusion of control, for we can imprison and hang the witch if we can but catch her. But the price for this false security is high, it is hatred and murder and ever more mounting fear – until we distrust all about us, until we suspect the very shadows of each other!

Our fears are bred in the stinking stagnant dogma of our Age and hatch like blood-sucking larvae. By my troth, this boiling seething hell-broth of suspicion and lies and mass held fantasies that we have long brewed in this land is far worse than the blackest witch's cauldron could ever be!

30ᵗʰ August 1594, entry by Hannah

The perfect promise of Beltane was not fulfilled. June, July and August all wet – ensuing a bad harvest, the worst for a decade. We have laboured with our scythes from sunrise to sunset but with little Lammas return, not one fifth of the seed planted has yielded growth.

Other promises have proven as false knaves as was spring's for summer. I do not know what Ralph murmured into Kitty's ear when he took her into the woods last May but her petulant pretty face is now tainted with bitter rebuke while his boasts only arrogant indifference. Her belly is beginning to swell and the village speaks in whispers and covert glances. Hers will not be the first babe conceived out of wedlock but while the Church and congregation are lenient when marriage is to follow, censure and retribution are cast upon the girl with no man willing to husband her.

Kitty has fallen to her knees and pleaded for the protection of his name, if not for her sake then for his child's, but Ralph coldly denies paternity or interest, fouling her name abroad as a "conniving little slut". The Crouches have pulled together, as always in disclaiming guilt, to vent indignant outrage at the slander of a "lewd and light woman of filthy behaviour who has played the bawd." They're a powerful family, much esteemed and curtailed to, whereas the Kemps have only the pity of a few and respect of none. The father is a bed-ridden drunkard who would wallop his disgraced daughter within an inch of her life had not infirmity immobilised him, while the mother just wrings her hands and weeps, ever bewailing "the shame, Kitty, the shame!"

A heavy scowl mars Hugh's angelic countenance and he rages like a tethered bull at the violation and dishonour of his sister. So hot is his anger, I offered to approach Ralph myself but Hugh only turned on me.

"It is folly to speak so! If the blackguard will not heed Kitty's tears no other woman's pleas will move him. But perhaps the actions of a man may! I will confront Master Crouch myself and this very day!"

With that he pushed me aside and left, running with such great strides that I could neither hinder nor entreat him to refrain from violence. I do not know how the encounter ended.

31st August 1594, entry by Hannah

Something is wrong. I am frightened for Hugh. I have not seen him and I cannot find out what has occurred. When I walked down into Durlow this afternoon, to sell the flax we'd spun into linen upon the treadwheel, I came across villagers whispering in huddles who ceased abruptly on seeing me. I begged Nan to tell me what was flying in the wind but she said only "I will find out." After sundown she set off to the tavern to gleam what she could.

I was left perturbed and pulling at my hair. Finally, I could sit still no longer, waiting in idleness for Nan's return. As a long shot, I resolved to go out into the night and search for him. I know his favourite haunt, a Norman hillfort, now but a few mounds and some fallen stone blocks left lying on the grass. He has often gone there to think or dream.

It took me a while to reach this place; on and off it's black as pitch for the gibbous moon keeps slipping behind impenetrable cloud, causing me to trip and stumble across the uneven ground. Sometimes I'm brought to my knees where I pause, listening hard to convince myself 'tis nothing but the scurrying of shrews in the scrub growth that I hear, before I stagger on.

But as I approach the ruined fort, I hear sounds that surely come from a larger animal, perhaps the nasal grunting of a wild boar. I creep up the steep grassed bank and, flat on my stomach, peer down. At the bottom of the ditch I see the shadowy outline of two figures in a fierce combat, rolling around in the belly of the earthworks, who curse and groan in the struggle! The broader man forces down his adversary, who screams out in an increasing extremity of agony – I am appalled to recognize Hugh's cry! Unheeding of danger I shimmy down the slope as fast as I may, the noise of my descent disturbing the men who scramble up and turn to me in alarm.

At first, I cannot comprehend what my eyes behold, for both men pull apart with their male members standing erect and naked, thrusting clear of their breeches which are undone and falling about them! We all three stand frozen in shock and horror! In acute dismay I look away from Hugh, whose eyes I cannot bear to meet, and towards the other man. His face is as loved and familiar to me as Hugh's own. It is my father.

1st September 1594, entry by Martha

Hannah is in bed and I will not disturb her. Her good-for-nothing father, a worthless scalawag who never brought his family aught but trouble, loafs by the fire, our tomcat purring upon his knee, and my blood boils to see him taking his ease there!

He and Hugh Kemp brought Hannah home in the early hours this morning, her face pale and blank. It reminded me a much younger Hannah, stricken and frightened after her family had left the shire. Hugh also appeared dumbfounded and would not stay, but sidled out of the door tongue-tied and ashamed. Only the scoundrel Jake Greene smirked and oozed felicity at his return "to his own little flock". He had the nerve to embrace me, catching me unawares – for certain, he won't do so again!

Well, the restoration of the head of the family has brought us little cheer. He brings only ill tidings, of my daughter Tamsin's death a few years back, dying of disease and poverty in London City's foul alleys. My grandsons have gone God knows where, one joining the lower ranks of the army, the other leaving his father without a word.

As for Jake himself, he has been coarsened by years of rough living, no longer flaunting that charming smile that once caused so much mischief, when he parts his lips now his mouth is rotten and half his teeth gone. He has joined a band of homeless vagabonds, at present camped on the uplands, who have not the price of a tankard of ale between them, or if they have 'tis not earned by honest means!

Hannah has told me of the sordid scene she chanced upon amongst the old ruins last night. *So,* the father returns bringing his daughter a double loss – the loss of her mother's life and of her sweetheart's love!

I have heard other rumours of Hugh Kemp from the tavern gossip yesterday. It appears that he did go to Ralph Crouch to entreat on behalf of his sister but somehow commenced declaring his own enamour for him instead! As to be expected, Ralph pushed the younger lad away and spat upon him, and is now bent upon spreading the muck around the district.

Hugh, the foolish boy, has played straight into the hands of the Crouches with his unbridled passions! The scandal is like to rock the village.

4th *September 1594, entry by Hannah*

I did not see Hugh again until this morning. Over the past few days, my thoughts have been plaguing me like gnats scudding about my head and biting on the tender tissue inside, injecting bitterness to sour the sweet of my memories.

I have painfully re-examined every meeting and conversation I can recall, and I've come to the bleak conclusion that I wilfully mistook his friendship for the more ardent feelings I so desired. Each time I acknowledge this and beat down any silly false hope that weakly wavers, the tears will prick beneath my eyelids and sting as I blink them away. I even tried to talk to my pa but he just shook his head and patted my cheek, "he's not for you, lass," was all he'd say.

Hugh hasn't come near me so at last I myself go down to the Kemps' cottage. As I approach, I hear the sound of vexed voices raised in anger. Amidst these are the plaintive high-pitched sobs of Edith and Kitty's hysterical laughter. When I knock the shouting is instantly snuffed out like a candle, and only after some hushed whispering does Hugh cautiously open the door and step out to join me, closing it firmly shut behind him.

We sit side by side beneath a holly tree, not touching. I with my knees up under my chin, he as unmoving as if he's cast in the hard stone of the hill, and both of us seemingly intent upon the view. I ask none of my questions, silenced by his remoteness. It is at this moment it fully dawns on me that Hugh wants no place in my life! And I am struck dumb with misery.

Eventually he sighs wearily and begins to speak, still not looking at me and his voice as unmoving as his stance. But I catch each word like pebbles in my heart.

"Hannah, I am profoundly sorry I have hurt you. I never meant to deceive you, rather I battled always to deceive myself. I have been lost in a gloaming life of suppressed yearnings, of searing secrets and of a burning frenzy in my blood. I heeded nothing of what you might have been feeling. I have no excuse for my selfishness except to place my torment before you.

"Throughout these past years I've torn myself from limb to limb, bound myself with biting shackles of my own forging, smothered myself in suffocating garb to disguise my agony from the eyes of others. I have loathed myself as gross, dirty and offensive. Believe me, none of the foul obscene taunts Ralph spewed out compare to the abuse I have long chastised myself with! And yet, throughout the years, I have *fought* to be the man expected of me, the suitor you deserved, the brother Kitty needed but always my own self rose up against me."

He sighs again, and I press his hand in sympathy.

"Could you not have trusted me, Hugh? Did you think I would judge you so unkindly that you feared to confide in me?" I have to ask him.

"Oh Hannah, you've been the one stable, noble thing in my life. I have been so stretched upon the rack that I've not known who or what I am! You – who are so pure and loving, the best and truest of friends – I have clung to, though you did not know it, as if to a ship's figurehead left afloat after the ship has submerged into the murky depths. You represent the straight and narrow, the goodly and safe, the harbour I sought but could not anchor in. If I had spoken the truth to you there would be no more hiding from myself! But blood will out anyway you see."

I am so stirred by his anguish that I propose, in a voice that's weak and puny, "We could try, not a real marriage, of course, but to keep you safe from the ill-will of others…" But my words falter, the sentence unfinished, as even to my own ears it sounds the plea of a tearful child, and I cannot reach him.

Hugh glances sadly at me, "It's too late, my dearest of friends. And it couldn't have been, you would have married a dead man, wasting your love upon a corpse. Again and again, the hollowness of my reactions would smite you, until it embittered and warped you own honest nature. To love and not be loved is to be sucked down into a swamp, slowly and helplessly, until at last it covers over your head!

"Our marriage would be a sham, Hannah, and I've worn a mask long enough now to know how it poisons the life behind it. Whatever the consequences there can be no more deceit." He speaks with tired resignation, and again turns his eyes away from me. If only to break the crippling silence that cuts between us, I gingerly ask about his relationship with my father.

"There is no relationship!" he snaps, as if exasperated by my obtuseness. "Your father stumbled upon me drunk and half out of my skull after Ralph had spurned me. I'd sunk so low in my mind that a debased animal coupling in the ditch offered some transitory but degrading relief!" Hugh offers me a wry half-smile, "Your coming unexpectedly upon the scene put a quick stop to any respite from that, I can tell you! But it shocked me to my senses."

Then, in a voice racked with both pain and passion, he proclaims: "It's Ralph, it has only *ever* been Ralph! Even in childhood I worshipped him, tall and disdainful, haughty and handsome. I hungered even for his blows and bullying, his jibes and jeers. Oh, the ecstasy of wrestling with him! Body to body, to feel his muscles under my hands, to flex mine against him!" He sucks in the air and then lets it out slowly in a groan, before confessing, "I would do anything, Hannah, to provoke a response in him. But it was never the response I craved. And now I cannot bear the humiliation of his scorn."

Whilst he's speaking, I grope towards an understanding and seeing the depth of his suffering I attempt to move away from my own.

"Dear Hugh, please don't despair! It may not be Ralph, it may need be hidden and behind locked doors, but one day you will find the love you seek. You too will have your chance of happiness. It is not too much to ask!" I try to comfort him, again pressing his hand but he shakes his head hopelessly.

"I love only Ralph. I love him with my body and soul. Wherever I go, and I will not be tolerated here, my heart will remain in his unwilling custody," Hugh replies.

We let go hands and sit quietly, looking down into the depression where the Crouches' farm lies.

18ᵗʰ September 1594, entry by Hannah

Hugh and Kitty have left Durlow. Hugh was right, the villagers drove them out. On the next Sunday after his disclosure the vicar denounced them both, sullying their names in church. Kitty was described as a wanton, tempting men to sin, her lust arising from "the low instincts and weak moral control that women are subject to". The congregation was warned to "lock up your daughters and beat the hot humours out of their bodies lest it defile their souls!"

Kitty is banished, the customary fate of distressed girls in her condition. If she tries to return after her confinement, the prescribed churching will be refused her and she will be left impurified by childbirth – a mortal sin by our Christian doctrine. The child shall be denied baptism and so condemned to Hell.

Hugh is pronounced a sodomite, a capital offense in English law, on a par with murder, manslaughter, arson and larceny. From the pulpit the Reverend Gifford proclaimed sodomy to be:

"The most abhorrent of the execrable carnal cravings, a debauched aberration, a bestial act of abomination in the sight of God!"

Only Edith, the mother, amongst the Kemps attended the service that day and for her 'twas a mortification beyond bearing.

That night a gang of men and youths armed with sticks, and banging pots and pans as they assembled in the village, climbed the hill "to deal with the degenerate" for fear his corrupting presence should imperil the crops. Kitty saw their approach and Hugh slipped out just in time to escape a beating and arrest. The men wrecked the house, thrusting the pregnant Kitty forcibly aside with lewd insults and mocking the cowering whimpering mother – who stood like a sheep bleating her grievances to the wolf at the door. The bedridden Tom Kemp struggled to his feet in fury to protect his furniture but he fell, hit his head, and later that night breathed his last.

Kitty and Hugh have fled to the itinerant camp out on the heathlands. Edith would not go, to live among the country's castoffs and ragamuffins is unthinkable for her, she would rather die alone in the gutter. My father also is to go back to his former companions, his return to Durlow has not been a success. I had hoped he would resettle here and be of service as a mole catcher and netter of choughs, rooks and crows, but old habits of begging for his ale are too strongly ingrained it seems and alas pilfering also. There have been brawls and disgraceful scenes outside the tavern at night and many villagers hold grudges against him.

Nan says Trouble is his Gemini twin and I think she'll be glad to get him out of her hair for she spends most days tutting and chiding him. Dad is good natured for all his faults, he grins at her throughout, calling her "his old darling". Yesterday she boxed his ears.

23ʳᵈ *September 1594, entry by Hannah*

The departure of the vagrants has been delayed by bad weather. After a wet summer, the rain has poured in torrents throughout September causing the riverbanks to burst and flooding the meadows, so that mud and grunge swept through the low-lying hamlets. The road south's been impassable but a brief lull in the tempest allowed my father to set off this morning, and I accompanied him to say my farewells. I went with a heavy heart, though Pa whistled and sang rollicking songs as we walked, calling me "his pretty little sweeting".

The rough-and-ready settlement shocked and grieved me. Destitution and want is appallingly evident as the way of life for this ragged collection of roaming beggars. The children are thin as twigs and they watch you with hungry eyes too big for their pinched faces. Several of these poor drifters are maimed in body, a few deranged or lacking in mind, some are scrawny old folks too frail to labour and without kin to sustain them. And yet I was amazed to see a substantial number, more than half perhaps, of able-bodied men and women in the prime of life.

Hugh led me a little beyond the noise and bustle of the encampment. I asked him why all these people had strayed from their communities.

"Not through choice, Hannah," he told me. "They've come because there's no work for them, or else they would have starved. Respectable folk say they're all rascals and ruffians but 'tis not so. These are dismissed servants, redundant labourers, unwanted petty craftsmen or husbandmen like your father cheated out of their smallholdings. Each winter, famine and hardship swell their numbers, as does the enclosure of common land by greedy landlords. These poor souls are driven to tramp hundreds of miles of rough road by dire necessity alone. And by the unjust laws of this land. And by the savagery of its citizens."

I spoke hesitantly of alms for the impoverished but Hugh just laughed.

"There are two types of poor: God's and the Devil's. The former are given licenses to beg and receive farthings from the Poor Relief. The latter are clobbered by the ruthless hand of the law and spat upon by the populace! As a child were you not taught to pray for the 'deserving poor' alone? But we here are of the other sort. We are the undeserving.

"*The King's Book* ordains that those who beg whilst still fit for work are 'masterless men, rogues and wasters', breakers of the Eighth Commandment. No matter that there's no work for them to do, nor employer willing to take them on. The 'sturdy poor' are imprisoned, sent to Houses of Correction or whipped from the parish – bound naked to the wheel of a cart and beaten red by its virtuous residents, rolling them out of their precious streets! Hannah, there are even tiny tots here whose ears have been branded through with a hot iron, the gristle burnt right away by official instruction!"

Hugh spoke with the vehemence of the new convert, the fire back in his face and the haunted look gone from it.

"Are you happy with these people?" I asked him, feeling a sharp barb of jealousy, along with shame for my pettiness.

"I'm one of them," he answered. "We're all outsiders and outcasts, hated by the authorities, condemned by the Church and shunned by those who lead settled law-abiding lives. And I must stay here. For if there are two sorts of poor there are also two sorts of men." He drew a sharp breath and spoke next with a caustic barb to his voice, "The world declares me the wrong sort, and I must be punished for it, by God's people even before God Himself gets the chance to do so!"

I edged closer, for I'm scared for him and for what his fate will be. I wished, with a heart full of pain, we could but be children again! Hugh put his arm about me as if to ward off harm. He then spoke with real concern in his voice and look,

"And you too must take care, for the same Good Book that declares me an abomination states also *Suffer not a witch to live*".

I looked into those light blue orbs I love so well and longed for time to stop forever.

"But you ask if I am happy," Hugh continued. "I do not believe it is in my nature, any more than anger or hatred is in yours. I will always be longing for what I cannot have, continually seething in my chest, ever torturing myself upon spikes of my own choosing. My life as a vagrant will be short and brutal but I'm grateful not to be alone anymore. I am with my own kind at last. I belong."

Smiling, he gave me an affectionate hug and said, "But you, Hannah, yours is a sunny nature! The lost and condemned will always huddle around your warmth. You are true and content in who you are. Your path of happiness is assured, unless the world itself does rise up against you out of envy and spite. You are loving and loved. I'm glad for you, my friend."

These were his last words to me, and there was some comfort in them.

23ʳᵈ October 1594, entry by Hannah

I've clocked up eighteen birthdays to my name, but we cannot afford the loss of a day's pay at present so I will forgo celebration this year. 'Tis little loss, I rarely require vision time now, my dreams have been trampled underfoot since last October.

This autumn has been a miserable one. I miss Hugh every dawn and every dusk and all the hours between. I no longer greet life with pleasure. Something true, some flame that burned bright, has gone out. Winter is already breathing down our necks in chilly gusts but the barns are half empty. This year's meagre harvest will take its toll before the next one. There are rumours of plague south of the county. Disease spreads fast in times of famine and feeds upon hollow stomachs. I pray my father, Hugh and Kitty are safe from it!

The weather has been in keeping, we've hardly seen the sun for weeks. Thunder clouds hang over the fields, casting all in gloom. They lie so low in the menacing sky, it is as if they would press down upon our shoulders! Every branch and drystone wall stands out starkly against the skyline. The light has been weird of late, with strings of strange angry yellows across the horizon and grubby pink smudges at sunset. People look up to the ominous heavens and mutter fearfully, God has sent his legions of wind and water to chasten us.

The demands upon Nan are manifold, the villagers turning to her with their troubles as always in times of struggle and hardship. She has a grim, worn look about her like twine stretched tight and fraying, strand by strand, under the strain. When I urge her to rest, she says that she is an old battle axe and well used to the grind. But she tries to cover too much rocky ground, like the mountain goat that is her ally and totem.

Until recently I've been winnowing the grain, while the men were out planting the winter crops of rye and wheat. But there will be little call for hired farm labour from now on, so the corners of our two roomed cottage are piled high with carded wool to be spun into serviceable thread. Winter is an isolating time for me, when our lives are dictated by the thin hours of light squeezed between the massive dark. I miss the easy warmth of the summer and the hurly-burly companionship of others working in the fields beside me. But most of all I miss Hugh; sometimes smarting raw, always with the dull ache of a chronic malady.

Each morning I collect firewood beneath a daunting daybreak, time and time again with cold rain trickling down my neck. Some days it pelts my face like piercing needles and I think of the spears of the Spriggins. Later, I sit hunched up for long weary hours, working the spindle until my fingers tingle with pain and stiffness. We toil without speaking, pausing only to trim the candle wick. As we work on into the night, I hear rustling words from the walls and spy spindly sprites peering down from the rafters. Their whispers come in rhymes:

"Poisoned froth of the black toad's spawn,
The poor pale maid is now forlorn,
Beware the hounds that hunt at dawn!
Born and bred of a brackish age
We'll come a-tapping on your cage!"

When the distant chime from the civic bells announces nine of the clock we stop. I to cut our bread and cheese for supper, Nan to rake over the embers, before saying our evening prayers, taking off our kirtles before the last of the fire's warmth and falling onto our pellets to sleep grateful oblivion.

31st October 1594, entry by Martha

There's to be a festive gathering in Farmer Baddon's barn tonight; 'tis likely to be a lively one for we're in much need of some light-hearted relief. Faces have been grave and troubled of late, and many are looking lean though the hard winter is not yet upon us. But even this brief chance to forget our worries and woes does not suit our rigid moralist, Gregory Gifford! His last sermon was all a rant on the wickedness of dancing.

"What clipping and culling, what kissing and bussing, what smooching and slavering one of another, what filthy groupings and unclean handling is not practiced in those dancing!" he accused in full hellfire and damnation mode.

By gad, he would condemn smiling and stamp out laughter if he could! The children's games of autumn lob-nut and tick tag would be outlawed! The very chestnut trees would hide their crop in chagrin! He would have us all muffled in black fustian, with reddened knees from kneeling. But, nevertheless, the kissing and smooching will go ahead with or without a dance, and Gifford might as well join King Canute in ordering back the waves!

'Twould be but a fine jest if it were not that his grim hatred of joy is shared and spreads like sickness throughout the land. The last lingering echo of the horned Pan, our gay goatfoot god, with his healthy appetites and love of music and dance, is being driven from our lives forever. He has long been renamed Satan and we must shun him along with sex and our bodies – especially women's bodies. Man must enforce dominion over the natural world, and suppress the natural within ourselves. I foresee a gloomy future for Merrie England.

I am dismayed to find that Hannah, who once was wont to go to a party with a hop and skip, is reluctant to go at all to this one. She's not turned Puritan but is missing her old playfellow, the Kemp boy, and there is little I've found to console her during the month gone. With Hugh's departure she lost the life she'd wished for and hasn't yet found a new one to replace it. But she will. Such a nature as Hannah's is not meant to wither upon the tree before her love has borne fruit for the world.

I hope the revelries will bring her some pleasure and blow the bloom back to her cheeks. I remove her linen coif and comb out her hair 'til it shines like copper beech leaves in the rushlights of the barn, and I bid her enjoy herself on peril of my grouching all the way home if she does not!

There are several youngsters amongst the company and I'm pleased to soon see Hannah gabbing along with her old playmates. Even Parnella Colebatch, bloated in self-consequence since her marriage, hovers about the girls, keen to brag of an Anticipated National Treasure due in the spring! In addition to her exalted expectations, Parnella still preens herself over the downfall of her arch antagonist Kitty Kemp. The local lads are also blatantly glad of Hugh's removal from the scene, for I watch in some amusement at they compete for Hannah's gentle attention. Soon she takes her place in the square set as the music starts up.

Later in the evening, when things have heated up and cooled down again, and the hair and faces of the guests are untidy and flushed, I sneak out of the barn with my mug of mead to breathe in air unsaturated with sweat. I've seated myself upon a comfortable hump beneath a bilberry bush, preparing for some sensible peace and quiet after the inane ramblings of the addle pated and self-satisfied drivel of the tipsy, when I see the silhouette of my granddaughter's graceful form stepping out into the calm night, leaning against the wall and gazing up at the stars as if she too is thankful for a space apart.

As I hesitate to disturb her, Ralph Crouch slouches out the central doors, scanning left and right as if seeking some quarry. In his satisfaction at spying Hannah, he fails to notice me sat upon my knoll in the dark. Ralph bears down and stands towering over her, one arm barring her escape.

"You look like a celestial lily bathing in starlight," he gushes. (In faith, at times you can see the resemblance between Ralph and his soppy sister!) "Do you watch for the dead to return this All Hallow's Eve? Best beware lest they spirit away such a lovely mortal maid as you! There must be a dearth of such beauty in the spheres beyond unless the ghouls stray from Paradise itself!"

Hannah moves to go (no doubt to vomit!) but Ralph puts a restraining hand upon her waist.

"Wait, I have something for you, look here! I saw your exquisite eye reflected in is sheen when I bought it," and he offers her some jewel which glitters in his hand.

Hannah stumbles on words of refusal but the lusty lad seizes her wrists, pressing her against the wall, and urges his suit more forcefully.

"Hannah, my love, give me your vow that you'll be mine! I will be a good husband to you, no one will come between us, I promise."

She shakes him off and speaks sharp rebuke, "Do you forget what harm you have done to my closest friends that you suppose I will listen to you now?" And there is an anger in her voice I'm unaccustomed to hearing in Hannah's mild tones.

"But why do you chide me, my sweet? How could I settle for bold little Kitty Kemp while the divine Hannah Greene walks within my dazzled vision? You could not ask if of me!" he pleads.

"So need you have destroyed her? Or did you take the sister to revenge yourself upon the brother?" she scathingly reproaches.

"Hannah, you must stop this foolish raving and come to your senses!" Ralph is becoming angry himself now for she hits him at his pride. "We have seen the louse Hugh Kemp as the scummy low life he really is! Surely you cannot still be taken in by his sham facade? He tricked and mislead you with lies and falsehoods! He never had anything to offer, but if you plight your troth to me, I will give you all I have to give!"

His words end almost in tears as the extent of his feelings ring out. I'm almost sorry for him – an unusual emotion where the Crouches are concerned.

"Forget him!" Ralph urges, "The worthless whimpering cur has slunk away with the riffraff and will pester us no more. Be glad! You are a woman of fire and water, Hannah! Do you delude yourself into thinking you could have wasted your life and love sitting holding hands with a boy who could do no more than ruminate upon the stars? You need a man, a man who adores and desires you, who has red passion flaming through him!"

I have to admit to myself there's something in what he says, but his words only whip Hannah to fury for she is as loyal and steadfast to her old playmate as to kin. As he moves to grasp her to him, she flings out a stinging retort.

"Get away from me! I'll have none of you! Did you suppose for one minute that I will stoop to the slime of your shabby vendetta? It was your public allegations and heartless inhumanity that cast him from his home and community! Remember, Ralph, Hugh was man enough to strike you down in fair fight, despite your five years majority, to leave you grovelling in the mud with the whole village looking on!" Hannah speaks with a blighting forthrightness that leaves no doubt of her contempt.

Ralph hardly knows what to do with himself, so choked up is he and torn between his ardour and his fury at the scorn heaped upon him. He can do no more than shout a threat "I will show you a real man!" as he thrusts himself upon her, forcing fiery kisses onto her unwilling mouth. At this, I hastily scramble to my feet to pull him by the hair off my granddaughter. He's so taken aback to see me there he can only stand impotent, out of control and shaking, before tearing himself away and running, a dangerous and distraught figure, like a squall blown into the night.

I put my arm around Hannah to lead her indoors, whispering soothing platitudes as I do so. As I turn, I catch a glimpse of the hem of a dress disappearing back behind the solid doors. So, I am not the only witness to the drama just played out! And I recognize that fine fancy fabric whisked so hastily out of sight. It belongs to the flashy gown worn this evening by Alice Crouch. It is the mother of the rejected suitor who has been silently listening behind the open doors.

Back in the hall, I see Mistress Crouch's thin mouth shut tight and her eyes snapping daggers at us across the room. Hannah has made an enemy this night.

26th January 1595, entry by Martha

I'm feeling old. Well, I am old, the oldest widow in the village. But now it's telling on me. My skeleton's shrivelled to a rickety frame, like a chair that's long past its useful service. After a day's rough graft, I scarcely have strength enough to haul myself to bed.

But it's not only the physical slog that tires my bones and weighs down my spirit, it is the deprivation and misery I daily rub against. I have seen *too much* suffering in my long life! I am *worn out* by it. But the people keep coming with their ailments born of this winter famine. The price of food has risen higher than a poor man's wage. We barely subsist on barley bread, beans and oats alone as our staple fare. Indeed, I know of families forced to forage for bitter acorns, like pigs in the forest, to relieve their gnawing stomachs!

When I walk through the village, I hear children cry in hunger and their emaciated faces, hollow cheeked and frozen with cold, haunt me in my sleep. In such conditions the frail and sick weaken 'til they can keep no grip on brittle life. Ravenous Winter crouches and howls outside the thin wattle walls of our homes, picking out its easy prey from within.

These pitiful peasants come flocking to me to magic away the illnesses of famine and I send them away empty-handed to once again seek poor-relief. And with profound guilt, for I know the parish charity has already been stretched beyond its limits. Though the shame of it is that some grow fat upon the starvation of others!

The larger landholders, whose extensive acreage has yielded surplus despite the bad harvest, are reaping double the price for their crops and are rubbing their hands greedily. Some days, as I lean over the churchyard wall and watch the almost fleshless white corpses lowered into the frost-hardened ground, I think I can hear the rich sprawled upon their lush cushioned beds, laughing from their full bellies!

My heart aches as I sit at my wheel brooding. I'm losing my will to action and wish only to slip away myself. I've spent sixty-eight years in this difficult world, labouring to heal and weave my little spells on behalf of the good (and silly and selfish) residents of Durlow. Isn't that enough? Must I again tighten my belt and face the toughest challenge when I am most tired and battle sore? My very soul is despondent.

When I was a young woman, with blood flowing through my veins instead of the weak aguish water that drips through them now, I would endeavour to explain to my customers the true nature of magic. I would optimistically sit them down and speak about the fluidity of the universe, of how thoughts have power when constant and repeated enough – and are lashed to a torrent when fuelled by emotion!

I would elaborate on how mystical symbols, embodying belief, can work as a key to open up what would otherwise come as a struggle or be denied completely. I would solemnly urge, while illusions of glory gilded my judgment in splendour, that if we but *all joined together*, man and woman and child, to employ the strength of our unified minds, united in dedication, we might *solve all our ills and misfortunes* through a disciplined programme of magical work!

"Only together," I would shout, "can we truly move mountains. But," I zealously assured them, "together we can!"

Open-mouthed and baffled, or bored and uncaring, I would watch them turn away, to slink back to their mundane activities, putting all their hopes and effort into their own paltry self-centred concerns.

And my wise old Ma, who taught me all I know, would scold, "Martha, you cannot change the world! Least not when it does not wish to change. At most, you may make just a small notch in it before you are gone. Do not expect to prise open the shutters across their closed eyelids. These are simple hardworking folk, they've no more time or energy left after fighting for survival 'til the next spring, for anything other than rare moments of harmless merrymaking and a few sleep bringing pleasures.

"They do not want the responsibility for shaping reality that you would thrust upon them! They wish to have faith in a good God who can defeat an evil Devil, as was given them when they sat upon their mother's knee. They believe in custom and it is customary to believe in us. Give them cures and talismans and they'll thank you for it. Give them difficult questions and challenging revelations and they'll not return, so the little help you could bestow will be lost forever from their short burdensome lives."

She was right, my dear old Mam. I can still hear her tenderly chide me across the decades for conceit in taking all upon my bony shoulders. She would shake her head and say, "Life will go on with or without you, my girl, with but little difference."

27th *January 1595, entry by Hannah*

Time has slowed to a cumbersome crawl, like a reluctant boy dragging his feet to delay the ill-natured inevitable. How can it be that the mirth and bounty of spring have gone so far from sight? Its rainbow colours were all washed out in autumn's drenching downpours.

Hunger has moved into Durlow and taken up rapacious residence here. In times of such destitution, of fear and distress, of loss and sorrow, how do we survive? How *not* to be defeated by desperation, not to let our little life force drain away? How to stand steadfast, working for the good of all, when the harrowing cries of the afflicted push us to the precipice!

I look now to Nan, so strong in her calling as if anchored in the still eye of the storm raging around her. And so I remember we have but this short life span to serve, to complete what we came for. Each night, as the impoverished day turns tail, departing before it ever fully arrived, I light a candle with a vow to rekindle the warmth within, whatever cold winter blights and pummels us from without. And I dedicate a prayer to gain the strength and unremitting courage of my grandmother. I know that at the close, brave Nan will leave a true mark upon the world while others leave only a stain.

10th *February 1595, entry by Martha*

I am afraid for Edith Kemp. Since her husband's death, whom she grieves for as a whipped mutt will grieve a cruel master, and following the calumny against her children banished from the parish, she is even less of the woman she was. Her wits, never keen, have now of a surety gone a-begging!

She wanders about the village, trapping people in the street with an endless babble of trivialities that stream from her like the vapours of a simmering crockpot. Folk turn tail when Edith comes in sight, and apart from Hannah (who has ever been kind to Hugh's twittering mother) and myself (less kind and considerably more irritated) no one goes near her lonely cottage.

So Edith has taken to tapping on people's windows, lifting the door latch to see who is within, and will sit mumbling upon the step until answered. When she wants something she will thump her chest in angst, bemoaning her fate with such grumbling and groaning, wailing and whining that people will pay up just to be rid of her!

In truth it is the begging which makes her presence most odious. 'Tis not that her need is not sincere (for you could play her ribs with your knuckles like glasses with spoons) but purses have been pinched this winter and public alms exhausted. Though no one thinks twice about paying the church tithes of wool, young livestock, fruit and crops which make up the clergy's comfortable income, we begrudge and fear the neediness of our neighbours.

And yet how to be denied? As Christians we are bade to practice charity and the scriptures demand:

> If thou in any way afflict widows and they at all cry out unto me, I will surely hear their cry, and my wrath shall wax hot against thee.

So people turn the matter inside out – they make the victim the culprit. "She is a witch," they cry. "We will hold no neighbourly bond with such a one, we will not admit her into our house, nor spare her a morsel from our table. Instead, we shall shun and spurn her for the safety of the godly!" And thus the righteous folk of the village are left in peace of conscience and in peace at home, free from troubling scruples and troublesome widows!

Already the irate inhabitants of Durlow are coming to me with their grievances about the tiresome Edith Kemp,

"It's not right, Widow Herrington," they protest. "Decent folk should not be pestered by this repugnant old hag," (and this to me who has more than twenty years on Edith!) "We sense her ill-will and evil intent, something should be done to curb her wicked capers!"

But I will have none of it! I'll not play their games for I have seen where they lead. If we cannot help our neighbours in times of adversity what hope have we for our community? And if we cannot bear with the foibles and weaknesses of others what hope have we for ourselves?

So, I speak out against their ploys, I prick them where their guilt lies hiding and smite them with the words of honest truth they prefer to deny. They recite the Reverend Gifford's denunciation of Satan's sorcerers and I retaliate with the Ninth Commandment:

Thou shalt not bear false witness against thy neighbour.

I have upset many an upright citizen in this way, and so often of late that incensed looks are cast at me and they take their offended dignity elsewhere. They go to a Peller like Bambrick, an expeller of curses, wearing the adder's ring upon his finger, who will collude with their stratagems and publicly proclaim a witch at work. Upon my troth, the man does more to belittle the Wisefolk than a whole host of avenging vicars!

The village is now trembling and raging against one weak minded widow, whom they've lived in accord with their life long. But these are times of scarcity and misfortune and somebody must take the blame. Edith Kemp makes a serviceable sacrifice, she is a nuisance to her reluctant neighbours and she is repulsive to them, with a squeaky whinging voice and white bristles upon her chin. So she shall carry the guilt of Durlow, and she will pay the price.

So it will always be. The scapegoats may vary from country to country, from one century to the next, but always the downtrodden, the defenceless, those who are deemed inferior, scorned and frowned upon, these will ever be fodder for slaughter. Nowadays, poor and needy old women without husband or male kin are despised and judged expendable. Edith will be imprisoned before this famine has passed and left to rot there long afterwards.

The ways of the world sicken me.

28th *March 1595, entry by Hannah*

Today I will not think upon the problems that plague us. For the sun shines and God did not make such a day to weep through! I have left my stitching to walk out across the hills, where the first signs of spring are flourishing their shy delight in a new cycle beginning. A flock of fieldfare circle over my head, close enough for me to hear the clamorous chack-chack-chack of their chattering. Early born lambs gamble and cavort as if life is made purely for play, while the dreary munching of their elders rebukes them for their folly.

Sitting down by the brook, in a place where the riverbed basins so the stream may pause to rest, I entreat the naiads to show me the secrets of my future for I have fresh hopes this day, and a keen desire to fulfil my covenant at Candlemas when I renewed my pledge. As I gaze into the dappled waters a curious likeness gradually takes shape, flickering in the shade from the willows wavering above. It is a woman's face, homely and plump, with nut brown eyes fixed intently upon me. Rising up behind her, I glimpse a faltering landscape of heathered moors with a tower like a giant's chimney. But before I can decipher the hidden message in this odd visitation the scene blurs and breaks up, carried downstream in dissolving segments.

The river nymphs will show me no more so I set back across the fields, tracing my way along the hedgerows. As the twilight recedes, I startle upon and disrupt the dancing courtship of a pair of leaping hares. They speed away in panic, the black tips of their long ears quickly merging into the shadows, while the white down of their bobtails linger longer, flashing like beacons in the dusk.

These mad March rodents trouble me and intrude upon my thoughts. Local folklore foretells that it is unlucky for hares to cross your path. 'Tis said to offer a dire warning to turn back from risky commitments before it is too late.

29th March 1595, entry by Martha

Hannah has gone to bed but I'm too restless to sleep, for all that my long-worn body aches. I sit outside, on the bench by the back door, watching the darkness thicken. A lone crow joins me, hopping about in the hope of crumbs; strange that it should be out after sundown.

Below in the village the church bell tolls, summoning people to pray for a departing soul. So it has rang many times throughout this winter, shattering the silence of the night and disturbing our dreams with foreboding. Before day breaks, a short sharp peal will announce the death.

So many endings, so much passing away. The loved and familiar slipping out of sight, leaving us empty and our lives shrunk. I wait only for my own withering to the dust of the earth. My cycle is surely complete, when will the bell strike for me so I may be done with this hard life?

Hannah calls me a wise old owl. Aye, but a bird that sees into the darkening gloom may be a curse more oft than a blessing! Perhaps our mortal eyes are not meant to see more than a step at a time. Maybe the veil is pulled across the forthcoming for our own protection. To keep us from the shades which dismay and warp and paralyze. To hinder our surrender to despair.

For today I took down my scrying mirror to seek out better times ahead for our stricken county. Hoping we might borrow some good cheer, until the warmth returns to heal us and the crops grow to feed us. Instead, I was shown only wretchedness! I saw but more and worse to follow.

I held the oaken surround, letting my thoughts fade and flee, until I fell into a trance. The disc glimmered across its reflective face, then clouded in fog, revealing images and omens waxing and waning – each crueller than the last. Three more wet summers and failed harvests will beset us. Famine without reprieve will gobble up its victims to leave half of the parish destitute.

I saw the nation's vitality drain away as the old century dies. Good Queen Bess will not be long in following. As certain as day and night, the mirror's malevolent round revealed the disappearance of the Old Ways of the countryside. The ancient beating heart of this land will finally be silenced and lost to the people of England.

I saw stern laws and harsh restricting ways weighing heavy upon them. Dressed in sombre hue, they will be afeard to partake in nature's joy and fettered to mourning evil in every deed. I was shown a diseased city burning, and once the glass reddened with bloodshed ripping our homeland apart.

I put the mirror back upon its shelf and will look in it no more.

21st July 1595, entry by Hannah

When the wind blows through the corn there are words in it. I strain to catch their import but hear only muttering without matter. As I walk home at the day's end, dark pulsating shrouds of murmurating starlings cause a rush of turbulence above my head, each following where others lead.

All is scarce now – the miserly grain crop, the absent sun which hides from us behind surly cloud, and the companionship of dear friends gone from my life. Maybe I can no longer muster the effort to meet with my remaining chums, or perhaps they avoid me for my sombre countenance is as unwelcome as the never-ending rain.

24th July 1595, entry by Martha

The gossips of Durlow, the gabbling geese and crafty cats, are out in force in the village. There is a great cackling and hissing, yowling and spitting! The geese gasp and gape with open beaks fed full upon the tantalising food of slander. And the cats creep along on sly bellies, spying their chance to pounce, fat whiskers quivering in anticipation of a bloodbath!

The rains persist, for the second summer the wheat grows stunted and feeble, and the quaking villagers look over their shoulders for the bogeyman behind. Edith Kemp is gone from their lives but the community's curse continues. Anxious eyes are feverously searching for another source of evil. And they are alighting on me. For decades they called me "Wisewoman", now they whisper "witch".

During the past weeks, rumours have been spreading outwards like ripples after some furtive hand has dropped a stone into the calm of the pond. I have watched them gather momentum and fly, each more outrageous then the last and thus a single spark does ignite the forest fire.

Behind the suspicious looks and cold backs turned on me, I see the venomous stealth of Alice Crouch – the scheming spider behind the web of intrigue, busy weaving her poisoned threads to trap us all in her net of malice. She has waited long for revenge but she's chosen her moment well. Like an adept, she gauges the mood of the village and whips it up against me. She has the ear of our matrons and her puppet, the pompous husband, wields the weight of wealth and prestige amongst the men. Reverend Gifford lends his pulpit as a weekly lobby for my downfall. Bambrick too must be basking in all the calls upon his Peller's trade; I trust the Crouches pay him well.

I have cast a spell of protection about us and summoned the spirits for their support. But the tension rises over Durlow like a monstrous black wing. I, who always advocated the power of the many, now find the crowds are pitted to destroy me! Alone I may not weather this storm of mass hate, my last desperate stand is swept away by the mounting menace.

5th *August 1595, entry by Hannah*

I found the broken and battered body of my darling black cat this morning. He was but a little way from the cottage, where I searched for him when he did not come to my calls. He'd been beaten to death, for sticks and lumps of rock lay around his mangled body, with ripped fur and white bone protruding.

Poor Whisper, he was ever a loving and loyal pet. He has purred upon my lap, stretching out a paw in his comfy way, since he was a kitten and I a child. He was always a sweet natured, timid cat. I remember how when something untoward startled him, his eyes would open up into great green pools and he'd skit away in panic. After which he'd return contrite, to mew and rub up against my legs.

It was a cruel death for him. What had he done to deserve it except to give us his faithful affection? Who would do such a needless vicious thing for point or sport? I knelt on the ground and held his poor mutilated body to my breast and wept.

28ᵗʰ *August 1595, entry by Martha*

On the way back from market today I was set upon and hustled by a group of women, all from the village and all known to me. I had my sturdy staff about me and made good use of it to stave off my attackers. They've left gashes across my face and neck, and have succeeded in collecting my blood beneath their fingernails. For a recommended antidote to combat a witch's curse is by: *Banging and basting, scratching and clawing to draw the blood of the witch.*

Later at home, while Hannah was cleansing my cuts, smoothing on ointment and soothing my exasperation, we started up on hearing a frightful crackling from the ceiling. Hurling ourselves out the door we saw the roof ablaze and the culprit fled! I beat at the flames with a broom while Hannah drew up water from the trough to douse the burning thatch.

The fire is out but we won't sleep easy in our beds tonight.

4ᵗʰ *September 1595, entry by Hannah*

We were arrested at dawn and taken to the county gaol at Hereford. Strange, but now that our worst fears are fact, after the cold sweats and terror of the past few weeks, I feel almost nothing.

No, that is not true. Two things have filled me since we were thrown in here.

One is the chill and dimness of this place. With its thick stone walls and tiny barred windows through which the late summer sun can hardly creep in at all. As if the daylight resists penetrating such horror and misery as found within.

The other, which clogs my lungs and appals me with each breath, is the stench.
I have urged and retched with the putrid foulness of it!

8th September 1595, entry by Hannah

The first act of our gaolers was to remove our shoes. Throughout the days and nights that followed, we have been compelled to walk back and forth across the cell. Back and forth, unremittingly, with neither rest nor sleep, never pausing for a single minute. We are denied food and drink, refused even a sip of water! We must walk barefoot over the jagged bricks of the rough uneven floor. Forever to and fro across this accursed cell!

Our feet are torn red raw and bloody from burst blisters and open sores, each step jabs like embedded nails. My throat is too parched to any more beseech mercy from our captors. Nan has become weaker with each hour. They will not let me give her the support of my arm, nay, nor even hold her hand! When she stoops and her knees buckle beneath her, the thugs scoop her up by her hair, sending her reeling on her way with such violence that she crashes back down again with force enough to break her bones!

I keep my eyes on the floor. I cannot bear to look into my grandmother's strained face, to see the whiteness about her gaunt mouth as she grits her teeth against crying out. But the rasping gasps of her frantic breathing reverberate throughout this tight suffocating space, desperately palpitating from wall to wall. I cannot block her intolerable torment! My soul is ripping apart! Anguish fries my blood dry!

My God how could this happen to us!
Help us, oh Lord on High! I beg Thee!
Help us!

9th *September 1595, entry by Hannah*

Nan has passed the point at which she can stand. Each time they drag her to her feet she collapses in a heap on the floor, mute and unmoving now, except for the thinnest whimper as she falls. Their failure to shift her shattered, broken body infuriates our sadistic gaolers who turn on her with savage ferocity, shouting thick oaths, kicking her with steel cap boots.

I cannot bear to see her frail frame so assaulted. I throw myself full length over her as a shield against the brutal blows. But I am tossed aside like a rag doll.

I scream and plead and weep. I am cuffed in the mouth, again and again, with the back of a heavy hand.

I can only watch her painful contortions as she receives each murderous blow.

It will surely kill her! I cannot *bear* it!

From the pit of me I screech like an inhuman thing, *"I will confess to anything you want but for the Christ's sake leave her be!"*

I had to do it. I had to!

Though I know what follows will be worse.

After we'd made our mark, they left us alone. In exhaustion, I slump on the cell floor with my back against the wall, cradling

Nan's limp body in my lap, her head on my shoulder. With bone-dry eyes, I would weep blood if I could.

For I have failed her. I have convicted us.

11ᵗʰ *September 1595, entry by Martha*

The midwives are here, sent by our accusers to seek for Lucifer's mark upon our bodies. They will discover no extra teat springing up in the genitals from which Satan may suckle in exchange for demonic power, but my skin is a mass of freckles and brown marks of age, while Hannah bears a rounded birth mark upon her right breast.

I think I glimpsed a flicker of pity as my numerous purple and yellowing bruises were exposed, but it's speedily wiped away again beneath the mask of their stone faces. After we've been stripped and shaved below, and each crevice probed, the elder midwife pulls the Witch's Needle from its velvet pincushion, taken from St. Oswald's vestry where it ordinarily resides.

"Agnes Waterhouse," I challenge, for she is well known to me and I to her, "Are you intent upon plunging that four inch shaft of rusty steel into my sagging old flesh? Have you forgotten me then that you can do so? Have you and I not laboured side by side to bring forth many a tenuous young soul into the world, through the night and into the day together? And was it not I who blended you a healing potion to combat the malaise of your first born before he was yet two seasons old?

"By Christ's Wounds, Agnes! Where is your backbone! Would you side with the forces of infamy and corruption? Will you condemn an innocent young girl who should have a full life before her? Or even a long toothed old biddy, who has been sour tempered and pig headed at times but has always struggled to assist others, albeit in her cross crabby way?

"I know you will not! I know you will champion justice and the truth that beats in your heart! For I knew you well, my dear old colleague, you will be a true friend to us as I have been to you in your hour of need. Stand by us now for the love of God!"

Mistress Waterhouse blanches and makes no reply, nor will she look me in the face, but sets about her work with that spiteful needle, drawing fresh blood as it pierces the vessels deep under the skin.

I do not know, as they leave, if they are satisfied or ashamed, but they have what they came for.

21ˢᵗ *September 1595, entry by Hannah*

We were hauled before the Assizes today. The courtroom seemed unbelievably light and airy after the cramped, squalid conditions of our cell. At first, I did not look at the rows of people at all, so rapt was I to see the golden September sun streaming in through the high latticed windows.

Nan is still weak from her battering. But there is some life back in her eye, which for days resembled the dull glassy eyes of a fish upon the chopping slab. I saw her measuring up the enemy with a grim determination on her face.

"Look Hannah, here are all are good neighbours, dutifully assembled to see injustice is done. They will be hoping for caterwauling and frothing fits at the very least, we mustn't disappoint them," she derides, directing my attention to the expectant assembly.

To the side of the carrion crows come from Durlow for the show, were seated the jury, respectable tradesfolk and artisans of the town. "All pea brain and plumped-up plumage," was how Nan described them. For a moment I saw the whole assembly as a sundry flock of birds, nestling on the benches, squabbling amongst themselves, seeking out tasty titbits with beady eyes. And led by a mighty raven, Judge Moyle in his black robes.

Desmond Moyle is a wealthy lord who owns a grand manor house, set in its own park and passed down through the noble family for generations. He rarely comes in contact with the villagers, though some of the young folk gain employment on his estates. I have seen him ride past on a magnificent dappled grey mare when he hunts with the pack on the moor. He has been about the world and bears the reputation for being an astute man.

I trust it may benefit us.

22nd September 1595, entry by Martha

The case against us continued into a second day; the broadsheet writers will have much to elaborate and distort. Except, in this case, there's really no need for what was said in court was all a great phantasm in its own right! Hannah looked ever more aghast during the lengthy legal process as if she could not believe what she was hearing. As for me, it merely confirms my opinion of human nature. Foolish or vicious throughout!

Many are merely deluded, led along on leads by those wielders of petty power. They quailed and quivered, surreptitiously crossing themselves whenever I glanced their way. Utterly pathetic! Why were we given minds to think with if we forsake them to curtail to the whims and ill will of others? I would like to see these sapheaded lubberworts on trial for the gross neglect of the small abilities they were born with!

The leaders of the pack – the Crouches and their cronies in enmity, with Gifford and Bambrick snarling behind – have mobilized their attack with some precision. There must have been many a secret meeting at the back of the alehouse while Hannah and I were rotting in gaol! They're careful to maintain a pious front, calling themselves "meek servants of the Lord" come to shield the innocent. But behind that bogus humility lies a sticky treacle pot of malevolence, I see it oozing behind each lie they spout. And they savour and feast on our ruin like gluttons, bloated with self-gratification, palpably drinking it in as a tangy wine!

The most iniquitous of the crimes incited against us came from the Crouches' unstinting donation. Alice Crouch spoke on behalf of her daughter Parnella Colebatch, who apparently was "too distraught with grief" to level the accusation herself. Earlier in the year, Parnella had born a misshapen baby, a sickly infant with a contorted back and bowed limbs which will never be robust enough to bear weight, who writhes perpetually and mews like a kitten. The child, should it live, will always be a slur and burden upon the family. At its birth I'd kept away but Hannah, out of kindness and loyalty to an old friendship, visited the mother. So the child's deformity is to be laid at my door with Hannah as my tool in the infanticide!

The depiction of me that Mistress Crouch presented to the court was as accurate as if she'd held a hand-glass before her own face and did report what she saw in it.

"This widow is a cunning and treacherous woman. Her heart is rotten and swollen with rancour and vindictiveness against her fellows! Her words are underhand and steeped in concealed turpitude! She pretends to help in order to harm. She has long been a wellspring of discord in our harmonious village, a brawler and uncouth drunkard. Her thoughts are eaten with spite, her actions driven by vengeance!"

I almost laughed aloud at so precise a self-portrait as she could paint, and I looked around the benches to see a spark of ironic recognition amongst the villagers. There was none. Not an eyelid flickered, nor a mouth twitched. It's as if they are so caught up in the web of falsehood and intrigue, they see fantasy where reality should be and reality where lies only fantasy!

Mistress Crouch commenced her attack with: "Widow Herrington's malignance has well-nigh destroyed my innocent grandchild! But with the justice of this court, your Honour, God will be avenged!" And I wondered what divine justice will be meted out to *her* as she sets her devious trap of hateful lies to destroy *my* innocent grandchild!

Her lumbering tedious husband, the Yeoman Crouch, delivered a long-winded catalogue of extensive damage to his property arising from the floods that I had undeniably evoked as "so unnatural and infernal in their ferociousness were the storms". Faith, if he thinks me that proficient in the Craft, such that I can raise tempests, I am amazed he dares to stand and berate me thus – does he not fear a thunderbolt to the seat of his breeches!

The Reverend Gifford was called up next to deliver his tirade. He must have taken long over its rehearsal for it was as sweltering and inflamed as Hell's brushwood, incorporating grandiose gestures, sinister head shaking, fierce finger pointing and tortured grimaces! But though the jury seemed impressed with his dramatic performance, I noted the eyes of his parishioners glazing over, they're all too used to his sermons.

He sited the *Malleus Maleficarum,* "The Hammer of Witches". This, the acclaimed authority at witch trials, dates from the last century and has bedevilled the lives of honest women ever since.

"All witchcraft stems from carnal lust, which is in women insatiable," he quoted from it, and ranted hot on his favourite theme of bestiality in *"the weaker and corrupt sex".*

Leonard Bambrick, as village Peller, declared that I had worked in collusion with the convicted witch Edith Kemp, hence my refusal to connive in the campaign against her. Another with a vested professional interest in denouncing me was the physician, who would much profit from ousting the midwives and Wisewomen from their traditional work in healing and childbirth. The physician's contribution was a medical assessment of my constitution.

"The Herrington crone is exceedingly melancholic, with a marked excess of black bile which defiles her blood and pollutes her emotions."

There were many from Durlow who stood up and spoke against us. Not one dared to speak in our favour. Maybe they feared to be sucked in themselves as witchcraft prosecutions, like plague and disease, erupt in fearful clusters and spread swiftly.

The worst accusations cited against us were grotesque indeed, some were merely bizarre. I was said to fly at night in the dark of the moon to attend blasphemous rites. I'm supposed to possess a magic broom that sweeps on its own and levitates through enchantment. Whisper, my granddaughter's cat, was depicted as our familiar exciting us to fornicate in black sabbats. Little Annie Lissett described how her perry cup had a suspicious white sediment in it conjured by Hannah's envy. I saw Judge Moyle's glance shift from Annie's commonplace countenance to Hannah's beautiful face and back again with a lift of his lofty eyebrows.

Husbandman Higman (the great oaf!) stolidly credited the broken leg of his shorthorn cow to my bale influence. The cheese was prevented from forming after I'd been seen in the distance, while two gallons of cream refused to turn to butter. A calf had mysteriously sickened between morn and nightfall, while another was wont to kick over the pail of milk – all testimony of my malicious grudge against his persecuted cattle!

"Nay", I countered, galled that such an ale-soused apple john as Higman should be even listened to, "'twill be well-nigh the next century ere each wronged milk-bearer has its case heard and disputed! Why not invite the whole bovine herd into the courtroom so they may bear witness first-hand? 'Twould only add sense to the proceedings!" The solemn jury frowned at my levity but the ghost of a smile briefly disrupted the judge's impassive demeanour.

Parnella Crouch, recovered from her bashfulness, started spitting forth her spleen, swearing she'd seen a waxen doll in our cottage. Mary Gloving, the miller's wife, told of having "fallen into a grievous fit, alike violent and diabolical in its peculiarity" after encountering me one evening in the lane. Jane Wilkins related how Hannah had once given her young son an apple to bite upon, after which he developed "a dry tickling cough and was struck down with little knobs like warts over his eyelids which were drawn awry." And so it went on.

Throughout these outlandish and ludicrous outpourings, Moyle looked coolly on without comment. Though once or twice, I caught a shade of contempt as he listened to the blustering ravings of these ignorant common folk. His sharp eyes were often turned in our direction as if summing us up in a detached scan. Though I noticed they rested more often, and lingered longer, upon Hannah.

I hope it is harder to condemn healthy young lives then decrepit old ones.

8th *October 1595, entry by Martha*

The judge's verdict was the expected one: "Martha Herrington, widow of the late Timothy Herrington, cobbler, and Hannah Greene, daughter of the vagrant Jacob Greene, you have been found guilty of the charges of witchcraft and sorcery by the authority of this court and with the holy sanction of God.

"You are sentenced to a year's imprisonment, during which time you shall be taken, once in every quarter of the said year, into this county town of Hereford upon market day or at such times as a fair is to be held, and there shall be shackled to the pillory for a space of six hours and shall openly confess your error and offence."

So we were returned to the gaol sluice pit to live amidst the filth and excrement. But today we're back out, released for our allotted slot of public taunting and humiliation in the stocks; pinioned at the wrists and neck by the weighty wooden slat, on the banks of the Wye beside the cheerful array of peddlers' stalls.

The residents of the town and surrounding villages, out on a spending spree, mill around us and lap up our discomfort.

"See, Hannah, we have a prime view and clement weather for our outing! All we need now is the generous young master to share his refreshments!" I say, not just for a wan smile from my granddaughter but also to raise a laugh from the onlookers. It's worth an attempt to win them on our side. It might even deter that grubby urchin from throwing his overripe fruit at our heads!

Intent upon pleasure, the people pause in passing, with a jibe, with curiosity, or with vengefulness and loathing. I am most wary of the men who roll out from the ale tent, for Hannah's beauty attracts much attention. Wrinkled old crones in pillory are two a penny but comely young women raise novel and licentious interest. There are many bawdy jests and lecherous propositions,

"By cock and pie you're a tempting ladybird! Let me feel some of your enchantment, me saucy bud!" And they sidle up behind her when no one is looking.

Hannah stands as a statue, her face unflinching and her eyes cast down, though my own flesh creeps as I see them put their smutty hands upon her, fondling her in soft places and whispering obscenities in her ear.

The young lads I can shake off with a muttered threat, the dirty old men are harder to scare away. I summon up every curse against their manhood that I can utter, forewarning the filthy swine that: "The callibisters dangling between your legs will be shrivelled up and impotent by morning if you don't take your stinking paws off forthwith!" All eventually spit a lump of gob at me and slope away, uneasy with my jinxing. For once I am glad of the fear of witches.

Many from our village are here. Some give us a wide berth, either out of shame or fright. Others swoop in like vultures for the kill. Parnella Colebatch has come with a riled gang of Durlow's youths. She stands before us spurting out noisome insults, screeching to the crowd:

"Behold this depraved harpy!" making a grab at Hannah's hair as if to yank it from its roots. "You would not think to look at her that she's a devourer of innocent infants, in collusion with the fairies who stole my child and left me a deformed changeling! But so she is I tell you! Yet she will be free to resume her witchery within a year whereas I, the aggrieved mother, will endure sorrow and tribulation my life long!" she whines piteously.

There are some murmurs of sympathetic horror from the crowd that has freshly assembled, attracted by this new spectacle. Hannah continues to stand motionless and deathly pale until, during a pause in which a spent Parnella gathers wind, she lifts her honest eyes to her old playmate and quietly entreats her charity.

"You do me a great injustice, Nella," using the nickname Parnella had as a child. "On my most solemn oath and in the hearing of my Heavenly Father, I swear to you I bear no ill will to you or your own and have never hurt, nay nor could I, a hair on the head of your child! I beg you to accord me your compassion, as one who has ever stood your friend."

To this Parnella waxes hysterical like a madwoman, roused to frenzy (I fancy) by knowing in her heart that Hannah speaks truly. She is so beside herself that her husband has to restrain her, dragging her away worried for her sanity.

Her brother, Ralph, has remained silent and rigid throughout, his eyes never leaving Hannah's face, his own taut and pained as he watches her at the centre of the mob's rage. He also turns tail after this scene, bolting off in the opposite direction to his overwrought sister.

It was some hours later, as the stores began to pack up and the crowds to drift away with the daylight, that we saw Ralph again. We were being released from our manacles and Hannah was rubbing her chaffed wrists to bring back the blood flow, when he swaggered by with a giggling hussy leaning heavily upon his arm. The chit was in a slatternly state, her footsteps tottering and her provocatively clad body swaying under the influence of too much ale.

The wench's unruly progress caused them to lurch towards Hannah at one point, and Ralph was brought up close to her. She lifted her head and I saw a look pass between them, at which he careered sharply away as if smitten and shaken by the interchange, pulling his bit of floozy behind him. But after a few yards he stopped and shook off the girl who collapsed, her legs sprawled, in an ungainly heap on the ground and he retraced his steps purposefully back to my granddaughter.

"Hannah!" he cried, urgently seizing her hand and seeking her eyes. "I will wait for you, Hannah! I will be there waiting at the gaol gates for you, I swear it! I will make everything so well again that you will forget this evil day and these bad times. And then I will cherish you, my darling, and keep you safe for the rest of our lives!" Hannah just looked away, too weary and low in spirit even for scorn.

Out of the gathering shadows stepped Mistress Crouch, and she stood alongside and laid her hand upon her son's arm, saying coldly to him:

"Best wait at the church lych-gate then. Both young and old leave prison in a box by that route more than any other."

She's right of course, prison is a hotbed of fever and disease, few leave it alive.

12ᵗʰ *November 1595, entry by Hannah*

This gaol is a dire, dismal place for any creature to be confined in. Life within its thick walls is remorseless and godforsaken indeed. Even in the summer it is as grim as winter and now, through the portals of November, life here is one of gnawing hunger, miserable cold and backbreaking labour. And each day brings more of the same.

But the nights are worse. Sleep upon boards in the dank air, which leaves any wood sodden, and spongy fungus spores upon the brickwork, is fitful and long in coming. Within this bone-chilling icebox, the victuals of oatmeal gruel and the coarsest dry bread are too meagre to keep warmth in our bodies. It is never quiet here. In the bleakest small hours, the moans of the dying and the demented wails of the insane echo in waves of low despair mounting at intervals to intolerable crescendo. In the blackness, 'tis as infernal and tortured as the dungeons of Hades!

We've been moved from our solitary cell to the cruddy communal quarters holding the women. You can tell which inmates have been here the longest, for the last vestige of human resemblance has deserted them. Amongst the raving lunatics is our neighbour, Edith Kemp. She rushes madly about the chamber, prattling incoherently about her brown goat and her best bonnet. Or she cringes in a corner, wringing her hands and casting sly side-glances from darting shifty eyes. Her words are all nonsense or worse, instilled into her mind during the trauma of interrogation.

"Ssshh! I am Lucifer's whore! The Devil's concubine! He sucks upon my nipples! He chomps on the sinews in my flesh. Oh shhhh! I'm a wicked, shameful woman!

I'm naughty and nasty, naughty and nasty,

a naughty, naughty, nasty hag!

Naggy haggy, saggy naggy,

saggy baggy naggy hag!

Please Sir, can I have my bonnet back?"

Thank God Hugh cannot see her now.

When we first encountered Mistress Kemp in this state, I regret that I turned away in shock and sorrow, but Nan sat down and spoke to her,

"What have they done to you, lovey? Where is that dizzy young miss who used to giggle and gossip with my Tamsin? Such a slip of a girl as you were then. And where is the pitiful worrying woman, scrubbing and slaving for her bullying husband? Teased and ridiculed by her smart tongued children? You were always such a good little soul, always so anxious to please! Always so obedient to your loud-mouthed boor of a father or thuggish brute of a husband. Never daring to question their tyranny, even in your own mind. Did you do the same with your interrogators? So eager to admit to whatever they accused that you began to believe what they said?

"Poor harmless obliging Edith! See what becomes of being dutiful? Of submitting to their decrees of good behaviour? Of trying to do what they say a virtuous Christian woman must? Look what it has brought you to! Cast off by your community, condemned to Hell by your Church – aye and put there early by your country's courts of justice! And you never even allowed yourself any fun in your docile life. The big 'Him' or the little 'him' might not have liked it!

"Come on, Eddie, you go tell them fry! You scream and swear at the cockalorums! You'll feel better for it, my dear."

The crazed widow clung onto my grandmother with perpetually clawing hands but gradually Nan's presence seemed to quieten her, the twitching abated and, for a space, she ceased chewing and manically working her bleeding gums.

Talk amongst the women is either angry and violent or low key and desolate. I have heard some sad histories since we joined the others. Emily Pole, a destitute beggar, flung her two-year-old infant down the well last March. For some inexplicable reason the wretched girl has taken to following me around, recounting her crime over and over, and sobbing hysterically upon my shoulder – as if I had the power to make her peace with God! I let her talk, it can do no harm, she's to be hung next Saturday.

"I couldn't abide it, you see! I couldn't abide to hear the little mite crying for food I didna have. Food to put in his stomach that bulged out in hunger like a boulder! I couldn't bear to pick him up and feel the bones all sharp-edged and poking out. It was like his flesh hadn't grown enough to cover them! I tried to keep him dry but he always got that wet and muddy, and shivered in his soaking clothes, fit to break your heart it did! He was sick'ning and I could na watch it, I was afeared to see it. I asked God to take him up to Heaven quick like, he didna deserve to suffer so, he was just an innocent little lamb. Not like me.

"I doth bitterly regret it, what I did. They won't kill me, Mam, will they? Not afore I've a chance of redemption? I'm a-frightened to die, I'm mortal scared of the rope! Don't let them hang me, please Mistress!"

There was another here convicted of child murder. She spoke hardly ever, her face always sullen and set, and she scowled and turned her back if you approached her. She refused even to see the priest to make her confession. Her name was Jinny Symonds, she was just fourteen. She'd been a maid servant, taken against her will by the gentleman of the house, who did deny it when she became large with child. She tried to hide her abasement from others and gave birth alone in the cow-brier one night. Then, as soon as it cried out, she smashed the babe's head against the wall, her own twisted away so she would not see the skull shatter.

They say that she spoke in the end, just before the stool was kicked out from under her.

"I rejoice to be gone from this cruel world!" were her final words.

19th December 1595, entry by Hannah

Nan has taken the fever. Gaol fever is pernicious and unrelenting, and I am afraid.

Malignant disease is as pervading in this death trap of a place as is the rank air. I have seen it eat away the strands of life like hatching moth eggs eat through woollen garments locked in a chest. It's not the only killer her, some are carried away by the consumptive lung ailment, others by putrid inflammation and still more by slow malnutrition. But it is the one I fear most.

I never thought of Nan as old, so strong was she and keen in mind, but in this harrowing penitentiary the years have galloped up on her like Roman Legions from behind. Skeletal, her skin dry and flaking like ancient parchment, her body has at last betrayed her spirit.

Now her cheeks are burning scarlet, her hectic eyes overbright in sickness. Her heart pounds against her ribs as if it would break out! How long can it withstand such an onslaught? Her soaking steely hair is plastered to her like a tight-fitting skull cap. With the hem of my kirtle, I try to wipe away the sweat from her brow but more oily beads spring up at once. As she groans in delirium, I can only stroke her head on my lap and beg, "Nan don't leave me! Please don't leave me here alone!"

I know this is cowardly and selfish. But I cannot face life without her.

20th December 1595, entry by Martha

Even before I sickened, I knew that my time was running out. Indeed, I have been in this world too long by far, no wonder I have been such a cantankerous old harridan for much of it! I would leave with a blessing and sigh of relief were it not for my love for Hannah.

She is my joy; she has been the solace and treasure of my old age. I had always hoped to see her cared for, in the arms of another who loves her, before I died. Instead, am I to desert her in the most dreadful period of her young life! For how will I reach her from beyond the grave? The chasm between the realms of life and death is a sweeping canyon, across which you may shout with all the force of your being to be heard only in the faintest wisp of a whisper, or but in silence on the other side.

What have I brought her to, my sweet loving girl! This is the thought that *torments* me amidst the heat of the fever! Who am I to disparage the likes of Edith Kemp who tried to play safe by the rules! Was it not wilful perversity and stubborn deviance to ignore the narrowing attitudes and tightening chains of our era? Did I not turn my eyes from the omens given me? And scorned to peer into the encroaching shadows? Oh foolhardy, foolish old woman that I am!

Why did I not trust that the destiny of this land lies in the wise hands of the Goddess? When I could have held faith that history unravels as it must, did I not in truth throw my puny pickaxe against Her? You cannot fight the whole world, nor stem the storm when in full flood. But I tried to. Was it all vain glory then? Is this a biting lesson to me, the punishment for which my darling grandchild must pay? Then it is bitter and merciless indeed!

Now must I heed the Crone of the Triple Goddess who ushers in death and decay, who brings a cycle to a close so that in time a new spring, a better world, may be born.

I will not enter the new century and it will not be found there.

21st December 1595, entry by Hannah

For the last few hours of this night Nan has been clear in mind. I would hope for a recovery but, in a cracked wheeze, she bids me accept that the end is awaiting her, ready to lift her up out of her wasted old frame. Unable to relieve her turmoil, I can do no more than promise her that she has always been my strength and trusted guide, and that it was she who bequeathed meaning to my life. Without the compassion and integrity she showed me, all would have been fallow as acrid dirt. Like a beacon so I could see the way, she's forever my touchstone and talisman.

Tears spilt down Nan's face at my words, and she breathed more quietly. Then she again opened her eyes to mine and said:

"Do not grieve for me, dearest. My life has been full and useful and good. But thou, Hannah, thou art like beautiful blossom frozen by frost – a frost that comes out of its time, to strike down faith and hope. Yet, you are unfaltering and true. You will survive it. And when you leave this lion's den do not look back, but live quietly out of the world's sight.

"Remember this, my angel, above all things: you are made to love, Hannah, and to be loved. Don't let anything or anyone thwart thy destiny. My dear."

She has little strength left to say more but she begs me to sing to her, the Winter Solstice song which is bleak and melancholy but it seems to bring her comfort. Each time I come to the end she signals to begin again. So I do, over and over, while the prison around us grows hushed and recedes from our vision.

Winter in solemn stillness pauses.
But we dare not stop to hold our breath,
We work with cold and clumsy fingers,
Often in darkness, too near to Death.

We fear for all the old and ailing,
With long thin lifelines, ashy white,
And brittle bones, like crisp frost crunching;
Beneath their feet lies treacherous ice.

We tremble for the young and new-born,
Their vulnerable softness in swaddling bound,
That a bitter season yet may harden
Or else may bury underground.

We're troubled for the ill, still gasping,
Their racking cough throughout the night,
While we wait for the wake of the dawn bell tolling,
Dreading a silence at the end of the fight.

And we fear for ourselves, hunched and brooding,
Burning damp wood in our home's chill hearth,
Breathing dim corners of mildew about us;
Our larder is empty with mould on the shelf.

For as long as the Grim Black Reaper is with us
We cling to our kin, our village, our past,
We cherish the Yule tide feast and its rituals,
Traditions that bind us we'll trust to hold fast.

The warmth in our hearts will ward off winter!
The wolf that howls will be kept from the fold!
The love that we bear will bring us new courage,
Till hope, pale and pinched, breaks up through the snow.

22nd December 1595, entry by Hannah

Martha Herrington has gone to the Summerlands she always yearned for. I will miss her like half of myself. But I am so glad she was a part of my life.

It was my grandmother who guarded my childhood's stumbling steps, who scooped me up and soothed my hurts, and my bruised feelings too. It was she who gave me a loving home to grow in, and she brought the whole mysterious, marvellous Universe into it! She opened my eyes to what others do not see, through her I met Nature as if it were a friend and tutor. It was she who taught me to trust in myself and in my own discernment, which grants the freedom and self-respect I see denied to others.

Dear Nan, she gave me the love every little girl craves, and she gave me the treasure to carry through my adult life and beyond. The gifts of the soul.

1st January 1596

My grandmother's death, like all gaol deaths except for executions, was attributed to "natural causes". But there is nothing natural about our mouldering existence in this depraved underworld! And it killed her as surely as a hangman's rope. She deserved a better parting from a life dedicated to helping her traitorous community!

My stomach is steeped in venom. During these interminable days of oppressive half-light, I find myself dwelling upon vengeance, the most tainted and festering of desires. My thoughts in this desolation, like my blood in the numbing cold, have congealed and set into an unknown substance. I do not know myself, I do not like myself, and I *hate* them.

24th January 1596

There was one day darker than all the rest. So dark it was as if the sun was blotted out, fallen in upon itself, and I have been a dead thing since.

One loathsome night, the turnkey (there was but one on duty for once) unlocked and came into the women's quarters. He shook off those who fawned and begged about him and sought me out, hauling me roughly to my feet. I was dragged off to a solitary cell, the size of a long narrow cupboard, and there I was raped.

The man was coarse and foul, throwing me against the wall to wind me, knocking me down to the floor with an iron punch in the stomach. When he had me pinned beneath his weight, he thrust his hard engorged jockum between my legs tearing the tender flesh there. Throughout the pounding that followed, he groped and squeezed violently at my mangled breasts. His breath stank of decayed gums as he panted into my mouth and, in the thrashing transports of his arousal, he dribbled a stream of spittle onto me. The thick slobber slithered down my cheek into my ear as I tried frantically to move my face, for I was certain I would suffocate.

This is so dense and jagged a memory it sears my mind, leaving me butchered, my body charred and angry meat. I am filthy and violated. I feel like a pig, run through with a skewer, roasting over a pit.

The next day the judge came.

23rd January 1596

Lord Desmond Moyle arrived at Hereford County Gaol this morning and took me out of it. Riding alongside the carriage, he spoke to me at intervals but I failed to comprehend what he was saying. The glaring sunlight, after months of prison gloom, shone too blinding to bear. Disoriented and dazed, I could not take in the green countryside rolling past the window, stretched out like a garishly painted canvas. I could not accept that these things were real and I do of a surety think, had somebody led me by the hand, I would have submissively stepped back into the dung and abomination of the prison cell as if it were the only world I knew.

However, when we reached Laslett Hall I recognized it, for it brought back some hazy memories from childhood, though as insubstantial now as dandelions turned to fluff. But I can vaguely recall Kitty, Hugh, Leah, Bessie and I following the supply wagons in, keeping out of sight behind the laurel bushes that bordered the imposing driveway, and gaping in wonder through the iron gates at the magnificence of the honey hued building with its castellated archway and cobbled courtyard beyond. Today, through the gaps between my fingers, I peered at the high walls mellowed in the radiance of a wintry sun.

I was escorted by a servant through a side door and up a small spiral staircase to a whitewashed bedchamber. A ewer of hot water was brought to me and a clean night garment laid upon the chair. I did as I was bid, stepping out of my reeking rotting clothes thick with prison muck, and strove to scrub off the grime and stench that clung to my skin and hair from months of subsisting there.

25ᵗʰ *January 1596*

Yesterday I was given a sleeping draught and left alone. Indeed, I slept heavily through most of it, the dreamless oblivion of drugged sleep, such sleep as I had been starved of through all those fitful, tortuous nights in gaol. Pulled down into the void, escaping for long thankful hours from my tumult, splintered my thoughts apart to re-settle like dust. Except for the most detestable remembrances; these have sunk to the bottom of my mind where they lie – a thick layer of stinking stagnant mud.

I feel a limp thing to which the blood is sluggishly returning.

26ᵗʰ *January 1596*

I know the maid who came to my room this morning, carrying a plate of vittles and a pitcher of water for washing. Her name is Beth and she is from Durlow, the tavern keeper's youngest daughter. She opened her eyes wide when she saw it was me, but then looked away without a word until I caught her arm, beseeching her to tell me whatever she knew. My pressing plea made her pause and answer me, though she refused to say much and she kept her voice down to a whisper.

"They're saying in the servants' hall that the master has taken leave of his senses and my mistress is livid, calling him an old dotard who's put their good name in jeopardy for the sake of gaol scum." Beth murmured nervously, keeping her eye on the door.

So – I am Judge Moyle's mercy mission. But without the support of his wife. It used to be common report in Durlow that Lady Moyle is much feared by her servants for her blistering tongue and infamous rages. Beth confided that her mistress is in a delicate condition and they fear the scandal might unhinge her.

"Lord Moyle has ordered new clothes for you, I'll fetch them," she added in a normal voice. "He says to inform you he will visit at noon."

This he did, tapping politely at my door and waiting until, in a shaky voice, I bade him enter.

"Good day to you, Miss Greene," he greeted me, bowing as if I were a noblewoman. "I am delighted to find you in such improved looks and health too, I hope. We were seriously worried about you, my dear; I feared your ordeal might have robbed you of your reason as sometimes happens alas. But you are much recovered I see and let us rejoice in that."

Asking my permission, he seated himself and folded his hands in his lap.

"I must tell you, Hannah – if I may call you so? – I have failed to obtain the pardon I sought on your behalf. After I heard of your grandmother's death from fever, I dared not wait any longer but got you out through bluff and blustering. But you must understand you're still legally a criminal and need to lie low, for it would be unsafe for you to return to your village at present. Pray think of Laslett Hall as a safe sanctuary and your home for the time being. "I'll leave you to rest now but I would solicit you to join my wife and myself for dinner later."

Thrown into appalled confusion by this I tried, in great agitation, to excuse myself. To which he replied archly but with decisiveness: "Nonsense, young lady, her ladyship will be delighted to receive you." And with those words he left the room.

Now, as the clock chimes seven, a footman leads me through a maze of lime-washed passages and oak doorways to what he calls "the small dining room". Though it appears a very grand, elegant apartment to me, with Flemish carpet underfoot and decorative tapestries on the walls. Intricately cut crystalware and silver cutlery are laid upon smooth white linen. A three-pronged candelabrum stands in the centre of the table and there are other beeswax candles lit upon the mantelshelf and on sideboards about the room. I am bemused and discomfited to find myself amid such affluence. Indeed, I'm as perplexed to be in the stately manor of a lord as I was when first thrown into gaol! Surely neither has anything to do with *me?*

Lord Moyle rises to his feet at my entrance, again as if I were a real lady and not a peasant girl dressed in a frock above her station. Her ladyship turns an angular profile to look at me, snapping her black eyebrows together as if she does not like what she sees.

"Ah Hannah, welcome to our table, I take pleasure in presenting her ladyship to you, my wife Barbara." his lordship says blandly.

I bob a curtsy to Lady Moyle, feeling anxious and uncouth. She does not acknowledge me, though her cold stare doesn't waver.

"Pray join us," my host continues, indicating the vacant seat into which I sink, fervently wishing to be swallowed up by the floor! I'm placed opposite her ladyship with her lord between us at the head of the table. "Permit me to pour you a glass of wine, my dear. We will drink to your new home amongst us, may it be a felicitous one."

He raises his goblet and waits for Lady Moyle to do the same. There is an uncomfortable pause before his wife picks up her glass, during which his commanding eye meets hers while unspoken conflict hangs entrenched in the air between them. At last, she sniffs and toys with her glass. Nevertheless I notice, although lifted to her mouth, no wine passes her lips.

A choice meal is served us of salted beef, roasted capons in an herb sauce with boiled vegetables, followed by apple tart, cheese and fruits. The female company eat in silence, I sparingly, unused to such richness after the near starvation of a prison regime, while his lordship speaks idly of his business upon the estate that day. Throughout I smile and nod nervously while her ladyship responds not at all, never once turning her head towards her husband but looking haughtily over my shoulder throughout. I'm completely unnerved by such treatment and have to stop myself from making a frantic bolt for the door! Though it does occur to me, that Nan – who was never one to stand in awe of her betters – would enjoy the whole scenario as hilarious as it is unlikely.

Lady Moyle is a rather sharp-featured matron with tight curled hair streaked with grey. Her face has aged badly, lined and sagging beneath the lead and arsenic concoctions fine ladies put on their skin to whiten it or to cover ravages left by the pox. She is elaborately dressed in a heavily brocaded puce gown, its full sleeves slashed at intervals to show puffs of lawn undershirt.

Her bearing is one of great pride and, on this occasion, barely suppressed wrath. As she pushes back her chair my eyes fall to her lower belly and I remember she is said to be with child. I'm surprised as she must be over forty, though perhaps ten years or so younger than her partner in marriage, and I know they have two grown up children already, themselves married and living in Worcester.

To my overwhelming shame, the judge notes the direction of my glance for he comments upon his wife's condition: "As you can see, my wife is in an expectant state. It's a late pregnancy

you understand, no doubt a final blessing upon our long union."
The dryness of tone is unmistakable.

I flush in acute discomfort, much heightened when he glibly
proposes:

"Perhaps, Barbara my life, we might ask Miss Greene to be
a godmother to our fortunate little issue? She is charmingly at
hand and might be a third, or fourth in time, daughter for you
and a comfort also as you so oft complain of being much left on
your own."

Lady Moyle, rising angrily, flings down her spoon at this
deliberate provocation and with a vexed flick of her hand sends
her goblet spinning across the table.

"Enough of this buffoonery! What other indignities have
you in store for me? Pray don't hold back, Desmond, I've come
to expect any outrage – however demeaning – from you!" she
shrills, heedless of the wine dripping down her gown.

"Oh well, no matter," he replies indifferently, snapping his
fingers for a manservant to clear the soiled cloth. "Would you
care for a sweetmeat, Hannah?"

After Lady Moyle has stormed from the room, I remain
frozen, overcome by the evening's events. I sit looking down
at my lap, appalled at my role in his lordship's design for his
wife's annoyance and his own entertainment! I have no wish to
play it. Indeed, I feel some sympathy for the untenable plight
of her ladyship and can better understand her ready temper. A
wife is reliant on her husband in all things.

"Sire, I do not seek to bring discord between Lady Moyle
and yourself," I contend, as firmly as I dare. "It will be best, I
think, if I leave in the morning and take my chances back home.
I thank you for your aid." And I stand up to take my leave.

His lordship steps over immediately, takes my arm and
reseats me, saying in a contrite, softened tone "I am sorry,
Hannah, you were subject to that display of atrocious bad

manners. It was ill done, and I promise to ensure your path doesn't cross my lady hornet's again."

I cannot be untouched by the kindness in his expression and sincerity of his apology. Who am I, after all, to criticize a gentleman's relationship with his wife in his own house? Although I again beg to return to my room and to be gone by the morrow, he will have none of it and bids me resume my meal.

I'm greatly puzzled by such confusing impressions of my host, and am not a little alarmed as to the use Lord Moyle intends for me. Taking my courage in both hands, and hoping to understand something of this perplexing nobleman and of his unaccountable intervention in my life, I ask:

"My lord, I am at a loss to understand why, after finding my grandmother and I guilty and sentencing us to imprisonment, you have since gone to such lengths for my rescue?"

"Are you angry that I convicted you? No doubt with good cause but I'm afraid the evidence was too strong against you. Justice must be *seen* to be done," he answers with some irony.

"You do not consider me guilty of the dark arts then?" I cannot prevent myself from probing further.

Lord Desmond smiles and shakes his head, "Hannah, my child, the world is not so black and white as young minds make it. If only it were! But for your peace of mind, I hereby officially acquit you of flying around the moon on a broomstick and of tampering with some yokel's prize milking cow!" And he laughs gently at his joke.

I sit sombre faced and uneasy, unable to share his humour on such a subject. His lordship observes me for a moment and then leans across the table, patting my hand in a consoling way.

"Do not be perturbed, Hannah, I vow no harm will come to you. After I'd seen you in court, so young and innocent as you are, I could not rest at night until I had secured you a pardon.

And I was troubled enough to ensure your release without it in the end.

"Pray excuse my flippant ways. I'm a selfish pampered old man, too used to living with persons who are as scratchy and acrimonious as burrs to know how to behave in a decent way anymore. Do not think though that I am unmindful of the atrocities you have suffered, or that I do not feel genuine sympathy for your bereavement and grief. I will do all I can to lighten it, my dear."

I stammer my thanks, rise to curtsy and bid his lordship goodnight. Thus ends the most extraordinary evening.

1st February 1596

Since that disturbing supper, I've kept largely to my room and life has settled into some sort of routine here. Although at times, I harbour a troubling misgiving that I am merely wandering bewildered in a baffling dream and will awake to find myself still incarcerated within the clammy walls of Hereford Gaol. But thankfully, more often than not I feel the exact opposite, that I've just woken up from a long-troubled sleep, riddled with ghastly nightmares, and I am deeply *grateful* to be alive and free!

Each morning I fling open my window casement to breathe in the fresh pure air of sunrise and it is nectar to me. Over and over, as the day ebbs and evening enfolds us in its restful embrace, I lean out across the sill and savour the delicious smells of wholesome food cooking, wafting up from the kitchens below. And I'm filled with *so much gratitude* for every joy that was denied me in captivity! Such simple pleasures I will never again take for granted my life long.

I'm not allowed to join the servants and work for my keep, though I would give much to have the company of my own rank, but Lord Moyle says they will not tolerate a convicted witch in their midst. Before I could close my mouth on my hasty words, I heard myself censuring him, "But you expected your own wife to accept such a felon at your table?"

"I expect my wife, who has the benefit of a superior upbringing and education – for all she hides it! – to be above the superstition of rustics," he answered somewhat tartly. And then he laughed and pinched my chin.

However, at my repeated appeal I've been given the household laundry for darning. I spend long hours sitting sewing at my window which overlooks a small enclosed courtyard, where I stitch and think and watch the servants scurrying to and fro in the course of their busy day.

2ⁿᵈ *February 1596*

The Moyles are out visiting today, so I availed myself of the chance to leave my room, and by way of the backstair, to steal into the family chapel. 'Tis Candlemas and I too wished to welcome the spring and to honour Mary the Mother.

Entering the small chantry, furtively and afraid to be seen, reminded me of stealing into St. Oswalds as a child, desperate to perform my personal pilgrimage but feeling dreadfully guilty at such barefaced intrusion. As if places of worship are not meant for little girls any more than for convicted witches. Once more my luck held, permitting me a whole afternoon there in uninterrupted bliss.

And so it was – bliss! Before my life went awry, I used to often marvel at this gift of rapture that is wont to descend upon us at rare moments, neither at our command or supplication, nor from cause which can be caught or created. From whence comes this divine boon? Does an angel walk unperceived beside us? Did some wild earth spirit follow me in, leaving the open moors of its natural abode to venture into bricks and mortar? Or was this majestic Presence here afore me, pressed in between ceramic floor and ceiling trusses, and charging the space betwixt with the tremor of enigmatic ecstasy?

For as soon as I'd slipped through the doorway and sank into a pew, the tears overflowed and I felt for the first time since the arrest that I'd come home. A homecoming of the Spirit, born of the Mystery and without chorus to herald its return. For the golden glory always speaks to me alone and in silence.

As the sublime reverie gently passed, I sat peacefully admiring the charm of this old chapel, with its ornate stonework and tall gothic windows. The February sunlight gleamed across the polished tiles, set in emerald and amethyst diamonds along the short aisle. I pulled out a prayer cushion from beneath the seat, it was of faded blue silk delicately embroidered with silver bells and tiny pink rosebuds. It seems there are many things of real beauty in this great house, each concealed away as if forgotten.

14ᵗʰ *February 1596*

Although I've never again been in her ladyship's presence, Lord Moyle visits me often. For this I am thankful for it is lonely here. Their outraged mistress has forbidden the maids to converse with me and, though Beth or another brings me meals, I rarely get more than a clipped word from any servant. But Lord Desmond comes frequently, especially at midday, tapping on my door, bearing a tray and saying "I've come with your luncheon, my dear." It has become a joke between us, this ritual greeting.

I find him to be a courteous and considerate gentleman, distinguished not just by his cultured manners, his precise refined speech, his neat black attire of the best cloth but also by the respect and benevolence with which he treats his inferiors. Despite his extensive learning and vast experience of the world, he strives to set me at my ease so I feel increasingly comfortable in his company and less like the ignorant country girl I know myself to be.

He's generous too. He has promised to teach me my letters, and today the housemaid brought me a petticoat of the softest peach wool, a new pair of cotton stockings and smart buckled shoes trimmed with ribboned edging. I have never known such luxury!

It is only in doubtful moments that I hear Nan's sceptical voice whispering into my ear: "Don't be so naïve, Hannah!"

28ᵗʰ *February 1596*

Lord Desmond escorted me around the gardens this morning and set me a task to seek out the patches of sunshine falling between the billowing white clouds! I was glad to get out, though some days I feel like a dog in a kennel waiting for my master to reward me with recreation. For I've been warned against going out alone; Lady Moyle would not hesitate to promote my re-arrest if outside the manor and safe custody of her errant husband. I doubt not 'twas she who watched us from the upper window this morning and I wasn't sorry to leave the flower gardens, which terrace steeply down to the river in full view from the house, to enter instead the enclosed kitchen plot which is less overlooked.

As we walked, his lordship described how delightful the grounds are in the full bloom of summer, the walkways ablaze with lavender scenting the air with perfume. There is a rose garden too, with trellis arches and an ornamental lily pool.

"Great orange pumpkins grow here in the vegetable patch, and below the herbary is a pond filled with carp to add variety to our dinner fare. Within the walled orchard yonder is a rounded dovecot, as old as the earlier manor and festooned with creamy honeysuckle by June."

As we ambled our way back, he spoke of farming and I told him that my father had been a husbandman when I was a child. On reaching the courtyard gate, he paused to request.

"We shall talk more over dinner later, if you'll be so kind as to grace me with your company for the customary banquet of Shrove Tuesday?"

"But her ladyship…" I began to remonstrate in alarm but was interrupted.

"My wife will be leaving this afternoon to spend Lent with our daughters in Worcester. It is an annual visit; I believe she finds it easier to be dutifully devout when out of temptation's way. I'm the irritant flint of her inflammatory temper you understand!"

"She may not like me to supp with you before the servants," I demurred again. "I think it would be more fit for me to eat in my chamber as usual."

"Not another word, my girl! There's really no need. I've already told Barbara of my intention to dine with 'our pretty little houseguest'. I thought it might lend a thought to warm her during the journey for it may turn cold later."

He spoke airily as if 'twere but a pleasantry, and then bestowed a smile and bow on departing.

It's now evening and the footman leads me, not to the dining room, but to the Great Hall where I'm met by Lord Moyle as I enter.

"I hope it pleases you to honour the occasion in the grand manner," he says and offers his arm to escort me around, describing its history and pointing out antique features. It is the original part of the present house dating from 1445 and I am much impressed by its size, and by the height of its lofty vaulted roof which makes a complex maze of intertwining timbers above us. It has three doorways set beneath stone arches at the far end and a massive moulded fireplace along the central wall, above which hangs the Laslett coat of arms.

"My mother was cousin to my wife's father, the former peer," he tells me, as we both stand looking up at it. "Despite the possession of this magnificent manor, the Lasletts were in somewhat straightened circumstances by the time I'd grown up, while the wealth lay within my own branch of the family. Hence my hasty marriage, which 'none may put asunder', to the last of the Lasletts. My wife Barbara was their only surviving child and dreadfully spoilt! We wed as soon as she reached fourteen as arranged by both sets of parents, each bent on their own advantage; one sought manna, the other inheritance of the ancestral home. Alas neither lived long enough to vicariously enjoy it, but I have been tasting its blighted pleasures ever since. And some days am heartily bilious of them!"

I know not how to respond but the judge smoothly continues, "But let us pass on for I see you are sadly confused for a reply, so shall we turn opportunely to the superb painted glass window of six lights, with its late fifteenth-century heraldic panes upon which again you will see the family's arms emblazoned at the top. In medieval times, you know, a Great Hall like this would have provided eating and sleeping quarters for all the family and household. I would suppose such communal living must have been decidedly irksome, don't you think?"

The meal is served, with his lordship sitting at one end of the long oak table and I to his left. It is a sumptuous feast and I partake too much of the heady burgundy perhaps, for I hear myself quizzing:

"Had you a productive afternoon, my lord?" as he'd visited the Assizes, "And did you convict many witches? No doubt to give yourself the wearisome task of rescuing them later!" I catch my breath at my own audacity and curse the rich red wine that has so loosened my tongue.

But the judge only laughs, his eyes crinkling in genuine amusement, "No, young lady, I have saved myself the trouble by sentencing no more than a beggar and a couple of boys for filching a handful of nuts and raisins."

His words instantly sober me as I remember the poor wretches abiding in such a turd pit as Hereford Gaol. I reproach myself for my frivolous levity, 'tis all too easy in the secluded comfort of Laslett Hall to forget that life goes on outside it. And that it is a pitiless one for many, indeed for most of England as the long famine still holds the country in its hungry grip.

Lord Desmond, ever perceptive, senses my change in mood for he speaks again but seriously this time.

"No doubt you think me heartless, Hannah, without clemency for my fellow man? And it is true there are some who are dealt rough justice, though none more innocent and lovely than yourself. But for the most part it is at least partly deserved. Order must be kept and without these punitive measures, turmoil would rock the nation into chaos and carnage. You are young and still have hope in human nature perhaps, but I have witnessed too much of it to trust the country to its keeping. Believe me, my dear, I regret it is so."

After pondering his words, I question him again:

"Did you think my grandmother was likewise blameless of black witchcraft?"

"Oh Hannah, Hannah, there are no such things as witches! 'Tis all superstition and old wives' tales. Silly hokum dreamt up to frighten children and scare simpletons." he dismisses.

"And thinking thus you could still condemn her to her death?" I cry, too horrified at such cold bloodedness to guard my words.

"Ah, my little one," he replies, his voice full of sympathy for my distress, "It was not I who condemned her but the spite of her own neighbours. Do you suppose me so powerful that I could have prevented it? If I were to acquit one in such a well-presented case I would lose all credibility. People would deny the justice of the land, saying it is but a wealthy man's whim and the grumbling would grow to the clamour of riots, with crime and butchery following hard upon their loss of trust.

"No, Hannah, I'm afraid my job is not so much dispensing justice as maintaining public respect for the law. We are all in the volatile hands of the populace. Even the monarch on the throne will blanch at the rumble of disgruntlement and civil unrest beneath the surface, for her own life as well as the State's existence rests upon such a turbulent bedrock."

I brood over his reasoning and though I know myself to be an unschooled peasant set against his scholarship, I still feel puzzled by it.

"I am sometimes cast into the shoes of Abraham commanded by God to slit his own son's throat, but alas it is no god that guides my hand and upholds the peace of the land, 'tis instead an illiterate and barbarous rabble. Mob violence is an ugly thing, Hannah, even more savage than our ghastly gaols," he concludes, with weariness.

"And will only the spilling of innocent blood cause the tension to recede?" I pursue, caught up in the hostile picture he paints.

"On occasion, yes. It is what the classical Greeks called catharsis, a peak of pain witnessed by the onlookers, which allows the throng to go quietly home, their bloodlust turned to the meekness of lambs who've escaped slaughter," he explains, with a vague wave of his hand.

"You describe a bleak world without compassion," and I speak in despair at such ruthlessness.

"There is hope, Hannah," he promises, eagerly leaning towards me. "The future will be a triumphant one when England comes to maturity, leaving behind the puerile fallacies of this credulous Age. The way forward is through Reason! – The objective endeavour to scientifically understand and so control the natural laws that operate in the world. Then we need fear no longer, nor attribute ill fortune to a vengeful God who must be mollified. *The time is coming,* by Jove! Already the haze of muddled thinking is clearing amongst the educated classes, eventually the enlightened mind will ripple down until all mankind is free!"

I'm surprised out of my despondency by the change that has come over Lord Desmond, and curious at the reverence with which he speaks – so different is his manner from his usual languid urbanity and acid humour. He gets up and goes to a cabinet placed against the wall and forages amongst some pamphlets kept there, returning with one in his hand.

"Permit me to read this page to you; it is the discerning account of a respected Kentish scholar, Reginald Scott, reviewing the subject we have been debating together this evening, that of the treatment of old women like your grandmother who are accused of witchcraft:

These miserable witches are so odious unto all their neighbours, and so feared, as few dare offend them to deny anything they ask. They go from house to house and from door to door for a pot full of milk, mead, drink, pottage or some such relief, without which they can hardly live.

It falleth out that many times their expectations are not served but rather their lewdness is by their neighbours reproved. And further, in the tract of time the witch waxeth odious and tedious to her neighbours so as sometimes she curseth one, and sometimes another, from the master of the house, his wife, children, cattle, to the little pig that lieth in the stye.

Thus in the process of time they have all displeased her, and she hath wished evil luck unto them all, perhaps with curses made in form. Doubtless at length some of her neighbours die or full sick, or some of their children are visited with diseases that vex them strangely as apoplexies, epilepsies, convulsions, hot fevers, worms, which by ignorant parents are supposed to be the vengeance of witches.

I listen intently, feeling sick at the atrocity of such *witch hunts*.

"Indeed Sire, the knowledgeable gentleman describes just what occurred to a neighbour of ours, by name of Edith Kemp. But Nan was made of sterner stuff. 'Twas not vexation at beggary which turned the village against us but rather resentment and revenge, a fear that she rivalled the Church and the coveting of others who wanted her pickings for themselves. Alongside all this, was the distrust for any who think independently and follow different beliefs of an older faith. These were the ingredients that set the brew boiling in our own persecution." And I speak resentfully for the perjury and bile of our trial are forever branded through me.

"And malice from personal jealousy also me thinks, from green eyed envy of your astounding beauty, my dear," his lordship adds softly, his agnate grey gaze upon me.

5th *March 1596*

During Lady Moyle's absence the manor seems lighter, as if a holiday mood pervades it. I bask in the extra freedom, picking up my skirts and breaking into a run along the passageways, setting the shiny floorboards clattering beneath my feet! I have noticed an uplift of spirits amongst the servants too, who often hum or whistle now as they go about their chores. Beth seems more inclined to pass the time of day with me, instead of shunning my company tight lipped and stiff as before. Though some of her disclosures are disquieting and bode ill.

"The mistress likens herself to Queen Catherine of Aragon, forced to witness 'the sly antics and artful cajoling of that royal slut, Anne Boleyn, stalking Her Majesty's rightful husband amongst the rose bushes.' And sometimes she works herself into a rare fury, screaming at us 'but just look whose bastard sits upon the throne now!' Though we're forbidden to mention you, she watches everything you know," Beth divulges.

And indeed, although I'm able to roam the gardens at my leisure since her departure, I still catch myself warily looking up to the mullioned leaded windows of the upper story, which glint strangely in the sun like multiple winking eyes.

16th *March 1596*

Along with my letters, Lord Moyle has been teaching me a little astrology. He says it will help pass the time, which lies heavy on my hands now that her ladyship has returned and I am again confined to my room.

"It is an ancient discipline, Hannah, which can serve as a lens held over our complex selves, allowing us to dissect each trait in turn before reassembling the whole," he tutors me. "Let us begin with your natal chart, which I've drawn up for the time and place of your birth. The most obtrusive feature is the conjunction, just three degrees apart, between your sun in Scorpio and Venus in Libra."

"What does that portend, Sire?" I wish to know, though suspicious for the judge has a gleam in his eye.

"*Venus*, Hannah! The fairest one of all!" he quips playfully. "The enchanting jewel star of the evening sky! Aphrodite, the Celestial Goddess of love and desire! But then how could *your* sun be bedfellow with any other but the most graceful of planets? She endows you with the bequest of charm and loveliness and seductive fire. See, alluring Venus even burns in your hair," picking up a strand of it.

"Copper is the metal of Venus – and behold your shining tresses, bright with the burnish of copper straight from the forge! Your mercury is happy to be there too, in the blue harmonious skies of Libra, ruling melody and enticing words from honeyed lips. Were you anything other than Heaven's most illumined star you would be a copper crested nightingale, my beauteous girl!" he effuses with mock rhapsody, hugely enjoying himself.

"Indeed, Lord Moyle." I reprove, for I am embarrassed by his extravagant sallies and looks of admiration. "Perhaps, when you have done with flattery, my lord, you might tell me something of my Scorpio sun? That doesn't sound quite so fair!" I counter, hoping to spare myself more blushes.

"Not so fair but deep, dark and passionate! It makes me question what else are you hiding that you feign to be a snow princess?" he teases.

With an uncomfortable smile, I beg him to cease his brazen banter and be serious.

"Oh, but I was! But never mind, you wish me to be grim and insulting so let us see what I can do for you." And his lordship considers me, his expression inscrutable, before proceeding, "Your sun lies low, deep down where demons lurk. Placed in the treacherous Eighth House of Fate, it is the spark within the black cave. It rules the knife that cuts and the wound that bleeds. Scorpio battles against the Monster and pierces her heart upon its claws. It is the sign of death by burning and rebirth through the phoenix arising from the ashes.

"But you have courage, my little scorpion, and endurance. Enough to survive the worst ordeal. Haven't you already done so?" he discerns with a penetrating look, and I wonder if he knows of my violation in that hateful prison cell.

"Now tell me something cheerful, I beg of you!" I plead, wishing to leave such grating nightmares buried.

"Certainly, my dear. Your moon is in Pisces, where its love and tenderness extend beyond the expanse of the vast ocean itself," he tributes with quieter esteem, lifting my hand to plant a kiss upon it.

18th March 1596

Thoughts of Hugh have been haunting me this day. I recall how insightful he was, always seeing to the hub of the matter beating beneath. What would he say to me now, I wonder? I look about me as if through his eyes and I find myself recoiling. The loving substance that once blessed my life has all been gobbled up, leaving only this flimsy affair fringed with futile luxury.

When I think back to the Hannah who lived in the little cottage on the hill, safe with her good kind Nan, I do not recognise her, so strong was she in her sense of self. But the once sturdy greenwood is riddled with wormholes! For everything that happened in that hellish prison was as a scourge which eats away healthy life, leaving me shrunken – smaller in mind, lower in spirit, my nature warped from within.

It stole my past *and* it stole my future. My chosen path blockaded, the stampeding herd has turned and the horde has marked me out. So I must break my pledge, turning traitor on my family birthright and betraying Nan's trust. Am I a coward then? Or is it not as heedless as spitting in the wind to so throw away my life?

But truth be told, it's neither. If I'm being brutally honest, the miserable fact is I no longer *care* enough! Why should I help those shameless backstabbers of Durlow who robbed Nan of her last years? But it's worse than cold indifference. Sometimes it boils up and disgorges hot hatred like a leprosy. Hugh used to say I was his good, kindly angel – he would not know me today! The thief has pilfered the goodwill and love from my heart. What is left? Who am I now?

I woke up last fall to find myself below Life's unbearable bottom line. I have lived with the dammed and desperate. I know the foulness of this world. I have bedded it. The stench of humanity, the greed and cruelty of people, guzzling upon others' downfall, savouring another's travail! Albeit stemming from a secret relief that they need not share it.

We are such shallow selfish creatures, living such little burrowed lives, turning away from the suffering in our neighbours' eyes. Only the rare, the exceptional, stand out from the contemptable crowd. The far flung few who risk all to change all. To raise us up a mite out of the mire. It takes incredible courage to face the world instead of weakly following it. I am proud that my grandmother was such a one!

But what of Desmond Moyle? He risked his own neck to rescue me from gaol. And yet he also put me there. He saved my life. But not Nan's. What of him?

5th *April 1596*

One midday, his lordship caught me crying. He "came with lunch" as he has many times before, but cut short his usual greeting when he saw me brush away the tell-tale drops from my cheeks.

"You have a fit of the megrims, my poor maid," he said briskly. "And no wonder, locked away in this room with only yourself for company, except for the annoying obtrusion from a tedious old man come to plague you! What you need is a trip away, new places to visit and fresh sights to see. A little shopping for some pretty trifles and plenty of walks to enjoy the mild spring air. It shall be so, I will arrange it forthwith.

"But for now, let me tempt you with these choice delicacies upon my tray. Look marzipans and sugar almonds! I am determined you shall not lose those sumptuous curves you've gained since you came to us as a walking skeleton."

I ate the almonds and the judge kept his promise, for today we're off to Gloucester which His lordship maintains is far enough away for safety.

"Though heads may turn when you walk down its streets it won't be because anyone knows you!" Lord Desmond assures me, his eyes twinkling.

Gloucester is said to be a fine walled city, larger and wealthier than Hereford. It's situated in the next shire, which in itself is marvellously exciting for I had never yet set foot farther than my own county of Herefordshire!

"Do you know Gloucester well, my lord?" I ask of my coach companion.

"I rent a house in Cathedral Close for a season sometimes," he tells me. "Though for our present visit we will lodge at *The Queen*, which I judge to be the best of its twelve inns."

"Will you tell me something of the city's history please?" I implore, for everything is of great interest to me.

"I'd be happy to, my dear," he courteously complies. "Gloucester is an early Roman settlement, and second only to Bristol amongst the great provincial towns outside London. It has the foremost corn and grain market, serving the Vale of Tewkesbury, the Forest of Dean and the Cotswold Hills. But wait until you see the shops, Hannah! It trades exotic wares shipped from the Mediterranean and beyond; tomorrow we will seek out some ornate gewgaw for you, such as worn only by the sultry beauties of the Far East!"

7th *April 1596*

So to the shops we went, his lordship was determined to indulge me! Gloucester is indeed a busy, bustling thoroughfare serving the heart of England; the hurly burly of the street market, with its dazzling array of merchandise, is thrice the size of any I have seen. We visited, I in wonderment, the resplendent and prosperous shops by the High Cross where I poured over the luxurious array of wines, dried fruits, foreign oils and intriguing commodities from distant shores. The city fashions, flaunting low necklines, were frankly shocking to my unsophisticated eye but the judge insisted I should be measured for a gown. I protested in vain and eventually gave in when my lord began to pout like a thwarted boy. Though forsooth, I find like Aladdin, it's hard to resist such fascinating temptations as are hoarded up in these man-made treasure caves!

This evening we've been joined at the table by two gentlemen of the town. The elder, a portly merchant and borough councillor, is visibly puffed up in self-consequence by the honour of supping with a lord. This Horace Corbet, for such is his name, extols the merits of his hometown at some length to us, pompously effusing that "there are more literate men in Gloucester than in any other place throughout the country. It's a damn fine city and by God's blood we've worked to make it so!"

Lord Desmond laconically regards him a while, before idly turning the conversation to various hushed up scandals that he knows of, casually undermining each offended defence Corbet attempts. He seems to enjoy antagonizing the bumptious townsman and I am reminded of a cat toying with a mouse.

"This worthy liberal policy of alms that you speak of, my good Sirrah, would that be the same reserved corn stocks for which Alderman Garnons was found guilty of fraud to the profit of £160 last September?" he enquires with his suave purr.

"Well, um… I know there was that one case… but I can guarantee…" the flustered councillor stutters.

"It's not as if he had need of the funds surely? Is it not the case that the Gloucester aldermen do very nicely for themselves in procuring the leases of prime municipal locations at absurdly reduced rates?" Lord Moyle sardonically interrupts.

"Now I can assure your lordship that whatever you've heard is grossly exaggerated and furthermore…" Corbet, red-faced, tries to muster his arguments.

"Do you recollect, during the bubonic plague outbreak of '93, impoverished mourners of your besieged town were obliged to bury their dead in expensive civic shrouds to be bought only from your Mayor's own shop? A fine way of making money out of grief and misfortune, was it not?" the unrelenting judge quizzes, ever with the same acerbic soft-spoken tone.

Corbet bites back an indignant retort, while the hostelry potman serves us with lamb broth and pours out the claret cup.

At this juncture the merchant's companion leans forward, a John Davies, an earnest looking youthful gentleman who has so far been silent and diffident. Though I've repeatedly noticed his reticent dove grey eyes shyly looking at me before modestly dipping down to his plate whenever I glance his way.

"Prithee, your Honour, you've heard bad reports," he acknowledges, "and the corrupt conduct of the cathedral clerics I will not attempt to defend. It has long been a matter of concern here but the citizens of Gloucester, for all their faults, have never been afraid to call for religious reform! Even half a century ago it was Gloucester at the forefront in dismantling the false doctrines of Catholicism. Truly, we've earnt our reputation as radicals and we have plans to reform our City on the Hill until it will one day become a centre of spiritual order, a godly inspiration for all to see!"

The eager fresh-faced attorney is fairly glowing with his vision by the end of his speech and I warm to his fervour and noble ambition.

"Do I detect a disciple of the Puritans in our midst?" Lord Moyle wryly queries, with a lift of a satirical eyebrow.

Master Davies flushes and answers a little stiffly to this placid mockery.

"I think you will find, Sir, that there are many here who are supportive of the high-minded tenets of the Puritans, for we are a sober hard-working people. Our goal is to achieve a simple honest way of life for all, working shoulder to shoulder for the common good!"

His lordship reclines back in his chair amused and bent upon further drawing out the diligent young councillor.

"And will you be banning travelling players and – that bane of decent society! – country dancing from your new Jerusalem?" his lordship flippantly ridicules.

"When such brings excess and debauchery in its train then yes, we would lief do without." John Davies asserts, more upright and stiffer than ever. and I feel for the young man being goaded so.

His elder colleague, finding himself neglected, cuts in here.

"These riffraff performing troupes serve no purpose except an excuse for brawling and drunkenness! And as for the alehouses – they're a public outrage, dens for every pickpocket and cut-throat from the backstreets! But, as one who sits on the magisterial bench in her Majesty's Quarter Session Court held at the castle yonder, I can tell you, your lordship, we are vigilant here, our beadles weekly whip the beggars from town and our stocks are rarely idle!" he lauds with satisfaction.

As one who has been held in pillory, I then speak out for I cannot sit dumb before these affluent gentlemen whilst remembering the unfortunate victims of this famine.

"I have seen the overcrowded squalid housing of your impoverished parishes of St. Aldates and St. Mary de Lode, Sire, for we passed through that way. Shoddy, broken-down buildings built haphazardly upon unhealthy marshland. They say the people there are wholly bereft of hope. The resolution can no more be to flog and imprison the destitute for their despair than 'tis possible to cure poverty by emptying larders of all remaining crusts!"

There is a moment's stupefied silence in which all three men stare at me, amazed at my unexpected outburst. Lord Moyle inclines his head in silent applause and slightly raises his glass in my direction, whilst Horace Corbet's face swivels round as if set upon casters. I can see he is as much taken aback by my unrefined accent as by my critical words, and he darts a sharp look of suspicion at his lordship. I can almost hear the sordid accusations of "proliferate" and "adulterer" pass through his mind and yet his expression, with sneering lips compressed tightly together, suggests he fully expected to find such dissolute behaviour amongst the nobility.

John Davies, however, takes courage and looks me full in the face for the first time.

"I pay tribute to your feminine tenderness, but pray do not suppose us blind to the deplorable conditions our fellow men and women must endure. Or too addlepated not to realize that the devil behind the unrest is not ale but impoverishment! During this last tragic year, we have levied statutory poor rates rather than relying on charity alone such as has run dry in other boroughs. We have set up alms-houses for the homeless and revamped hospitals brought under our control. There is much left to do but please believe me when I vow to you that I for one will not slacken in my endeavour!" he betroths, with a return of his heartfelt ardour.

"If you are to stay a while, Mistress, I would gladly show you the measures we're taking to combat pauperism," he suggests shyly and with a blush.

I listen to him with respect and admiration. Oh, that there were more such compassionate men to be found in our councils! As we exchange smiles, he leans in my direction as if to speak to me alone:

"May I recite to you a prayer from the early Celtic Christians? I aspire daily to abide by its humble wisdom and charity.

Remember the poor when you look out
on fields you own,
on your plump cows grazing.
Remember the poor when you look into your barn
at the abundance of your harvest.
Remember the poor when the wind howls
and the rain falls,
as you sit warm in your dry house.
The poor have no food except what you feed them,
no shelter except your house
when you welcome them,
no warmth except your glowing fire."

The judge coughs derisively, as if at adolescent folly, and so breaking the gaze between us.

"Hmm, well... It's time we were retiring, my lady, we have an early start back to Laslett Hall tomorrow," he says, rising to his feet and waiting for me to follow.

1st May 1596

I'm sitting on the window seat in my room, looking out through the small squares of glass. I think I will never forget a single brick of the little confined courtyard leading to the manor kitchens, for I spend most of my days staring at this restricted view.

As ever, I take care not to intrude upon her ladyship's sight but, even on such occasions when she is out visiting, I still fear to bump into the servants if I stray about the house, for they look askance at me as if they are about their proper business whilst I'm an interloper up to no good. His lordship is always kind and spares the odd hour to sit with me or to take me for a walk about the manor grounds, but of course, he is a busy man with much demanding his attention. So, I'm lonely and blue – though as fed and pampered as a pedigree pet.

I feel guilty and ashamed of such ungrateful thoughts, and I admonish myself to count my blessings. And there are many, without doubt I'm one of the few lucky ones. And yet I sigh again as I look out of the window, whilst the long-drawn-out hours slink slowly past.

Today especially my spirits are low for it is the first of May and I cannot help dwelling upon so many other May Days which I laughed and danced my way through, with dear kind Nan and my beloved Hugh beside me, his arm linked with mine. Then the tears come, which I try to stem, for if Lord Desmond notices the lingering signs, he will look concerned and try to put his arm around me in solicitude. Which I must shake off, rejecting his comfort, and see again the hurt look in his eyes.

2nd *May 1596*

This night I dreamt. I am younger in my dream, thirteen or fourteen perhaps. I'm humming with happiness, lying on my stomach making daisy chains in a summer meadow. All is fair skies, golden sunshine and a pretty profusion of wildflowers. My hair hangs loose with a garland of bindweed wound through it. An unlikely plant to have woven into a headdress, with its pulpy perishable blooms and trailing tendrils.

Suddenly the ground beneath me gives a great rumble and splits apart! Into the widening chasm I fall, and am swallowed into murky shadow as the earth closes above. Down in the Nether Kingdom, I find myself in Hereford Prison, with lunatics wailing about me, their naked bodies white and luminous as ghouls. The clank of keys in an iron lock cowers the inmates, who – all in unison – turn their anguished eyes toward the heavy door studded with bolts. It swings open and in glides *Lord Moyle* at his most decorous, bearing a silver tray of sugared almonds!

"I've come with your lunch," he smiles.

I awoke in a cold sweat with my heart racing.

3rd *May 1596*

His lordship has been summoned to Court. He said, with a sigh, that it's time he put in an appearance,

"It's never profitable to displease her Majesty. But I am sorry to leave you, my dear. I hope you won't miss me – or rather I hope you will! Barbara's confinement, she's due any time now, will give me excuse enough to make this a fleeting visit."

My heart sank with the prospect of his absence, I foresee many lonely days with hardly a word passing my lips. I who once gloried in roving the hills alone now detest my own company. My memories, marred by dark monsters, loom up in my isolation and wrap their clinging tentacles around me, pulling me under, down into the inky black.

It's been raining all day. My eyes have followed each raindrop hit the window and trickle down the pane as if somehow my life depended on it. I have watched the puddles slowly spread across the cobbles of the courtyard below, and the kitchen maids curse as they lift their petticoats to cross it. The sky has shifted between all shades of grey, from dark and vivid as wet blubber to washed out and pale like lambs' brains beneath the butcher's knife.

And I cannot abide the long night once the daylight slips from reach.

6ᵗʰ May 1596

Late this afternoon I crept from my room, along the upper corridor and around to the nursery where Beth and the other maidservants were busy preparing for the expected baby. I so longed for the sound of chatter and mirth that I determined to risk their displeasure and offer my help. After all, I reasoned, I share the same humble country upbringing as they do, surely they would not begrudge me the sound of their voices? I've dearly wanted to hear how farest the people and places once so familiar to me!

So I went, hastening my steps as I heard talking coming from the bedchamber. The door stood ajar and I was just about to enter when I caught a glimpse of her ladyship within, stopping myself by a hair's breadth in my tracks, standing paralyzed, too petrified to move forwards or back!

"There 'tis done, Madam, 'tis all prepared. I've placed the pig's heart in the nook above the mantelpiece and bricked it in. The waters have been sprinkled along the window sills and all will be safe now for the birthing," the maid assured her mistress, dipping a curtsy.

Lady Barbara had been pacing back and forth across the room as her servants worked but at this she swung round and glared at the serving girl, snarling:

"You witless imbecile! What use is sealing the windows and securing the fireplace against witchcraft *when the witch is already in the house!*"

Then, pointing her finger hysterically towards the door behind which I stood, she shrieked: "See there! Through the crack! She has sent her spectre to spy upon me and abort my efforts!"

With this the motion returned to my limbs, I picked up my skirts and fled back down the corridor.

Midnight

It is dark and I am the Darkness.

I am the Sickness in the churning stomach of the nation!
I am the Banshee who shrieks through the night!
I am the Fiend of the swamps and quagmire!
I am Fury! I am Hate!
I writhe, I loathe, I hanker to kill!
For I am consumed with Rage.

I flood with torrid liquids and bitter rancour.
My mulled anger, perpetually whipped down, forever caged in, erupts into a crazed beast rearing up in agony to slash and claw.
I see my grandmother's kicked face, imploring pity.
Her body pummelled, bruised from joint to joint, bled purple beneath thin ripping skin.
I hear the screams of Hugh and Kitty pursued by the howling mob, snapping and chewing the flesh off their ankles.
I hold the twitching hands of Edith, wringing out her lamentations, sodden with the gob-spit of her captors.
Torn apart! My legs forced open. I eat my disgust. I drink his mucus.
I gulp down the grime of debasement. I spew shame.

I will call up Catastrophe! I will summon bloody Carnage!
I will tear into their throats with my fingers,
I will puncture their lungs to suck out their hissing breath,
I will scrape out their rotten blackened hearts,
I will gorge upon their rancid slimy entrails!
I will fly through Durlow raining a deluge of curses!
I will be Vengeance!
I will be avenged.

8ᵗʰ May 1596

The serpents have slid back to their lair. The ravaging aberration abated. The mad moon has past, with its tide of evil receding from my conscious mind. But I am appalled at what has become of me! I have nourished vipers from the abyss. Hecate hath coupled with me in all her malefic power of destruction. Nan would have been ashamed of me. Oh, how I hate myself for that!

In my misery and heartache, I shunned the Healing Wisdom of the Old Ways. In my bitterness and anger, I scorned the Sacred Lore I'd pledged to honour. In my loneliness and desolation, I spurned the Numinous Gift bequeathed me. In its place, I drowned in a whirlpool of annulling passions, I gave myself to life-disowning obsession. Oh Nan, what have I done!

I have been so mistaken and blind. I'd thought the Craft served in my life so I could help others, now I know it was there to save myself. And I cast it aside.

I sit broken and forlorn, with my cheek against the cold glass, watching the storm clouds gather. As the light wanes, I listen to whispered words, singing over and over through the evening air:

"It is never too late to return to our roots. They are part of us."

11ᵗʰ May 1596

Lord Moyle is back, bearing gifts and good cheer.

"Here is the gown we ordered at Gloucester. See it is of the brightest, richest crimson, the colour of life and vitality! And here in this little leather box lies a scarlet jewel, a precious drop of blood, set amongst the shimmering white pearls of purity. Wear them tonight my dear and we will celebrate returns and rejoinings!" he gaily petitions, not listening to my thanks but whisking me outside into the May sunshine so welcome after weeks of rain.

We meander through the orchard, my face upturned to the pink and snowy blossom of the spring trees, startling against the blue of the sky. Sitting in a wall arbour, looking across Nature's beguiling display, his lordship proceeds to make me laugh with a droll account of life at Her Majesty's royal court.

"Oh Hannah, I wish I could take you there to see it all with your clear sight and natural honesty! You would think the grand courtiers a pack of poodles, prancing about in paint and powder, bobbing their empty heads to pomp and fashion, wagging their little pomaded tails to the tune of the most absurd fad of the moment! The profound matter of cloth, cut and style occupies the vain deliberations of noblemen and ladies alike to the exclusion of all else (excepting the romping of illicit rendezvous!)" And he winks an eye at me.

"Court dress is becoming ever more preposterous. The breeches of these stylish gentlemen are so ballooned out with horsehair that their lower legs, clad only in hose, look ludicrously spindly underneath such a girth of padding, the overall effect resembles nothing so close as that of a turkey!

"The fashionable ladies also have a fowl look. 'Fowl' in the sense of poultry you understand! Moving downwards from the cartwheel plaited ruffs, the stiffened bodice supports the breast of prime meat and tapers towards a pertinent point below the waist. Under this is the famous steel-inserted farthingale petticoat, shooting the dress out to the furthest hemispheres of the known world! Ropes of pearls, pomanders, girdles and jewelled books are hung upon the skirt; no wonder such sturdy scaffolding is required to bear so lavish a load! And jaunty little hats bedecked with feathered plumes complete the lady's ensemble. One court wit likens the whole to 'trussed chickens set upon bells'!"

"And would you speak so disparagingly of the Queen herself? Is she also a breed of farmyard fray?" I quiz him in amusement.

"Heaven forbid! She is far too wily an old bird to be likened to a species of poultry! She has all the proud plumage of a peacock at the very least and the vanity also. In her younger days she would forbid the ladies of the court to adorn themselves in any colour other than white or silver so as to flash her own flamboyant feathers to better effect. She was always one to rule the roost!" Lord Desmond daringly confides.

"For shame, my Lord! Do you not fear death for treason?" I laugh.

"Aye, and worse to precede it! John Harrington, the Queen's godson, has been heard to say (well out of the Queen's hearing!) that he would rather face a whole fleet of the Spanish Armada than Her Majesty in a rage! Even Barbara's fuming fits are nothing in comparison but a flame to an inferno. Talking of which, I'd best let her know I'm home and suffer her scalding reproaches and peppery embrace," he concludes, as we retrace our steps back to the house.

I am bid to dine with his lordship this evening Lady Moyle, the footman reported, is indisposed and will not be supping. To be honest, I'm glad to put the night terrors of recent weeks behind me and to be light-hearted once more in my lord's carefree company.

When I count eight chimes from the clock tower, I put on the handsome red dress and fasten the pearl choker, with its gleaming ruby drop, around my throat. I hardly recognise myself reflected in the glass!

"Is this really me?" I marvel, giddy with such finery, "I counterfeit a grand lady indeed, I – a vagabond's daughter – clad in velvet and jewels!"

How much my pa would have revelled in this opulence strange Fate has handed me, I can see him now, chuckling in glee! And I deem I am surely my father's daughter, for I take pleasure in the luxurious fabric beneath my fingers and delight in its brilliant scarlet blaze, so warm and radiant in the glow of sunset.

By the time I reach the dining room the candles have been lit, mirrored in the sheen of the oaken wainscoting and causing the ruby at my throat to flash. As I pause in the doorway, my lord comes forward and leads me in by the hand.

"Behold, the red rose has opened her petals in full! How breathtakingly beautiful you look, my bonny maiden." Lord Desmond praises me.

I blush rosily and disclaim but the judge chastises me for this, "No prudery, my lady, even in the tattered rags of prison there was no hiding your loveliness. And tonight you shine like a gem lustrous beyond all others!"

I, in my frivolous mood, argue no more but give way to indulgence, supping on the finest foods, feeling myself quite at home in the company of a peer of the realm in his elegant manor! The talk runs merrily between us, and over sweetmeat I recount my dream of being swallowed down into a subterranean shadowland, making joke of his appearance there bearing a luncheon tray.

"Does this denote you as a Knight come to my rescue or as Lucifer come to tempt me with favours, such as velvet dresses and ruby necklaces?" I quip.

His lordship contemplates my nocturnal adventure, with his head to one side, gently stroking his neat goatee beard.

"It's clearly a Grecian Persephone myth and I undoubtedly figure as the wicked Lord of Hades, who has stolen you away to be held captive in his debauched Underworld! Ah, but who can blame poor Pluto, craving a little of the freshness and sunlight of spring in his dismal dark realm? Hell must be a tedious mirthless domain, riddled with cynicism and disillusionment, what man or devil could resist sharing his pomegranate with fair Persephone, a delectable ray of youthful grace piercing his heart and hearth? I cannot see him willingly giving her back." And he looks at me thoughtfully.

At this point a manservant enters, approaches Lord Moyle and speaks quietly in his ear. His lordship nods dismissal and with his usual stately languor turns to me saying,

"Ah, please excuse me, Hannah, I must leave you. It seems I have more progeny come into the world." He drains his goblet of wine, fastidiously wipes his mouth and fingers upon a napkin, rises sedately, bows and leaves the room.

12th May 1596

Her ladyship bore a healthy, and huge for she was overdue her birthing date, boy. The whole house has been caught up in celebration; it even rubbed off on me a little, for I found myself hoping that someday I too will be blessed with children. I will wish for it, and for the dearly desired love that heralds it.

Quite late, for darkness has fallen, there comes a knock at my door. Considering yesterday's momentous event, I am surprised to see Lord Moyle there but he straightaway explains his intrusion,

"This cannot await another day, Hannah, nay nor even an hour for the heavens do not pay tribute to the little deeds of man! There is to be a lunar eclipse this night, pray accompany me to witness it. It will be well worth the excursion."

I am instructed to wear my thick cloak, though the evening is warm when we step out into the garden. I can smell the exquisite fragrance of lily-of-the-valley, commonly called "Mary's tears", in the calm air. His lordship guides me to a bench on the terrace, someone has placed rugs and cushions upon it and a flagon of hot mead stands on the path close by.

"We will drink to Mistress Moon, my dear," he proposes, pouring the steaming liquid into two cups.

And indeed, she is at her most alluring, a full globe glistening upon the tiered lawns sloping down to the silver river band below. The wondrous starry arc, *the White Lady's Pathway*, wands across the sky. My lord points out the constellations, showing me where the stars throng, lacing the Abyssinian black with ivory tresses. He speaks well and before long I begin to see the night's dark dome anew, as a cascade of mythological creatures jostling for their place in the firmament. The Babylonian Bull, the Egyptian Ram, Ophiuchus the serpent-bearer, the Phoenix and Centaur; each conjured up against the jet backdrop of the vast vault of Heaven.

"Such a majestic celestial sphere belittles all our petty differences and decries the false divides we erect between ourselves! It binds us all as one, breathing with a single breath! Do you feel it, Hannah? Can you sense our essence entwined?" Lord Desmond invites, leaning close to me, his eyes gleaming like the orbs of a sphinx.

I feel dizzy from staring up at the awesome night sky, with my head tilted back and neck arched. The moment feels unreal and I detached, as if I were not in my body at all but floating amongst the shimmering star-mists above. I cannot bring myself to move, though I know his lips are about to press on mine. But then, from behind his head, I see a dark shade creep across the edge of the moon maiden's face. The ominous intent of this crawling shadow reaches me, I take a sharp inbreath and draw back.

We watch in silence as the blackness begins to blot out the lunar light. The bleached landscape below is repainted in deeper shades of blood red and ebony, while the stars sparkle all the brighter. But to me it feels like a shroud of ice slowly encasing my heart.

"Is it a bad omen, Sir? What might it portend?" I beg in hushed dread.

"Oh Hannah, Hannah!" the judge impatiently reprimands me, "Have we not spoken of this? When will you cease filling the world with green gods and goblins! They are nowhere but in the minds of gormless clodpoles and doltish old dames! Civilised mind seeks to work within the cosmic order, only the primitive tries to placate it by whimpering to their gods! Intent and consciousness have no component of its workings."

"Wait, please!" I plead. "What is it that you're saying? The Divine Consciousness of our Creator, what are you saying of that?"

There is a pause before he answers, "I fear, my sweet girl, the Age of Reason that I would see dawn must needs be preceded by an era of disenchantment. The Almighty is as distant and untouched by you and I as are the mountains; 'tis not a popinjay to be bribed with impassioned pleas and prayers! Neither is the world a piece of cloth to be tugged this way and that between God and the Devil!

"The clergy will lose influence and the Wisewomen and Cunning Men will be out of business once the news gets around. No wonder it is unwelcome! Why even the Queen, who pays outward homage to the pursuit of knowledge, keeps John Dee in her employ – a court alchemist who uses occult practices. A fine example, is it not, to lead the country forward!

"But, by my oath, we *will* break through in the end, for rational thought must ultimately win against the walls of ignorance! Richard Hooker's great treaty proclaims that *The Laws of Nature are the stay of the whole world.* Let us throw off our superstitious tomfoolery and strive to discover them!" he advocates in triumph.

With his rising elation my spirits are cast down, and I cannot forbear from protesting,

"But until we can command these laws you speak of, does this not leave us merely pawns with no impact upon our fate? How helpless and pitiable that is! How sad and cheerless life is without the aid of prayer, without the relief the Old Ways lend us in our suffering!"

"It is generally agreed that the time of miracles is past," he answers gently. "And permit me to again quote Hooker in that *order, moderation and reason must take the lead and so bridle the affections.* We must be content with what is, it is infantile to hanker after what is not."

I sit frowning down at the ground, rolling the small stones under my feet in disquiet. What he so proudly promotes makes a charade of all the effort of Nan's hard life! Likewise, it denies the truth of my own experience and the convictions of my heart. I ache to challenge his vision for it is determined to strangle my own,

"Then I, Sirrah, must join the ranks of those who would resist the advance of Reason! I must displease you more by saying I do not believe in all that you say. Yes, nature follows established paths, just as the sun rises and sets, and spring follow winter. But maybe it is itself a natural law that we can impress upon our environment a little? My grandmother used to say that the world has less substance and our thoughts, fired by feeling, more solidity than we give credit to! How else could she have mended the sorrow and bettered the lives of the poor people who came to her?"

Gaining courage, I cross him further, "And I do not believe in your remote God who you acknowledge but cannot approach. The Blessed is just within a hairbreadth of us. – No, it is closer, it is actually in us, linking all life and form! Even the lofty crags themselves are aware of us, for they are awareness!

"Lord Moyle, deep in the midst of Durlow Woods there stands an old beech tree. It has a spiralling trunk and generous canopy sheltering all below. When I was a small girl my family left for the city, leaving me bereft and my world tumbled down. In those times of loneliness and grief, when goosebumps of fear set me quaking in my little boots, I ran to this noble tree and leant my back against it. 'Talk to me, Grandmother Beech!' I entreated. And I felt the pulsing of the years, her roots receiving nourishment from the earth, her branches reaching high above. And the serenity that blew through her leaves rose up in me."

"Childhood fancies, my little one, nothing else," Lord Moyle says placidly, stroking my cheek in compassion.

"When I was older," I persevere, "when I stood more firmly upon my feet, I would skip out onto the moors just as the sky was bursting into flame. I knew I could chase my dreams there, like skylarks ascending the rays of sunrise. I flew with the wind and I called to the hills 'Speak, I am listening!' And they echoed through the ages with possibility, promising me the sun and the moon! I took home that courage in the breath of my lungs."

"The enthusiasms of youth, doomed to disappointment with encroaching age," his lordship smiles, giving my hand a kindly squeeze.

I make one last attempt, "Not so many years ago, when maidenhood was whispering its secrets into my ear, I often sat beside a trickling waterfall which fell between two moss-coated rocks. And I would listen to the lyric of its falls until I knew their melody; rippling through me like a musical refrain, making my heart beat and my spirit leap! I recall now, just in time perhaps, the song it bade me live by."

The tears spring to my eyes as I remember that early promise of love. And I resolve to never again deny the blessed presence of the Land for it has never denied me. It strikes me then, with the resonance of a ringing bell, that – although only yesterday I declared myself my father's daughter – I now know I am in heart and soul my grandmother's child!

Lord Moyle speaks at last, breaking the quiet peace that has enveloped us.

"Oh my beauteous Hannah, you undo me with soft words, you bewitch me with your fluid voice! You will convert me to the heathen if I listen any longer!" he declares. "But perhaps it is not so bad to keep a little of the irrational in our lives if we hold it in the hearts of women. I think, with your hazel-green eyes, your fluttering hair the colour of autumn leaves, your young form as slender as a sapling and your love of all things mystical, I will name you 'Wytch Hazel' my enchanting wood nymph!"

He hesitates, and then again breaks the night's silence to humbly ask of me:

"And may I not come to you, when I am weary and downcast, to find rest and solace beneath the sway of your caressing branches and to find sweetness once more under your loving spell?"

14th June 1596

Lady Moyle paid me a visit this morning, bursting into my room like a surging torrent. I rose hastily, curtsied and stood before her, while she flashed a searching eye around as if seeking something hidden here.

She fixed me with a hard stare and I shivered under her cold scrutiny.

"Sit, girl. I want some straight answers and no impertinence from you," she barked, much as if she wanted to sink her teeth into my flesh! "Is Lord Moyle bedding you, doxy?"

"No, Madam," I replied, my voice trembling with apprehension. "His lordship is charitable to me as a gentleman who's taken pity on the unhappy plight of a peasant girl, nothing more."

Her lips curled contemptuously, "He was ever one to play a waiting game. He likes to watch his prey before darting out his tongue. Fie! 'Tis the Lizard Man himself forsooth! And, of course, the appetites are less pressing with old age and decrepitude.

"He's a disappointed man you know. He had hopes that my birthing bed would double as my deathbed. Did he enlist your sorceress ploys to entice things awry? You failed then, no coronet for your slatternly head now!" she sneered, and I knew not how to disabuse a mind so set in suspicion against me.

"To be sure, it would have been the perfect farce – and so like him! – to put a lowly strumpet in my place. Pah! To so degrade and demean the noble estate of Laslett with a trollop from the pigsty is just the sort of perverse sport the shameless cad would revel in!"

When I attempted a remonstrance, she cut me short like a whiplash.

"Why else has he not tumbled you in the hay like any other cheap slut? Did you suppose him a knight in shining armour then? You're an idiot, girl! He is nothing but a carpet knight on the lookout for a bit of available fluff!" and she laughed curtly in scorn.

She left as abruptly as she'd entered, leaving the room resounding with the cutting sound of her mockery. I could not settle to my sewing after. My thoughts scurried round and round like rats in a trap.

23rd June 1596

Lord Desmond has taken me into the summer garden, placing me upon the marble seat overlooking the lily pond. I watch without words as he plucks a flower and kneels before me.

"You yourself, Hannah, are Nature's fairest bloom! I know you to be tender and pure, blessed with rare goodness and grace. I offer you this rose to symbolize the full heart I have to give. Will you accept it, my love?" he asks, with his eyes raised to mine in beseeching hope.

"My lord, it is not yours to offer. Your wife sits within the house nursing your new-born child," is the only answer I can return, though the bald facts sound taciturn and callous.

"Little one, it's too late to bid me save the wasteland of my wedlock. It would have been too late thirty years ago! And it has been a bitter pill of acrimony I have swallowed each day since." And if ever a voice could be soaked in sadness so he speaks now, "Must I never sip from the cup of happiness? I am a parched man fearing death, you are an oasis of radiant renewal, a fountain of soft salvation that I've crept towards in wonder and longing. Will you turn me away to perish?"

At my silence, he begs in desperation: "Alas, I cannot give you marriage but you shall be showered with all else! What would you like, Hannah? The finest things a lady could wish for? You shall have them, chests full of dresses and jewels! I'll take you into society, somewhere we're not known. To all others we will be as man and wife."

I can only shake my head.

"What then?" he cajoles. "Do you wish to return to the life you're used to? Then you may! I will build you a cottage, my darling, as simple and rustic as you choose. With chickens clucking about your feet, and a nanny goat to milk and a plot for growing vegetables. I will come each day. Soon the children will arrive and I'll cherish and care for them in equal measure as my own precious Wytch Hazel!"

I fix my eyes upon the waxy petals of the water lilies, for I cannot bear to meet his pleading gaze. Neither can I bring myself to respond as he desires. This benevolent man had done so much to ensure my comfort; much more so, he has taken such risks to secure my life! But I do not love him. And I know my body also would rebel against submission. I cannot be intimate with him. As if he senses something of my physical repulsion, he lowers his voice to divulge:

"My love, do not suppose I'm ignorant of what you went through in that obscene cesspool of a gaol. Don't be afraid, nothing will be forced in haste upon you. I will worship you as a goddess, I shall sit at your feet and love you from afar. You will be as a serene and lovely swan that glides down to the sea only when the time is right for you, my dearest."

Oh, the keen perception of the man! The kind, courteous consideration he has always shown me! But I cannot give myself to him. I realise I must try to make him understand, and I must banish any hope.

"My lord, I beg you in your generosity to heed me! I cannot go against my heart. It is the star on the horizon I have set my trust upon and must follow. Everyone holds a dream most precious to them. That which makes us want to live! That which ignites us so all else glows!

"For some it is splendour and riches, or success and fame, for others a quest for foreign vistas, the yen for adventure that pounds through their veins. For my grandmother it was the ancient faith of our ancestors, urging her to bend her knee in glad service from childhood to old age. For the good attorney at Gloucester, it is to cleanse and restore his beloved city with his Puritan values. Our minister at Durlow is compelled to burn the fiery cross of religious fervour and so to bring us into his fold. For you I think 'tis the pursuit of knowledge, the Banner of Reason and Truth to which you have nailed your hopes, to enlighten us out of our slavery, to calm the blind howl of the mob! Is this not the bourne that raises you to the heights?

"But mine is love. The miraculous bonding between two, when both are visited by the blest enchantment which cannot be willed or chosen. This is no great crusade. I will make no waves upon the world, nor touch other lives except for the very few to whom I'm conjoined. But it is my lifeblood. And I know that somewhere in my future it awaits me.

"Where there is no vision the people perish. When I heard this passage read from the book of Proverbs I trembled from head to toe. Without our vision we are straw, we dry up inside. We may live but it is just a life sentence we suffer. I am sorry. I cannot again surrender my creed. I cannot betray the song of my heart. Forgive me!"

Without a word Lord Desmond gets up and walks away.

Evening

I cannot stay here any longer, it would be unfair to him. It's too late now, I'll go with first light in the morning. I reach for a shawl and place a few items within it: a small loaf, some fruit, a couple of candles and a flint. I do not know what may be left at the cottage, I hope it has not been burnt to the ground.

A tap at my bedroom door makes me jump, my nerves are in shreds. I know Lord Moyle's knock like I knew the sound of his voice. And I must make the effort to express my gratitude, wanting and ungracious though it will sound! But on entering, he immediately sees the shawl on the window seat and unceremoniously cuts through my gabbled prepared speech, which comes out all back to front.

"Hannah, you cannot leave yet! It's too dangerous! I implore you, wait at least until September when your year's sentence is up," he urges. And I feel a fiend to make him so prey to anxiety.

"Don't worry about me, my Lord, I have friends who will harbour me. I cannot hide behind you any longer," I stammer and, though I try to look away, our eyes lock hard.

There is a long and impenetrable pause. The air reverberates with the fast pace of my breathing. And of his. I do not know how to end this. Perhaps neither does he, for at last he shifts uneasily, opens his mouth to speak and then stumbles towards me, his arms outstretched and eyes tortured. Without thought, I step aside and put out a hand to hold him back. I realize at once this was the wrong action for I see hurt and anger contort his face, and I fear him.

"Please, let me depart freely, Lord Moyle. I know I owe you so much, but please let me go..." I blurt out, panic rising.

"You do, Hannah. You do owe me." he warns, his voice grim.

I fight with frantic desperation but he forces me down under him, tightly squeezing my hands together in one of his, the other creeps over my body like a hound sniffing out a scent. Hysterically, I scream and scream until he clamps my mouth, grabbing a cloth from the pile of darning and stuffing it in, pushing it back towards my throat and making me gag. No one comes to my rescue though my cries must have been heard throughout the house.

I see his face when he's done. It's red and greasy in sweat – but he does not look satisfied. As soon as he's hauled himself off me, I roll onto my front, pull out the cloth and vomit over the rug.

"I'm sorry, Hannah," he mutters, panting heavily.

He straightens up, dragging his hands through his tousled hair, and attempts a feeble justification for his lust.

"I couldn't help myself. You are too ravishing for any man to resist forever! You should not be beautiful, my love." He gives a weak laugh, but he won't look my way.

"Then I curse my beauty!" I spit at him. "If it brings to me such a harvest of violence and degradation then I wish it gone! On bended knees I entreat God on High to grant me such plainness of face and form that no man will ever again look at me!"

Nightfall

I escaped from Laslett Hall directly after he'd left the room – blundering out in shame, tugging his dishevelled clothes about him. I fled across the moors with a vestige of light lingering, for tonight is Midsummer's Eve. I did not stop running, pacing my heaving breaths, until I reached the woods. Here the trees forced me to slacken my frenzied sprint but I stumbled on, pressing deep into the forest, crashing through the undergrowth like a hunted animal fleeing the trap. Not without suffering the barbarity of its captors.

I am sore and dog-tired and can go no further. I crouch down beneath a tree, with my cloak drawn tight about me, to wait for the grey fingers of dawn. Hunched up against the trunk, sore and nauseous, I am sick with the world and with myself. Dupe that I am! Pitiful and pathetic! A prey to every snake in the grass! A simpleton! I despise myself as much as I despise my fellow man. The taste of vomit is still in my mouth. I try to spit it out. Then the tears come, like rivulets over the dry dust that I am.

At last, and in weariness, I stretch out on the springy moss to ease my stomach cramps, and look up into the tree above me. I recognize it, from what seems another life now. This is the twisted beech of my childhood, its hoary trunk spiralling as it turns on itself like a woman swirling her skirts around her. It has stood here since the last century or the one before perhaps. Where the trunk is smooth someone has chiselled names: "Margaret and Mark 1558".

Seeing the indented inscription, I am both pained and appalled by my aloneness. For an insane moment I want to leap up and carve out the words "Hannah and Hugh 1594"! To leave a scratch asserting the goodness that can be found in another. To proclaim that love can quicken for a heartbeat in all our lives! Instead, I remain passive and defeated, listening to the rustling of the flute edged leaves in the midnight breeze, letting my eyes wander up through the high branches to glimpse the night's sky above. The moon appears, unveiling her sympathetic wan face from behind the clouds. Filtering her lonely light in moon metal strands through the tangled canopy, dappling the leaves in stellar silver.

As my exhausted brutalised body stills and becomes heavy on the ground, and as the hours slowly slip by, something sinks out of me, seeping into the earthy bank upon which I lie. Something shifts. Something offensive and sordid falls away until I can scarce remember what it was. Something ancient, a strength from the tree's core, reaches me. The evening's events, and all the deeds of my short life, shrink down to doll size, small and fuzzy and irrelevant. Impermanent miniscule moments, tiny things in the great Wood of the World. With an unshakeable certainty I acknowledge that noble endeavours, for which we give our all, stand out brighter than the tarnish. Without question I will withstand, as I have withstood long before.

They will not extinguish who I am. They cannot encase me in brick for I yearn towards the intangible. I have sailed forth from an ethereal abode with gossamer boundaries. I wear the mist of immortality, veiling a soul not of this time and place. I will pass through this life plane like a wraith from another dwelling, born of an unknown element, forever free in my soul. Returning to my homeland. Back to my kin.

Sunrise

When the sun came up, I was changed. I was rooted in tranquillity. I rose up and walked the remaining distance to Durlow.

8th July 1596

Our cottage was as we left it, except wreathed in cobwebs and covered in a musty blanket of dust. It was also full of cherished memories that brought both joy and sorrow. Nan once said, "the young are more nostalgic than the old." Sure 'tis so, for I spent a few brief treasured days revisiting those special places Hugh and I used to call our own. But there was no time to pick up the pieces, the most vital elements of which have long since gone, for I was arrested and am now back in Hereford Gaol.

I have been tried for new allegations of witchcraft. Lady Barbara Moyle presented herself at the assizes to proclaim I had bewitched her husband and made him impotent. Desmond Moyle was not in court, I hear he's now residing in London. This being my second conviction as a witch, I was sentenced to *death by hanging*. I will die before my twentieth birthday.

13th *July 1596*

I am spending my last night in one of the single cells, "the darks" as they call them. I was promised the privilege of solitude but at seven o'clock Betty Bawden, the gaoler's wife, intruded upon my seclusion bringing her knitting and baccy pouch with her.

"Well my chick, I always try to spend a bit of time with the lasses like you on the night afore your 'anging," she wheezed, plonking her ample backside on the floor besides me. "Bit of company will stop you moping and dwelling on t'morror."

She then proceeded to talk about my execution in the morning. Her monologue was interrupted every other minute as she took a draw upon her clay pipe, noisily sucking it in and letting the brown smoke leak out through stained, toothless gums. Sometimes I heard what she was saying, other times I was able to block it out by concentrating on the clicking of her knitting needles.

"It's to be at noon by the town clock, me dear. You'll 'ave a big send off by the look of it! The roads 'ave been chock-a-block with carriages, carts and wagons since daybreak, all come to see you, lovey! The posh inns in the 'igh Street are filling up with the gentry, and every tavern and alehouse is overflowing with common folk, full from cellar to attic! We've not seen a crowd like this since Bludgeoning Bill was 'ung for triple wife murder. The peddlers be settin' up stalls and ale booths all 'long Fore Street, we might even get a bit of a fair if we're lucky. The pickpockets are gonna be 'appy too!" and she cackled at that.

"Jim Pike the 'angman reckons 'e can double the usual price for snips of your 'air and slithers of t' rope after you get cut down. Folks believe 'twill ward off rheumatism and the ague you know, and 'tis said to cure the King's Evil!"

She appeared greatly chuffed by the attention my hanging was stirring, and seemed to feel some congratulations were due to me, for she leant forward and patted my knee,

"'Tis 'cause you be so young and pretty, me dearie'," she complimented me. "And Jim'll do 'is best for you, don't you be afeard of that. He's got the knack of stretching the neck so it breaks in a twinkling. Not that it always works mind, some days they do writhe and twist upon the rope end and convulse something awful! With their eyes bulging out of the sockets and their poor limbs flailing and feet scraping the air! The crowd do dearly love it, but I 'ope it'll be quick for you, pet.

"When 'tis over, they'll 'oist the black flag and that do bring a lump to me throat every time! You'll be left to swing for an 'our afore they cut you down. There's a nice deep 'ole been dug ready for you in prison yard."

At last she stopped, "I best get going, Bert 'll be wanting 'is supper, awful grumpy 'e gets when 'ungry! Lookee, 'tis a goodly sunset, 'twill be a fine day t'morror."

After she'd gone, I went to the small window and stood looking out through the grid at the fiery red streaked sky until it darkened. Now I crouch and watch the moths flutter around the candle Betty has left me. The silly things will not fly to their freedom and I have no will left to brush them aside before they burn their fragile wings upon the flame.

For I am afraid. Deadly afraid. My skin is cold and clammy with terror. The evil hours before dawn. Life's lowest ebb. Death waiting at the gallows, relentless. I try not to think of the rope tightening about my neck. I dare not think of gasping in vain for air when the power to breathe is taken from me. Of the panic, the desperation! The unutterable terror of it! But I cannot think of anything else. My body is full of it. I dread this dying. For a hundred years, this has been the fear of witches.

22nd July 1596

At a quarter short of noon, the bell started to toll. I was led out by the hangman, escorted by the gaol governor with a church minister following behind. I walked a dozen yards across the courtyard, screeched at and booed by the excited crowd, their anticipation gathering momentum at the long-awaited sight of their prey. They were perched up in hedges and trees for a better view, as well as clamouring against the barricades. Many jeered and shrieked "Witch!"

But now they're hushed and silent, even the children, as if holding their breath for the clock to strike. Keeping my eyes fixed down upon the ground to avoid seeing the hanging rope, I mount the stool and hear the Reverend speak the words "the peace of God that passeth all understanding".

I look up but once, with the noose about my neck, to see the bluest of summer skies.

Part III

Back in the Box

Chapter Eight

Moira Box was back in the pit.

A winter of Regression Sessions had been a great diversion from her life. And it was a real thrill to find she'd been a stunning beauty once! But the sixteenth-century Mega Alternative Reality Trip was over, Hannah Greene dead and hung, and Moira was back to being Moira. Alas for Moira.

"Oh piddles," she summed up without surprise. "Definitely no more pleas to the Almighty Stage Producer about being so gruesome no man will look at me! Witches always say be careful what you ask for – you'll probably get it..."

To be on the safe side, she wrote out a carefully worded request for her next incarnation, set fire to it and blew the red-hot ashes across Time (and across the new carpet, somewhat disastrously). Now all she had to do was wait.

Moira got fed up with waiting. It left her with too much time to look back on her life. Revisiting Moira's life was not a riveting experience. Moira thought that had it been the other way around, Hannah would have stopped going to the P.L.R. man after one or two sessions. Through total discouragement. And sheer boredom. Given the option, she'd like to go back to Day One of her life and start again, preferably as someone else.

However, as you'll bound to bump into an empath blocking every turn (she put it down to that 1968 *Star Trek* episode in season three) it wasn't long before Moira was helpfully signposted towards *Develop your Self-Esteem* books, complete with handy exercises. She wasn't doing particularly well. Pat walked in on her one day to find her manically scribbling.

"The book says '*it is imperative to appreciate your many brave attempts and achievements*'. It suggests writing a *I Have* list to credit yourself for all the things that you have done." Moira explained. "Before coming to Cornwall, I couldn't find anything to write other than 'I have a cat'.

So, I'm writing a *I Haven't* list instead. It pages long! Just listen:

I haven't had much fun
I haven't played many games since peek-a-boo with mum's midwife
I haven't got into drink and drugs and trouble
I haven't got into an online chat room
I haven't got properly chatted up, except once by Psycho Zac on glue
I haven't really got much past GO yet to be honest
I haven't got into my jeans for years
I haven't won respect
I haven't won on a scratch card
I haven't one flattering photo of me, not one
I haven't broadened my mind with useless qualifications
I haven't much minded missing my birthday more often than not
I haven't ever walked past wolf-whistling workmen
I still haven't worked out my good points
I haven't broken limits
I haven't broken my chocolate spread crisps addiction
I haven't crossed frontiers
I haven't crossed the line or stepped on the herbaceous border
I haven't created anything of beauty, not even a baby
I haven't eaten by candlelight, except on my own
I haven't slept under the stars
I haven't laughed till I cried
I haven't …"

"Enough!" Pat shrieked, decisively removing the wad of writing from Moira's grasp and depositing it in the wastepaper bin.

"How old are you Mogs?" she demanded sternly.

"Forty," Moira admitted.

"Well then – Life Begins."

As a kick-start for her new preferably-positive life, Moira enrolled on a *Mythological Pathway* weekend, a residential workshop near Bodmin. This was scary. It was scary because it meant the stranger-danger of having to make polite conversation and sleeping in a dormitory. And there was the awful probability that she would have to introduce herself and try to say something interesting or witty to a whole circle of unknown faces – all looking at her! Or worse still, she might have to play "getting the group to bond" games. Hideous! Also, she'd come with Gwen and Rianne in Gwen's car, which meant no escape unless she hitched across Bodmin Moor. And hitching was scary too, though not usually (in Moira's case) hazardous, except for long term exposure in freezing weather.

Everyone said the workshop was powerful, with women weeping and baring their souls (and underwear, plus private parts at times) but it took Moira straight back to where she was before. Back to plain Moira Box. Back to heading backwards. She felt stuck and insular, unloved and unlovable, outside the outsiders.

They all had to pick a totem 'intuitively' – i.e. dipping into a bowl of labels with their eyes closed. Moira had expected to get Mole:

Mole digs blindly down into our depths, unearthing the long buried, bringing up what's been covered up, upsetting our perfectly manicured façade and leaving little muddy mounds on the lawn. Mole medicine is to gorge on decaying matters, digesting our hidden past that is still eating away at us, preparing the soil for new growth.

Just what Moira had been doing all winter but said better. But Moira didn't pick Mole, so maybe she'd done all her gorging. (Fat chance!)

"But fingers crossed. All those rebuffs and rejections," she recalled, glumly looking back over her life. "And definitely no rich pickings on my skinny skeletons under the stairs. The only tasty morsels occurred when I was a Tudor!"

Instead, she picked Spider. She recognized it instantly. That feeling of being a small insignificant crawling creature, that people go "ugh" at, suspended in some dingy forgotten corner. Living in dread of a clumsy hand brushing you aside like a web in their path. Leaving you immobile on your back amongst the broken strings, defeated and disconnected yet again. Stuck in a sticky tangle. Oh woo and boohoo! But Spider Spirit myth offers a spindly strand of cheer for the wretched arachnid:

Spider is the Weaver of the Web of life. She knows we create from our own weaving. Spinning our lives around us from the little we hold within. Spider endures against all odds, forever rebuilding her broken web. Interlacing our dearest dreams into the darkest places. Spider hangs on invisible threads and waits.

Moira thought it improbable that she'd get her lacy veil and long white dress (Sir Gawain and the Loathly Lady not being a modern male archetype) but she could at least begin connecting to herself a bit better. It was worth a go. Additionally, as always literal minded and to follow up the spider web theme, she resolved to take up spinning as a hobby.

"So next time I have to introduce myself," she optimistically averred, "I can say: *Moira Box, spinster.*"

That night Moira had unsettling dreams (possibly due to the loud snoring and guttural walrus sounds in the dormitory). Throughout her dreams she was anxiously searching for a doll.

She scolded herself for being such a baby but she couldn't rest until she finally found this tatty old rag doll in a dresser on the top landing. Pinned onto its pinafore was a scrap of paper which read "My name is Hope".

On waking Moira grabbed a pen and wrote her first poem ever.

Hope is the battered doll
I hold for comfort.
I pull it out of a bottom drawer
When the nights close in.

When bluer skies and golden dawns
Are blotted out.
When dull damp clouds
Clog up the stars.

When I open empty cupboards
Looking for memories,
Disturbing dust on the shelves.
In my life I've collected
Broken cups with seeping cracks,
Ever wanting a will-of-the-wisp.

Forty years gone,
Not flown but leaked away.
Yet I fear to let go of childish things,
Afraid to grow up alone.

Upstairs, through the window,
By the evergreen tree,
Sits an inner infant me
Hugging her Hope.

Chapter Nine

Moira spent long hours making mind maps about the recordings of her and Pat under hypnosis, (and even longer showering everyone with her rambling thoughts on the topic). She doggedly deliberated their hidden message as she stomped the cliffs. She persistently peered into the sea mists seeking their significance. She dived deep for underlying secrets whilst watching the gannets divebomb into the sea, like kids playing *"Dare you!"*, causing an eruption of mini geezers and traumatising the fish.

She diligently dug up every detail, vegetating over each as she chopped carrots, turnips and beets for warming winter soups. She was so busy stewing over possible regression sessions' lessons, she accidentally fed the front porch Peace Lilies menstrual blood – thereby ruining her scientific experiment. (Only the bedroom geraniums were allowed to sup on blood, the ill-done-by downstairs pot plants were on a dull diet of phosphorous nitrate.)

(She was testing a theory that dunking a used tampon in your watering-can makes an excellent plant supplement. This carnivorous flora investigation had been instigated by a local Earth Mother irate at orthodox Judaism for asserting that one drop of the obscene blood of menses will kill a healthy plant outright. It must be said that the upstairs foliage was flourishing, albeit a bit whiffy. They were planning to market the product as "Moon Blood in Bloom micronutrient grower" and contact *Breakfast TV*.)

Pat was insufferably delighted with her former self as Martha Herrington. Immediately after the first session she dashed off a postscript to her Gaia Goddess Tours' brochure; it read:

All guided walks to the megalithic sites are led by a reincarnated sixteenth-century Wisewoman. At no extra cost. Book now to avoid being disconsolate!

Friends also clocked that Pat had taken to wearing knitted shawls and kept dropping allusions to "her Ancient Lineage" into the conversation (any conversation).

But Moira had the bit between her teeth and she wasn't unclamping them without answers. Unravelling her newly unwrapped past, deposited on her doorstep like a surprise Secret Santa, felt like a never-ending pass-the-parcel. She figured if only she raked through it enough times, she'd be able to get to a Core Principle, Defining Essence and Ultimate Meaning of the whole experience, along with the definitive instruction sheet to sort her life out. Then she could precis this as a mantra and stick it on the mirror over the washbasin in her bathroom.

She'd discovered that by the 1590s witchcraft persecutions had reached a historical peak, determined to finally snuff out any female authority in midwifery, medicine and folk religion, perhaps a faint echo of a long-lost priestess role. The village Wisewoman still held sway in her little vicinity; a calling which Martha with her strong sense of community welfare embraced, as had her mother and grandmother before her. But, like the oppressed badgers today, she was a threatened breed.

Even the Church itself was losing control thanks to the Queen Dad's Reformation, and the extortionate charges for religious relics of saints' (or not) disembowelled body bits had gone out of fashion amongst the upper classes. The educated, aristocratic Desmond Moyle was a precursor of the coming Enlightenment, a forerunner for a materialistic worldview that spat out the old magical thinking so dear to our distant ancestors. And not without good cause Moira couldn't help thinking. The whole hullabaloo of sixteenth-century fear and superstition had got her well and truly into hot water (or treading air) once upon a time!

It was the common masses in Elizabethan England who were still clinging stubbornly to the crumbs of the old traditions; hence the marketable asset of snippets of a hanged woman's hair and the whole saga around the witch trials. Of course, the latter also had utility value as a practical means of settling village antagonism or disposing of impecunious widows.

With the Cult of the Virgin Mary superimposed upon the earlier Goddess, and an enduring adherence to the lingering pagan folkways, the old and new religions had probably been not unhappy bedfellows for several hundreds of years. But both had to make way for the approaching Age of Reason. The former to be jettisoned as ignorance and irrationality (the new sin), the latter to be trimmed down to fit in with the Civilised Age of church-kept-for-Sundays-and-the-wearing-of-hats, with God – not a noticeably rational deity – just squeezed in (nicely sanitised and possessing restricted powers of interference).

"And what," Moira wondered, "became of the axiomatic baby after ditching the grimy bathwater?" She talked it over with the Moon Group who had plenty to say before Moira had finished asking the question.

"Yes, we did *indeed* end up with the ultimate no-nonsense-it's-all-got-to-tally society, with man as master of the universe and a kitchen full of gadgets for woman's convenience, apart from the price." Pat got in first.

"Though I don't suppose I'm alone in finding our consumable, no-enchantment-allowed world all a bit flat." Moira, now an adept at coven conversation, managed to nippily slip in by positioning her face to block Pat's. "It's a modern malaise – alcohol, binge eating and the TV soap diet as a means of evading the tedium of our colourless, polythene and all wrapped up Clingfilm Age."

"But the automatons are rebelling," Pat interrupted and without further ado, preceded to hold centre stage for the next minute without hesitation or room for challenge. "Turning the tables on their parents' aspirations, having got what the previous generations strived for. It's not that they don't want it – they just want more! Female spirituality is ultra-chic, paganism is accessorizing into the commercial market, and these days it's more trendy than taboo to call yourself a witch. The media just laps it up, and it drives people in droves to find a bit of Good Olde Meaning in their lives!

"Even the denizen of science has turned traitor on its forebears. The classical you-know-where-you-are-with-Newton has been usurped by the raving mystics of Quantum Physics. Oh woe for the rational man! The universe is not what he thought. At its most fundamental level it is neither predictable nor ordered, the observer affects the observed and the quaint convictions of Martha Herrington don't seem so far off the mark after all!" At which point Martha's reincarnated self exuded self-satisfaction.

Moira reiterated the question: "So, will the twenty-first century be a Return to Wonderland? A Restoration of the Sacred, the Renaissance of the Magical but neon lit and metamorphosed by our zany new-fangled technological paradoxical paradigm?" (Moira's turn to look pleased with herself.)

On a roll, she kept her unexpected eloquence flowing – at a rate of knots so as to prevent Pat from butting in,

"Look, here we are plonked back in the garden of *mind stuff*. The physical reality of the Enlightenment was just a big conjurer's trick played on us. We've looped another full circle of the Spiral and we're revisiting our roots from the New Age of the unrestricted sub-atomic particle in all its whacky, chaotic kookiness! We're back to an unfathomable universe where anything might happen and frequently does. A mad March Hare's tea-party of a world for those as Weird as Witches!" And, waving her arms in a flourish of triumph, Moira popped the cherry on the cake with: "Are we then on the brink of a Mysterious, Mesmerising, Metaphysical Mind-Maze of a Mayhem Millennium!"

The Moon Group broke into applause while Pat, finding herself superseded, sniffed sneeringly and got up to let the dog in to knock over coffee cups and disrupt further proceedings.

Chapter Ten

The total eclipse over Cornwall of August 11th, 1999 was described by most as a wash out.

Since the closure of Wheal Crofty, the county's last working tin mine, and the decline of fishing, the Cornish had turned their attention to netting tourists. The eclipse had seemed like a Divine Tourist Board timely intervention. But inevitably all the hopefully greedy would-be entrepreneurs trying to rent out their semi-detached homes for ten thousand a week, while busy planning a Caribbean cruise, were disappointed. In the end it had been the farmers, by renting out their fields as campsites, who had benefited – so that was a first. The roads were occasionally blocked in places, though not gridlocked as predicted or seething with road rage from the Tamar to Land's End. In the actual event, the police looked slightly silly on their specially provided contingency mopeds.

The days preceding the momentous moment were pleasingly sunny and peopled by a complacent populace in shorts. The eleventh hour of the eleventh day itself however, saw only the primary colours of wet weather cagoules dotted over a puddly Penwith. The orbiting superstars of the day ungraciously hid themselves behind thick curtains of sulky cloud while their disappointed and dripping audience, without a glimpse of solar or lunar discs, sat – gutted! – under torrential deluge. (This despite the Padstow Sun Dancers best efforts throughout the preceding week.) Afterwards, the bedraggled eclipse fans returned to their uninviting sopping tents, shivering and fantasizing about hot baths, dry clothes and the Costa del Sol.

Moira, on the other hand, had loved every one of the three rain drenched minutes. She and Pat and Pat's annoyingly friendly but unwieldy black Labrador, Guinness, had arrived at the hilltop plateau of Trencrom by nine thirty to find it already inundated by a hundred or so sun-and-moon-spotters with flasks and sandwiches, nestled amongst the bracken or roosting up on the huge granite boulders.

While Guinness sniffed out the picnics, Pat and Moira pushed their way through to the southern perimeter overlooking St. Michael's Mount, as someone or other had forecast that the Eclipse heralded the incoming St. Michael's Dragon Energy and they wanted to catch a glimpse of him as he arrived. They were squashed between Brummy motor bikers on one side and a group of Hampstead yuppies on the other, who had hauled up strawberries, Pimms and a barbecue kit. A formidable Canadian woman in a red synthetic cape was balancing on a precarious rock on the steep hillside dropping away in front of them, from where she sang North American Indian chants – loudly. Moira was all for pushing her off.

At twenty past ten it started to drizzle and folk began muttering anxiously. By twenty to eleven it was more of a downpour and Guinness was looking miserable. At ten to eleven the skies opened and it bucketed down. Moira was soaked through to her underwear and a lily-livered few slunk back to their cars: "For we are, on the whole, a race who permanently hangs out in houses, offices and undercover shopping arcades, and hence has forgotten that Britain has natural elements which won't kill us," as Pat scathingly observed. Most people jettisoned their cardboard safety viewers in the mounting mud.

By eleven, hysterical camaraderie had set in and the drummers commenced a steady pulse, "the earth's heartbeat" as Pat interpreted it, who was measuring time with swinging arm movements not entirely suited to the crowded conditions. In the last moments before the sun was eclipsed the sky was spectacular. Mighty roller coasters of dense, slate black, bulbous cloud galloped overhead. An eerie light hovered on the sea and a tornado formation could be seen above the Mount, whirling down like the apocalypse! The assembled crowd were wound up like springs under the weight of such potency and peril.

Trencrom held its breath. The drums gave a final roll as the hill plunged into darkness. The birds stopped singing, not a car engine could be heard, and the temperature dropped several degrees. There was a flickering of camera flashlights all over Cornwall, like the land giving off white static. The boom of Concorde pursuing the eclipse shook the hill.

And it *was then*, when everyone in the county had stopped, switched things off and turned their faces up to the skies muttering "awesome!", right then in those extraordinary communal three mystic minutes, that Moira was visited by a cosmic cataclysm which cannoned her mind and shook out a new consciousness like a flag unfurling in the solar winds!

Right then and there, straight out of the black, Moira suddenly felt the presence of the earth, sun and moon as *conscious and aware*, as if *these* were the major players in the drama of life, whilst she was only one of those smidgy midges that are supposed to live in our eyelashes, or a single microbe amongst the billions of bacteria that inhabit our miles of gut.

It was clearly the pivotal point of her life and possibly, she hazarded, of human evolution! Along with all the shamans, priesthoods, holy men and hermits – dancing and shaking rattles, enacting high ceremony with reverence and incense, or sleeping with a rock for pillow – she could now see the Whole, within and without, that is so much more than our piddly fun-size selves! Breathless in expectation of epiphany, Moira realised she'd been studying an elementary Ladybird book all her life but now she'd accidently flipped a switch and been plugged into the cosmic web, a Universal database, a Galactic Gossip Blog through which she could access the Multiverse! At this totally WOW and Whoo-Hoo ecliptic moment, she – Moira

Box – was convinced she was about to get the ANSWER TO IT ALL!

The next minute, when the daylight returned and Moira was brusquely unplugged and switched back to being one of the disconnected little people with whom the world abounds, everyone spontaneously cheered and excited chattering broke out as they descended back to the carpark, sliding down the mud torrents in squelching sandals. The London socialites who were staying to party, lit their barbecue only to discover, while all human eyes had been fixed in wonder on the heavens, Guinness had eaten the burgers.

It was around this same time that anonymous threats to demolish the Cornish Sacred Sites began appearing in the local press, cumulating in Lanyon Quoit being doused in napalm (supposedly) and set alight, causing damage to the lichen and a gungy black mess. The stone abusers sent in a photo of the victimised dolmen on fire and described themselves as the "One Hundred Stone Avengers".

The witching community got heavily het up over this attack on antiquity, and were extremely preoccupied with drawing up improbable plans for guerrilla warfare across the Penwith moors, aiming to ambush all stone burners on sight. (As arsonists' organisations go, this one was along the lines of a guild of square wheel builders when you come to think about it – stone not being renowned for its flammable qualities!)

Moira had her doubts as the teenagers from Hayle Comprehensive School were pretty 'cute at concocting school lab combustibles but, after tortuous debate between the resident covens as to the ethos of cursing, a protective anathema curse was cast (promising the readers of *The Cornishman* that only the avenging vandals would be annihilated by it) and a nationwide Red Alert was sent out to all Pagan and Wicca groups across the net.

Following a visit to the local health centre, Moira (still unanswered) started examining the case for reincarnation. This was in response to her doctor suggesting her regression experience might be more a matter of mental health than of past life. His prognosis mentioned low iron levels and neurotic wish-fulfilment fantasies. He suggested eating spinach and offered to make her an appointment with the counsellor, though he ought to mention there was a long waiting list.

"Off the record," he said conspiratorially, "what you really need is something to keep you occupied, maybe a baby or a holiday in Disney Land, Florida." At this point he glanced up at her, for the first time briefly taking his eyes off his computer screen, and amended "Probably the holiday."

Belief in reincarnation, Moira unearthed, stretches far back in time, long predating our "one man one life" lottery system. The *Papyrus Anana*, an Ancient Egyptian manuscript, seemed to have it sussed right back in 1,320 BC:

Men do not live once only to depart hence forever, they live many times in many places, though not in this world only. The strength of the invisible time will bind souls together long after the world is dead. In the end, all the various pasts will reveal themselves.

Moira was pleased to find that some contemporary religions still uphold reincarnation today (as had Christianity until AD 553, when the Fifth Ecumenical Council of Constantinople had connived to re-write a whole wad of the words of God, and to ditch the awkward applecart which had allowed people more than one go at getting to Heaven). However, she baulked at the cross-species reincarnation beliefs of Indian Jainism, guessing it would be typical of her luck to return as a bluebottle.

Research has picked up where religion left off, with lots of Scientific journal entries and birthmark identification analogues. So many entries in fact, there was talk of "empirical verification of reincarnation" with an equally vehement backlash of "balderdash", proposing a neurosis of the "incarnation type personality" along the lines of a button phobia.

Personally, Moira was predisposed to any doctrine which didn't entail a *resurrection of the body* on the Day of Judgment – because if that meant a life-after-death eternity in her present bod she would lose the will to die...

Chapter Eleven

"I can't shake off this nagging niggle that I'm becoming a self-development junkie," Moira complained, having rashly signed up for another gruelling Inner Growth workshop.

"Don't worry," Pat consoled her, "It's just a phase you're going through. We've all been there. And a few of us have come out of it without rehousing to a yurt."

This weekend she was at Rosenwyn House in St Buryan, a fine nineteenth-century house with a genuine Iron Age fogou and ye quaint gypsy caravan in the grounds. Moira hadn't twigged when she sent her cheque in for the *Ritual Theatre Encounter* that this is cosmic consciousness jargon for "an intensive spitting-out-your-emotional-innards-and-cradling-the-pieces-afterwards group orgy".

At a particularly agonising point in the proceedings (lots of private anguish being passed around for sharing), everyone in the (now officially bonded) group was sitting in the standard New Age cross-legged circle on the carpet. It has to be said that Moira, whose lack of physical appeal was accompanied by a corresponding lack of confidence, did not dazzle in group situations. She usually checked the venue out first and dressed in accordance with the wallpaper. If there was any chance of good Old Age rows of seats, she'd reserve the one at the back behind the pillar.

She suffered most in getting-up-close-and-personal set-ups such as this one, in which the behavioural code was one of hefty hugs, close bodily proximity and intimate (practically mouth-to-mouth) confidences. Moira felt people shouldn't be obliged to fling their arms around her on arriving, departing or crying. Anyhow, she'd gritted her teeth and had survived to this point.

"Shut your eyes and visualise yourselves as a symbol within the group," had been the introductory exercise. The inevitable image that sprouted out of Moira's surly subconscious was that of a holly bush (stumpy and struggling to grow in a rubbish tip). All the other trees (tall and slender and gracefully swaying in time with the prescribed monosylip meditation music) were elsewhere, and seemed to be having a whale of a time stroking each other's leaves in an exclusive cluster.

Madeline (who was a blooming magnolia tree in Moira's cliquey top-notch wood) started expressing her feelings, while tears gently flowed down her peaches-and-cream cheeks. The men were listening intently. She described herself as a flower opening up in a hard vicious environment, aware of how fragile and vulnerable she was. Indeed, in Madeline's ritual performance she'd laid bare the delicious curves of her naked body, not – Moira charitably gave her the benefit of the doubt – to rub it in the noses of the less perfectly endowed but in an attempt to lay herself open to the critical eyes of others. Though eyes on stalks better described the male quotient of the audience! Moira, hanging on to her metaphorical holly leaves and substantial Angora cardigan throughout, thought that personally she'd rather publicly confess to piles.

"But of course, you feel vulnerable! That's the flower problem!" she piped up in spite of herself. "The whole thing about a flower is that it is a thing of *beauty*. It gives great pleasure in a stark ugly world as long as it's prepared to expose itself and risk being picked; hence beauty can be short lived. At least the holly with its unpleasant spikes and the yew with its unpalatable needles last a long time, there is something to be said for being obnoxious!" Moira stopped to recollect what point she'd been trying to make while the room patiently waited.

"What I'm saying is, I think," she held out, "that if you're born a flower all eyes will turn towards you either in admiration or envy. It's the fate of a flower. Society still sets great store on flowerhood for women. Men are always wanting to pluck them or put them in their flowerbeds. And it's not always such a benefit either," she added, thinking of Hannah Greene.

"But anyway, we can't all be flowers, some of us are born hedgehogs and no amount of prinking and pruning will grow us petals. – Though there are practical perks for hedgehogs. They're well equipped with survival skills for one thing, and provide a welcome habitat for small jumping wildlife."

"Sorry, I thought roses had thorns?" enquired Frank, unnecessarily facetiously in Moira's opinion.

"Well yes," she admitted, getting flustered. "But the fact is if you take the thorns off a rose, it's still a beautiful though defenceless rose, while if you take the spines off a hedgehog, it just looks silly and cold."

"So the question is," Frank proposed with a rather pronounced grin, as he continued to pick her metaphor to bits, "Is at preferable to live an exquisite short moment basking in the warmth of the world's adoration as a flower or to have a long life with fleas?"

"But either way you're stuck with it!" she snapped crossly, glowering at him. "Though, if you're born a hedgehog, you'll going to need your prickles – not a lot of people want to pet us after hibernating in the dung heap!"

"And if a flower risks being plopped in a vase on someone's mantelpiece," someone else asked (sniggering a bit), "then what's your fate as a hedgehog?"

"I'm working on it," a mulish Moira rebutted. "In the meantime, don't try to catch the eye of men in cars. They won't see you... splat!"

Later that afternoon, Moira – frizzling and fraying after a day of pushing her boundaries – sneaked off to sit by herself in the fogou. It was wonderfully cool in the underground chamber and she heaved a Herculean sigh of relief at escaping the communal cuddles (condensing too many people into too small a space for too long, some with sweaty armpits – grossly penalising the short in stature like herself). Maybe, she mused, it was the lull of the poor light or perhaps it was the high radon gas levels from the granite making her drowsy. Either way it offered a much-needed retreat from the Rosenwyn Retreat's psychodynamic but excruciatingly embarrassing *Ritual Theatre Encounter*!

Moira wriggled on her belly into the Creep, a little dirt-floored anti chamber which the pagans brag is the earth's womb, and sat pondering the flower-hedgehog dilemma. As an exceptionally ill-favoured dumpling of a child and poor pudding of a teenager, she had frequently wailed "why me?" Despite what your mother says, there's no denying that looks affect your life. In her case not for the better. But what's your best strategy if you fail to get past the bouncer into Vanity Fair? She sighed again and longed for easy answers to life's puzzles, and at this moment in time a chocolate cupcake wouldn't go amiss either.

As she adjusted to the dimness of the fogou, she noticed something strange etched into the cave wall in front of her. Squinting hard, Moira began to doubt her eyes – was she being fanciful or was that a face? She leant forward to peer closer. Just as she did so, the boulder moved! A gaping hole appeared in the rock! At this point Moira's mouth became itself a gaping hole and her eyes began to pop; she was feeling very queer.

The semi-transparent woman who had emerged through the opening and sat opposite her, motioned a greeting.

"In my time," spoke the visitation, "it was not so great an issue. Not that human nature has changed for we liked what looks pleasing as much then as now, but we required other gifts in our struggle for survival."

As soon as her heartbeat had stopped racing in the Grand National, Moira tentatively inquired of the possible Celtic priestess or Neolithic Deity.

"But then perhaps you weren't brought up with implausible magazine models and their glamourous counterparts on TV games shows? Plenty of demoralised youngsters respond by compulsive binging, while others literally starve themselves to death. Boys are doing it too these days, so does that represent progress?"

The Deity laughed, "Things will change again," she guaranteed. "Give it a hundred years or so."

"That's no good, I won't be around to see it!" Moira objected.

"Oh yes you will," the Fogou Guardian smiled, as she flickered and faded from view. "In one form or another!"

Post-supper found the torturous theatre group lounging on the lawn at the back of Rosenwyn surrounded by the voluminous white blooms of the rhododendron bushes, enjoying a full moon and a full stomach of rather too wholesome food. After swapping stories about spooky phenomenon and psychic happenstances in fogous and long barrows, Moira wrote her second poem. It was short, but it had been a tiring day.

Where the Winds Meet
Blue wind from the sea,
mounting the cliffs
beneath the lazy bellies of the gulls.
Wind brown from dirt field,
blown aground in rocky gorge,
circling cairn and menhir,
wailing through chambered tomb
white with the ghosts of our ancestors.

Wild winds whipping up
long gone feet dancing still
amongst the last stones standing.
A May wind tangling

ribbons of missing memories,
tempting wives to whisper old tales,
peeping into a forgotten fogou,
– where a lost lore waits
to be reborn.

Chapter Twelve

On a wet and windy morning, Moira met the Reverend Gregory Gifford in Chapel Street. She'd popped into Penzance to renew her library books and hurtling back to the car, head well down under her rudely assaulted umbrella, she didn't notice until she'd accidently impaled him. She recognised Gifford immediately and wondered why she hadn't made the connection before between St. Oswald's rampant vicar and St Edwyn's visionary missionary, David Hoskings (for such was his contemporary form), her squeaky-clean neighbour's personal guru.

She appreciated now why he was such a natural orator, he had at least one other lifetime of preaching experience behind him. And he was still on the same assignment it seemed; although this time without the weight of an omnipotent religious institution and the death penalty to back him up. She found him more likeable in his present mode as a little man delivering leaflets.

All sorts of fantastic possibilities struck her in that moment, Penwith might be full of reincarnated Durlow characters! Beverly herself could easily be the dippy Edith Kemp or the drippy Parnella Crouch, and maybe that sarcastic woman at the hairdressers was Parnella's bitchy mum Alice in a past incarnation? She even had a hunch the present Queen Elizabeth II might have once been Elizabeth I (with Her then royal courtiers now reborn as royal corgis).

She was stopped short in the game of superimposing unsavoury Tudor personalities onto all her least liked acquaintances, on realising that the lay preacher had already been enthusiastically addressing her for several minutes.

"As I was saying, Miss Box, I could drop off a church service schedule and maybe you'd like to come along with Beverly one day soon. It would be nice company for her, her husband not being as keen a devotee as herself. And..."

As he continued to pontificate, energetically bulldozing his views onto her, she discerned a similarity between his way of speaking and that of her friend Pat's. Of course, they shared a long personal history spanning the centuries. Who knows, perhaps in a future life they might even get it together?

"I'm sorry, Mr Hoskings, but I'm very tied up with my Minoan Goddess correspondence course at the moment. But would you mind calling in on Pat Trenoweth sometime? I know she'd like to discuss a possible ecumenical cross-faith meeting group with you," Moira artfully fabricated, before nodding angelically and moving on.

Driving home through the squidgy lanes, Moira reflected that we now live in a ridiculously air-headed and spaced-out era with all its quirky ideas and kinky fads. But at least it's got more *spiritual rights*. At long last, it's not illegal to practice alternative spirituality or even politics if you want to. At all events, the Craft is no longer a dangerous undertaking with high stakes – literally stakes – as in tied to over burning faggots!

During the most savage century, *The Burning Times* of 1550–1650, there were an estimated sixty thousand burnings and hangings in Europe, of which 80% or so were women. (And quite a few poor moggies thrown in. Such a come down from their Egyptian god status! – You can tell they've not forgiven us yet.) The last woman to be tried and imprisoned under the witchcraft law in Britain was the psychic medium Helen Duncan in the 1940s.

"The age-old fear of witches has all but crumbled away," Moira cogitated, sucking on a humbug. "The role of women in religion, long shoved down and marginalised, has re-arisen; transgendering the dog collar into a unisex neckline, wedging the Mother Goddess on the throne alongside an indignant God the Father, and squeezing her libelled feminine form between the wholly resistant Holy Trinity!

"The medieval churchmen erected grotesque gargoyles of the witch with which to terrify us and win their ecclesiastic crusade. But with the passing years, these have shrunken down to Halloween party props and the Witch is back! Wriggling out of the closet woodwork, giggling and garnished with glitzy witchy fashion accessories from eBay. Still obstreperous, stubbornly noncompliant, and probably up to mischief!

"There's no denying," Moira wound up with gratification, "that amongst our ancestors, the persecuted victims of Wiccaphobia are *not* a-quietly cooling off in the cinders!"

As she drove past the Noah's Ark gay friendly pub she thought of Hugh Kemp.

"If he lived now (and maybe he does)," she informed the empty passenger seat, "he could have a perfectly legal love-life with no other threat than being duffed up by delinquent gangs after closing time. Who knows, come the twenty-first century it may be totally O.K. to be any sort of well-meaning, optionally different minority group at all!"

And maybe pigs will *fly* after the Swine *Flew* epidemic...

"Life scripts tonight!" Pat announced briskly to the Moon Group, as they trooped into her higgledy-piggledy house and arranged themselves on cushions. (The cushions like the sons of Abraham had been multiplying greatly of late, so they all sat on three apiece to make more floor space.) They'd come in from the rain, secretly relieved but with some loss of face – witches are supposed to be a weather-hardy breed.

"What are life scripts?" Moira enquired, as she negotiated the shell and fir cone mobiles and clanging wind chimes that dangled from the ceiling, a precarious task when bearing a tray of full coffee mugs. Pat explained, swaying enthusiastically on the pinnacle of her tottering foam pile as she spoke.

"'Life scripts', coined by the Transactional School of Psychology, is a hypothesis that as children we adopt a particular fairy story and then adapt the rest of our lives around it. For instance, if you resonated with Cinderella, you'll live the life of a drudge and expect every good-looking affluent fella to do a Prince Charming job on rescuing you. I see my own life script along the lines of Rumpelstiltskin as I'm genius at getting answers to all life's big questions."

"You have Rumpelstiltskin's crotchety temperament too," Vicky commented.

"And his nose," Bea pointed out.

"And people do call you lots of wacko names!" Olive concurred.

Pat quelled them with a frown and added another cushion to her mound. Moira, who had been considering the idea in her usual persistently persevering manner, looked up and acknowledged.

"Yes, thinking it over, I'd say there's something in it! In all good fairy tales, the heroine has to go through trial and tribulation before the happy ever after ending. Well, life is like that. But without the happy ever after bit."

Several groans and soft furnishing missiles followed this prosaic statement. Pat fixed her with a hooking look and demanded, "What's your life script then, Mogs?"

"I don't know," Moira replied at a loss. "I suppose it might be *The Ugly Duckling* – but, like I said, I never turn into a swan. Just a bigger duckling. I've spent most of my life waddling around the water edge unable to get in. I look at all the glamorous lovelies with their healthy well-fed egos swanning it on the lake while I, with my poor starving self-esteem and tufty brown feathers, lurk out of sight like an unwanted clubfoot in a ballet company. Hoping that one day I'll also be so swanlike that people will flock to see me bringing bread."

There was an instant outcry and loud protests that she was nothing of the sort, was quite lovely in her own way, etc. etc.

Then Roz observed: "Well, it's time to show your face even if no one likes it." (Realising too late that could have been worded better.) "At least you're not skulking in the reeds anymore."

There was another round of agreement and congratulations until Pat called a halt.

"That's enough chit-chat. Though I must say, while we're on the subject, I think swans are overrated. Scrawny necks for one thing, and small heads. Anyway, people can switch life script and you've changed a lot since you migrated down here. Let's see what you get."

"Yes please," Moira begged, drooping dejectedly, "The duckling could do with a break."

Pat led them through the visualisation and brought them out again for the usual group share, passing around the speaking stick so Rianne couldn't talk too much.

"I was exploring a house," Moira described when it was her turn. "It was mainly empty, with lowered blinds across small windows, but I found a secret staircase leading to an attic with fantastic views. An old-fashioned record player was playing and when I looked at the label I saw it was *Snow White and the Seven Dwarves*. So that's it I suppose, Snow White – though I can't see it myself. I mean wasn't she *'the fairest of them all'*!"

"Epic stumper!" Nellie applauded, clapping her hands. "It's obvious really, you are the fair Divine Princess but for safety you disguise yourself as a scrubby, scruffily dressed scullery wench and loiter around in shady woods."

"What's more," Gwen collaborated with relish, "you live with a dubious collection of little men who possess a whole load of insalubrious or plain ludicrous personality traits, (grumpiness, debilitating shyness, bossiness, dopiness to the point of imbecility, narcolepsy, maddening nasal allergies and infuriatingly incessant cheerfulness). It goes without saying, these represent aspects of *your personality* which are unpleasant and farcical."

"Thanks," Moira grouched. "Think I prefer being an unsightly signet."

"And the dwarves are miners, creatures from the underworld. All stomping around with pickaxes in your subconscious!" Amyrah expounded for Moira's further discomfort.

"Exactly!" Jan nodded vigorously, "In my Jungian imagery class we learnt that an attic signifies spiritual potential. All your hidden rooms and panoramic views are the treats in store for you! Lucky you!"

"Hang on a minute!" Moira protested, wildly brandishing the talking stick to get their attention, "Didn't Snow White get poisoned and put in a coffin!"

Pat dismissed this with a shrug, "Oh come on, Mogs, you can't *always* expect to have it *all your own way* in life!"

Chapter Thirteen

On the last winter solstice of the century, Gwen gave a public talk with slides in the café at Tehidy Woodland Park, followed by a mini ritual besides the duck pond. There was a good turnout and Moira was delighted to count up how many people she now knew who she didn't need to dodge when spotted from a distance. The coven itself had become Moira's tribal clan and she finally got enough birthday cards for a mantlepiece.

They were all there that evening, being organised to help – either in a participatory role or in a "fundamentally vital capacity" of putting out the chairs and pouring the tea. Gwen herself was on high form; she had a new man at her side, husband the fifth, this time married by a pagan handfast ceremony for a year and a day (which meant they could omit the Christians and eschew legal fees both ends). He was a gentle, softly spoken man who was handling the slide projector and sweeping the floor, which boded well for their future chances together. Her public talk was teeming with references to birds, bees and Nature overflowing with sexual juices. Moira secretly missed the acid commentary and blistering recriminations of Gwen's post-divorce period.

New Year's Eve came up next on Moira's social calendar (no longer just a waste of money) and she joined the Millennium celebrators on Porthmeor Beach, St Ives. It was pretty bracing but this didn't prevent a very jolly Nellie, dressed as the Shamanic Woman in nothing but a few hanging bones, feathers and wolf headdress, from taking a swim at midnight. A bemused young policeman suggested she might be getting rather old for these pranks but Nellie, a voluptuous and sprightly fifty-year-old, just tossed back her long black beaded locks, looked at him with her big blue eyes and said: "You ain't seen nothing yet!" Her new faux fur calf-boots were quite ruined by seawater and had to be thrown out the next day.

Moira made her customary New Year's resolutions of giving up chocolate and getting on the bicycle more (i.e. once) and celebrated this with a fat chunk of chocolate log cake. Pat resolved to overthrow Patriarchy and re-institute paganism as Britain's national religion, with herself holding the Arch-Crone Crown Office of the new order. As her first act of Holy Benefaction, she announced with unholy glee, she would send the Pope a lion.

Anxious to find out what the twenty-first century had in store, Moira enrolled in an online astrology course. For one wet week at the end of January when she was off work with the snuffles, she sat on the rug in front of the fire surrounded with Millennium Prophecy info, zodiac cookbooks, an ephemeris and her new ten-year diary to mark don't-go-out dates in. She feverously dipped and dabbled into these all week, never once venturing beyond the front door. (Thank Goddess, she was well stocked up with essential medical supplies, i.e. albas oil, lemons, lozenges and chocolate swirl ice cream.)

It seemed a lot was scheduled to take place on the interstellar web in the coming years. Everyone was excited that Pluto was going into alignment with the Galactic Centre. Moira had no idea what this meant but conjectured it had to be super cosmic cool and hoped it might add to the currently available Galaxy and Milky Way confectionary. Neptune, Jupiter and Chiron would conjunct in 2009 to open up old wounds (she planned to build a large nest in the freezer and cryogenically freeze herself for that year). Pluto would move into Capricorn in 2008, where it would remain until 2024, having enormous fun digging up the dirt on financial and political institutions, and shaking the established order with hell-raising hissy fits. So Pluto – furious about being demoted from planet status – was to have its Revenge.

The in-coming Aquarian Age is all set to premiere the Power of the Collective (supposedly a bit like the Borg from *Star Trek Enterprise*) with its egalitarian weapons of social media technology and street demos. This was optimistic news for someone who always felt happier as an indefinable dot in a mass mob than she ever did standing alone on a chair.

There was also a great buzz on the WWW superhighway about 12/12. For a while, Moira thought this was a variation on an unreachable dress size, until she discovered references to the end of the Mayan Long Count Calendar on the December solstice of 2012. Everyone from the Ancient Mesopotamians to the Canadian Cherokees seem to have jumped on the Doomsday or Ascension (depending if you're the glass half empty or half full sort) bandwagons; each new prediction outsizing the previous, including claims of *translation or dematerialization to another sphere of the Universe* (Teilhard de Chardin), a *Human/ ET interface and the arrival of a new species or kingdom on Earth,* (Jon King), an increase of the Schumann resonance to 13Hz and *increasing tryptamine and beta-carboline neuro chemistry allowing us...mass out-of-body-experience,* (Geoff Stray).

Moira surmised that she'd need another course.

On the eve of Imbolc (possibly not significant) she had a curious dream, one of those peculiar ones which gets you speculating about its symbolic footnotes. Moira, who had always been intrigued by Monkey Puzzle trees, found herself wandering in a whole forest of these. She looked up in awe at the spiky boughs which reached high into the sky and down at the well-trodden earth underfoot. This perplexing exotic dream forest was empty of all sound except for a continual low hum from swarms of buzzing flies – like a black mist of irritants – that hovered in the air around her head.

"Such is life," a disembodied voice boomed through the trees, *"a Mighty Puzzle to fathom and Countless Aggravations to swat."*

She'd walked on through the bug-infested dreamscape until she came across an arched doorway leading to a large modern building, set within an Elizabethan style formal garden. To one side of this imposing edifice was a noticeboard which read: *The University of Greater Choice.*

Moira mulled it over the next morning, as she munched her way through a breakfast of eggy bread, fried tomatoes, grilled mushrooms, mandarin oranges and fresh coffee poured into her favourite wide brimmed yellow cup. She ate it at the kitchen table, where she and Tigger could enjoy the sunshine and look out at the year's first dandelions.

As she sniffed at the percolated coffee, she decided it was time to stop hankering after being beautiful. It had never been on the cards anyway. And it was just the ill-luck of the draw after all, if some got dealt the Queen of Hearts then someone had to be left with the joker. What's more, hadn't she grown enough over the last couple of years to accept herself with grace and even a little affection? She took a gulp of coffee, closed her eyes and resolved that she had at last arrived at a place in her life where she could step beyond other people's narrow definitions and find out who she really was. The she who continued over many lives and personas, shape shifting between incarnations and getting full-body makeovers each time.

"Of the three ingredients which create us," she ruminated, "we only get to keep our *soul inheritance* while our *genetics* and *environment* get ditched after each trip – so why let them hammer us into becoming who we think we are? It might be fun to obsess over having a beautiful *Spirit* for a change, less visible than the bod but infinitely longer lasting!"

Besides, there was a bucket load of stuff she wanted to do before she snuffed it. If nothing else the twenty-first century offers a baffling and bewildering range of possible options. On a postcard of St Nectan's Fairy Glen addressed to herself, Moira wrote:

"Whatever your limitations there are always multiple possibilities open to you. Either by working within your confines or by shooting far beyond them into the dazzling, astonishing, wondrous, azure stratosphere!" And she placed it to one side to be posted.

While she slapped marmalade on toast, Moira Box found herself humming a chirpy rhyme from a children's TV show she'd watched as a toddler, "Andy Pandy jumped out of the Box" it went.

Moira propped open her book on folklore and scooped up three big dollops of clotted cream, depositing one into her coffee cup, one in her bowl of mandarins and one in Tigger's dish. The birds in the garden sang. The blue sea twinkled in the distance. The morning sun streamed cheerily through the window. Both the stripy cat purred and Moira Box sighed in blissful contentment.

Part IV

Life Post 2012 and Past 50?

Chapter Fourteen

Rianne kept grimacing as she scrutinized her face in Pat's crone mirror, with much groaning and grumbling that the light in the room was unnaturally unflattering (i.e. daylight). No-one took any notice as the Moon Group had been going for well over a decade now and familiarity breeds voluntary deafness. In any case, Rianne still looked annoyingly good for her half-century tally, though she disagreed:

"I'm mutating into an intro-species and vegetation hybrid with my crow's feet, turtleneck and orange-peel skin!" she wailed, though not without hopes of instant rebuttal. Peeved at the non-response, she issued a pugnacious challenge: "Still, fifty is the new thirty so I must only be about twenty-five by now!"

The women lounging on Pat's plump cushions merely smirked at this. Roz for one knew Rianne's real age as she'd sneaked a peek at her passport, and *sisterhood* insists on *One for all and all for one*; i.e. it only takes one member to know some juicy titbit and within the hour they all know it. However, they put down their dream journals so Rianne had succeeded in getting the attention.

"Pah! Wrinkles, a rash of age spots, descending boobs and flabby buttocks – what do they matter!" Pat pooh-poohed, in her favourite role as coven astringent.

"You girls," she accused the mid-life (ish) contingent, who were all buckling beneath their fifty-year milestones, "are fussing and fretting about a few minor cracks and crumples on the outside. It's when things disintegrate on the *inside* that you've really got something to gripe about! You wait till you get inflamed joints, impacted intestines and leaky bladder! Then there's the encroaching brain shrinkage – half a percent per year apparently. It's just as well some of us had an exceptionally colossal intelligence quota to begin with!"

This wasn't what the flinching fifties ensemble wanted to hear – more bad news – so they blanked Pat and turned back to Rianne with atypical sympathy. Rianne flicked back her long still naturally corn coloured hair (grr!) and started fishing for reassurance, agonising that she'd thought she'd noticed not being noticed in such a noticeable way anymore, and did she look her age? (real or assumed).

"It's all in the head," Moira comforted her. "Seeing the way you *behave*, Rianne, nobody would *think* you're very old."

Missing the point, Rianne glanced curiously at Moira's plain podgy countenance, as if considering a jam roly-poly which was lacking the jam, "I don't suppose *you're* bothered about losing your bloom and going to seed, are you Mogs?" she probed inquisitively.

Ignoring the slight inflexion on the pronoun 'you', a decade of self-preservation exercises having finally paid off at last, Moira promptly answered "No, not at all."

Then a pause for reality to nudge in, "Well, at least not until I look in the mirror, then I curse and scream and shriek obscenities at the Gods of Time and Face." Further pause to recall another of her self-preservation strategies, "So I don't look in the mirror. Sorted!"

In fact, the dreaded disease of "Are we getting older?" (Which was sweeping through her peers like a tsunami, leaving them thrashing around in twitchy panic and checking their pubes on a daily basis for signs of grey) had done no more than dint Moira's body with a few furrows without denting her healthy self-esteem at all. This was partly due to becoming an adept in the awarding art of "Not Thinking About What You Might Think Other People Might Be Thinking if you Think they're Thinking About You. Though probably not. (As most people are mostly thinking about themselves most of the time.)" She'd learnt she got to do a lot more of the things *she* wanted to do that way; it was undeniably an all over win-win, fun optimizing chosen life discipline.

In addition, Moira had recently discovered the Secret of Eternal Youth.

Moira's recipe for holding back the clock, which she magnanimously shared on Facebook, was complex and convoluting. And, needless to say, in dealing Decay and Decrepitude a deathly blow there's always an attendant price to pay (traditionally it was killing virgins). Her prescription for hanging onto eternal, or slightly prolonged, youth was as follows:

- Anoint your face daily with a concoction of extra virgin (had to come in somewhere!) olive oil, ylang ylang, neroli and carrotseed. *Cost*: the oil leaves stains on your clothes and if someone comes to the door you're glistening and dripping like a chip pan.
- Cover your head with a stocking (or half a pair of tights in Moira's case), cut out nostrils holes and slip rose quartz crystals inside, said by the pharaohs to soothe and smooth wrinkles, while communing with the mineral elementals. *Cost*: bits of crystal *will* fall out and subsequently do havoc with your vacuum cleaner.
- Drink cranberry juice (*warning*: draw the line at rooibos tea, some healthy options can *go way too far*) and do your pelvic floor exercises. Best done while your boss is pontificating in the Thursday team meeting. *Cost*: The rest of the staff, noting your expression of intense concentration, accuse you of buttering up to the manager.
- Smear yourself with Manuka honey once a week. *Cost*: even for Pooh Bear honey is *excessively* sticky.

- Shake Old Age out the backdoor along with the duster on a windy day. *Advantage*: let's face it, we all need a blimming good incentive for dusting...
- Eat a nutritious diet and banish sugary food, as you would an ant infestation, from your fridge and bedside bottom drawer. *Cost*: you'll need a whole series of intensive Last Rites Ceremonies with the coven on the dark of the moon to say your tearful – by the bucket – farewells to chocolate. (OUCH!)
- Eat a gluttony of vitamin supplements every morning, putting your meagre bowl of muesli and blueberries in the shade. *Cost*: the cost.
- Try meditation, research suggests it can knock a staggering ten years off your chronological age! The best time, apparently, for tuning into the cosmic rays is after sundown. *Cost*: it's impossibly hard to turn the TV off and get up off the sofa to find your candle and incense stick.
- Facial exercises. *Advantage*: you can stay on the sofa with the TV on.
- Ah well, we have to come to it eventually... EXERCISE the bod. *Cost*: more a case of extreme reluctance than extreme sports. *Tip*: the longevity promising Tibetan Rites (google it) are a bearable place to start. You can do them in five minutes (by cheating a bit) without needing to leave the house or change into jogging bottoms and trainers.

Moira had waded her way through Patrick Holford's and Deepak Chopra's anti-aging manuals and assimilated that you may guzzle down a whole punnet of raspberries for only five GIs, and you can switch genes on and off by love and gratitude to tailor make your own physiology. In the hope that the gullible physical is indeed susceptible to what you're thinking about it, she doused herself with warm cosy vibes before going to sleep at night and on waking she jabbered kindly to her body while she dragged it out of bed.

Moira was a bit fuzzy around the quasi-science bit but there was something along the lines of lifestyle influencing the length of the telomeres on your chromosomes, and that controlling insulin levels in *Caenorhabditis Elegans* worms results in them living for the human equivalent of 450 years! Moira had every hope of being sweet sixteen again, except much sweeter this time round.

Chapter Fifteen

The summer of 2012 was glum faces all round. Wet, wintery, woeful weather throughout the supposedly promising months of April, May and June, while most of July and August were touch and go (i.e. when the faintest touch of sunshine is felt, out everyone goes, all hectically haring around the coastal footpaths for fear of missing a precious minute of it). BBC Radio Four had announced in the spring that even the birds were confused as to whether they should be feathering their teensy nests or flying south for the winter. Moira, watching the sparrows despondently poking around in the soggy garden, thought they weren't so much confused as just plain depressed.

She was wearing wellies and waterproofs 24/7 and had joined in the nationwide howl of "Where's our summer?" in post office and corner shop. Consequently, conversation flourished amongst the non or barely acquainted all across Britain. (The only time this bonhomie was topped in Cornwall that year was when Helen Glover, local lass, won gold for rowing in the 2012 London Olympics. That afternoon Moira had been travelling across Penzance when an excited lady with shopping trolley kept popping up from her seat to announce: "That's the ice cream shop that Helen Glover's parents own!" or "That's the road off the road that goes to Helen Glover's road!" to the top deck of the number 300 bus.)

Back to the dismal weather then, it was the dogs and dog walkers who fared worst and looked the most muddy and morose. Moira congratulated herself on having a cat. As for Tigger, still sprightly despite his sixteen years, he let the mice and newly planted seedlings off the hook for once and retired to the bedroom. Wealthy humans retired to their villas on the Greek or Balearic Islands, where they smugly sipped their cocktails, pitying their poorer countrymen. Meanwhile, the deserted Cornish beaches looked sadly naked without the usual shivering white bodies of lower income holidaymakers huddled on them. Moira could certainly see the advantage of being stinking rich that year and added this to her *Next Incarnation Wish List.*

And the waterlog kept her extra busy. While many women have to do "the school run" – Moira did "the snail run". As she was too soft and soppy to put down the toxic blue slug execution pellets, she would sentence her garden snails to Transportation instead; distastefully dropping them into a jam jar with perforated lid, tramping through several fields (as it's common knowledge the little b's return home in their own sluggish time) and depositing them in a dank hedgerow. If the snails were particularly plentiful due to their inexcusable reproduction rates (horrifically, 500 babies per snail per year!) or if they were extra bountiful due to excessive rain (as in 2012) or if there were too many slugs (even more slimy and yucky to pick up) she might be mean and empty the jam jar on the top of a drystone wall, figuring that at least she was providing the birds with a healthier meal then stale white bread.

It was on one of these snail runs that Moira discovered the Vortex. She'd driven the *Mollusca Gastropoda* jar well beyond human habitation this time as she was convinced some of the bigger b's colonizing her agapanthus looked suspiciously familiar. She'd parked by the Climbers Rescue Centre and slogged up Carn Galva Tor clutching her glass gaol of gruesome garden guzzlers. At the top is a granite maze of gigantic boulders – which looks for all the world like one of the legendary Cornish giants had long ago chucked a tub full of rocks onto the summit in much the same way Moira now deposited her snail collection there.

It was mid-August so the moors were peacocking with the ballsy pinks of harebell heather and the in-your-face yellows of the bird's foot trefoil and hawkbit flowers. The shyer blues of the scabious, attempting to tone-down all this clashing bling of an over-the-top hillside, bobbed their petalled heads here and there in an encouraging breeze. The narrow wiggling coastal road lay far below, where the Volkswagen camper vans of the visiting sightseers were wending along in trepidation of meeting a bus or tractor. From there on the land sloped down to the sea, now sombre grey under the brooding blanket cloud, in a hotchpotch of small grassed fields with the odd tin mine chimney stack or stocky farmhouse dotted about.

Moira sat in her secluded tor-top spot, munching on a snack of tahini coated wholegrain rice cakes with sprouted mung beans, and considered the dire forecasts for the winter solstice at the end of the year. Several websites claimed the earth was kicking back against the rude manhandling by mankind with highly stressed tectonics and OTT weather. She idly wondered if the world were to speak, without all these meteorological histrionics, what would She say? *At that very moment a deep sigh reverberated around the rocks!* Moira almost jumped into the astral in surprise and span round to see who it was. Nobody there. Scurrying in pursuit, she scampered about the outcrop to nobble anyone hiding amongst the rocks. Nobody there.

Besides, it had been too loud and strangely husky. She might say the unlocated voice was unearthly, but in fact it had sounded just that, very *earthy!* Of course, after her Epic Eclipse Experience of '99, and as a fully-fledged pagan who'd been doing rituals dedicated to the Earth Goddess for years, it was well within Moira's belief circumference that Gaia is more than a mere intellectual concept. But she baulked and boggled and broke out sweating at the Gargantuan Presumption that this planet sized life form might be trying to get *her* – little (comparatively speaking) Moira Box's – puny attention! So, having failed to find somebody crouching in crevice with a megaphone, she started telling herself it was just the wind. Still, maybe it was worth taking a last look from that table-top slab of granite with its vast vantage point.

Having scratched her way through the gorse prickles and hauled herself in ungainly manner up onto the ledge, the first thing she noticed was that the flat capped boulder was a Rocking Stone, balancing on the tips of the stones beneath and tilting from side to side depending on where you put your weight. But what happened next blew her circuits like an ecstatic shock through her dendrites! What felt like a tornado-force vortex coiled up from the granite, whirling around her in a sizzling spiral flux! As if the rock were a high voltage socket and she an insufficient amp! She felt dizzy, fully charged and invincible – convinced she could currently do *anything* from minor bread and fishy miracles to moulding time, space and inter-dimensional anti-matter as if it was playdough.

For as long as she could manage without pressure sores, she refused to move but lay flat on her back blissed out. If she had to describe it, she'd say it was a Rapturous State of Being beyond biblical records and anything saint Teresa could lay claim to. True, orgasms weren't her specialty but they came nowhere close! Eventually, as the mammoth power surge slowly wound down, she drifted back to disappointing reality and her mind started kicking in again, gibbering rabidly with headline queries. WHAT was the Vortex? Where had it COME FROM? What had it DONE to her? WHY? And was she now, like Harry Potter, The CHOSEN ONE?

She couldn't possibly go home to the washing up straight after Nirvana, so she stopped off at the cosy old pub at Gurnard's Head where she indulged in a cappuccino (yes, she *knew* caffeine promotes prune textured skin and she *had* limited her consumption to one cup a day, but was tenaciously attached to this last not-to-be-surrendered-unless-hospitalised-and-nil-by-mouth vice). Sitting in the corner, cherishing her coffee cup and trying to return to law-abiding normality, she casually glanced down at a tourist guide lying open on the timeworn oak table. It showed a pic of spiral carvings, a relic from the distant past, on a gorge cliff near Tintagel. Something kept her focused on the twirling image. As each clog clicked into gear in the long chuggy chain within Mogs' cerebral matter, it began at a painstaking pace to add up to an esoteric equation.

This was why, she calculated, the spiral icon is to be found on the walls of caves, burial chambers, menhirs and dolmans, in fact in sites of antiquity on every continent except (query) Antarctica. Inscribed in such famous locations as the Nazca lines, the temple of Tarxien, the Knowth passages, Newgrange and Gavr'inis tombs. It represented, *obviously*, the energy spiralling up from the earth used to catapult the Highest priestess, the Mightiest shaman and Moira into a different level of consciousness and maybe, if only suitably harnessed, out of time and place altogether! Jubilant, she jumped up and yelled "Atlantis, here I come!" before recalling she was in a crowded pub.

Of course the Moon Group wanted to try it out, so they had a Sunday afternoon picnic there, all capering over the hillside like a farmyard of clucking hens and quacking ducks, babbling in unison about their experiences in ear-splitting excitement. Most reported an energy rush, some an amplification effect of whatever they'd been feeling, and one brave soul insisted she'd had been spun into a parallel universe of fanciful vistas and alien critters (to which the rest raised their eyebrows at each other and someone whispered "Neptune sun quincunx" behind her hand). (Astrological shorthand for "pretentious and psychotic self-delusion".)

On mass, they were all highly chuffed at having found their own mini magnetic-flux earth fixture on their doorstep, and

Pat promised to add it to her Goddess Tours' circuit, claiming that it rivalled the famous vortex sites of Cathedral and Bell Rock in Sedona, USA. Moira suspiciously speculated whether Pat was planning to sell tickets and feared that visits might be by appointment only from now on. She rather resented the way that the coven had appropriated her private Find-of-Portentous-Importance for themselves.

"There are times," Moira sulked, which nobody noticed, "when their sheer individual and collective *cheek* makes one's support group downright *insupportable!*"

Chapter Sixteen

Moira had long since traded in her shop job, selling charmingly useless thingamajigs, whatnots and doodahs in a St. Ives curio shop, for employment in the caring professions in order to earn better karma. She now worked in a day centre for the elderly, an assertive one storey building advancing into Penzance's Penlee Gardens. Its large central room resembled a combat zone with the belligerent pattens on flock wallpaper and Axminster carpet at war with each other, and hosting a legion of oddly assorted armchairs, all congregating in small inward-facing conspiratorial clumps – as if each cluster of comfy chairs were colluding and, she suspected, spent the night hours gossiping about the old dears who had occupied them during the day.

Moira's work persona was a mixture of tea lady and Master of Ceremonies, i.e. introducing new members to the established chaired huddles, bringing refreshments and organizing the bingo cards. She'd been much heartened to find that her faltering opening conversational gambits were more gratefully received in the Day Centre than in society at large. Perhaps, with the onset of old age and general depreciation into loose skin folds, stooped stance and pearl-coloured perms, appreciation of a kindly word from a friendly if frumpy face increases? At any rate, Moira felt as whole-heartedly welcomed as a warm woolly in winter as she trotted around with the tea trolley and ginger nuts.

Getting to know the O.A.P.s was an unexpected eye opener. A curious thing seems to happen to the elderly, as everything else slows and dwindles, personality traits magnify. Many mellow with age, becoming dear old grannies or doddery old darlings, good naturedly accepting their increasingly unsatisfactory lot. Whereas others rant in outrage as their power and prestige is snatched from them, and resort to the sort of cantankerous growling and grousing that they might have exhibited as tantrum prone toddlers. Maybe we lose our inhibitions as we give up the fight to impose impressive impressions on others and out comes what lies beneath – matured or fermented like wine left in an underground cellar for decades.

What Moira found distressing though, was the uncomplaining suffering that many of her tottering octogenarians were plainly trying to cover up from polite society. One sweet old lamb would hobble painfully across the carpet, leaning precariously on sticks, while making apologetic mutterings about "the old rheumatism playing up". Or she'd watch a trembling wafer-thin hand groping for the teacup only to knock its contents flying due to failing eyesight and encroaching cataracts.

They struggled on relentlessly, expending so much effort (of the odds and ends they had left) just to maintain some vestige of human dignity! It seemed crappily unfair, in Moira's opinion, that at the end of a lifespan of hard work and hardship, surviving a lethal war or two, these long in the tooth folk should be reduced to this pathetic replica of their former selves – to be pitied and patronized by those same people whom they had once dangled and changed nappies for.

Maybe old age is our last and steepest learning curve. Our ultimate and most desperate attempt to reach true values to live our selfish and trivial lives by before time runs out. So we are slammed with everything most disagreeable all at once, with the assurance of worse to come! But along with the theft of our healthy robustness, there's just a chance at the close of life that we might at last surrender the heartless indifference of self-obsessed youth and vigour.

Undoubtedly, old age is when the physical knocks the socks off everything else. No wonder so many of the 2012 solstice forecasters were optimistically insistent that the imminent shift to the fifth-dimension pledges to bypass all these dodgy bits of the material plain! Nonetheless, as there is no guarantee we're get these Hugely Hopeful Prophecies, Moira took up yoga and thought long and hard about the two days fast that Michael Mosely had recommended on *Horizon* that week.

For a couple of doggedly long-winded weeks at the end of August, Moira had been awarded the dubious privilege of dog-sitting Guinness the 2nd, another cumbersome black lab, while Pat was up country visiting a new grandchild. Guinness provided more persistently insistent but less intelligent company than Tigger her cat (highly incensed at the choice of house guest) and seemed to rely on Moira for his every want, much like an overgrown baby who refuses to be weaned.

Just between themselves, Moira tended to agree with Tigger that canines are a good-natured but lesser species in the evolutionary chain. Moira thought, if domesticated animals went to school, then the sort of school report the Labrador would get would be along the lines of:

Very enthusiastic. Eager to please. Never intentionally causes havoc, didn't mean to break your Cretan snake priestess figurine with his jumbo tail, to wipe the slobber from his drooping jowls on the lady in the smart suit, to sniff out unsavoury substances and then lick your dinner plate the second your back's turned. Low graded deafness when called. Though normally outstandingly stupid, the Labrador does possess the ability to escape from the garden at inconvenient moments, making all your neighbours believe you're trying to get it run over. Best comment possible: means well.

However, seeking positives in every pesterance, a lumbering Labrador does give you authorisation to be out walking on your own. Moira had often noticed the sideways suspicious glances dog walkers would give her when she was alone on the moors, as if wondering what she could possibly be up to away from shops! It's only the serious German hiker who sees nothing amiss with a dogless walker; though even they would flash her unsuitably unsturdy footwear a condemning scan.

Strolling along the coastal footpath was one of Moira's chief pleasures (now she'd forsaken chocolate. The chocolate sprinkles on a cappuccino don't count, and, truth be told, the odd choc tiffin wasn't entirely absolutely an endangered species). On yet another soggy summer day, she took the well-trodden trail from Porthgwarra to the Minack clifftop theatre's coffee shop. The weather was typical of 2012, with cloud hanging like layers of sagging brocade above an oppressed ocean. However, there was just enough blue overhead to make sailor suits for a small paddleboat of hobbits, and Guinness outdoors was preferable to Guinness in her little lounge.

As she plodded along, she contemplated cultural attitudes towards form and matter. On the one hand, youth is highly profiled along with whatever body shape the current fashion aspires to (no longer, thankfully, by her which had improved things no end), while on the other hand there's the highly communicable fear of age and corrosion and a strong aversion to the end cycle of our life spin.

As for matter – historically, the denser the matter the more man disapproved! It wasn't surprising that many of the hefty granite boulders that jut out across the Penwith peninsula had been christened with captions such as *The Devil's Pebble, Hell's Balls* or *Lucifer's Pitch-n-Putt*. Whereas references to the Divine agenda are associated with insubstantial downy white feathers or powder-puff clouds and ethereal sunbeams. The pagans were an exception to this anti-matter ideology as they worshipped the ultimate matter of the Earth Herself and all things bone and stone. Hence their propensity to revel in the fleshy pleasures; Moira had observed this hedonistic tendency at the annual Pagan Federation Conference which exhibited progressively protruding tummies at each succeeding year.

On reaching the thirteenth-century church at St. Levan, Moira contemplated the medieval carved pew ends of jolly ploughmen, jesters and jumping fish, along with a slate plaque of the Lord's Prayer, full of *Father* and *Heaven* references, pinned to the wall. Sitting on a grassy mound outside (actually it was an unmarked grave but she was too intent on speedily emptying her pockets of all healthy snacks to notice), Moira began to hammer out an alternative version to this renowned religious petition, honouring all things earthly and feminine to redress the balance. After much brow-furrowing she came up with:

Our Lady's Prayer
Our Mother who art the Earth,
Lush and fruity be Thy Nature,
Thy fertile song, Thy reign be long
Till the sun doth supernova.
Give us our food from thy earthly breast,
Forgive us our greed against Thee.
As we eat what we reap
So we reap what we eat,
Lead us not into naughty temptations.
May we honour thy Bounty
By learning to share,
Deliver us from bad-mannered bullies.
For Thine is the cradle,
Our playpen of Eden,
All hallow Thy nursery garden.
Amen. (Awomen? So mote it be?)

She put the rest on hold for future inspiration. She'd ask Pat, who – inevitably – would have already done and dusted it.

Trudging back across the fields, with the elusive sun blessedly peeping through and highlighting the sea, Moira considered her relationship with her own non-prescription fleshy form. Luckily, although still susceptible to high pollen count and insect stings, the human irritant no longer bothered her with their snidey snipes about it. She'd extended her self-concept (she'd come a long way since Slough) beyond her outer form alone and she'd learnt to like herself, bod and all. So much so, that she was now prepared to do the nutritious diet/exercise/health thing in order to prolong its shelf life and stay earthbound for say another half century or so.

Also, her blunderings into quantum physics assured her (at least so she reckoned, as the gist remained pretty incomprehensible) that energy and matter, at a quark level of course, are interchangeable. For Sedna's sake! – She'd proved that herself when she'd jettisoned one of her physical vessels on the gallows at Hereford but here, she was four centuries later and trotting! Her energy essence had fluctuated between bodies as do taste buds between the different layers of a Battenberg cake.

At this point a text from Pat announced she was westerly again, so Moira shoved a mud-caked Guinness into the car and gratefully returned him to St. Just.

By the time she'd chugged into town (the Cornish get very uppity if you call it a village) there was no more than a slip of light lingering on the horizon. The front door of Pat's miner's cottage stood open and Pat could be seen loading up the car. She greeted Moira with a hug and a brusque order:

"Come on, we're going out. I've packed the flasks and your cardboard-tasting superfoods. Two dratted weeks of hospital wards and city streets, I need the fresh air of a bonfire!"

After a long day's driving, Moira had to admire the unremitting stamina of her older friend; who by anybody's standards has to be called elderly by now, though Pat herself used the term "Elder", invariably with the word "Wise" as a prefix super-glued in front of it.

They decided on Carn Galva Tor, although this meant lugging the logs and provisions up a steep bumpy path by torchlight. After huffing and puffing to the top, they built a respectable campfire on a flattish patch of sheltered ground. Though for once this was hardly necessary, there wasn't a whiff of even the most bashful breeze, and the smoke arose in an impeccably behaved vertical line instead of the usual boisterous blowing around trying to goad chesty coughs and smarting eyes.

It did in fact feel quite uncannily still, Moira reflected as she retrieved the foil wrapped but nevertheless burnt potatoes from the fire, grated the cheese and picked the twiggy bits out of the butter. Quiet too – as long as you blocked Pat's long tirade about the traffic, doctors and the rudeness of people in cities. (Pat claimed her obligatory civility to the in-laws had strained her through a colander and she'd finally been *forced* to give them "a piece of her mind" purely to prevent rightfully deserved murder and maiming.)

Like the shrill whistle of a steaming kettle (in the days before they courteously turned themselves off) Pat at last boiled herself dry, and the long-time pals settled down to some peaceful fire dreaming. As the flames subsided, and the dark thickened and encroached on a fireside seat beside them, a comforting silence returned to the hill. High above, the night's sky was filled with stars that had shone for millennium, shining all the brighter from their elevated position at the summit.

Moira started brooding on the ancestors who had once lived in the hut circles found across the land hereabouts. She often dwelt on the country's past – perhaps because she was still carrying around her previous Tudor lifeline, bulging out of the excess baggage pocket of her aura.

Pat opened an eye and fixed it on Moira. "You're thinking about the Bronze Age people who used to live here," she stated without a question mark, they knew each other brutally well after over a decade of shared ruminations. "They probably sat around a fire in this very spot once. But how different then! All wilderness, with only the odd pinprick of human dwelling in the dense forest or vast heathland!"

"In such an inhospitable and lonely terrain, clan and fellowship would have counted for so much more, with the nearest settlement a hard day's walking away." Moira remarked.

"Mmm," Pat agreed, picking up the theme but tweaking it with: "and magic would have been an integral part of daily life, not shoved to the outer edge of society like a stray cat with mange!" (Pat invariably harped back to the resplendent time when the Wisewoman played a venerated role, deeming that she'd been denied her inheritance this time round and harbouring an itchy grudge about it.) Moira interrupted hurriedly, before Pat could sink into self-pity and general angst, offering her the lemon and ginger tea flask and adding, "but the magic never completely disappears, it can't do, it's of the Earth Herself."

As she spoke a sudden gust of wind sprang up like a jack-in-the-box, though immediately after it was dead calm again. Moira's psychic antennae tingled and twanged madly, making her jump up with unusual alertness.

"I think I'll go and do a spot of meditating on ...um, the vortex rock." She announced, just preventing herself from calling it 'my vortex'.

While Pat maintained the fireside vigil with closing eyelids, a hunched figure in front of the dying glow, Moira clambered up onto the Rocking Stone. She spread her tartan topped, plastic bottomed metre square from Poundland across the smooth granite surface and seated herself comfortably, feeling quite warm in the tranquil summer air.

At first the blackness seemed impenetrable but gradually she was able to make out the crags to the east and the flat line of the sea below. By counting her breaths and relaxing each muscle in turn, she steadily deactivated herself into an inert blob. Her erratic thoughts began to slowly thin and falter as the theta brainwaves kicked in. Within a hiccup of time, she knew she was no longer alone.

The air around her revolved in rings of Life Energy, blasting up like a NASA space rocket through her tartan rug! The whole tor was impregnated with a *Presence*, a potent sentient Being, overshadowing and busting Moira's personal perimeter. Flummoxed and awestruck at such jaw-dropping company, euphoric from the high volt blast, Moira experienced A New Hope that *this time* she'd definitely get the celestial page with all the answers on! She heard words, deep toned, feminine and ever so slightly sleepy, like a Global Force awakening from a snooze.

"My child, I am your Mother, I am the Earth. I bring a portent of that which is coming. For you all to hear."

Moira responded with a ducky fit. The responsibility of delivering a memo from the Earth Herself to all humanity was just *too much*, and her remonstration came out in a panicky screech.

"But why me? (*Squeal!*) I'm not the right person for your message! (*Squeak!*) You need a national leader or a celebrity from the 'get me out of here' jungle who's got the world's attention! (*Squawk!*) I'm not capable of changing mass consciousness! (*Yap, yelp, gasp!*) If I want to change anything I have to ask the man-in-a-van to do it!" (She was in such a flap by now she even made the Rocking Stone throw a wobbly.)

The energy currents softened, as if soothing and smoothing her sorely ruffled feathers,

"It is exactly because *you* can change, because you *have* changed! It's *because* you've come so far in your little lifespan, in such a short speck of time, that I have come to you!

"For I need you *all* to change, all my human progeny, to change wisely and swiftly now. I need you to change in your hearts, in your thoughts, in your behaviour! To change your enterprises, your consumption and how you educate your young. For *I* need to change. I have held Myself back for eons, waiting for My children to grow up to what is needed. I feed and nurture you all in My cradle of Nature and I bear with your destructive and short-sighted ways, ever wishing that you will come forward with Me. The coming epoch will bear forth My Initiation, an Initiation for us all."

The next moment She was gone. The hillside returned to a slumbering summer night in western Cornwall. In one almighty hoo-hah, Moira cannonballed down from the rock and bulldozed helter-skelter through the undergrowth towards the fire. She woke Pat by smacking her, gushing out her Revelations in an incoherent choppy Gulf Stream. Pat looked at her in a bleary sort of way for a moment, unhurriedly pulled herself to her feet and then turned her back to start packing up the stuff. Moira was infuriated – what was wrong with the woman! Didn't she realize what she was telling her! In high dudgeon, she had to stop herself from more smacking.

"Mogs dear, I appreciate you've just had a tete-a-tete with Gaia," Pat patiently explained, "but the proper venue to treat your disclosure with appropriate attention and respect is my comfy lounge, with a suitable bowl of my special punch or mug of Green and Black's organic Hot Chocolate!"

Moira paused at this last suggestion, which oddly seem to ground her, and then began helping to extinguish the last charred logs before the hike back down and homeward. After all, she reasoned, if a personal audience with the Earth Goddess didn't warrant an extenuating circumstances relapse from the hot chocolate ban then nothing did!

Chapter Seventeen

A few weeks later (during which time Moira had been carrying the weight of the world on her shoulders), she and Pat attended an alternative archaeology lecture held at Truro College, organized by the local UFO group. The talk was about a Bosnian Pyramid, said to be twenty thousand years older and twice as high as the Great Pyramid of Giza, and Moira was enthralled to hear that nearby underground passages have negative ions of 43,000 (as opposed to the 1000 you get by the sea) which can mend breaks in the human electro-magnetic field as shown by Kirlian photography. She couldn't wait to add a trip down its tunnels to her Secrets of Eternal Youth inventory!

"Why the Hecate hadn't we heard about it before and why hasn't it featured on a *Panorama* special?" Moira queried impatiently, as they discussed the presentation over a healthy salad bowl and permissible pizza.

"Hmm," the more cynical Pat curled her superior lip. "Acknowledgement would have a whole job lot of thorny implications. They'd have to rewrite history to start with, as it outdates the oldest known Sumerian civilization while Ancient Egypt is a mere 5000 years old. (Though they're still failing to explain away the Egyptian engineering feats.) That's an awful lot of premises laid in stubborn stone for the Establishment to overhaul! And now they've got Gobekli Tepe in Turkey drilling yet another stink-hole in the hallowed bedrock." she pointed out with satisfaction, and (always keen to berate the status quo) continued with:

"Why give up the ostrich approach when it's served academia so well for so long? Think how much time had to pass and consternation overcome before admitting that the earth revolves around the sun! Anyway, if there's any chance of health care which isn't based on chemical consumption, the pharmaceutical companies are never going to let that Cheshire cat out of the bag! It may take decades to reach the mainstream."

"But we may not *have* that long according to what the Earth Goddess told me recently," Moira said tragically, though with a definite swelling of head circumference as she name-dropped on a grand scale.

Pat's eyes twinkled a bit but she managed to maintain a respectfully straight face aided by having a headache, before resuming her rant – this time extending it to the entire human race.

"Why everyone else is so incredibly stupid is beyond me! Even a bimbo or politician must realize that we can't just carry on polluting and damaging the planet without earth-shattering consequences! Gaia's returned with a vengeance, narked and hot under her crust, with a dose of floods, tempests, bushfires, droughts and melting ice caps. Amazing She hasn't simply shrugged off our pesky pipsqueak human race!"

"She cares about us, we're Her children," Moira, still embracing her role as Gaia's newly appointed PA, stated diligently.

"Nevertheless, we may be coming to the point when She has to chuck out Her entitled maladjusted kids or to let them kill Her and themselves with Her," Pat insisted, adding in her Wicca Wise-Elder voice, "And *this* is the fear of twenty-first century witches!"

Being human, Moira was able to happily ignore the terrible fate approaching her species and tuck into her stone baked Margareta with relish. While it lasted, life was pretty good for a contemporary Cornish witch. No threat of incineration (indoor screen showings having usurped bonfire bondage as weekend entertainment), a lovely landscape to live in (ignoring the ailing climate), a caring community of fellow witches (bearing with their infuriating foibles) and a best buddy who was always there for her (albeit with sporadic crabby spells and tetchy tendencies) (but she might be projecting here) and a successful vocation of Enjoying Life Despite All. With a grunt of gratification, she lifted her snout from the plate and turned to her durable chum to share an endorphin moment.

At first Moira thought Pat had fallen asleep mid meal. She was slumped in a crunched-up position against the window with her head on her chest. With mounting panic, Moira registered that Pat's breathing was strenuous and, scrutinising her face, she saw one side was drooping. Neither did she respond to being shaken like billy-o. In a crescendo of agitation, Moira waved frantically to attract staff attention but, as with all self-respecting waitresses, the Pizza Hut girls were well able to carry on crossing the room without once looking in the direction of an annoying customer they're not allowed to be rude to.

Hysterical now and hardly aware of what she was saying, Moira leapt up and let out a deafening bellow which drew all activity and conversation in the restaurant to a sudden halt.

"EXCUSE ME, BUT THERE'S A WOMAN DYING HERE! SOMEONE CALL AN AMBULANCE AND PLEASE CAN I HAVE THE BILL?"

Two hours later, Moira was sitting in dazed disorder in the waiting area outside the stroke ward at Treliske Hospital. The doctor had spoken about a *major cerovascular incident* and of a *cerebral embolism starving the brain of oxygen* alongside a *haemorrhagic burst blood vessel in the parietal lobe*. Pat had said nothing having failed to regain consciousness. When asked how she was doing, the nurse said "it was early stages" and suggested Moira go home and come back at visiting time tomorrow.

Moira, feeling sick and stunned, couldn't bring herself to leave so she deposited herself in the canteen with a stewed tea, and then paced the hospital corridors clenching plastic cups of congealed fluid from the vending machine once the canteen had closed for the night. Maddie, Roz and Shirl arrived to take turns in keeping her spirits up with well-meaning platitudes such as "Everything happens for a reason" (which might be true but it doesn't follow that you're going to like the reason) while alternating between "Don't worry, Pat will be fine, tough as old boots!" and "Let's be grateful Pat's had a good innings".

The next morning, she was allowed to sit next to her comatosed chum and squeeze her hand in the hope she'd squeeze back. Moira got very excited at one point when Pat raised an arm to pull out the naso-gastric tube stuck onto her cheek with surgical tape. This caused the frazzled nurse some vexation (though luckily Pat didn't get to the urinary catheter) but alas did not herald a return to lucidity.

On the third day the Registrar explained to the assembled coven (only allowed to the bedside in pairs and their fragrant floral offerings refused admission altogether) that it was unclear as yet what permanent damage had been done though it was possible (read probable) this would be considerable. At first the doctor had said he's only authorized to speak to family. On being told they were Pat's "soul family" and, fully taking in the middle-aged, menopausal militants forming a scary semi-circle around him, he accepted that he'd met his match and gave up the unequal fight.

As the days passed, it became clear that no quality of life was coming back and, though no one wanted to use the word "vegetable" to refer to their dearly loved crony, this was what it was going to amount to. The awkward issue of minimal medical intervention was posed, and a bout of pneumonia sent Pat into a downward plummet that was horrendous to witness. Moira was haunted by the fear that Pat was in there somewhere, silently screaming to get out. Despite repeated requests, not a single member of the medical team on the ward seemed sympathetic to the old superstition of opening windows and unlocking doors to aid the spirit's flight. It was October, after all.

Three weeks later, the mainly motionless Pat was shipped to a nursing home as her bed was needed for someone who could recover. The staff there were less stressed and it was more peaceful than the hospital; not that there were any fewer dementia patients who writhed and screamed through the night (it reminded Moira of Hereford Gaol in the 1590s) but here Pat got her own rather dour but private room. Moira was allowed to play CDs of harp music, waterfalls and blue whales wailing, and to leave crystals and amulets on her pillow. Nurses are a long-suffering breed and they let the entire Moon Group sit there for hours chanting protection incantations, accompanied by their Himalayan singing bowls.

It seemed indescribably sad to her friends that a woman who had been so verbal and erudite throughout her life should end up immobile on a two-foot six bed unable to communicate. To be denied a last chance of passing on pithy dictums from her deathbed seemed a cruel twist for a Wicca senior whose vision and creed had been largely unheeded in the modern era.

Moira spent her days on the creaky chair next to her unresponsive best buddy, and spoke earnestly to her in the hope something might trickle through:

"Pat dearest, I've never had the chance to tell you how much I love you to bits. Fourteen years just wasn't long enough! It was always going to be the heart to heart I've scheduled in for your last days, which weren't due until you were at least as old as Dumbledore. So, I'm going to say it now and trust that one way or another you'll hear me.

"Sometime in nearly everyone's life, there's someone who crops up and saves you from the worst that has happened. Someone who gives you a hearty shove to get you up off your bottom and to propel you in a better direction. It's rarely the person you expect it to be – some prince on noble steed or smooth dude in Ferrari car – but is invariably the person you unthinkingly rely on, and take outrageously for granted, but who's there for you in ways you don't even notice.

"And *you* are she in my little life! You picked me up when I was most woe begone and pitiful, you listened to my laments, and in equal measure you dished out helpful unpalatable advice – which I rather resented, and life affirming sympathy – which I greedily gobbled up, and you stood by me as I struggled to change despite the growing pains. And you've been there ever since, and I'm going to miss you like the summers we never have anymore. Like my support and companion who's kept me floating my leaky dingy across the squally ocean of life. Like the warm face I turn to, the listening ear who bears with me and the shrewd darling old crone who pushes me to keep on trying!

"And I'm never going to forget you because there will forever be a great gaping hole where you've been. Maybe in time my life will re-grow around it but the hole you've left will never shrink, and it will never be filled in with other people. That empty hole and you, darling Pat, will be part of me always."

Pat died two months after her stroke. Her ashes were scattered off the jetty at Cape Cornwall and just as the wind carried her last mortal remains over the sea towards Longships Lighthouse, the attending crowd all gawped and pointed up at the sky where a heart shaped cloud appeared in – and out of – the blue. No one doubted Pat had somehow engineered it from beyond the ashes urn in her usual grand gesture style. (They were only surprised it was a *silent* gesture.)

That evening a cacophony of Penwith pagans celebrated Pat's full life as Matriarch with mead, feasting and boogying in St Just church hall. (The vicar was fortunately not a David Hoskings of evangelical belligerence or he might have carped at the life-size chicken wire and papier-mâché model of the Boscawen Un stone circle set up in the centre of the hall in honour of Pat's work in the Goddess tourism trade). A glut of candles was lit in defiance of the Health and Safety regulations, as it was agreed that Pat should be granted her last chance to flout the patriarchal establishment.

In the company of the coven, who were all conspicuously rallying around her with anxiously buoyant expressions, Moira tried to be stoic, finding some consolation that Pat's death this time round hadn't been quite as harrowing as her death from gaol fever. Gwen put a compassionate arm around her but couldn't resist misquoting.

"To lose a friend to the grave *once* might be regarded as a misfortune, to lose her *twice* looks like carelessness!"

Pat's was their third Departing Party, cancer had chased dreamy dark eyed Jan till she slipped away on her ruby slippers, and Olive – her lively mum who became a lot less lively after the loss of her daughter – had joined her a year later. As with all pagan Rites of Passage, there was considerable carousing well beyond the witching hour that night with much swinging and swishing of emerald cloaks in time with the Celtic bodhráns, uilleann pipes and bouzoukis.

Moira managed to slip away at midnight, taking the lane to the Carn Gloose burial tomb and scrabbling over the turfed walls which ring the central cist of Ballowall Barrow, dramatically situated on the cliff edge. She was always impressed by the grandeur of prehistoric funerary arrangements and she started concocting a petition for planning permission to erect a similar monumental mound as a suitable memorial for Pat. However, as she sniffed around the central chambered pit, she twigged that it would probably be utilized as a public latrine.

The moon was a misty disc directly overhead and Moira huddled on the stonewall bank, pulling her cloak tight against the November chill (though the curtain it was made from was somewhat threadbare by now) and had a good long howl, safely out of range of sympathetic snuggles. She was badly missing her dear old confidante and doubted she would find such comfortable closeness and essential emotional back-up elsewhere, while as for the future – all Moira could see was a Big Bleak Beige Blank.

These reflections were only dunking her deeper down into the dripping dumps, so she gave herself a brisk shake and talked severely positively to herself, as Pat would have done had she been there. And maybe she was.

"I have a choice here. I can either wallow in the poor-me call-me-Job genre (been there and got the hairshirt) *or* I can evoke Artemis Warrior energy, cram up on a life-refresher spells package over the next thirteen moons, and get on with it!"

Moira rummaged in her bag to find her micro angel oracle pack (lightweight to carry around). She shuffled the cards, clumsily as gloved, and one accidently fell out. She clocked it was the "opportunity coming your way" card, put it back in the pack and then picked one, getting the same "opportunity coming your way if you grab it with both hands". This cheered her up a notch. Anyhow, she cogitated, it wasn't as if she wouldn't see Pat again, either between lives or in the next one.

Though comforted, there was just one piffling essential query worrying her as she walked back to St. Just and the merrymaking: would she and Pat still be able to chat over their one daily indulgence in the next dimension? Are any vices permitted in the Summerlands and do they have cappuccino machines there?

Chapter Eighteen

One sunny day in June 2013, Moira was blithely trampling amongst the honeysuckle and oddly named red campion flowers in all their perky pinkness and feeling at one with the world. Above her head a flock of fulmars milled around cackling with spring gusto. Over the past winter she'd slowly picked herself up, a toe at a time, manoeuvring her way round the manure heap by reasoning:

"It's just the way things go here, 'shit happens' and then you go back to growing the roses – or just growing. You complete the loves and lessons of one season and you progress on to the next grade; back at the bottom of the class but at least you've gone up a year, who wants to hang around with the tiny tots and potty training for ever?"

There were times, of course, when Moira massively missed Pat's trusty companionship but she continued to be fondly irritated by her eccentric Wicca pals, and had completed a personal-empowerment-with-your-power-animal programme (finding her Inner Cat had helped heaps in licking her wounds and clawing her way out of the doldrums). And even on really grotty days, when her optimism and self-confidence shilly-shallied under the bed, she could still congratulate herself that *at least she wasn't a muggle!* (Non-magical folk).

After a long trek across the moors Moira arrived at the Men-an-Tol. Clambering over the stile, she was rather put out to find some bloke sitting there on a rock (luckily for him not the famed crick stone or Moira might have obliterated him for sacrilege) eating a cheese and pickle sandwich.

"Hi," he said in a friendly, chummy sort of way (still a rare occurrence for Moira who featured an inbuilt male repellent). "Take a pew" he invited and gave her a sandwich.

Moira cautiously perched on the granite edge and nibbled on the bread offering. Sharing food – not a bad way to win friends and influence people she decided in his favour.

"I'm doing a recky of the site," he told her. "I've recently landed a job with the Ancient Sites Preservation Society and this is my first megalithic sculpture, it's a bit like a very early Barbara Hepworth, don't you think?"

"No!" Moira disputed, a little scandalized at the irreverent coupling. "Interesting work though, I often help with the Ancient Sites Committee's volunteer clear-ups."

(Actually, she had gone along once, only to discover it involved too much grappling with prickly brambles using dangerous looking but blunt metal instruments. And she had enough brambles of her own to grapple at the end of the garden.)

"Yes, it's a fantastic job," the amiable guy enthused, "archaeology has always been my passion. And much more enduring than my passions for persons!"

In surprise at the candidness of this confession, she looked him full in the face and what she saw there, especially in his light blue eyes, made her leap up and roar in recognition,

"But I know you! You're Hugh! You're Hugh Kemp! I'd know you anywhere! Even in the secondary Elizabeth's reign!" she gibbered excitedly, giving him a quick prod to check he wasn't a fata morgana. "Though of course you were quite a bit younger then," (he must be about mid-forties), "You were only eighteen when I saw you last."

"Oh!" he smiled in a hesitant sort of way, "It's fab to see you again. But it's Hugo. Hugo Kemble."

"Well now maybe," Moira kindly corrected. "And my name isn't Hannah Greene either."

Hugo looked distinctly puzzled if not a little alarmed.

"Um, were you living in Sussex too back then?" he fumbled his way in the dark.

"No, I was living in the village of Durlow, Herefordshire," she happily reminded him.

"Really?" he countered, none the wiser. Then coming clean, he admitted: "Er, I'm really sorry but I can't quite place you at the moment. But if I was only a teenager that was some time ago."

"Yes, over 400 years!" Moira babbled back in delight.

"Exactly how old do you suppose I am!" Hugo demanded indignantly, "and what's *your* secret for eternal youth?"

"Well, I do have a checklist for that as it happens, it includes Tibetan rites and Bosnian pyramids," Moira, momentarily getting side-tracked, flagged up with pride, "but don't get me going on that one! No, it was in the sixteenth century I knew you. And I'm not Hannah anymore – it's Moira, Moira Box. How do you do!"

"OH, MY GIDDY AUNT!" Hugo gaped in dawning stupefaction. "I've had dreams all my life about living in Tudor times, I always had a hunch it was a past life! And there was a girl called Hannah who cropped up in a lot of them! And do you know I just *feel* you're her. I actually knew there was something about you when you first hopped over the stile!"

"Even though," he tacked on imprudently, "you don't look anything like her. She was really prett... um, I mean she was really pretty loyal as my best friend in those days. But it's so fantastic to see you again! How's *this* life treating you? And how did that old life treat you since we last met?"

"Well, they hung me on the gallows as a matter of fact," Moira answered cheerfully, as if referring to a bout of flu, "But I'm much better now thanks. What about you? Do you still hang around with deviants, outcasts and vagabonds?" she asked conversationally.

"Pretty much," he grinned, and then threw back his curly head and laughed long and loud, "By Jolly Jingo, Hannah! Have I missed you!"

The following day, Hugo invited Moira to his place on the crest of Bosullow Hill, so as "to catch up on old times". Moira was frankly pea greenly envious of the isolated squat cottage tucked away on the craggy moor top.

"Whoa, what a view! You certainly got the prime location this time round!" she conceded, referring to Martha's hill cottage.

"It's super-doper spectacular, isn't it?" Hugo agreed, putting the kettle on, "Tea or coffee?"

"Do you have anything herbal?" Moira enquired with reluctance.

"Oodles," he said, showing a shelf full of cheerily coloured tea boxes.

"Oh never mind, fennel then thank you." Moira replied, mournfully accepting her healthy fate.

"Make yourself comfy," he said, indicating an armchair overlooking a Saxon quilt of fields flickering in and out of the sunshine. While he was filling cups and dousing teabags, Moira leafed through a *Megalith Monument* magazine on the coffee table.

"You've found my pet hobby," Hugo observed, handing her a steaming mug. "I'm the editor for my sins, we've got international readership now would you believe!"

"Mmm, that's... oh, Oh, OH!" Moira lit up in pulsating light like the Tardis as a dazzling idea hit her. "Do you have room for an incy article I'd like to write, by any chance?"

"Always do, exciting up-to-date news flashes about primeval antiquity, and big stones which haven't done a lot apart from standing around for a few thousand years, aren't that plentiful! What's your angle?" Hugo encouraged.

"Um, just a message about saving the world," she mumbled modestly.

"Honey! You sound like a Christian!" he teased.

Moira went on to explain about the Rocking Stone and Gaia's request.

"That's Fab!" Hugo commended impressed, "We can title it *Voice from the Vortex!* Much more fun than the usual carbon dating surveys."

Feeling a planet-sized weight slip off her shoulders, having at last found a means of completing her Mission Improbable, Moira heaved a humongous sigh and told her knight in shining armour (well a rather nice taupe linen shirt in point of fact) how she loved his new home.

"Yes, it was brill luck getting this place," Hugo agreed, "I've only just moved down, hotfoot from the infamous south-east. My unloving spouse went off with another man, a prime specimen this time apparently. They're honeymooning in some villa on a Greek island right now. I scuttled down here to escape, can't face all those vulgarly curious faces and awkward condoling comments!

"Anyways, I love Cornwall. It's so adorably rough round the edges. The home counties are simply too tidy for my taste, everyone's a paid-up member of the consensus culture club, it gives me cramp in the soul! Though, of course, you realize this is just the bitter spleen of the rejected speaking," he acknowledged with a whimsical scowl.

"I have to tell you, I was feeling dismally doleful when you came upon me the other day. It's like losing half of yourself; to say nothing of slicing up your shared property, splintering your friends into opposing lines of battle, splitting up the dinner service and matching bedroom furniture set, plus guillotining the wedding photos down the middle, along with the loss of my Significant Other – to whom I'm now supremely *in*significant in the shadow of the Great Gregg who superseded me in that role! I'd just like to get my heart back in my body if I could only retrieve it. I guess it's dangling around the happy couple on some sun-drenched Santorini beach at the moment."

"Ooh, I know that feeling!" Moira empathised. "Well, not losing a partner to another of course, but having that big gap in your life which someone special used to plug. Do you know, I've been working on a fresh-start goal agenda for ages and, apart from the obvious ones like 'Sufficient monetary means to avoid working full time' or 'A happy cat', the one I can't get away from and which keeps nudging itself up to top of the list, however much I try to bring it down a peg or two, is just that 'Someone who I'm special to and who's special to me'.

"And that's it – the Tricky Number One! It's so tremendously tricksy because" and Moira counted them out on her fingers, "of the following:

1. You have to find someone who you really like – and that's harder than it sounds.
2. You have to find someone who really likes *you* – and that's even harder.
3. And mere mutual liking's not enough on its own. Something has to click in place so when you hang out together it just feels *right!* That's the indefinable alchemy bit.
4. And it's no good being a close second, if it's not equal it won't work.

So, all in all it's a tough one!" she concluded forlornly.

"But without it everything's a tab on the drab side," Hugo agreed. "And rough going, like climbing up a scree slope carrying a rucksack of rocks. *Whereas* when you have that *special someone* your life's a playground, sorry to be hackneyed, and there's always the next playtime to look forward to.

"And what about you, Hannah darling? Where did your special mate go this time?" Hugo probed sympathetically. "He didn't run away to join a band of undesirables I hope?"

"Died. Last year, November," she said shortly.

"Just as well we've met up again then, isn't it!" Hugo warmheartedly commiserated, muffling Moira in a big taupe hug.

Moira was having a colossal fit of the collywobbles in front of the mirror. It was a week later, and Hugo had suggested going to a production of *The Red Shoes* by Kneehigh Theatre in their Big Top near Mount Hawke.

"What if this is a *date?*" she asked herself in petrified delirium, as she scurried around her bedroom completely unhinged. "I don't think I can cope with a date! Just does not compute! For one thing the nooky programme on my hard drive was deleted decades ago! *And what on earth can I wear?*"

She had already tried on her entire wardrobe twice which, although perfectly adequate yesterday, had suddenly become hopeless. Not a single garment gave her that fatal allure or turned her into Beyonce. In a right stew and kerfuffle, she picked up the tweezers and started feverishly plucking away at her eyebrows.

"Oh for Sekmet's sake! Get out of your Pickle Pot, Mogs!" an exasperated voice railed at her from the empty room.

"Aah...!!" Moira jumped, hair on end and skin goosebumping as she dropped the mirror in shock.

"I know that voice! Pat? Pat! That's your superior eyes-rolling-up-to-the-ceiling tone! Where are you? Pat, come on out!" Moira, reviving, commanded her invisible friend.

"Well, it's not my fault you can't see me!" the disembodied Pat reproached her. "If you'd only stuck at that psychic development NVQ, *like I told you to* if you remember, you'd have enough clairvoyance to spot us spirits by now! As it is, I've had to borrow a High Charge Ectoplasm Amplifier Unit to manifest enough psychic energy just to get myself heard. And it's on short term loan so you better sit down and listen to what I've got to say. I can't pop over every afternoon you know. Stop your fussing and pay attention!" (That was definitely the old Pat, no doubt about it.)

"And, by the way, it's a pity you can't see me," she added inconsequentially, "I'm looking much younger, quite spruce and spry. Our appearance reflects our nature on this side you'll be pleased to know. There are some beauty pageant queens here who look downright grisly!

"Now focus. We have a different concept of time on the next vibrational level. In fact, I can see quite a lot of what you'd call the future, or more specifically your future. It's *meant to be* that you and Hugo reconnect up again, you've always genuinely cared about each other so the psychic cords have been tugging you together, and I can tell you it's going to be much smoother sailing this time round. *And you can just put that mirror down right away!*" she snapped as Moira peered into it for any improvement in the eyebrow situation. "I don't know why you're in such a tizzy anyway, Hugo's last partner is called Luke."

"Uh-huh… Oh… Ah!" Moira cottoned on with her usual brakes-clamped momentum. "Phew! What a relief! We can just be cronies. Much more congenial. No fluids. And how are you Pat dearest? It's all true then about the pagan Summerlands? The Christian idea of a Heaven with harps is the hogwash you always said it was?"

Sounding as sheepish as a higher-plain apparition can, Pat admitted, "Hmm, yes and no in that order. In point of fact, there's plenty of room for alternative realities in this dimension. You can more or less take your pick. Just as in yours actually, only in the 3-D world we like to think our version is the only right one."

"Sweet Hathor's Horns!" Moira goggled, thunderstruck. "Why aren't you choking on your words? Never thought I'd hear you say that!"

"Only to you, tweety pie. On no account are you to repeat it to Preacher Hoskings mind, or I'll be doing a spot of poltergeist activity on your stamp collection!" Pat warned. "But I better say toodle pip for now, I'm meeting Old Mother Shipton for coffee and cake. (I hope she'll be more fun than Joan of Arc! All I got from her was fonts full of ever-so-saintly-oh-so-holy God talk, tedious woman, she really didn't deserve to be called a witch.) Be sure to remember all my sound advice and nifty tips, won't you. Tatty-bye. Be happy. Stay stroppy. Hang on in there."

"Thanks, Pat. Love you heaps!" Moira yelled at the ceiling.

"Love you too, Mogs" came back faintly, an etheric echo from infinity and she was gone.

"CRIKEY!" Moira – flabbergasted – summed up her paranormal visitation, continuing to ponder on its awesomeness while absentmindedly removing the remains of an eyebrow.

"Seriously Stupendous!" she concluded. "One of my lovely old soulmates has just re-enrolled in my life. Pat's well and spitting. *And* obviously you *do* get to have calorie free, insulin resistant, non-harmful (as not physical) to the body (also not physical) chocolate cake in the next dimension! For the Love of Witches what could be better?"

At this point Tigger, who like any proper witch's familiar had been utterly unphased by the spooky caller (merely glaring), jumped up onto her lap, purring and dribbling a bit (he was old). Moira stroked him fondly and beamed happily at the cosmos.

"Life was, is and will be simply out-of-this-world extraordinary!" she celebrated.

As she thought about Martha/Pat and Hugh/Hugo, Moira felt all warm and loving, loved and loveable. The closing ceremony of every witch's sabbat everywhere drifted into her mind:

"Merry meet and merry part and merry meet again!" she sang.

Part V

In Interesting Times

20th *April 2020*

Moira had been stopped in her tracks.

Well, her and the rest of the world. A third of the world's global population had been locked down already, with 200 countries effected by coronavirus so far. The human species – the self-doting, selfie-posting Homo sapiens – was waking up to the fact it was no longer the supreme master race of the planet.

This was a big blow to the Collective Ego. Certain individual egos weren't too happy either. Poor Trump went into thwarted tantrum mode when trumped by the incy wincy viral cells sweeping the USA and threatening his presidential election popularity poll. Even his billions and Big Man job status couldn't prevent Donald, who likes to blow his own trumpet, from looking small and ineffectual in comparison to a microbe. (*Human* opposition has always been so much easier for the elite to deal with; throughout history and the *Game of Thrones*, rebels could be beheaded, hung, shot, tear gassed or proclaimed "fake news".)

Only the astrologers were at all nonchalant, as they'd been twinkling on about 2020 as THE BIGGIE for years now. With the Saturn Pluto conjunction in January kicking things off and hotting up nicely in March when Mars joined in the tryst, they promised, basking in a bit of attention for once, that it'll go out with a bang; with Saturn, Pluto and Jupiter – the three planetary Mike Tysons – lining up in November and throwing their weight about.

"There's never been a time like it!" Moira spluttered into the phone during her daily natter with Hugo. He would have preferred to skype but Moira, though long since a fully mature if not always dignified swan on the inside, still didn't relish having her face on display. (On top of that, she wasn't a fan of chatting via technology full-stop, pointing out: "you thought human communication couldn't get any more riddled with confusion and misunderstanding, and then along came predictive text! What a mean cosmic joke.")

"Naturally, it's the poor and ethnic minority groups who are suffering the highest mortality rates, no surprise there." Hugo remarked despondently, drumming his fingers on the newspaper. "Wish we could meet up, Mogs, drat this social isolation," he tagged on kindly, momentarily taking his attention off the gloomy article on coronavirus and socio-economic status.

Moira conjured a wistful vision of meeting up for a naughty Cornish rarebit or slightly better-behaved avocado on toast, dished up by the local "Dog and Rabbit", now alas shut, along with all such blessed dens of indulgence.

"Yep, tragic shut down. I was just this minute thinking how much I'm miss our extinction-rebellion demos," Moira concocted with barefaced inaccuracy. (Earlier this year she'd made her first exciting entrée into political lobbying under Hugh's more experienced chaperonage. Though the lack of toilet facilities in the London blockades took some of the pizzazz out of disobedience and insurrection.)

Things had been fairly okeydokey for Moira during the pandemic as, since her sixtieth birthday last year, she'd ditched the daily grind and put her feet up in bunny slippers. Retirement had been an acceptable compensation package for the ticking clock Bonging at her and made possible by a small windfall, about the size of a Granny Smith apple, bequeathed by her good friend Pat. Consequently, she hadn't been struggling financially and was suffering far less than many – curfewed in confined high-rise accommodation with bored kids, sarky teenagers, narky partner and barky dog which didn't understand the "stay at home" 2020 mantra was the new virtue.

Without any outside activities, each day became *Groundhog Day* (though a deprived version as minus the featured cafe and coffee takeaway), until Moira lost all sense of which day of the week it was. She had to write reminders to herself to change the duvet cover before revolting her cat (Tigger's replacement after his tearful relocation to the Summerlands and under the hydrangea bush; another stripy tabby, named Snigger) who would pee in the middle of the mattress in protest. Being a no-nonsense feisty moggie, Snigger made it known from the outset that he wielded the ultimate feline weapons of mass destruction – claw sharpening and piddling on the soft furnishings – and wasn't afraid to use them!

Another double-edged development was the rare emergence from the shed of Moira's rusty bicycle, on account of gaining yet more pounds due to cancelled zumba classes and every evening spent alone with her fridge, plus the reality that the threatened food shortage had proved to be no more than a transitory run-on loo rolls. Though admittedly, during her once-daily permitted outside exercise, the bike generally trundled jauntily on beside her while she pottered along on foot. The countryside, with its lack of work activity and 1950s car levels, was abnormally quiet and this despite streams of walkers trying to avoid each other on the narrow cliff paths, now blue with bluebell and small squill flowers.

"And how astonishing that nearly everywhere is much the same," Moira marvelled, *"with a kind of hush all over the world!"*

The record number of walkers was attributable to empty pubs, shut theme parks and a flood of Londoners flocking down to their second homes in Cornwall, where covid cases were low, to sit out the curve flattening. (Often bringing the lurgy with them and thus giving the locals yet another angst against those who could afford a spare house while they couldn't clamber onto even the bottom-most rung of the property ladder.)

Amidst this man-made shush, the birds were in full chorus. The cuckoos in the fields above her garden were going bonkers Moira noted, as she battled with the scratching, clinging and stinging weeds outside the back gate (having, like so many stay-at-homes, been reduced to doing even those objectionable items right at the bottom of her *To-do-one-day* list). The bumble bees were in abundance too this spring, having bounced back after their own viral pandemic.

Today, Moira was taking advantage of the easing of travel rules, allowing her to go farther abroad than the locally accessible by foot or two-wheels, and joyfully leaving the bike behind to seize up again. Her destination was Carn Galva Tor, which she continued to climb with an agility her spiking year count hadn't yet impacted, still scrambling over its rocky outcrops with ease if not grace. In terms of appearance she hadn't changed that much either (though, for her, not such a big bonus).

She attributed this all to her Elixir of Youth itinerary, which had got quite a bit longer over time. A sea swim and a daily teaspoon of turmeric and black pepper promised to keep any arthritis at bay, cold water immersion being one of five ways to stay youthful as recommended by Dr Sinclair, Harvard's professor on anti-aging. This did require, brrr, a quick daily dip in a teeth-chattering rock pool throughout winter (surprisingly exhilarating in an excruciating sort of way) to get that brown fat going. Moira had been overjoyed to discover that there is a socially acceptable, even honourable, sort of fat. She'd swopped her usual self-defence when weighed by health professionals from the bog-standard "My bones are big" to her current boast of "Well you see, me and Wim Hof both have a remarkably large proportion of healthy brown fat!".

She was doing averagely well on the other four: good diet (ish), intermittent fasting (very intermittently), exercise (gently, gently) and positive attitudes (up and down). The latter was still a work in progress but so much better than the mopey Moira she'd been as a tweeny-whopper (in a decade that had exonerated Twiggy), a floundering teeny-bopper after being hurled at by puberty, peer pressure and poncho fashions, and a twenty-something full-bodied flop at a time before the Body-Positive Movement had really caught on.

Thankfully, she'd finally figured out that it wasn't a case of her getting the short straw life so much as *everyone* gets *a whole box* of straws, all of assorted sizes, and maybe – in keeping with the purpose of a straw – the more it sucks the better? At any rate, Moira now liked to make the best of things as, after all, you're not only born once.

Along with the gardening jobs, her daily spiritual practice had also benefitted from not having much to do. Lockdown is like being on an awfully long Buddhist retreat as there are no longer welcome unavoidable reasons to evade your devotional discipline. For today's meditation-in-nature she was aiming for her Vortex Rock at the hill's summit, one of her favourite spots (except on typical Cornish windy days when a ditch is better) as it always gave her an above-it-all sense of well-being and topped up her batteries. She spread out her waterproof-lined sheep's fleece, an upgrade from her Poundland tartan square, wrapped her fluffy lotus flower blanket around herself and started on Dr Joe's chakra-blessing breathing exercise.

After a few minutes her fidgety mind broke free and galloped away on its elasticated harness, and she found herself dwelling on the surreal times everyone's been pitch-forked into. So many deaths. Of course, for Moira death wasn't a wasteful dead end but rather the long-awaited chance to get a new body out of mummy earth's wardrobe (non-returnable). But the tragedy as she saw it, was the loneliness of dying without your loved ones and how agonising for family to be kept away from the hospital, constantly worrying what mum or dad might be suffering and not even able to hold their hand!

Tapping into this vast world grief took her way down into herself, deep furlongs below conscious thought, syphoning into a primal sinkhole where the turgid heightened emotions of the contemporary collective unconscious were swirling. Huge tidal waves swilling around in an immense whirlpool of loss, loneliness, helplessness, hardship, frustration, division, anger and most of all fear. Fear perpetually whipped up and frothing in the 2020 collective cesspool.

Suddenly, without even a polite warning, a waterspout sprung up from the eye of this emotive twister and Moira experienced a soul shocking jolt, an existentialist slap – perhaps comparable to the one occurring just before life ends – as a basement casement in her mind was flung wide open! Like stampeding buffalo, through the gap galloped memories of a long-gone time, of an age echoing today's panic in a denser form again. Not a whole life as in her sessions with Alec but a short episode, a sharp wake-up call like a quick slap in the face, but as startling and gaspingly real as her daily plunge in the ocean.

30ᵗʰ January 1349

I'm making my way back home. Even in normal times, never an easy task as it means picking your way over the garbage and excrement dumped in the streets, holding your gown up all the way, all whilst keeping a vigilant eye out for the emptying of a chamber pot from the overhanging gabled windows above.

Really the London streets, and given that I live in the more prosperous side of town, are a disgrace! Clustered rows of overcrowded houses congested in a maze of winding lanes, tightly crammed side by side and drunkenly leaning across towards each other from their upper storey. Pigs, dogs and rats, rife in our dirty alleyways, add to the filth. Most of the refuge flows into gullies and sloshes into a slow-moving, foul-smelling sludge. The King himself ruled that something must be done to address these unsanitary conditions, but the town council had to tell him this is impossible now. For nearly all the city street cleaners are dead.

It would be amusing, were it not so desperate, that *'noisome stench'* is recommended by the doctors and learned men as a means of *repelling* the Pestilence – in which case London should be utterly plague free! But it's far from.

I'm thankful to reach my husband's family home, a fine stone-built residence with deep solid walls that keep out the weather better than the usual timber framed and thatched roofed but today, and for two months past, I've been in no mood to admire and hurry in with a sigh of relief.

My beloved Aldwin is in the passageway so I run across the flagstones, as if my feet have a will of their own, to thankfully press against his comforting chest. We were married this November past, at the Feast of All Saints, and it was on this very day the Plague first reached the city. I would quake 'twas an ill omen for our wedding, were it not my blessed good fortune to have married one the most admirable, generous and steadfast of young men. Tall and handsome too!

"Aldwin, it's getting worse; the market has been closed down and the price of food from wayfarers has gone through the roof!" I launch immediately into our problems. Indeed, for many weeks, throughout the capital, all conversation has been urgent and all speakers afraid. Except only in the intimacy of our bedchamber, once the wintery sun has set upon London's troubles for the day. During those exquisite hours of the night nothing of this troubled city touches us, for then no world exists beyond our bright wedded joy.

"I'm told Parliament is to be prorogued due to fears of contagion spreading there, leaving our poor country without guidance in its hour of need," he imparts, after slackening a long loving clasp and leading me to the fire blazing against the January chill.

We sit close, and talk gradually ceases as we link hands, intertwining fingers, to watch the afternoon's light dwindle away.

2nd *February 1349*

The Great Mortality, as the Pestilence is called, has spread eastward and all the pleading prayers of London's clergy and congregations have failed to prevent it. Mass panic infected England long before the real infection landed on our Dorset shores. Fearsome rumours have flown from town to town, village to village, brought home by travellers on trade routes carrying tales of Death's black hand mercilessly reaching across Italy and then France, leaving a trail of putrefied corpses in its wake, and creeping ever closer.

This last year has been one of portentous threat, when fleeing families have been barred from entry here, left to starve outside the city gates. And now that plague has breached our walls, neighbour shuns neighbour and children fear to visit even their parents, or parents their children, abandoning them to die each alone. It has made enemies of us all, suspicion and terror have turned us into snarling feral dogs!

This morning a peasant woman, not known in this part of St Dunstan's Hill, was beset upon by some rowdy lads throwing stones in the street outside. With the new instinct of callous indifference, grown of necessity out of disease, I had almost shut the door on the wretched ragged matron when I caught sight of her face beneath a dirty shawl and her desperate eyes sought mine.

There was something compelling in her silent plead that I could not deny, or else a fleeting memory of happier times spoke to me, and I recalled that today is Candlemas. Without doubt I have acted recklessly – may God grant clemency if I have invited danger into our home! – but in honour of the Holy Virgin Mary whose day this is, I beckoned her into the house.

The infuriated gang of youths accused me of colluding with the Pestilence and spat at us as they departed.

"Too late to close the stable door after the horse has long since bolted to London," I murmured in reply, as I turned the lock on them.

I bade our servant bring food and more serviceable raiment, and seated the poor woman in our cosy parlour. Her name is Joan Elford, yet recently wife to a farm serf and running from a Wiltshire wholly devastated by plague. All her family and friends, and the greater part of her village, are now but a reeking pile of rotting flesh; too many for the remaining handful of inhabitants to bury, who fled with the unstoppable Scourge chasing behind them. My heart goes out to her, as to all our ill-fated fellow countrymen living through these demonic days!

When I confessed my rash behaviour to Aldwin, my good husband forbade from chastising me or throwing Mistress Elford back onto the street. Instead, he took both my hands in his and, holding me in his intent gaze, earnestly entreated:

"My kind, warm-hearted Roesia, how am I to chide you for those very qualities for which I hold you most dear? But I beg you to take a care for your safety, pray remember my happiness also rests upon it! Death now hovers close by, grown monstrous in power and within a hairsbreadth of striking us down, and I am too selfish to lose you!"

Aldwin drew me to him in a fond embrace, pulling off the net caul confining my long hair, which fell down my back in what he caressingly calls my "silken nutmeg cascade". He slid his hand gently down its length and tenderly kissing my lips, he said simply, "I would give my life to protect you, my sweet loving wife."

Every day, with each dawn breaking, I rejoice in the godsend of such a husband! If only there were some magic talisman I could purchase which might ensure our lives unfold in full.

The weather has worsened this evening, with rain turning to sleet and hailstones. I kept busy with household chores until late, and now our maidservant has gone home, we sit down with our new guest around the fire. My husband and I on the double-seated settle as, like so many newlyweds, we seem pulled together by some intangible force and find it difficult to resist touching, if only a shoulder against arm.

Aldwin throws on fresh logs to awaken the flames and the shadows flicker up the wall panelling and across the floorboards. We talk of Mistress Elford's sad history and she asks after our own families. My parents still live in Threadneedle Street, may our Heavenly Father in His benevolence preserve them, while my husband lost his from ill health a few years back.

Aldwin is a merchant, though currently halted from trade, as for so many in these treacherous times. God's bones! We have heard of ships found floating the sea with all the crew dead within! People say, not without a shudder, that the Plague was first brought to Sicily two years ago when a whole fleet of these *Death Ships* floated like a swarm of evil ghosts into harbour there.

For a little relief, we strain to talk of lighter things, of how this holy day in ordinary times sees processions of women dressed in white, each carrying a lighted candle to church for the Purification of Mary. Saint Bride, also honoured today, protects the household; on yesterday's eve I placed an offering in the hearth and sent her an ardent prayer.

Still seeking respite from London's heartache, I make jest about the old wives' tale that you should bring someone or something into the house on the morn of Candlemas afore anyone goes out of it.

"That makes you a blessing to us, good Mistress." I smile at our unexpected visitor.

But before long talk turns back to the great menace which here and now overhangs our perilous lives.

"The town's death toll is rising steeply," my husband tells us with a sigh. "Some estimate two hundred die each day! Graveyards are full and the Bishop has opened a new mass burial site at Smithfield to accommodate the dead. The pits there are immense, allowing corpses to be stacked five deep and several across."

"Pray the Lord have mercy on their souls! Who knows how many will be left before this diabolic disease departs, maybe but remnants of England's people?" I query, quietly reaching for Aldwin's hand.

Joan catches the tremor in my voice and hastens to say, "You are young and strong both, and have many happy years ahead. One day you will recount the bitter tale of 1349 to your children."

It is a pleasant picture and I'm grateful for her reassuring words, but as I turn to thank the good matron I see a sudden stillness about her, while her eyes seem to glaze opaque, as if she's been swept far away from this room and place.

Her next words are slow and faltering, spoken in a stricken voice:

"We can only trust that all is as it needs be, though the ways of God are inscrutable to us down here on mortal earth."

Hope turns to foreboding, and dread bleeds coldly through me. Looking away from the sorrow in her face, I glance at the candle on the dresser to see its flame is burning blue. My old grandma was wont to warn "spirits stray close when the flame changes hue".

We all fall silent, a thick cloying silence you could pick up and smother life with.

Perceiving my distress Joan attempts to console me,

"My dear, know that you're not alone. Your devoted grandmother says take courage, she is watching over you always."

At last I whisper, the air weak in my chest, "Are you a seer then? Do you have the gift of speaking to our loved ones gone before us?"

But Aldwin, suddenly alert, puts a restraining hand upon my arm and says with command.

"It is late in the hour; let us all seek our beds and things will appear more cheerful in the daylight."

3rd *February 1349*

The following morning I sought out Mistress Elford, though not when my husband was close by, for he is wary as the Church frowns heavily upon such Otherworldly communion and would declare her a thing of the Devil to be hung from tree or gallows. For myself, I believe the present world is brimming full enough with fear without adding phantoms to the real!

Our guest was anxious to speak only succour, begging me to hold faith and promising that better times will return to our homeland albeit calamity now engulfs us. I readily believed her, for there is something decent and honest about Joan Elford, simple peasant though she is, which makes me implicitly trust in her goodwill.

Alas, this was but the last leaf of hope before desolation. For during the evening, I was knocked down as hard as a punch can deliver and as low as a stone could drop, when the baker's boy brought a dire message to our door. The lad was passing my parents' home when the window was wedged open a crack, and through it my father shouted out for me to cease all visits from henceforth as the black sickness has befallen them! In shocked terror, I ran straight to Aldwin who said nought but held me closely bound to him, while I cried long in tribulation and despair.

All through the interminable appalling night I wrestled with demons, tossed like a homing pigeon between the harsh creed of the living to spurn the contaminated and a crushing compassion for my condemned parents. Lying grief-stricken upon our flock mattress, the cold-blooded reality of their fate closed ever in upon me until I felt myself a helpless trapped creature vainly struggling. In the long silence of the darkness I made my grim decision, but I had one small pilgrimage to perform ere morning broke.

When I heard Aldwin's breathing slow to sleep, I got up and crept along the corridor to the tiny boxroom at the back of the house. I have secretly visited this little room, at quiet moments when no one was about to see me, many times since becoming a wife. For it contains a treasure casket, awaiting the blossoming of our union, in the shape of a rocking cradle – sturdy and of dark endurable oak, standing under the eaves. I stood there a while, unwillingly dropping the golden thread leading to my future. With great sadness I set the empty cradle gently swinging to and fro.

I dressed before dawn, left a letter to Aldwin into which I poured all the love and remorse I could convey in a few sentences, bundled some necessities into a shoulder-sack and soundlessly left the house. I paused for a moment on the doorstep, knowing I would not pass this way again.

4ᵗʰ *February 1349*

My parents are in a horrendous state! The gross swellings (buboes, the hideous hallmark of this plague) bulge around neck, armpit and groin, seeping pus and blood. They lie side by side on their canopied bed, thrashing about in pain and racked by fearful bouts of coughing. The sheets and pillow beres, and their weak sore bodies, are stinking and soaked in diarrhoea and red-stained vomit; which I set to clean up as best I may, wiping away the defecations and gently bathing their chafed skin with rosewater.

My poor tormented mother seems hardly with us at all, delirious and whimpering, but my father is conscious and much distressed both by my presence and by the human excrement he could do nothing about. With a colossal effort he manages a feeble whisper.

"So sorry, so weak, I couldn't get up, so sorry, you must leave, Roesie, go go go go!"

Tears ran continuously down my cheeks as I tend them, no longer guilty for coming, I now curse myself for not coming sooner. Unforgiveable that I waited a whole night while I debated over the implications for myself and my marriage! When fetching water from the pantry, I can no longer hold back the sobs which convulse me. I am overcome, collapsing on the floor, and know not how to bear the great pity for my parents with such abominable misery upon them!

Not much more than an hour later, a loud hammering sounds upon the door and a fresh shock strikes me as I recognise my husband's voice insistently calling my name. In panic, I plead through the window gap,

"Please Aldwin, I cannot leave my parents while life lingers, please do not ask it of me! And once 'tis extinguished I will not return to you for surely I would bring this putrid fulsome decay with me!"

"Oh my darling, my cherished wife, I have not come to drag you away but to give my support! Just as it behoved you to stand by your parents in their utmost need, so I would be by your side all our married days however few these may be. Open the door and let me in, my love, otherwise I will beat it down!" he demands.

I know, despite – or maybe because of – the gravity with which he views life, there is a hidden streak of recklessness in him that the world fails to see. In his secret soul, Aldwin is a man of passion and I tremble lest he heedlessly throws all to the winds for the sake of a doomed love.

"Heart dear, pray understand, I cannot let you in! This is death, this is loathsome, most ghastly death! Grant me the solace of knowing you will survive this abhorrent disease! Live on my beloved! It will make some meaning of it all if you do." I beg, desperate to protect him.

Wasting no more time on words he leans forward, wrenching the shutter from its hinge, and climbs over the sill. Before I can hinder him, his arms are around me and I cry anew for such devotion as this.

6th February 1349

The skin around my parents' mouths and fingers is a dense jet black, decomposing even while life clings to their wracked bodies. Huge bruises stain limbs and torso where stale blood is pooling beneath, and fresh blood trickles out through every orifice. Mercifully, my mother no longer suffers having sunk deeper into oblivion; her breath thin and shallow now, with no other sign that life remains. But my poor, poor father retains sense of what is happening, constantly flinching in the agony of decaying flesh.

Throughout the last relentless days, he kept muttering his gratitude and of his bitter regret for the ruin he's inflicting upon me. I had to lean close to catch his appeal for his voice was no more than a rush of rasping air. Even after speech ceases altogether, his distraught eyes seem to be piteously begging my forgiveness. I cannot express what unimaginable grief this has brought me! How cruel is this scourge! What misery it wreaks!

I sought to find words to ease his anguish of mind, though I can do all too little to relieve the corruption of body,

"Don't fear, dear father, assuredly the Angel of Mercy is even now winging across infinity to reach you! Hush, can you not hear the soft brush of ethereal feathers? Soon you and I will meet up again, out of this earthly realm of pain and sickness, I know it, and in but a heartbeat! Don't doubt it my own good father, we will find a meadow in paradise, sunny yellow with our favourite buttercups, more delightful even than those you used to take me to, sitting high upon your shoulders, as a little girl. What a wondrous, fine childhood you gave me and I thank you! Be at peace now, dearest, just a little while longer, for soon Heaven will open wide its blessed arms to welcome you home!" For a brief instant I felt a tightening grip on my hand clasping his.

As the day wore on, his eyes closed and there seemed no awareness left to torture him. My beloved mother has now gone from us and this world forever.

Late in the afternoon a pale wintery sun filtered through as if to lure us outside, where we sat in my parents' enclosed courtyard, with a small quietude amidst our fatigue, knowing there is nothing more we can do for my father and his release too will be soon.

Some benevolent, kind soul has been leaving food and fresh water upon the doorstep each day, knocking and swiftly departing before we open up. I wonder who this may be, our maid Agatha perhaps or a brave neighbour who has defied the Plague's survival code of eschewing all contact, leaving each damned soul to die without aid or compassion.

We have taken some of these victuals and a jug of ale into the backyard, empty now except for the washing tub standing neglected in the corner. Despite the returning chill as the sun sinks, we huddle together beneath a blanket, reluctant to return to the noisome air within. My husband is exhausted as am I, and sombre, speaking little. I lean against him, grateful for his presence as never before. I implore him to tell me his thoughts, for I wish to share everything betwixt us for what little precious time remains.

"Is it not strange, Roesia," he replies slowly, "that the one certainty above all others is the very thing we will not heed? We're all heading the same way. To Death. This is our sure destination, for one and all. And yet we refuse to think on it! We spend our lives with averted faces, we put up screens to hide away the inevitable. And although the Church is forever rattling our mortal chains to cower us into obedience, this only makes us look away in greater apprehension.

"Is this not sheer absurdity? Do we really suppose that if we forbear from considering it, we can put Death off the scent – our scent! – so it may not hunt us down? But behold how our ludicrous defences have collapsed like tinder! This is what epidemic does, this is where pandemic leads us. Picking us up by the scruff of our necks and marching us right up to that Dreadful Encounter we've so desperately shrank from!

And now we must keep close company with that which is most atrocious. Now we must all together lift Death's hood and face the skull beneath, we must look into its hollow eye sockets, put our hand willingly into the gaping mouth, run our tender fingertips along the cutting edge of its scythe!"

As he speaks, I see the spectre of Death grown supreme, stalking the world as never before. Surely now the Grim Victor, as humanity is all but wiped out from the earth.

"*Why* is this our ultimate fear?" Aldwin questions. "What is it to die? Body gone, possessions gone, identity gone. What is left? What if there's really *nothing* left? Is this not the most frightful thing, to lose everything, to lose ourselves? No, it isn't. There's a worse fate even than oblivion, yet more diabolical than obliteration. What if death is but the prison portcullis to an everlasting Hell of everything most hateful!"

We both pause, reluctantly thinking upon the pathetic fate of the hapless human as we have been taught it, from pulpit and bible, and from our infancy.

"What you said to your father, do you believe it, Roesie?" his frank brown eyes beseech me. "The priests have proclaimed the Pestilence a punishment for our sins. Seeking to appease this Divine wrath and in true martyrdom, men have joined processions to flagellate themselves, flailed blood dry by leather straps studded with metal shards, but to no avail, God will not pause in His Retribution! Truly, if He can so chasten even such honest worthy folk as your parents, it fills me with trepidation as to the damnable vengeance awaiting us in His formidable dominions beyond the grave!"

I recall my last conversation with Joan Elford and I tell him of this.

"She believes all that we are told in this narrow time and place is not the whole nor even the real story." And I cautiously ask, "Could it not be, Aldwin, that our leaders – the king and ministers of government or of holy cloth – are but like the rest of us beneath their pomp and grandeur, straining to see their way in the fog?"

"Sweetheart, not so long ago that would have sounded hot headed heresy to my ears," he wryly smiles, "but today, with death lying within the house behind us and spreading unrelentingly across our country slaughtering all in its wake, I doubt everything I had once believed certain! All that is unprecedented is shocking us daily anew in this cursed city, and that which was unthinkable is now being challenged by rich and poor alike.

"Many tormented souls, defeated by this vile disease which blackens the body even before it dies, have turned their backs upon religion and succumbed to immoral depravity. Others go rabid, gathering in rampaging crazed mobs, scapegoating thousands of innocent Jews massacred all across Europe." he acknowledges with sorrowful regret. "Goodness knows, all we pitiful citizens of London have need of something strong and uplifting to believe in, to uphold us in these ugliest of end times!"

He cradles my hand between his, lifting it to his lips, and avows, "For me it has been you, my adored wife. Your love and my love for you belittles all else, even the Plague itself! This is why I could not be separated from you, what you call my sacrifice is, in truth, my salvation."

Before I can answer and from a full heart, a sudden stabbing pain cuts through my gut like a chopping blade and I bend over double, crouching in a tight ball upon the dirt floor.

"Roesia, what ails you?" Aldwin cries in alarm but as I look at him, once the spasm has passed, and reach up to stroke his flushed face, hot and feverish to my touch despite the chill of dusk, I give no answer except a kiss upon his damp cheek. We both know.

10th *February 1349*

My head is pounding, my throat is on fire and I feel I'm burning alive in an all-devouring furnace! Aldwin's skin is aflame with an angry rash which he can't cease from scratching, until the old flea bites on his arms are red raw pits. My body is pockmarked with countless black dots and I have lost the will to continually dab at the plague-boils, bulging in every fold of my body, as the oozing pus seeps through the linen of my shift. Most frightening of all are the ferocious seizures which sporadically grip my husband, during which he turns rigid from head to toe whilst shaking 'til his teeth rattle! This malaise leaves him limp and almost lifeless after each attack.

Indeed, an indescribable weakness of limb has beset us both, becoming increasingly disabling with each hour. We can barely move about the room and for the second day have failed to make the short walk from parlour to front door. What would be the purpose? Even had either of us the strength to lift up any supplies left there, the sickening nausea and violent vomiting which incessantly drains us makes any food repugnant. Added to this, all excretions stink with the foulest, most offensive fetid stench you could ever gag upon!

At noon we heard the familiar knock upon the door, vaguely listening for the sound of footsteps hurriedly withdrawing. Instead, the click of the latch being lifted sounded loudly in the quietness of the house and in walked Joan Elford. Astonishment that it is this kindly matron, scarcely more than a stranger, who has been our secret benefactor at first kept me speechless in wonder. Then I, and Aldwin beside me as if in one accord, struggled to sit up from our prone position, painfully with aching joints and enfeebled muscles. Joan hurried over and besought us to lie back, though I laboured to thank her for such charity beyond all conceivable selflessness.

"I have seen it all before, my dears," she answered, "and no more will I go on fleeing while the Great Mortality mocks my futile flight. I cannot outrun so mighty a foe! It is time to accept the fragility of the body against this world domination. Here I will rest my tired bones with gratitude that the vain chase is over."

With much solicitude, Joan has attended to our care throughout the day and finally, now midnight approaches, she gently raises our useless bodies, sore to the touch where the infected buboes – swollen to the size of chicken eggs – protrude, to rest up against the wall with a rug placed to soften it. She has lit many candles giving the room a yellow halo, while dryly apologising for stealing our entire month's store to bring here. I laugh weakly, a sensation of which I had no longer believed myself capable. Aldwin turns his face a fraction towards me and I see a faint smile upon it.

"It's goodly reprieve to hear you laugh, my own Roesie." he avers.

Joan stays close and talks to us, speaking of such wondrous ideas that the nightmare of our rancid flesh diminishes a little, the agony seems a fragment less unbearable, and even the candlelight glows more golden, keeping this dread night at bay. She knows not of Heaven as reward, nor Hell as damnation, but of our eternal Spirit home where we live and love without pain or distress and with a freedom unimagined here.

"Ever since I can remember" she tells us, "I have been talking with my companions who reside out of body as much as with those who reside within it. When this atrocious sickness ravaged through my village only my Spirit helpers remained at my side, with such words of encouragement as enabled me to carry on whilst others, distraught and helpless, drowned in the desperate well without foothold."

Her belief in the company of our unseen kin folk – and she speaks as if they are in this very room beside us – brings me comfort and her visions lift my heart.

"When you watched your parents suffering their last hours, take solace to know all but a remaining residue of their soul energy had already left and was set free from the atrocity of their physical trial. You too will depart soon, as easily as slipping off a smooth silken shawl, and you will go home gratefully holding hands one with the other," she assures us.

Despite the throbbing trauma of my decomposing body, my Spirit expands beyond it and the horror of the Plague falls away to but a bump in the magnificent journey of our souls.

I remember nothing more until, awakening in the hour before dawn with Aldwin asleep, unconscious or dead beside me, I felt a cool hand upon my face as Joan lent over and raised my head, spinning in fever, to rest upon her lap and began wiping away oily beads from my forehead with the hem of her kirtle.

Moira came to after a couple of hours to hear her tummy rumbling furiously, gushing like white water rapids through a subterranean cavern in a bid for attention. She had been so engrossed in the whole new (even older) lifetime opening up from some bottomless recess of her mind (direct download from the Quantum Field? the Akashic Records? a celestial Wikipedia?) that she'd forgotten to eat. The sun had dropped down in the sky and her legs were practically tin-man rusted solid from sitting so long, so it was a squeaky, stiff legged stagger back down to the car. Home and hot parsnip soup was very welcome.

While regalvanising on the sofa that evening, with Snigger purring on her lap and looking harmless (as long as she didn't attempt to move), Moira scribbled down all her retrieved memories before they slipped away forever on the merciful River Lethe. A forgiving river of forgetfulness without question, to wash away such an overwhelming emotional overload!

With the monstrosity of Roesia's last days still in her, Moira found herself crying. Not just for Roesia but also for Hannah, for herself, for *everyone* in our endless myriad of forgotten lives. We are so much older, we go so much deeper, we have borne so much more than this millisecond life we're living! She gulped on a wave of pity for all that suffering gone before, an aching burden hidden within, lost from conscious memory but carried from lifetime to lifetime throughout the eons. An endless cycle in which we return, over and over, to the frail human lot of disease, war, persecution, exploitation, poverty and famine. All so savage, cruel, debasing, deadening, intolerable!

"Are they embedded in our DNA, sealed in our subconscious, soldered into our souls?" Moira asked herself in despair. "Will we never escape, when still today we're again facing our old enemy, epidemic, still dying all across the world?"

"The Cataclysmic Mystic would say," she reasoned in an attempt to heave herself out of the trough, and referring to the ultimate kick-arse psychic pundit in cyberspace, "our hope is ourselves. Humanity, as a species, is lifting itself up

– infinitesimally – with each passing century, throughout millennium, transforming the circle to a spiral."

She was feeling so traumatised from reliving the Black Death first-hand she finally got *exactly* why the unbearable weight of our past lives is normally kept from us, and wondered how she'd managed to sidestep this cosmic safety valve twice now. After serious deliberation she came to the discombobulating conclusion that, for the first time at any rate, it had been a last resort from her exasperated oversoul as the *only* remaining way to budge such a stubborn stuck-in-the-muck mule as she'd been up till then! Not that she wasn't grateful but *how humiliating!*

As for the characters involved, she picked up the common thread weaving between her three (known) lifetimes straight away, recognising via sensation rather than appearance (she must remember to tell Hugo what a hunk he'd been in the fourteenth century!) her husband Aldwin as Hugh Kemp and currently her dear chum Hugo. And how apt, she mused, just as she had taken in the fleeing Joan Elford so had Joan, returning two centuries on as Martha Herrington, repaid this hospitality by giving little Hannah a home when her parents deserted her.

Considering Mistress Elford's mediumistic abilities, it now made total sense why Pat had insisted on dragging Moira to spiritualist churches over the years; including the aptly named Oddfellows Hall in Redruth and the quaint little loft church in Bread Street, Penzance – originally and for many decades decorated by wall covering of pegboard to which somewhat pathetic bunches of yellowing plastic flowers were pinned.

Of late there had been a drastic refurbishment, the pegboard and plastic floral offerings had rather sadly gone, while the truly awful hymn book had been replaced by purple plastic A4 folders of Abba, Johnny Nash and The Carpenters songs. The united rendering of "I can see clearly now the rain has gone" and such like, are now accompanied by CD player replacing the late elderly church pianist. Doris does still attend Sunday service at the Loft but she wafts over with the deceased flock now, all politely elbowing each other to get to the front of the Spirit queue to the medium. Pat, since her death, had been particularly apt at getting her terse criminating comments in first (much to the entertainment of a giggling congregation), advising Moira on such things as her wind problem and delivering sporadic etheric slaps for minor misdemeanour.

"Still, whatever the pleasures of the fifth dimension," Moira explained to everyone during the tea and custard creams get-together in the kitchen afterwards, "Pat must be missing the real thing, nothing is as satisfying as a fully 3-D smart smack across the back of the hand!"

Despite such irritating idiosyncrasies, Moira greatly valued her three-lifetime old friend – more than ever in fact, as she'd been a real brick in this newly exhumed incarnation too. Regardless of century, Pat /Martha/Joan had always been there when she'd most needed her, with a wider perspective on life/ after life/the cosmos, allowing Moira/Hannah/Roesia to loosen the ill-fitting, tight-laced corset of cultural dictates which was making living so awkward. (While on the subject of corsets, Moira remembered she'd once worn an early Tudor version while living at Laslett Hall and had decided, there and then, that whalebone stays served the same function for women as sackcloth and ashes did for Lent!)

In medieval London, poor Roesia found herself in an abysmal era during which half the population of Europe was wiped out by the flea, lice and rat carried bacteria Yersinia pestis; all of whom died thoroughly godawful deaths, shut up in their solitary houses with only their household, down to the last one standing. Right in the nick of time, Joan had shown up with introductions to her Spirit family waiting to greet Roesia as she passed through to the living other side of death's door.

"Hmm, I might owe you, Pat" she conceded to the ceiling. "Promise I'll make the special punchbowl next time round!"

In Joan's honour, and as a little thank you for the gift of benevolent belief, e.g. death is not just loss, it's also gain – and so easing the trip over no end – she dashed off a short verse.

You are not alone.
Your Spirit guides are nudging your elbow,
Your guardian Angel tugging at your sleeve,
Your ancestors snooze not in sleepy barrows.

We are plagued with epoch turning times,
When the microscopic
Toppled the apex predator.
We learnt again to be vulnerable,
We learnt again we stand best
together.

Though the Jury was still out as far as Moira was concerned, having lived during two worldwide pandemics of fourteenth-century bubonic plague and twenty-first century coronavirus, as to whether the Chinese proverb "May you live in interesting times!" is a covert blessing or just a really, *really* spiteful curse...

21ˢᵗ *April 2020*

Moira was agog to tell Hugo all about it, so she phoned first thing in the morning and a drowsy, slightly grumpy voice answered her call.

"Mogs, what are you thinking of! What's the point of no work, no pubs or clubs, and no visitors if not to wallow undisturbed in bed in the morning?"

"Ha!" she retorted, "and to think you used to be the perfect gentleman when we were first married! I knew it wouldn't last!"

A pause, and then: "Oh blooming heck, you're going to explain that at great length aren't you, hang on till I get a latte," he stalled and put the phone down.

Ten minutes later a more civilised Hugo rang back, by which time Moira had her notes out ready to pursue after a polite swopping of pleasantries. (These consisted of enquiring how her feline fiend was doing without its human scratching post – Hugo himself – to which Moira retaliated that he shouldn't turn up with no catnip and wearing tempting stylish clothes that snag.)

"The Black Death! Holy Heifer!" he exclaimed, post medieval disaster reading, "Seriously, Mo? London in 1349, Wuhan in 2019 – just not the place to be!"

"I know! I know!" Moira wailed pathetically. "*So* need to work on my timing!"

"Have you ever considered dying comfortably in bed as a senile old biddy?" Hugo grinned down the phone waves at his impossible buddy.

"It's scheduled in for this time round," Moira confirmed (crossing her fingers).

"Come on then, spit it out! A reason for the season. Give us your pet theory. Know you didn't sleep last night till you'd worked it through to the last why and wherefore!" he teased.

"Well, I do have the odd thought if you'd like to hear it," she offered, aiming to sound humbly diffident but not quite making it. "This is what I reckon: Time is thought to speed along a nice consistent straight line right? But what if it doesn't? What if our history (personal and collective) loops in the slowly ascending coils of a spiral? And at any point along the time curve, you can just reach down and reawaken the echoes of a past era at the same point in the ring below it, or the one below that and so forth? The exact spot that shares the same refrain, the same calamity, the same mortal dilemma visited and revisited and revisited again, as we gather fresh insights, try out better solutions and hopefully edge forward an iota or so each time? Maybe?"

She decided against sharing her thoughts as to why *her*, figuring a little omission between old pals is perfectly permissible.

"Sounds sound. Einstein wasn't into a fixed lineal space time either, he reckoned it's relatively bendy." Hugo accredited, to which Moira inflated like a bouncy castle.

"And how's your research into the ANSWER TO IT ALL coming along while we're at it?" He couldn't resist, after endless convoluting late-night discussions on that one.

"Um, that's still a job in progress, give me another lifetime and I'll have it pat." she replied, with a slight twinge of dissatisfaction and deflating a smidge in smugness.

"Anyways, it's tote thrilling for you, poppet, but must say I'm a trifle peeved at my performance as the dull husband!" Hugo griped. "Where is my style, my effervescence, my wacky left field perspicacity? Just a dab disappointing. who wants to be goody-two-shoes? Though, I suppose at least it shows I've come a long way in character development over the centuries. Glory be! Reincarnation is more than just another trip on the merry (or in our case not-so-merry) -go-round after all. *Voila! Me voici!* Progress!"

"What do you mean 'disappointed'! You were a real dish when you were Aldwin, and you simply *adored* me!" Moira refuted outraged, "Not completely sure I wouldn't swop back to the earlier model!" But appending post-haste, as she understood that Hugo is a wee bit sensitive under the persona, "Just joking, hun!"

("But am I? Really, really? He'd been *gorgeous* and how fab to be cherished! Oh pooey the Plague!" she muttered mutely to herself.)

"He just sounds a bit boring," Hugo grumbled on, having taken exception to her little joke. "I mean *me* – a pious churchgoing prig! No wonder I opted for a real shake-up life in the fifteen hundreds. Hugh Kemp was a truly mixed up, inwardly tormented, deviant soul – so much more likeable!"

"Aldwin was a hero! Bravely facing the Plague in order to support me when everyone else was not very safely in lockdown, and I won't hear you criticised." Moira insisted reproachfully.

"Nor you, sugar plum. But must dash, gotta catch Miss Marple; divine Geraldine McEwan, so omniscient! We'll chat more later, say hello to the little furry Freddy Krueger for me," he wound up, but tagged on before ringing off:

"Oh, by the by, and apologies if I've not said it for 671 years, but *still* adore you, Mogs!"

1st *May 2020*

2020 saw a very demure, maypoleless Beltane – difficult getting up to shenanigans with social distancing (not that these ever featured in Moira's daily planner app) so she went on a solitary pilgrimage to Madron Well instead. The day was sunny with clear skies, like so many days had been since lockdown as if determined to rub it in, and the path between the white bloom of hawthorn bushes was lace-bordered with wood anemone. The authentic sacred spring actually bubbles up in a marshy gully some way into the tangled thickets, reached only by squelching your way through bog determined to suck the wellies off your feet, so Moira settled for the muddy puddle under the clootie tree for her May Day ritual.

This darling month of buds and blossom and floral fashions has seen thousands of pilgrims coming to the well, stretching back to time immemorial. Legend says by hanging up a clootie dipped in the hallowed water, your ailments will disappear as your clootie slowly rots away. Whilst once these consisted of strips of woven cloth, today the multi-colourful tree is festooned with keyring trinkets, nylon ribbons, the odd sock, hair bungies, a dog collar and sundry other twenty-first century knick-knacks that the modern-day pilgrim might have at hand.

After performing her solo ceremony for world healing in these sad uncertain times, and dangling a tissue from the lowest branch, she went to sit in the little granite chapel, now a ruin with roof long gone. It's built upon the site of a fourth-century Celtic structure, dating from the arrival of the early Christians in Cornwall who – with what Moira condemned as the usual reprehensible cover-up by the invader – rededicated the well to St Madern, usurping the former goddess or Nature Spirit who had presided there for eons and putting a lot of ancestral noses out of joint as they turned in their graves.

With the present mortality rate for COVID-19 being 288,000 globally (and rising exponentially) Moira was in sober, contemplative mood as she sat on the old stone alter, listening to the tinkling water flowing melodically into the corner basin. Over and over, she reviewed, unstoppable epidemics have swept the planet in deadly waves. TB, cholera, smallpox, the 1918 influenza, Ebola, AIDs (33 million), MERS, SARS and many more mass killers forever beating humanity back into a subservient position beneath the multitudinous mutating microorganism! Even throughout the rest of the fourteenth century there were further outbreaks, including "The Plague of the Children" which targeted the young in the way coronavirus meanly picks on the elderly today.

"If *the meek shall inherit the earth*' the infinitesimal corona pathogen is certainly holding its own," Moira reflected, "and *I've got a really bad feeling* about this one!"

Today's encounter has come some way since the sheer sordidness of the Black Death, with advances in hospital care, scientific understanding and public information (though misinformation – to say nothing of downright lying! – was itself currently spreading across the web like a badly R-rated contagion). And even in the modern era of medical marvels, disease is still able to wreak mayhem, turning millions into a mass of jitters and sending us reeling from the shock of sudden loss.

"We're being shaken out of our self-gratification and habitual shopping," she postulated. "With the shutdown of department stores, hairstylists and beauty salons we're compelled to reassess the BBLs, cosmetic preening and swanky designer labelling of our superficial consumer society. What *really* matters is not so different today than it's ever been. And so we carry on, humans are a resilient species."

That is those who are left. Moira sat in the remains of the little chapel and thought about all those millions of people who wouldn't made it through.

The Sadness of the World
rolls round in a great wave,
drowning us, country by country.
A ceaseless tsunami of sorrow,
through century after century.

The streets empty in incomprehension,
the crowds are gone, each alone
counts the cost, day by day,
from behind closed doors.

The air is emptying from their lungs,
life is fading,
slipping out in the wan March sunshine.
All is dreadful here.

Life is precarious in 2020.
Life is precious always.

7th *May 2020*

The coven was doing this month's full moon circle on Zoom. They'd skipped the April one altogether, as since the ban on social gatherings members had been all atwitter, flapping about and generally failing to get their heads around the technology. Now that Everest had been conquered, they were each sitting expectantly in front of their PCs with a candle.

The biggest disadvantage of a cybernetic meeting proved to be the lack of speaking stick (all talking at once and nobody listening). This was further compounded by the Hollywood effect of being on camera. It was noticeable that everyone was looking a smidgen more glamourous than usual, wearing their plushest cloaks and sporting fetching appendages of malachite or amethyst jewellery. And this enhanced appearance achieved despite the embargo on hairdressers (though fortunately long and scraggly is still the trademark of the witch even if the wart and bristly chin has gone out of fashion).

Moira kicked off with her latest poem, unwisely mentioning it was written at Madron Well which shifted attention to Rowan who was born in the village nearby. (Once 'Rianne' but she wasn't one for the same-ol'-same-ol'; although her mum Shirl – who secretly prefers the name she'd given her – usually addresses her as RiUmRowan.)

Rowan displayed her collection of orb snapshots taken around the renowned spring (and a chance mention of the surrounding medieval landscape even succeeded in catching Moira's attention, 'medieval' being her new personal buzz word). These curious pics had caught hovering discs of tinted light as the ethereal de-cloaked itself for a photo shoot, and starred materialising misty apparitions open to a colourful plethora of interpretations.

"See that blue orb there? It followed her home one day," Shirl corroborated her daughter's claim, "we're sure it's the Archangel Michael."

"But what's more surprising," Rowan excitedly chimed in, "is that physicists actually report an interface between orb and photographer, they respond to human prompt! So I'm prompting Michael to be my personal PA (Parking Angel) –

always good to bring in the Big Winged Guys when looking for a parking space!"

"That makes me recall a talk I once went to by the late dowser, Hamish Miller," Gwen snuck in quickly, annexing the metaphysical limelight. "He demonstrated how ley lines evolve to repeated dowsing. Fascinating! The earth isn't just listening, it's talking back!"

"Yes, now you mention it, She has spoken to me on occasion." Moira, who had a t-shirt printed to that effect in 2012 and been wearing it ever since, acknowledged with a show of sham reluctance.

Ignoring this completely, Gwen continued, "And if we could just take a quick peep at this month's transits before we start, I think I can find my ephemeris," – placing her hand on it, right in front of her on the desk and fixing reading glasses more securely on nose.

"Pluto, Lord of Hades is dallying with the Almighty Zeus (Jupiter) in a planetary show-down. The Pluto Jupiter conjunction is infamous for popping up in pandemic years: 1918 Spanish flu, 1981 Aids epidemic, Russian Plague 1777 and the Black Death when it was in full swing," she briefed everyone, rustling through her wad of notes. "And it's not over yet, triple line up in autumn, we've only just got going I'm afraid."

"Drat, it's not as if I haven't done my fair share of mass pestilences," Moira mumbled to herself.

"What's it all about then, witchy friends?" Maddie posed the hundred-dollar hundred-answers question. "What are the circulating coronavirus conjectures and which ones can we swallow with a G and T?"

"Censorship," Amyrah suggested, "the internet dictators are blocking podcasts in an information drip feed by the status quo?"

"Back to the mainstream media spooning us diluted slops! Why can't they let us make up our own minds?" Rowan, who combined a liking for combustible conspiracy controversy with her love of matches, moaned.

"Hmm, hate to sound a cynic, but not sure we've *have* got the necessary 20-20 vision yet, even in 2020," Vicky appraised sceptically. "I'm just not convinced I *can* trust other people to sift through all the online twaddle and tommyrot in order to make the right choices to protect my health – not if their election preferences are anything to go by! Just look at some of the politicians we voted in to rule us across the globe! We might as well hand over world domination to Larry the cat!" referring to Downing Street's most famous and possibly most intelligent resident.

"Sedition prohibition then," Roz countered. "Subversion diversion. No more crowds allowed. How can Extinction Rebellion take action when we're isolated in our separate cells? Take away our right to gather and we're powerless, aren't we?"

"But ironically a lot of its aims (reducing human activity which impacts on nature) have actually been achieved *through* lockdown! Nature's the all-round winner at the moment. Spooky that!" Bea wryly pointed out.

"And pretty unprecedented," Nellie chipped in, using *The Word* of 2020.

"I tell you what *isn't* getting 24-hour media coverage," Rowan contested (as a perpetual blond who's always got a panting male following, provocation was ingrained by now) "the twenty-one thousand people who die *every day* due to poverty! Kicks COVID into the bucket don't you think?"

"You wouldn't say that if it was *your mother* killed by the virus! Not so insignificant then!" Bea argued hotly. Shirl nodded, having to side against her daughter Rowan on that one.

Maddie intervened at this point to avoid the usual coven squabble (generally settled in the end as "equally valid differences of opinion", though 'the end' could take some time coming...) and edged them back on track, "So *why* this world pandemic which *has* got our full attention?"

"Try this one on for size," Moira tentatively offered. "All those deaths, in a sense they're all really suicides!"

This was met with a rare but definitely disapproving silence.

"All deaths are suicide in a sense," new moon clan member Gill finally volunteered, kindly saving Moira from further social ostracism, over and above what the lockdown had already achieved for a single lass living on her own. "If we opt for life in the tough third density we need an exit strategy. If death didn't exist we'd have to invent it."

"Exactly!" Moira agreed thankfully, "What if all these thousands of people are enrolled in a *social revolution?* A planetary insurgence. What if on a soul level they're making a mass political statement in the form of a biological boycott? (i.e. by dying.) Look at all pandemics, if you view them as demonstrations against prevailing social injustice then the major reforms which invariably follow can be seen as the hidden agenda. All those deaths *achieved* something! They weren't coincidental or pointless, they were the lynchpin of human progress!" she yelled at the computer, raising the volume tab in an attempt to sound more convincing.

"Mmm, there might be something in that," Gill continued mulling over, ever game, "The 1918 influenza followed the terrible futility of the Great War. People had lost faith and left life in droves through the pandemic. Our attitude to war changed after that, re-edited as 'The War to end all wars'. It didn't, of course, but at least it was no longer considered 'Good and sweet to die for one's country' and war stopped being exonerated." (Gill had done Wilfred Owen for her English O'level exam.)

"And after the Black Death, serfdom was phased out and so things improved for the peasant majority." Moira informed her online hub, thrilled at the opportunity to exhibit her newly acquired expertise in fourteenth-century history with offhand nonchalance.

"There's still plenty of deprivation going on in low-income countries but coronavirus has hit the *developed* nations first and most heavily, at least for the moment." Nellie queried.

"Life isn't just about one species – us! It's about how we treat other creatures and our damage to the earth itself." Roz steered the conversation, whittling away at her own agenda. "And, yes, China has already improved it's laws concerning wet markets and animal welfare."

"I'm not saying it's a conscious choice, more a decision on the psychic level to make their deaths worth something." Moira went on to explain when she got the chance. "Probably put in as a footnote when drawing up their pre-birth life plans. By exiting in such massive numbers, it can't slip under the rug unnoticed, the world *has* to create change!"

Maddie eventually said what they were all thinking, "This is all a bit too deep and profound for you Mogs, huh? HUH?"

"I got it from Jane Roberts' *Seth Book*," Moira owned up, "you can find it on YouTube."

"There you are then, back to the zodiac's three heavies! Pluto pushing transformation and Saturn reaping karma, the consequences of our actions. Jupiter just makes everything bigger to grab our attention, in this case COVID going viral across the media and globe." Gwen clinched the debate.

Vicky, the group's Virgo, seized the moment and called order for the ritual, including a power-raising to be sent out into the ether with an automated task of squishing the virus, in the air and on every surface, with an energetic blasting agent generated from everyone crooning Christy Moore's cover of *Burning Times* loudly into their webcams. The libation was dedicated to their own wonderful NHS heroine, nurse Gill, with everyone raising a glass of bubbly to the pc screen; Rowan wickedly held up a box of chocolates for virtual reality partaking – *not* gratefully received by the rest.

13th *May 2020*

The first baby bunny hops towards coming out of the lockdown cubbyhole and everyone's snug-fitting shrunken comfort zone, included being allowed to meet up with one friend in the park and shouting at each other from a distance of six feet or so. Hugo and Moira utilized this to reacquaint themselves with the non-pixel version of each other, taking independent picnics to Tregeseal stone circle.

Swopping notes had become a different experience for everybody since March; nothing happening in the outer world in terms of work dramas, who's cheating on who, what's showing at the cinema, next holiday booking etc, meant that conversation had to shift to one's inner world. (Moira had always ranked her internals over her outside anyway.)

Personally, she looked to her nocturnal dreams to find out what was really going on with her (her inner psyche usually sent her daleks, orcs and White Walkers, while featuring her local library staffed by a swarm of Dementors). Despite missing her soothing, soporific Friday evening dream group, held in a Morrab Road attic with comforting nibbles, cushions, fleecy blankets and kindly soft lighting, Moira had still managed a dash of lucid dreaming during lockdown.

Becoming awake and aware in the right brained dreamworld promises all sorts of perks and spin-offs like divine guidance, miraculous healing, enlightenment, Nirvana, etc. Though admittedly, each time Moira broke through the unconscious barrier in her dreams she'd kind of got stuck on eating chocolate – heaven! – and maybe even better (delish *and* calorie-free) than the forbidden thing in the real (possibly) world. EUREKA!

Hugo was more macho about the whole thing and had been experimenting with Out of Body experiences, since the-world-put-on-pause allowed him extra reading time to research. After a lot of laborious breathing exercises and trying to squeeze himself through a door in his pineal gland, he'd finally got a taster and was keen to share.

"Weird or what! I woke up in the middle of the night and, remembering not to move a muscle, I succeeded in elbowing my arms out of my arms (if you see what I mean) but just couldn't budge anything else. Then I heard a voice say 'roll out' which I did and Bingo – I'd made it! Out-of-this-world spectacular!

"Before my body got a chance drag me back to its physical lockdown, I ran away from it and went out into the garden. Everything looked in mint condition, as if it hadn't been taken out of the wrapper yet. And I was just getting the hang of the flying thing and wondering which direction to head for Machu Picchu, when this giant – armchair size – bee with a supersonic buzz appeared heading straight at me! Blast! Must have been in a dream all along. Just bog-standard phantasmagoria."

Moira sympathised with his aborted lift off to interdimensional travel but then came up with a happy idea.

"*Or* you really were out of your body but instead of being in the etheric, which after all is just a carbon copy of the physical, you were actually in the astral!" she suggested, feeling quite chuffed with herself (she'd been doing her reading too).

"Hmm," Hugo considered, not as obviously ecstatic and bowled over as Moira deemed he should be. "Well, the payoff would then be that I've had my first O.B.E. but on the flip side if I'd strayed into the astral by mistake then I have some serious psychological glitches to fix!"

"Uh?" Moira queried, with her customary blank canvas look.

"The fourth dimensional astral realm is super plasticine malleable, as impressionable as *Sunday Telegraph* readers. Our beliefs, thoughts and feelings imprint there, like a duckling to ma duck or werewolf to Bella Swan's baby. I must have been buzzing with an awful lot of aggro for ages to make that gigantic bee, and it's probably about to manifest in this dimension – yikes!"

"Well, have you?" she demanded, not feeling like letting him off the hook after his failure to acknowledge the genius of her etheric/astral dichotomy inspiration.

Hugo looked distinctly uncomfortable, even from a two-metre distance.

"Spoiler alert then! I realize that you think I'm a cool, take-it-in-my-stride sort of dude but, to be honest Mogs, I'm afraid I've still got a dash of Hugh Kemp stashed away in my psyche's sealed up cellar," he grudgingly outed himself. (As if she didn't know, bless him!)

"OK petal, if I must, here goes with embarrassing icky confession time!" he managed to muster, rather red around the gills, "I'm ashamed to say I suffer from an unhealthy mental compulsion. I'm addicted to brooding on resentment and revenge – just can't seem to stop! It's cos I always end up with such pants relationships. It's like I've got the *Big Mug, psychopaths dock your twisted dagger and bloody axe here* Syndrome. (Is that a real syndrome? If it isn't, it should be! I know I'm not on my own here, me and half the world end up shat on and *narcissist* is the new normal for the other half, right?)

"I appreciate that my various *objets d'amour* are just immature, nappy modelling, toddler souls on the spiritual development scale and one shouldn't expect much above pee and poop. And I don't really object to the complete selfishness and all-consuming self-absorption, we're all human at the moment after all. Or even the titanic entitlement that what's mine is theirs and what's theirs should be considerably more! I can just about stay afloat with the obvious fact that they don't give a didley-squat about my feelings – but what really gets me miffed is the jubilant kick they get from trampling all over them with their spikey muddy football boots! By the time they've dumped me,

I've been wrung out like an overused and abused floorcloth, continually mopping up someone else's muck!

"Hate to say it, but I'm still feeling *mega shirty* about it all. Flaming Nora! I've been so steamed up and hot under the collar all my polo necks have scorch marks! Oh, I know, cross with me-the-mopper-upper too but I can remember in dismal detail, yonks after the shipwreck, every single little comment made and action taken – or failed to be! You just wouldn't believe how much mind space I waste coming up with what I should have/could have said/done in 101 long-been-and-gone-and-best-forgotten scenarios. And then I start bashing myself up for trashing my brain with all this flotsam and jetsam junk!

"Ahh! Botheration this *interminable infernal internal prattle!* Beam Me Up to a planet where we don't have cerebral matter with perpetual negative thought circuits to get into a neural rut with! Less touchy-tender feelings would be a relief too. I want to be one of those Greys on Mars next time, just for a break!"

From her anti-contagious safe distance, Moira held her arms open wide,

"Metaphorical hug, hun!"

Back home after dark, Moira racked her brains for some way to cheer up her tortured-soul pal. To be frank, with one MAJOR EXCEPTION (her fourteenth-century self), all his love-interest picks had been hands down minging! On a par in fact, with that up-his-own-backside Ralph Crouch or the greasy gummy Jake who she had to admit, even though he was her dad, was a wholly disreputable character.

"Hecate's herpes!" she groaned, "this reincarnation business can be pretty messed up when you start spotting all the re-runs! And the Law of Attraction is just a sneaky cosmic rat-trap; we end up sharing the sofa with some guy stuck on the same knotty impasse but from the other side of the coin. If you're brill at looking after others but as for self-care – you just nail yourself to the wall and hand out darts, then you'll fancy someone who never gives a nanomite about anyone else but has got looking after their own interests down to a tee! (Though maybe not really, as who wants to be The Mean Girl?)"

Clearly, Hugo needs to swop his rose-tinted spectacles for a shite detector, learn the "No" word, set up passport control across all his slip roads, build healthy boundary fences where his "open house" signs are now, and rent out his subconscious dungeon of masochism to a self-esteem coach – but *what do you do* when you're irresistibly attracted to scumbags? Or even just the wrong people? She truly sympathised having been in love with her male best friend, who was gay, in her last life.

The answer came to her after she'd fallen asleep, still on the sofa so as not to incommode Snigger. (Feasibly her own shadow cat – possessing claws *so* could have sorted Moira's people problems!) In her dream she was in an infant school playground with other five-year-olds, all engaged in hopscotch, chalked out on the tarmac. They each threw a stone at the relevant number and, in the tradition of the game, had to hop and jump up to and then leap over it. Just as in the Game of Lives we progress through a sequence of experiences in an Evolutionary Hopscotch – in order to focus our attention, perfect our skills and win the match. For sure, the farther away the square you're aiming your stone at, the harder to hit target and the more times you get stuck and keep missing a go, but eventually you land it, leap over and move on.

The difference between the game she was playing in her dream and the game we're all playing in life, is that kids enjoy hopscotch! Perhaps that's how life's meant to be too but we make such heavy work of it. Or maybe the human as a soul host is just too damn sensitive, like a mushy marshmallow susceptible to all that ucky pain from even the slightest, let alone the hard knocks of life, in a way the jolly discarnated soul merrily planning its next trip couldn't quite envisage when out of body?

"Just as our outer world reflects our inner self," she inferred further, "so does the journey into the incarnate paint us with the pale face of Pierrot, frantically juggling his multiple life theme balls and crying in the rain.

"But," Moira grinned at her scratchy cat, "we're all laughing clowns in the Spirit!"

On waking, she sent Hugo a quick email along with her seven-century-long love:

"Dear darling Hugo, kind, dogged and brave master class hopscotch champion! Have figured out that what we should do, as soon as first contact is permitted, to fix relationship probs and smooth out inner wrinkles, is to start up a games club. Board games, kids' games, non-competitive tag and tiddlywinks, whatever – as long as it's FUN!"

1st June 2020

Another heavenly spring day, with radiant Nature knee-deep in a lavish luscious floral spread, saw Moira buoyantly bouncing down a path lined with the bold magenta of lofty headed foxgloves. Lots of little blue butterflies, like confetti cut from a summer's sky, flitted on the breeze. Swallows swooped about in glee, announcing the arrival of the sunny season despite border closures and forced quarantine.

Moira had just had a quick refreshing (well, invigorating) swim in the crystal-clear sea beneath Pendeen lighthouse. This is a short chunky lighthouse painted a genial white, to which she had always felt some personal affinity; there is something comfy and comely about the squat and well-rounded after all.

She lay out on the grassy clifftop, amply scattered with fat pink cushions of thrift, soaking up the warm sun and happily warbling *"I have a song to sing Oh!"* from *The Yeoman of the Guard*. High above her head a Peregrine falcon spread its tail feathers to hover soundlessly and Moira relaxed her whole being, sighing in sleepy satisfaction while the world hummed on in its present pandemic pandemonium.

Her musings today were all admirably blissful and complacent. Where had life taken her? More or less to where she wanted to be. And more or less to *who* she was ok to be (or could at least grouch along with on a tart crab apple day). Her life, she reflected, had been threefold like a cheaper set of Russian dolls, the first opening up to one lived before and another before that.

Each had spun her in a giddy helix, flipping her horizons topsy-turvy, revamping her from tip to toe and creating havoc in the neat orderly drawers of her taken-for-granted reality. Lifting the lid on a triple tiered scrumptious chocolate-box, with a holographic forever fluctuating picture on top. Taking her deeper into herself and out the other side (to where another 'herself' was impatiently waiting), unfurling layer upon layer of Shrek's onion!

Moira deliberated on how the current world scenario is likewise just an itsy-bitsy bite of a bigger plus-sized picture.

"Life itself is really just one long lockdown," she lazily speculated. "And you'd think once everything's gone – all the parties and picnics, lunches out and trips to Barcelona – you'd wouldn't be left with anything. But it's not like that, for it's *then* that you find something there you hadn't even noticed before; maybe not solid, nothing you can put your finger or foot on *but really there*, in a nebulous gloopy sort of way!

"It's as if after emptying Pandora's box, having chucked out the refurbishments and taken the sundry costumes to the charity shop, there's still something at the bottom, hidden underneath all the paraphernalia of life, and when that something shows up it's *way too big* to have ever fitted in Pan's chest in the first place! (Back to the Tardis more-spacy-on-the-inside transdimensional engineering paradox.)

"As if that's not preposterous enough," she continued cogitating, clinging onto Ariadne's thread for dear life as she groped her way through the befuddling mind maze, "the next thing that happens, by some freaky unearthing beyond all hitherto accepted applications, is that you then find IT's actually neither in nor out of the chest at all anymore, now IT's in YOU! Now IT's a bottomless well you're carrying around, which you suddenly *feel* inside your own physical chest, as real as dripping concrete, like it might bubble up and overspill into tears at any moment. And yet not sad, more *soulful*."

After puffing and perspiring through this mental workout, straining to get a hold of ever fluttering fancies and pin them down on the pinboard long enough to examine them, Moira was getting peckish so she stopped trying and backtracked to the main point: here she was, Moira Box (affectionately aka "the moggie basket" to friends) in 2020, alive and kicking madly each day in the wild green sea!

Later on after supper, with an orange orb gleaming on the skyline and a dainty lunar curl above, she strolled down the lane to watch a rowdy badger family romping and rollicking outside their set. She'd discovered that if she sat on the wall looking like a boulder, they didn't notice her and she could watch their adorable antics. These mainly consisted of the cubs snuffling around and bickering in high squeaks, while mummy badger sat on her bum scratching her tummy with long thick claws that could really do with a pedicure.

Back in Slough in her wasted youth (wasted in terms of not doing anything, not as in having a debauched good time), even if it had ever occurred to her, watching bunglesome badgers would not have been her notion of a good night out. But then again, she hadn't been happy in the prescribed social scene either – basically big brick boxes packed with people clasping drinking glasses. And made unpleasantly stuffy by a narrow world view and society's shallow values, still rolled out like a faded red carpet today. Somehow, she'd always had a hunch there's a whole load more they're not telling us...

Thinking back on her lives, Moira surmised that history has swung between the fear-mongering superstitious to the sterile scientific (excluding the crazy quantum maverick) and boring basic textbook explanations. But sparkling within both, the dangerous and the tame, nestled amidst the dull and dowdy, the little and limited, the prescribed ordinary – sometimes revered in temple or ashram, sometimes hidden in shady grove or behind cottage door – but always *somewhere* has been a glimpse of the Mystical and Magical.

"*This* is the mystery which unlocks unfathomable far out possibilities," she told the black-and-white short legged guys excitedly (despite long faces). "The downpour of rain in a parched desert suddenly abloom with a cornucopia of latent life, little lizards and flamboyant flowering cacti! And a spaghetti junction of access routes to what lies beyond limitation are open to us: witchcraft, meditation, mediumship, tarot, dreams, past life hypnosis, astrology, human design, near-death experiences, and so on, on and on and on through the Violet Vale, to faerie gate after gate after gate standing open. The exploration kit to expand our consciousness and revitalise our lives is just jammed packed full of quirky developmental toys!

"But beyond all the fun mind stuff and yet more exquisite," Moira, profoundly touched, went on explaining to the badgers who still weren't interested but at least didn't keep interrupting the way people do, "is the Beauty, the Awe, the Quickening. Bringing unbidden tears rolling down your cheeks – the *heartfelt!*

"This is nature *not* under our dominion, that which has been banned from the mainstream, outlawed outside our manmade walls, forbidden, ridiculed and unexamined – our culture's blindspot! Here lies the enchanted Lothlorien of the eternal feminine, the fair arcane domain of yin, Neptune's deep watery realm," she pensively affirmed, surreptitiously wiping her eyes. To Moira, this was the soul-soaring Transcendence, the Arkenstone, the most precious; that which gives meaning, gifts wonder and orbits the divine.

The last tip of the red sun was sinking into the ocean. Moira drifted away on Brendon's sixth-century voyage to the Isles of the Blest, she raised up the lost land of Lyonesse off the very West Cornwall coast she was standing on, and she sailed the westerly seas to the Celtic Otherworld following Conla in his ship of glass.

"We have always yearned for the Splendour, the Sublime, the Rapture beyond normal reach," she wrapped up. "Found wavering above the horizon, far out over western waters and wafting back to us upon the wind."

As she stood there gazing into the glorious sunset, and after more than twenty years of laborious searching and lengthy pondering, Moira finally came up with the simple formula to IT ALL, the summing up ANSWER, personal to her and containing the Essence of her life. She raced back home through the twilight, repeating her all-inclusive affirmation of enlightenment-according-to-Moira-Box so as not to forget it, till she could write it down on a post-it note and proudly stick it on the bathroom mirror above the washbasin:

Beyond the mundane, a billion stars blaze,
Outside the closed box, a Multiverse beckons,
Past here and now, lost lives linger,
Leading us through Time and our selves.

The Mystery has crept back from the west,
The witch has crawled out of the woodwork,
Aha! Magic is brewing!

MOON BOOKS
PAGANISM & SHAMANISM

What is Paganism? A religion, a spirituality, an alternative belief system, nature worship? You can fi nd support for all these definitions (and many more) in dictionaries, encyclopaedias, and text books of religion, but subscribe to any one and the truth will evade you. Above all Paganism is a creative pursuit, an encounter with reality, an exploration of meaning and an expression of the soul. Druids, Heathens, Wiccans and others, all contribute their insights and literary riches to the Pagan tradition. Moon Books invites you to begin or to deepen your own encounter, right here, right now.

If you have enjoyed this book, why not tell other readers by posting a review on your preferred book site.

Bestsellers from Moon Books
Shaman Pathways Series

The Druid Shaman
Exploring the Celtic Otherworld
Danu Forest
*A practical guide to Celtic shamanism with exercises
and techniques as well as traditional lore for
exploring the Celtic Otherworld.*
Paperback: 978-1-78099-615-8 ebook: 978-1-78099-616-5

The Celtic Chakras
Elen Sentier
*Tread the British native shaman's path,
explore the goddess hidden in the ancient stories;
walk the Celtic chakra spiral labyrinth.*
Paperback: 978-1-78099-506-9 ebook: 978-1-78099-507-6

Elen of the Ways
British Shamanism - Following the Deer Trods
Elen Sentier
*British shamanism has largely been forgotten: the reindeer
goddess of the ancient Boreal forest is shrouded in mystery...
follow her deer-trods to rediscover her old ways.*
Paperback: 978-1-78099-559-5 ebook: 978-1-78099-560-1

Deathwalking
Helping Them Cross the Bridge
Laura Perry
*An anthology focusing on deathwalking and psychopomp work: the
shamanic practice of helping the deceased's soul pass on to the next
realm.*
Paperback: 978-1-78535-818-0 ebook: 978-1-78535-819-7

Bestsellers from Moon Books

Keeping Her Keys
An Introduction to Hekate's Modern Witchcraft
Cyndi Brannen
Blending Hekate, witchcraft and personal development together to create a powerful new magickal perspective.
Paperback: 978-1-78904-075-3 ebook 978-1-78904-076-0

Journey to the Dark Goddess
How to Return to Your Soul
Jane Meredith
Discover the powerful secrets of the Dark Goddess and transform your depression, grief and pain into healing and integration.
Paperback: 978-1-84694-677-6 ebook: 978-1-78099-223-5

Shamanic Reiki
Expanded Ways of Working with Universal Life Force Energy
Llyn Roberts, Robert Levy
Shamanism and Reiki are each powerful ways of healing; together, their power multiplies. Shamanic Reiki introduces techniques to help healers and Reiki practitioners tap ancient healing wisdom.
Paperback: 978-1-84694-037-8 ebook: 978-1-84694-650-9

Southern Cunning
Folkloric Witchcraft in the American South
Aaron Oberon
Modern witchcraft with a Southern flair, this book is a journey through the folklore of the American South and a look at the power these stories hold for modern witches.
Paperback: 978-1-78904-196-5 ebook: 978-1-78904-197-2

Readers of ebooks can buy or view any of these bestsellers by clicking on the live link in the title. Most titles are published in paperback and as an ebook. Paperbacks are available in traditional bookshops. Both print and ebook formats are available online.

Find more titles and sign up to our readers' newsletter http://www.johnhuntpublishing.com/paganism

For video content, author interviews and more, please subscribe to our YouTube channel.

MoonBooksPublishing

Follow us on social media for book news, promotions and more:

Facebook: Moon Books Publishing

Instagram: @moonbooksjhp

Twitter: @MoonBooksJHP

Tik Tok: @moonbooksjhp